THE
RAGNARÖK
CONSPIRACY

A NOVEL

THE RAGNARÖK CONSPIRACY

A NOVEL

EREC STEBBINS

SEVENTH
STREET
BOOKS™

59 John Glenn Drive
Amherst, New York 14228–2119

Published 2012 by Seventh Street Books™, an imprint of Prometheus Books

Cover image © 2012 Media Bakery
Cover design by Nicole Sommer-Lecht

Inquiries should be addressed to
Seventh Street Books
59 John Glenn Drive
Amherst, New York 14228–2119
VOICE: 716–691–0133
FAX: 716–691–0137
WWW.PROMETHEUSBOOKS.COM

16 15 14 13 12   5 4 3 2 1

Library of Congress Cataloging-in-Publication Data

Stebbins, Erec.
    The Ragnarök conspiracy : a novel / by Erec Stebbins.
        p. cm.
    Includes bibliographical references and index.
    ISBN 978–1–61614–712–9 (pbk.)
    ISBN 978–1–61614–713–6 (ebook)
        1. United States. Federal Bureau of Investigation—Fiction. 2. Terrorism—Prevention—Fiction. 3. International relations—Fiction. 4. Conspiracies—Fiction. I. Title.

PS3619.T4323R34 2012
813'.6—dc23

                                                                                            2012019051

Printed in the United States of America

For Anna Maria and Christina

In today's wars, there are no morals. We do not have to differentiate between military or civilian. As far as we are concerned, they are all targets. If inciting people to do that is terrorism, and if killing those who kill our sons is terrorism, then let history be witness that we are terrorists.

—Osama bin Laden

Choose your enemy with wisdom, for him do you become.

—ancient proverb

PART 1
TARGETS OF VENGEANCE

1

Near the back of a seedy bar in the Bronx, in one of the deeper recesses and darkest corners, FBI agent John Savas hunched over a shot glass, a caramel-colored liquid halfway to the rim. His slumped posture and a deep-blue Mediterranean fisherman's cap obscured most of his features. Dark hair flecked with gray spilled out from under his cap and partially melded with the rough layer of stubble on his face.

The smoke in the bar created a dense fog, infiltrating every open space, staining curtains and nearly obscuring the obligatory "No Smoking" sign. Here in a rundown basement, New York City health regulations held no concern for those seated around the jazz band.

A second group of patrons displayed no interest in the music. Huddled in dark corners, their faces turned inward and away from the room, pairs of often foul-looking men spoke of matters suited to the obscurity of the location.

Savas clenched his jaw. He'd been waiting too long, and this was a dangerous game. His recent injuries tore at his concentration, and fatigue began to set in. He should not be here; he knew that. His choices had not pleased the physicians. *But they don't understand.*

He stared at the whiskey in front of him. Now only a prop. Once poison and self-medication. Beginning on a rain-drenched night at the Church of the Holy Trinity in 2001, he had nearly drowned in a downward spiral, skipping work, drinking himself into numbness each night. He had known it was wrong, but he couldn't find his way out. Soon he had lost more than just his job. Or his home. Or his wife. After his son's death, he had lost himself.

He hadn't touched a drop now for nearly a decade. Not since the day he'd made that life-changing trip to the FBI. Thank God for friends in high places who had believed in him. Friends who had connected him to a new and experimental division of the FBI seeking unusually motivated recruits. Friends who had brought his file to the attention of Larry Kanter, the new branch chief, a man determined to rewrite the rules of antiterrorism, beginning with unorthodox methods and staff. Kanter had seen something in Savas, his past record of achievement at NYPD and the spark in his eyes at the mention of antiterrorism. As he would do with many others, Kanter had taken a chance on John Savas, and he had been amply rewarded. Savas had been granted a new lease on life. *Beyond that.* He had been given a *mission*.

At the sound of a moaning door hinge, Savas returned sharply to the present. He glanced up discreetly, his slovenly posture belying his inner intensity.

A large man stepped inside, his appearance clashing sharply with the interior of the bar. The battered trench coat poorly concealed his expensive tailored clothes. His skin was a sandy brown, his features faintly Arabic but obscured by the fat deposited over many years of high living. His stance indicated a man of power, now unsure of his footing. As the door closed behind him, two hulking bodyguards remained posted outside. The man nodded, almost imperceptibly, toward a lone drinker near the door, a carbon copy of the two guards outside. The man had obviously sent in a scout and had brought more muscle with him.

Savas swiftly returned his gaze to his drink and smiled to himself. His contact was anxious; frightened men were far easier to manipulate. *Now the trap will be set.*

The Arab walked slowly toward Savas at the back of the room. His eyes darted in several directions, and he approached the booth like a hunted animal. He slid into the opposite seat, placing his hands on the table. "This place is not safe."

Savas looked up from his whiskey and nodded, his olive skin blending subtly into the stained wood behind him. He scratched the three-day growth of beard on his face, a useful contribution to the role-playing game he undertook with his criminal contacts. Along with his dress and body language, it had become part of the dangerous act often required to infiltrate terrorist networks that were all too real and growing in America. His friend across the table was as big a fish as Savas had ever hooked.

"What place is *safe*?" he replied, a false Greek accent, modeled on his immigrant grandfather's, partially garbling the words. He spread out his hands on the table. "You want to be *safe*, sell smartphones. You want to bring in your *shipments*, talk to me."

The Arab once again glanced around the room.

He is very frightened.

"Dimitri," began the Arab, "I have my connections. We must know *who* we deal with. Your name doesn't show up on any shipping records. Your prints don't match *anything* in any database. You don't seem to *exist.*"

Savas mulled this turn of events. His contact was indeed becoming paranoid. He thanked his own paranoia that forced him to insist on the latex false-skin worn over his fingertips. He only hoped these guys didn't have access to DNA analysis. "Ambassador Hamid," he began with his most crooked smile, "I have been a disservice?"

The ambassador rumbled deeply over the bar sounds. "No. But before we go further, we need to know more."

Savas shook his head slowly. He hoped his cover had not been blown. He felt the bulge from his pistol and wondered how he could survive a firefight if the man turned his goons on him. "If you know more, it's not so good for me, *katalaves*?" He held up his hands. "No one knows these hands, Ambassador. My business is better with shadows. Not you, not the Americans, no one knows Dimitris."

"Is that your real name?"

Savas only smiled. "I have boats. Good boats, also shadows. Never traced. We pay good money so they stay shadows. If you change your mind, then find other boats." He paused dramatically. "If you can."

The ambassador looked distinctly uncomfortable. Savas did not envy the man and the two-faced game he played at the UN. His position gave him tremendous opportunities to exploit weaknesses in US security. But he risked much to play the role of a terrorist pawn, whatever they paid him. Savas didn't fool himself that Ambassador Hamid was any kind of idealist. He was simply the greedy scum that enabled the monsters.

The ambassador whispered tensely, "We would have been less uncertain if you hadn't *disappeared* for a month!"

Savas had anticipated this. His injuries from the Indian Point insanity had pulled him off the street. Hamid had asked for meetings he could not honor. Dimitris the smuggler had simply disappeared. "It was, as the Americans say, too *hot*, Ambassador. Dimitris was in danger."

The look of fear in the ambassador's eyes was unmistakable, and the depth of it shocked Savas. "Danger? From where? Who knows about you? Can they connect you to me?"

The fake Greek captain waved his hand up and down toward the ambassador. "No danger, no discovery. After those bombs at Indian Point, the FBI was very busy. Nuclear power plants make them very nervous, no? Everyone was quiet."

"*FBI?*" the frightened man asked, almost desperately.

"Yes, FBI. Who else?"

The man visibly relaxed. *Relaxed!* Whatever Ambassador Hamid was afraid of, it was not the FBI or discovery by US law enforcement. On the one hand, Savas was relieved, pleased that his cover was not blown, that he still had a hook in this big fish. He was also disturbed. What would frighten this man so much that arrest, and possible life sentencing by the FBI, seemed a relief in comparison?

"Who, indeed?" said the ambassador, a false and awkward smile forced onto his wide face. Again he glanced around nervously, then checked his watch. "Then we are still good. If you do not disappear again! But we must meet in more protected locations." Hamid seemed to have finished an internal argument of some kind. "Captain Dimitris, we will have our deal."

Savas put on his greediest grin, but he was also smiling internally.

Swallow the bait whole, Ambassador. Soon the FBI would have a catch of unprecedented visibility, but only after they had exploited Hamid to obtain all the underground contacts this octopus's tentacles reached. Then they would crash on him hard, force more information out of him to save his skin, and toss him in jail until he was too old to remember his lucrative moonlighting. Diplomatic immunity be damned.

The ambassador continued. "We will contact you when we are ready. It will be soon. You will come to a place we designate." Savas groaned inwardly; the ambassador was introducing complications.

"Of course, *Ambassador.* But, after Indian Point, business is much more difficult. More *expensive.* You understand?"

The ambassador hardly frowned. "Yes, of course. This was anticipated." Savas nearly laughed out loud. *How predictable the criminal mind.* "What are your terms?"

Savas knew he had to drive a hard bargain to cement his character. "Double, Mr. Ambassador, and a quarter in advance."

"That's outrageous!"

"So is whatever you want to smuggle in."

The man nodded. "We will consider it and be in contact."

Hamid rose, having never ordered a drink, and checked again with the bodyguard by the door. He then walked with his nervous glances back across the bar to the exit. The seated goon followed him out, and Savas could see them through the window standing together, waiting for their driver.

Savas pushed his untouched drink to the side. There was much to consider, much to plan in this setup. He would return to the FBI and talk to Kanter. They would need enormous resources to bring in Hamid. After two years of tedious work, slowly bringing to life the character of Savas's Greek smuggler, luring several interested parties into the net, Savas had hit the jackpot. The monsters needed gremlins to sneak them in, and there were always greedy men like Hamid to serve in those roles. Relying on them was a weakness, a trail back to the hive. Savas intended to exploit it.

A sharp sound tore through his consciousness—a strong slap from outside. He could instantly visualize several possible weapons involved, but his mind lurched away from the details, and he stood up, looking through the window.

The music had stumbled to an awkward halt. People in the bar were screaming and backing away from the window. Like the first stages of a Jackson Pollock commission, red paint seemed to have been flung sharply across the glass, thick, languid drops tracing slow paths toward the sidewalk from a central bull's-eye. Crumbled on the ground against the glass was a figure in a trench coat, three large forms bent in panic over it, screaming into cell phones. The back of the coat had a fist-sized hole blown out of it and, like the window, was stained in bright red.

Savas was dumbfounded. Within seconds, years of work had collapsed along with that form. Important and carefully orchestrated openings into international terrorist organizations had slammed shut. As chaos erupted and patrons scrambled to exit the bar, Savas stood still, staring at the downed shape outside, knowing too well that it would not rise. The shot was perfect, through the heart, the bullet chosen and aimed by a professional.

Ambassador Hamid had been assassinated.

2

Through the window of the bistro, Savas could see an elegant woman in a gray pantsuit step out of a cab. Her highlighted hair shone a rich golden blonde in the May sunlight, and she walked with a quick and confident step across the sidewalk to the restaurant entrance. She spoke politely to the maître d', who directed her toward a table at the back. He watched as she surveyed the establishment—tables well separated, sounds absorbed by the old woods and carpets—approving of his careful choice. They were ensured a private and comfortable conversation. Savas smiled when several heads turned as she made her way to the table where he waited.

"Dr. Wilson, it looks like your medical training has paid off."

She sat down and looked at him sardonically. "OK, John, and the punch line?"

"Well, I saw at least three men look your way. At forty-eight, you must've developed some serious antiaging formula."

She smiled curtly. "Requisite flattery: check. Quotation of age: Uncheck. Decent digs for lunch: check. And the check?"

"Check," nodded Savas.

"I think you owe me dinner for this one."

"Lorrie, this case is three years, five agents, several hundred thousand dollars . . ."

"And one dead diplomat."

Savas frowned. "He was plugged into terrorist networks I'd give my right arm for!"

"He was plugged, alright."

Savas sighed. "Somebody wanted him out of the way. I don't know if it's a competitor, another government, or what. But he was taken out for a reason. I want to know who and why."

A waiter came over to the table, and they quickly ordered, resuming their conversation when he was out of earshot. The woman pulled out a manila folder and slid it across the table. Savas put his hand on it.

"This is everything?" he asked.

"Jeez, you're one greedy bastard. My husband is alive because of you, but there have to be *limits*, John."

Savas was already flipping through the pages. "How is Mike?" he asked absentmindedly.

"Fine. Look, John, everything you need is there. I've looked over it. They didn't get much from the crime scene. They recovered the bullet —high caliber—damn thing blew right through him. They traced the angle of fire to a rooftop a block away. A long-range shot. The shooter was thorough—not a print, not a shell, not so much as a hair anywhere up there. The diplomatic turbulence on this pushed them to work overtime. Top forensics team. Several people flown in from other crime labs. I wouldn't be surprised if they brought in a board-certified psychic. *Nothing*."

"Mmmmm," said Savas, reading through the file.

"But you *are* right about something."

Savas glanced up from the papers. "Yes?"

"Somebody wanted him dead very seriously. The ballistics report is eyebrow raising, if you know much about guns."

"Go on," said Savas, irritated at her dramatic pauses. He had forgotten how she liked the stage.

"7.62 by 51 millimeter, .308-caliber hole and bullet."

"Sniper rounds?"

"Yes, standard issue US Army and civilian law enforcement. With a twist," she said coyly, sipping from her water, her attractive face angled slightly. Savas just stared at her. "A slight variant on the ammunition. Ballistics had to call in help. Turns out it's a limited production of the cartridges used only in the beginning stages of the Iraq War. Couldn't get much more information on it. Definitely *not* civilian ammo."

Savas leaned back in his chair and squinted at the physician. "You're telling me that my contact was gunned down by a limited-edition military bullet from a high-powered rifle, fired over a block away with enough accuracy to strike the man's heart?"

She flashed him a winning smile, obviously enjoying the look of confusion and surprise on his face. "That's it, Johnny-boy. This is a weird one."

"How the hell did *that* end up in New York City?"

"I don't know, John. That's *your* job. This CSI shit isn't what I went to med school for. Now, the rest is there for you to read at your considerable leisure." She glanced purposefully around the restaurant. "I'm hungry—for food and for a drastic change in the topic of conversation."

Savas nodded, still fixated on this absurd piece of information. Sniper rifles with obscure military rounds. The assassination of a dirty diplomat in the pocket of international terrorists. Blown apart outside a Bronx dive by a mysterious and highly skilled sniper. *What the hell was going on?*

3

CIA agent Brad Thompson squinted at the monitor, watching a large crowd gathered restlessly around the mosque on the outskirts of London. They seemed to strain to hear the words of Imam Wahid, broadcast over the loudspeakers yet drowned out by surrounding noise and distance. He didn't know what worried him more—the imam's inflammatory rhetoric or the number of people the nut could draw who were eager to hear it.

He approved of the heavy presence of British military to keep the peace. The task was underlined by the boiling unease and anger simmering beneath the surface of the youthful and mostly male crowd.

Agent Thompson cursed the faint rain that misted over the people, the streets, and the rows of cars lining the curbs, making their surveillance that much harder. At least they were hidden. He imagined how it looked from outside: a few hundred feet from the edge of the crowd, a wet and rusted white van parked roughly between two cars. Everything about the vehicle said that it was in disrepair, neglected, and of a very limited life span. Only a thick black antenna on the side of the van might give any hint as to the reality within the vehicle.

Inside, it was a very different story. Behind the deeply tinted glass, several rows of computer monitors displayed video feeds from many angles around the mosque. Members of Thompson's team sat in front of these monitors, earpieces relaying audio, microphones over their mouths.

He had been assigned only three months ago to investigate Imam Wahid. He glanced back at the monitor, shaking his head at Wahid's angry words, his youthful charm. *Your charity fronts don't fool us, buddy.*

The man was a powder keg of Islamic radicalism. They would stop him, but not before finding out the bigger picture.

The words of the imam's speech were broadcast at a low level throughout the van. "The United States wants to control our world," rang out a charismatic and strong voice. One video feed showed the passionate gesticulations of the imam; another, the rapt attention of the young men in the crowd. "Yes, with the dollar and the sword they seek to subdue every nation, every people, every religion. But what chance does an empire, however grand, have next to the power of God? No, God will channel His great power through each of you. Each of you becomes a soldier of Heaven against the armies of Satan. The world will be Islam!"

An agent in the van whistled softly. "The bastard is really on. How many future martyrs has he recruited today, I wonder?" Thompson leaned over one of the monitors, staring at a pan of the crowd near the speaker. "Keep an eye on those close ones—the ones he acknowledges, singles out, greets, walks with. Let's get face shots, front and side. We need to ID these people. They're possible nasties, folks."

An agent at the back spoke up. "Hey, you all hear that they've come up with a new punishment for suicide bombers?" He paused for effect. "Death penalty."

There were a few scattered chuckles and several rolled eyes. "Stay on task, Johnson," Thompson barked. Chastised, the agent quickly returned his attention to the monitor in front of him.

Suddenly, a woman's scream wailed over the speaker system, and everyone in the van stiffened involuntarily. A man monitoring the speaker focused intently at his screen and nearly shouted to the others present.

"Wahid's down!"

"What?" Thompson gasped.

"Switching to stage angles."

All the monitors lit up with images at various angles of the platform on which the speaker had stood. The podium was empty now, the crumbled body of the imam near its base. Figures leapt onto the stage and raced to the body, turning it over as panicked screams rose from the crowd.

"Oh, my God," whispered Thompson. The video feed made it very clear that the imam was unlikely to return to the podium ever again. Figures around him were tearing at their beards, several covered in Imam Wahid's blood. One cradled the man in his arms, the body limp, a large bloodstain over the left breast visible on the video. The rain washed softly over their forms, diluting the red.

Thompson mobilized his team. "Move people! We have a hit on Wahid! It's long range, rifle shot, and from high ground, I'd put money. Sync with the Redcoats! Rooftops, exits—we need it all covered! I need agents moving *now*!"

The van erupted in an uproar of sound and activity, voices over the speakers in ears, commands shouting into microphones. The crowd outside was turning violent, with men grouped and chanting angrily, fists raised in the air. Several men pummeled the car next to the van, smashing its windows.

Shit. Thompson thought quickly. "People, this will get ugly. Radio British police that we have a riot brewing. Let our people out there know where the violence is and how to avoid it."

The van began to shake, fists impacting loudly against its sides and the dark glass. Several shouts announced the arrival of the mob.

"Don't panic! The glass is stronger than the walls." Thompson pulled out a gun, its dark metal gleaming in the lights of the computers. Except in training, he had never used it before. "The door isn't going to last. Michelson, let's try to get this piece of junk moving!"

He checked the cartridge, released the safety, and moved to the front seat of the van. Daylight spilled into the dark vehicle as several angry arms forced open the door. The CIA man aimed the weapon and fired.

4

"**J**ohn, I think I might have something."

Savas leapt over to the console next to a shy-looking man sporting an awkward grin. The man's face turned back to the screen and was partly obscured by an enormous beard and long, disheveled hair curled down below his shoulders. The sounds of keys clacking burst from underneath the hair. Savas had to suppress a laugh. *What did the team call Hernandez? "Our very own Jesus." Yeah, exactly. Except for the pornography.* Savas frowned as he tried to decipher the multiple open windows, filled with database output, open web pages, photographs of crime scenes, and more.

"I don't see it, Manuel. We're looking for known hit men with MOs that might match what we have on the Hamid assassination."

Hernandez nodded. "That's how I started. But it was a long shot, John, like we discussed. I've been in front of these databanks for *three days* cross-correlating materials and methods from every known killer we have in there with the forensics. Larry's got us drawing from FBI *and* CIA records. If there's a known assassin with any consistency in style, it would show up. Three days and nothing. Gets boring, John. I always get in trouble when I'm bored."

"That why they tossed you out of graduate school?" Savas asked absentmindedly, still squinting at the screen, trying to see the pattern.

Hernandez sighed. "No one believes me that I quit! Honestly, John, there were weirder people there than me."

"Yeah, but not so much trouble."

"Can't a man just want to serve his nation in the war on terror?"

Savas smiled and waved his hand at the screen. "I give up. Don't have a computer science PhD. Explain."

Hernandez opened several windows from online news organizations. All were dated reports, weeks to months old, from diverse locations across the globe. Each had an image of a dead body and police. The headlines in every case contained the word "assassinated."

"Manuel, what are we looking at here . . . and why?" asked Savas.

"Since I wasn't getting anywhere looking for a *who*, I started looking for a *what*. What unsolved crimes in the last two years might have matched the MO we have in this case? Honestly, after drawing a big zero in the database, my feeling was that our killer, or *killers*, weren't in there, that we are looking for something, someone new. Our fancy intel databases were useless. Where else left to go but the papers?"

Savas nodded. "OK, what are we looking at?"

"It's thin, John, but there's something. Remember the Al Jazeera reporter killed in Atlanta, right as he exited the airport?"

"Mohammed Aref? Of course I do. Larry reassigned the case while I was in the hospital. *Lighten my workload*, he said. Aref was a real tap dancer. He had been implicated by the Sheikh in money laundering through some of the East Coast mosques."

"The *Sheikh*?"

Savas smiled. "My little double-agent friend."

"The one we don't mention, whose real name not even Larry knows?"

"That one."

"So, he ratted out Aref?"

"And several others, as he collected from them, too, no doubt. The Sheikh's a real charmer." Savas grinned. "Second-generation Syrian street punk. Broke away from his conservative parents, but not before he picked up enough Arabic to make him very valuable to certain underground elements. Kid's addicted to gold and adrenaline, and likes to feel smarter than everyone he's conned."

"*That's* what you call charming?"

"Anyway, the Al Jazeera job was a cover for Aref, for his real work.

He had a good scheme going. Charity dollars from many uncharitable sources. We used Aref to trace an assassination plot against a diplomat from Pakistan. We're still planning to move on the entire operation, as far as I know." Savas glanced down at the computer scientist. "The connection?"

Hernandez gestured toward the screen. "Aref was gunned down by a high-powered sniper rifle. Single shot. Right through the heart. Sound familiar?"

Savas furrowed his brows. "Coincidence?"

"And so's this, I suppose," said Manuel as he enlarged another window. Savas read aloud from the web page.

"Raahil Hossain, a lawyer and lobbyist for a Saudi construction conglomerate, was gunned down today in Egypt on a business trip. Known for his outspoken stance on Arab rights of ownership of oil and gas sites developed by foreign powers, he had become a controversial figure in the international community. Condemned by many Western governments for alleged ties to jihadist movements in several countries, he had found his ability to travel outside the Middle East increasingly restricted."

"Skip to the next-to-last paragraph."

Savas paused and scrolled the text up on the monitor. "Reports claim that Mr. Hossain was struck by a bullet as he exited his hotel in Cairo and that he died instantly, suffering a direct hit to the chest. The gunman was never found; police speculated that the killer had fired a high-powered rifle from a distance and escaped in the ensuing panic."

Savas was quiet for a moment. Hernandez used the silence to bring up a list of names, dates, and locations. He rolled his chair backward and let Savas lean in closer, reading through the file.

"All killed by snipers," mumbled Savas as he read silently through the list. "All taking direct hits that killed them instantly. Each a player in the underground terrorist network. There must be twenty names here, Manuel. You think that they're all linked?"

"I don't know, John. Some don't exactly fit—head shots, for example, even though in some of those cases the bullets were identified to be military grade. Not the special ordnance you discovered, but we don't know how careful the ballistics teams were, whether they did their homework like your contacts. Half these kills were in parts of the world where they likely don't even do a full workup, let alone release the data."

Savas put on his best Larry Kanter voice. "This is *really* thin, Manuel."

Hernandez nodded dejectedly. "Yeah, John, I know. But it's all I have."

"I didn't say I thought it was wrong." Savas sat down and breathed out slowly, lost in thought. "Do you remember those studies at Army Research focusing on soldiers in Iraq who had a high rate of survival?"

"Not really, John."

"I do, because I found it fascinating. A large number of those soldiers were characterized by strong emotional responses to environments, having *hunches* and *gut feelings* about danger. The studies showed that these guys tended to have hyperactive attention to detail, keen sight and other senses, noticing absurd details others missed, yet they were not consciously aware of it."

"Yeah, now I remember. Like the soldier who thought 'the concrete slab didn't look right' and inside was an IED waiting to blow them apart."

"Exactly. He had processed a lot of data subconsciously about the slab—imperfections, mismatches in colors, location, and so on—and without knowing why, his brain sent an alert. All he knew was, it *looked wrong*."

Hernandez shrugged his shoulders nervously. "So what's that got to do with this?"

Savas looked back at the list of names compiled by his computer systems man. "After reading that article, I started believing in intuition, Manuel, that it's often much more than simple flighty emotion. Sure, in some percentage of the population it *is* flighty, useless stuff, and that's why we get nut-jobs paranoid about things that aren't there, conspiracy theories, and people afraid of their own shadow. But for those with a history of survival, or of finding solutions to puzzles, let's say, with few clues, I think it's real, representing a lot of neurological processing we aren't aware of."

Hernandez simply stared at Savas.

"What I'm trying to say, Manuel, is that I know this is thin," he said, gesturing to the list. "I can't justify it logically, but my gut tells me there's something here. I think yours did, too. There's something in that list. Like that cement block, it doesn't look right. There's something there."

"What?"

"I wish I knew. There are a lot of dead men on that list."

5

Kanter stood up and leaned over the table, an exasperated expression on his face. "*This* is what makes sense?"

Standing up was the first sign that things were not going well for Savas. Kanter didn't usually stand unless he was upset. Once Kanter began running his fingers through his graying hair, Savas knew that he had lost him. It was only a matter of time before the lecture began.

"This is the special meeting of Intel 1 you called me in for? You *do* realize that I manage other groups in this division?"

"It does make sense, Larry! They're using guerilla-style methods. Removing those who are the key links in the international terrorist web! What else could unify all these attacks?"

Kanter threw up his hands. "John, that's the point—I don't see that they *are* unified. That's your task, to prove it to me, and, *damn it*, this isn't very persuasive!"

The rest of Intel 1 was very quiet. In addition to Hernandez, the group was fully assembled, torn from different tasks and assignments, interrupting their work of digging out international terrorists. All because Savas had called a special meeting with high priority. With their eyes on him and Kanter's dismissal, he felt like an idiot.

They had all listened intently to Savas as he had presented the information. A list of assassination-style killings, all of which were connected in one way or another to the international criminal underground that supported and enabled terrorist activity. Some were middlemen, some were spokesmen, and some were fundraisers. All were significant players, and all had met untimely deaths in similar ways. The MOs were very similar. *It was so clear!* Someone was moving systematically and ruthlessly, brutally crushing the pressure points to cripple the ability of terrorist groups to function. The silence he received was maddening.

He glanced around the room for support. *Any* hint of support. J. P. Rideout and Matt King had their eyes cast down. The dark-haired Rideout, trim and stylishly dressed, had been Kanter's steal from Wall Street and Bloomberg monitors. Rideout retained a residual superiority inherited from his French forbears, his style sharply counterbalanced by the analytical bookworm named Matt King. King, a former energy lawyer for big-oil firms, had turned do-gooder after witnessing the 9/11 attack on the Pentagon from his hotel window. Both Rideout and King clearly thought he was nuts.

Across from them at the round table frowned Frank Miller, the hulking ex-marine. Miller clearly wasn't onboard with him, but he held his gaze with a thoughtful expression as he parsed what he had heard from Savas.

Last of all he looked over to Rebecca Cohen. She sat on his right, her deep-brown eyes troubled and nearly lost in the thick mane of chestnut hair that swept across her face and down her shoulders. Her small stature seemed dwarfed by the solid wall of marine next to her. Cohen had moved up through FBI counterterrorism for a number of years and was snagged by Kanter because she was so bright. She had come to the states as a small child, her father immigrating after several family members were killed in a bus bombing in Tel Aviv. Her motivation was keen, and her analytical skills had made her his "right hand" at Intel 1.

"Mad John." A voice from the back of the room.

An uncomfortable silence fell. Savas glanced toward the source of the voice. He smiled as he glimpsed a young elfin woman in her midtwenties, long, ironed-looking orange hair to her waist framing a needle-thin body as pale as undecorated china. She wore a plain dark-blue dress that looked like it came out of an Amish catalog, complemented by bright-orange sneakers with flashing lights built into the bottoms. *Children's shoes.* She stood apart from the group seated at the table, staring absentmindedly outside the window, seemingly caught in a trance of some kind.

"Greetings, Kemo Sabe." The young woman spoke as if sensing his gaze, yet she never took her attention away from the glass or left her trancelike state. *Angel Lightfoote. Brilliant and pulling out important connections in data no one else could see. Larry's latest find.*

The awkward silence continued. "Don't everyone act so shocked," said Savas at last. "I've heard the name. *Mad John* Savas. Nice ring to it."

"Does seem you're out to earn it," grumbled Kanter. "You might have gotten a call from POTUS for your recent *heroics*, John, but back here we need you to *make sense*."

Miller interrupted. "A series of coordinated hits—what about organized crime?"

Savas felt his frustration boiling over. "No! Not mob! I saw my fair share of mob hits when I was on the force, Frank. They're brutal, but blunt. These hits were surgical. The methods the same: single shot, high-powered rifle, military grade, professional work—*beyond* mob. Assassination style."

"John, you would be talking about an organization with enormous resources," Cohen interjected. All eyes turned toward her. "These are not a series of isolated murders. If this is all part of some broad conspiracy, the killers have to have an international scope, finances, skilled personnel, an ability to conduct intelligence and mission planning that would rival the best government agencies of the world!"

"How do we know it *isn't* governmental?" asked J. P. Rideout.

"Not possible," scoffed Matt King. "You're talking about a series of coordinated assassinations. No reputable nation would dare."

"Maybe one *not* so reputable," grumbled Miller, his broad frame tense as a result of the new direction of the conversation.

"Which of the disreputable nations do you think cares enough to undertake an effort to *stop* terrorism?" quipped King.

Rideout turned toward him. "What makes *any* nation reputable? What about us? Didn't we have a vice-presidential CIA hit squad trained for this very purpose?"

A long silence fell over the room. The weight of that statement in connection with the assassinations sank in deeply. Even Kanter sat down and looked sharply at the former Wall Streeter.

"Well, *didn't* we?" Rideout echoed.

Kanter looked troubled. "If you're talking about Cheney's death squads, that's all documented. So is the fact that they were *never* activated. That entire idea was only a *hypothetical*."

J. P. Rideout laughed. "Sure! For eight years of the Bush presidency, these guys were being prepped—that much is on the record, too. Larry, that's a hell of a long training program. *Eight years* readying themselves to kill terrorist leaders and never once going on the job? Must have been a frustrated bunch of dudes."

Kanter's face was stern. "You can speculate all you want, J. P., but at the FBI, in *my* division, we deal in *facts*. And let me tell you, even the speculation of such activity by the US government is a serious matter."

"It would surely make a good framework for hanging John's linked assassinations, though, wouldn't it?" added King.

Cohen shook her head. "Come on, guys, this doesn't make sense. It would mean that the current administration had put into motion the clandestine murder of numerous US and foreign targets."

"Bin Laden. That's all I have to say," broke in Rideout.

Cohen rolled her eyes. "Damn it, J. P., that's *completely* different! *Bin Laden? These* are kills on US soil, some of them *American* citizens. CIA killing Americans *in America*? That's 1984 material, folks, really scary stuff."

Rideout wasn't fazed. "2011, Defense Appropriations Bill authorized the indefinite detainment of American citizens arrested on American soil for *suspicion* of terrorist activities. 2012, Obama has his attorney general justify killing Americans *suspected* of terrorist activities. Due process be damned."

"That authority has never been used!" said Cohen animatedly. "And now you're going from hypotheticals to documented murders? It *is* a crazy idea!"

"A crazy idea for which there is absolutely *no* evidence!" banged out Kanter. The others began to speak out of turn as the argument escalated.

Savas shouted them down. "They're right!" The eyes of Intel 1 turned to him in surprise. Savas held his palms up, trying to explain. He lowered his voice. "Larry and Rebecca are right. It's too outlandish. It doesn't feel right."

"*Feel* right?" asked Rideout.

"No, it doesn't, J. P. Let's just say these death squads were still around, *activated*. They might make hits on foreign soil, not *here*. Even the craziest antiterrorist zealots would think twice about that. For God's sake, we don't have to shoot them here! Why not just pick them up, extraordinary rendition and all that? We do it all the time, whatever you think of it: grab a suspected terrorist, take him someplace far away, interrogate him. Maybe worse. A hit on someone abroad, maybe, but not like this."

Cohen picked up his thoughts. "And not with this frequency, this thoroughness. Such a group might make a hit here or there, take out a particularly important target. But the list of possible kills John is showing is too long. It's *absurdly* long. It would begin to call attention to the murders. That's the last thing some covert death squad would want. Bad for the US, bad for them, bad for their long-term goals."

Savas refused to let go. "I still think these deaths are linked, but it's not governmental. It's something else; something else is driving it forward."

"John, what the hell are you talking about? Something else *what*?" asked Kanter. He seemed beyond frustrated. "How do they magically appear in the span of half a year in ten or twenty different places around the world, bringing down the target—often a highly protected target, by the way—without leaving any trace? Are these *ninja* snipers? Who funds this? What's the unifying motive for your imaginary marksmen with the special bullets?"

Savas was silent. He didn't know if he had the words for this intuition, the connection between his own experience and the pattern he was seeing in these murders. He wasn't even sure it made sense to him. Then the word just came to his lips.

"Vengeance." As soon as he spoke, Savas felt his stomach drop—he could almost feel the disbelief in the room.

"Vengeance, John? *Who?*" asked Kanter incredulously.

"I don't *know*, Larry! But if *I* struck back for everything they've done to us, it might be something like this. Hell, it might be worse."

The second the words left his mouth, he knew it was over. Savas knew he had blown it, shot to hell any hope of objectivity, any chance of persuading a group of analysts that he was correct. Their expressions confirmed his fears, the downward glances, no one looking him in the eye. Kanter moved quickly to resolve the issue.

"John, we appreciate that many of us here have had personal experience with international terrorism, and we use that every day to motivate us. But we can't let it cloud our judgment. I don't like to go over this in front of everyone, but too much has been said," Kanter noted, glancing over the table, "by too many of us here. We've ended up in no man's land of speculation, serious accusations, too much emotion, and too few facts. There's the beginning of a coherent linkage between these murders, but only a beginning. I'm torn about how we proceed. Good detective work is often shot to hell if heads are clouded by emotion."

Kanter seemed to mull something over in his mind, then he stood up abruptly. "John and Manuel will continue looking into this idea of a link between these murders, at least for the time being. But we'll hear no more of international death squads and the like. I've got to fly to Washington for another one of our interagency summits this weekend, and the last thing I want on my mind is wondering if my agents are out and about trying to prove the CIA or whoever is involved in an international assassination program. Honestly, folks, I'm too young for forced retirement."

There were nervous smiles around the room, but Savas merely stared forward, unable to focus on Kanter's words. "Let's call this a day. I'm late for a twelve o'clock. Get back to your posts and saving the country."

Awkwardly, the members of Intel 1 got out of their seats and headed for the door. Lightfoote brushed past Savas and whispered in his ear.

"It's OK, John. *I* think you're right." She smiled blissfully at him and danced out of the meeting room. The irony was total—his main support came from the most *eccentric* member of this team.

He glanced up. The room was empty. Kanter entered and closed the door.

"Is there anything we should talk about?" Kanter began.

"No, Larry. Maybe I *am* biased on this, but you might consider that I also have an advantage."

"Which is?"

"If I do happen to be right, I'm the one who would understand the motives better than anyone."

"Vengeance?"

"Yes, and more. A removal of the threat and obsessive cleansing of the world." *Hunting the monsters. Showing no mercy.*

"John, you're essentially telling me that if you are right, you'll be very right. That sort of tautology doesn't really give me much to base things on."

"I know that, Larry."

"Besides, even if you are right, I think our hands are tied."

Savas looked up, his brows furrowed. "Why?"

"Jurisdiction. If this has the scope you think it does, it's way beyond FBI. In addition to the thirty or more US agencies involved broadly in criminal activities outside the country, there are the international ones."

"Well, we'd have our part to play."

"Yes, but to break this case, it will require access to and investigation of places and people we can't go to."

"Well, we pound the beat we know, Larry."

Kanter nodded. "OK, John. That's all I'm saying. Stay in your boundaries on this one. If there is something to this, you'll dig it up." Savas watched his boss stand up and leave the room. The message was clear.

Savas felt exhausted. In the span of less than half a workday, he had run a roller coaster of emotions from his own elated certainty to the embarrassed rejection by his peers. He glanced at the presentation on his computer, closed the laptop, and dropped it into his bag. As he left the table and walked to the door, Rebecca Cohen entered. Her eyes told him too clearly what was on her mind.

"Is this a therapy session?" he asked sharply.

"John, please. It's not like that."

"Isn't it? I saw all your faces. I could hear it perched on their tongues: *Mad John*. Useful in a pinch, but a little too wacko at times. Wasted on his own grief and anger. Unreliable when it comes to certain topics. Ready to see in others all the things churning inside himself." He marveled that all this spilled out to her. "Doesn't that about capture it?"

Cohen sighed and looked crestfallen. "Yes, John, it does. But I didn't come here for that."

"Then what?"

"I came to tell you that whatever they think, whatever doubts anyone might have, we've all come too far with you not to back your play. Take it slow, John, but we're behind you."

Savas was strangely touched. "And you're speaking for the others?"

"I'm sure I am, but it wasn't put to a vote or anything. I know I speak for me."

Her earnest eyes burned into him, and, not for the first time, he felt them pierce through so many layers of armor and anger. It was a place that couldn't be touched. Not now. Not anymore. *Not after Thanos*. He was shaken by it, by the *goodness* of that touch. It made him recoil all the more.

Cohen sensed his withdrawal, and her face tightened slightly as she watched his eyes.

"Thanks, Rebecca. It's good to know." He turned quickly away from her and left the room.

6

Across the world in the mountains of Afghanistan, darkness had fallen, and the one called Kamir felt a chill descend. His group of mujahideen sat quietly around a small fire, several smoking, weapons at their sides. He was exhausted from a long day of drills, scrambling to keep ahead of American squads tracking them through the rough terrain. Their leader had posted guards at two positions around their camp, and three others at high and low points more distant. He grunted. They would see no Americans tonight.

His mouth formed a sneer. His group lacked any high-tech equipment—motion detectors, night vision, satellite surveillance—expensive toys used lethally by their spoiled and arrogant American hunters. Instead, they used an older set of tools: their eyes, ears, nose, and skin. Truer tools given from God, each a more finely tuned instrument than anything assembled to take their place. They learned the land; memorized its pulse, the night sounds, the scents that belonged, and those that did not. His troop remained several steps ahead of their pursuers, mocking the grand collection of technology arrayed against them.

Tonight, his senses were charged. No, they would not see the American army tonight. The last few days, a nervous tension had grown within the group. Grown within him. Normal banter had been replaced with sharp whispers, and movements were made with unusual caution. No one spoke of it. There were no reasons, no evidence of danger. Yet all felt it, a sense of encroaching violence. Kamir felt like the prey when the predator was near.

Too many training cells had disappeared. Only months ago, theirs was one of the most promising training centers, already receiving praise from terrorist groups seeking their fighters. He was proud of the demonstrations of their prowess and the respect they had earned. Suddenly, everything had changed. Groups stopped returning from missions. At first, it was explained as American interceptions, until they became too numerous, too frequent, and often occurred in locations not patrolled by United States forces. Not once had they recovered the bodies of their slain brothers. The mystery fueled a growing superstition: of dark forces, demons, spirits sent out by the Evil One to undermine the jihad.

Today, his small training cell had slipped past a second American patrol just that morning, and the sense of threat had only grown. The Americans were not the threat. His mujahideen brothers began to mutter old nonsense from grandmothers and pagan times to ward off the evil. *Fools!* They did not even understand the words.

Kamir signaled to a haggard man stirring the fire. "Jawad, see that there is little smoke." Jawad grunted but showed no other sign of having heard him. Kamir stood up and quickly walked over beside the fire, crouching low.

Finally Jawad spoke. "I don't like it. We have not heard from the scouts for too long. We should wake the others. Something is wrong."

Kamir nodded and muttered a curse. He glanced anxiously around the campsite. "Not even the insects speak."

The men around him stirred restlessly, and several rose from their pallets and fingered their machine guns. Whatever it was, whatever had been following them like a wraith, it was here now. He felt it.

A harsh cry sounded out from one end of the camp. Kamir turned his weapon toward the sound. He jumped back as a mujahideen warrior staggered into the light of the fire, his hands covered in blood, his neck sliced open. He fell suddenly into the blaze, scattering the logs and tossing sparks into the air, his dry clothing bursting into flames.

From around the campsite, muffled shots were heard, and, one by one, the trained guerrilla fighters around him fell. Kamir spun in circles, unable to identify the attackers. Next to him, Jawad cried out, having been hit simultaneously in the chest and head, and fell backward several feet to land roughly on the ground. Kamir dropped to a prone position and scanned quickly outside the camp for a target. A blur to his right suddenly came into focus, a metallic gleam of a broad blade glinting. He turned rapidly to aim, fired wildly, but he knew he was too late. He felt an icy burn in his chest, and several gunshots thumped against his shoulders and abdomen. Momentarily, he passed out.

Opening his eyes to a fog of sound and pain, he tried to move but found himself unable to do so. He watched helplessly as several others managed to fire into the darkness, his eyes discerning only blurred shadows and motions. Each man soon fell, brought down by weapons unseen, controlled by hands unknown.

A silence fell around him, and yet he watched. A body continued to burn, now in the center of a circle of bodies, the stink of charred flesh carried on the soft breeze. His vision receding, he heard rapid shuffling sounds from the darkness, and several man-sized shapes sprinted into the camp. The fire was doused, and darkness infiltrated the area. A faint light from the stars weakly illuminated a group of active shadows that seemed to drift above the bodies, dragging the dead forms away. He felt his ankles clamped tightly.

He knew no more.

7

Savas struggled in a dream like a man drowning in water. It was the same nightmare. Dimly, a part of him recognized this, but his unconscious was in control and doomed him to walk through it again.

It was late September, 2001. He felt the storm rage over New York City. From above, he saw a depression, born in the Gulf, crouched over the Atlantic like an obscenely stretched octopus or some giant thumb of cloud-form pressed firmly on the eastern coast. Slowly rotating, its counterclockwise motion drew in the colder air of the north and built a storm system as cold winds mixed with the moist, warmer air from the sea. Savas's omniscient perspective contracted from the heavens to the streets below. He felt the pull in his stomach as he fell. Rain and thunder blanketed the concrete landscape of the city, and he came to rest near a small church in the Greek American enclave of Astoria.

A blue-and-white car was parked in front of the building. Inside, he saw the metallic finish of a handgun reflecting the orange streetlights at opposing angles, facets blinking underneath the rain-swept window where pouring water blurred the lighted icon of Christ on the church door. Worshippers trailed in, crossing themselves, dropping coins or bills to pick up candles, lighting them with short prayers, kissing the icons before entering. Inside, Savas knew, incense and chanting filled the air. Warmth and the damp smell of wet bodies and clothes mingled. Outside, only the incessant drumming of the rain, swallowing all other sound, blurring all images within the NYPD blue-and-white. No light shone from within. He followed a male figure as it stepped out of the official vehicle and entered the church.

As the doors opened, he saw an old woman inside, barely five feet tall, draped in widow's black as she hunched over candles, harvesting them, pruning those that had burned too low in the supporting sand beside the icons. She turned with arthritic slowness toward the door. Its opening brought a cold blast of moist air. Savas followed the shadowy man, the soaked and disheveled outline of his police uniform hardly recognizable.

As the dream continued, Savas felt himself approach the form, merge with it, until he felt himself striding with a mad purpose, drenched and chilled in his ruined uniform. He marched past the icons and candles, stepping through the narthex onto the red carpet that ran alongside rows of parishioners. He focused on the iconostasis and the altar, gripping a wet gun in his hand.

A priest was bent over the altar, hands cupped before him. He spoke the prayers before the Eucharist in a soft drone.

> *Behold I approach for Divine Communion. O Creator, burn me not as I partake, for Thou art Fire which burns the unworthy. Wherefore purify me from every stain.*

John Savas, dripping from the pouring rain, walked past the Royal Doors into the nave of the church. He looked neither left nor right; instead he focused intently straight ahead toward the altar and the figure of Father Timothy bent in prayer.

> *Of Thy Mystical Supper, O Son of God, accept me today as a communicant; for I will not speak of thy Mystery to Thine enemies; I will not give Thee a kiss as did Judas; but like the Thief do I confess Thee. Remember me, O Lord, in Thy Kingdom.*

Several heads turned in Savas's direction as he moved toward the altar. Eyes glanced up from prayer books like the wake of a boat, a flowing distraction from the climax of the liturgical service.

Tremble, O man, when you see the divine Blood, For it is a fire that burns the unworthy. The Body of God both deifies and nourishes; It deifies the spirit and nourishes the mind.

Savas passed three-quarters of the pews, walking underneath the high dome painted with the icon of Christ Pantocrator, Christ Almighty. The low prayers of the priest were increasingly disturbed by a surge of murmurs from the faithful, a slowly cresting wave of chaos drowned by the thunder rumbling outside.

Into the splendor of Thy Saints how shall I who am unworthy enter? For if I dare to enter the bridal chamber, my vesture betrays me; for it is not a wedding garment, and as an imposter I shall be cast out by the Angels. Cleanse my soul from pollution and save me, O Lord, in Thy love for men.

By the time shouts rose to warn the priest, John Savas had scaled the four steps to stand within the Sanctuary itself. Chanters and front-row worshippers who had moved forward to take action froze and slowly backed away. A gun was raised, aimed at the back of Father Timothy. The priest paused, perhaps sensing something or perhaps confused by the sudden swell and fall of noise in his church. Hands still raised in supplication, he turned slowly, his eyes at first unfocused over the many faces in the pews. Then they sharply pinpointed on the barrel of the gun not five feet in front of him.

The inside of the church was utterly still, silent, rocked softly by the receding thunder outside, lit brightly in slaps of lightning over the soft candle flames. Water dripped from the policeman's cap and began to form small pools on the white marble in front of him. Savas spoke.

"He can't have my son."

The priest stared down into the dark tunnel of the weapon, water beading around the slick metal. His eyes began to glow a deep red, and a demonic grin spread across his face. Savas screamed, pulling the trigger repeatedly as the robed figure laughed manically before him.

Savas awoke suddenly, shaken from sleep by a crack of lightning and a deep roll of thunder.

Where am I?

A loud knock accompanied the noises from outside. His watch displayed 10 p.m. He was in his office. He had fallen asleep at his desk, the fatigue of nearly constant late evenings catching up with him. The pounding on the door continued.

He rubbed his temples as he stood up from his desk, walked over to his office door and opened it. An extremely agitated Larry Kanter burst into the room and sat down in the chair beside the desk. He was dressed in his travel clothes—gray suit and briefcase, computer bag in hand. His thinning hair was in disarray, and he sighed loudly, slightly out of breath.

"Sit down, John, please."

Savas cautiously complied, wondering what emergency Kanter would drop on him.

"I'm off to DC a little earlier than I expected," he said. "You want to know why, John?"

Savas merely waited for him to continue.

"Because I was foolish enough to take you seriously. Crazy enough to call up my good friends at Langley and ever so subtly raise the issue of a connection between these seemingly disparate assassinations."

Savas felt his pulse quicken. "Yes? And they said?"

Kanter laughed. "First, they said they'd get back to me. Then my friend called back and told me to get a good lawyer. The next thing I knew, there was the head of the CTD oversight committee telling me to get my ass up to DC on a special flight chartered out of LaGuardia. Before the JTTF meeting this weekend, I'm going to get a special one-on-one with the entire Counterterrorism Task Division overlords. All because I *speculated* on your cracked idea."

"Did you mention anything about internal hit squads?"

"*Hell*, no, John! I'm not suicidal. But I don't really need to raise the issue, anymore, do I?" Kanter paused ominously.

"What do you mean?"

"Isn't it obvious? A few minutes on the phone linking these attacks gets me hauled up for questioning. What on earth could have them that jumpy?"

"You can't believe this is a possibility, Larry," said Savas, his smile fading quickly as Kanter remained serious. "But it's *crazy*!"

"I don't know what to think. But if there *were* assassination teams behind these killings, this is *exactly* the kind of response I would expect. That, and my upcoming reassignment to the Alaska division office."

"Calm down, Larry. We all know this doesn't make sense. There has to be another explanation."

"There sure as hell better be another explanation, John, or we've just opened a can of Texas-sized worms."

8

The door closed behind Kanter, leaving him alone in the room with six other people. He was already fatigued from his last-minute sprint to the airport, flight, and subsequent rush to the late meeting. *They couldn't wait until morning? Who has meetings at midnight?*

Now he had to face this table of officials overseeing the antiterrorism activities of the United States. The setup was inquisition-style with a single, lonely seat for him facing an array of questioners around the semicircular polished wooden slab.

Kanter felt his knees buckle as he scanned the faces around the table. Even the phone conversations and summons had not prepared him for this. One next to the other, he saw high-ranking representatives from critical US agencies, many exclusively counterterrorism. He ticked off the offices associated with the faces: the CIA Counterterrorist Center, the Office of National Security, Homeland Security, and his own superiors at the National Joint Terrorism Task Force. He was surprised to see a representative of the National Security Agency— he couldn't imagine why they'd need a communications angle on this story. If he was perplexed to see an NSA representative, he was stunned at the final face present—the deputy secretary of state. That *she* was here raised the stakes to feverish levels.

"Please sit down, Mr. Kanter," began his FBI superior.

Kanter noticed that he had been standing in front of the chair, nearly at attention. He smiled and sat down. He was too damn old to be acting like a freshman.

The FBI representative continued. "We apologize for calling you out here on such short notice, but we understand that you would be attending the Task Force meeting this weekend anyway."

"That's correct."

"As you are probably aware, Mr. Kanter, you are here to answer some of our questions about your comments to CIA counterterrorism personnel and, if possible, to aid us in solving some frankly disturbing mysteries."

Kanter suppressed an urge to sigh. "I'll help in any way I can."

The NSA man cut in. "We have printouts and digital samples of your conversations earlier today. However, as I understand it, the CIA wishes to proceed without an in-depth analysis."

"Not necessary; there's nothing complicated," said the director of the CIA Counterterrorist Center, her voice strained. She turned from the NSA officer toward Kanter. "Your special-ops division has come to a startling conclusion, Agent Kanter."

"No conclusions—nowhere near that level. Purely speculation. Some of our agents had stumbled on what they believed are connections linking a set of crimes, assassination-style murders of a number of pro-Islamic extremists in the US and abroad."

"Yes, we've seen the transcripts," cut in the CIA woman. "Why did you feel it necessary to contact CIA agents if these *connections*, as you call them, were purely at the speculative stage?"

Kanter frowned. "That seems the best time to me."

"Wouldn't you have preferred to have obtained some more firm evidence before making such accusations?"

"Accusations?" asked Kanter.

The FBI man swooped in quickly. "I don't think Mr. Kanter is making any accusations, Susan, only asking questions."

There was a very uncomfortable silence around the table. Kanter had a bad feeling about where this was headed, and he wished they would just open up the black hole and get it over with. The deputy director of state obliged him.

"Look, everyone, there's no point in tap dancing. Before we go any further, Agent Kanter, these members of your staff—how would you characterize their relationship to this hypothesis?"

Kanter gave her a knowing look. "Extremely committed, perhaps emotionally so. That's why I called this in, frankly. One of my best agents, John Savas, strongly believes in this connection. Many others do not. Frankly, I've been skeptical myself, but Agent Savas has a track record that is anomalously productive. I felt I should follow up on his hunch."

The deputy director smiled. "You say you've *been* skeptical. Has this changed?"

Kanter looked her in the eye. "The moment you all jerked me up here."

Several faces at the table appeared irritated, but the woman from the state department laughed. "After all the doublespeak I hear every day, Agent Kanter, your lack of diplomacy is welcomed. John Savas has been well-known to many over the years, and the recent events at Indian Point have refreshed any poor memories. Your division—as unorthodox as it has been—is unmatched in its contributions to counterterrorism efforts. The White House has decided to make you aware of some highly classified information."

Wonderful. "I don't suppose I might have the opportunity to decline?"

The FBI man laughed. "Wise man."

"Legally you can, of course," continued the deputy secretary of state. "But then we would have to make sure that in your ignorance, you did not make this classified information known—you or your group at the FBI."

Kanter felt his stomach drop. There was no misinterpreting those words. Either he was in, or he and his "unorthodox" group, including Intel 1, were toast.

"You can be persuasive."

"I have to be; this is too important," she said. "Susan, this belongs to you for the next few minutes. Your mess."

Kanter turned his attention to the Counterterrorist Center director. She had the look of someone who had recently learned of a relative's death.

"While it is well-known that the CIA, along with numerous US agencies, undertook extraordinary antiterrorist measures in the years following 9/11, it was only recently appreciated that some of these efforts took on the form of targeted elimination teams."

"Assassins," corrected Kanter. Here it came.

"Yes. I'm not here to examine the ethics or policy wisdom of such actions, but they have been a part of covert operations for decades. They have been vetted by several agencies, congressional oversight, and therefore have been answerable to the American public."

"Until Cheney," whispered Kanter.

"Yes, I can see that you know where this is going. During his tenure as vice president, Dick Cheney instructed the CIA to form an elite core of assassins, specifically designed to go after high-level targets in al-Qaeda and other terrorist groups threatening US interests. He took the unusual step of concealing this plan not only from Congress but also from nearly every other agency and governmental branch. These men and women were highly trained for years, awaiting orders that never came."

"Never?" asked Kanter.

"The records have been made public, Agent Kanter. Not a single kill was ordered. The program was terminated." She paused and removed her glasses. "Or so we believed."

She sighed and continued. "This connection you make between the killings of Islamic radicals has come to the attention of the CIA and other agencies as well. We are particularly concerned, because the methods used are right out of the training program of these assassination teams."

"Certainly other assassins could employ similar methods?" asked Kanter.

"Yes, of course. However, there is more, beyond the killings you know about. While the growing success in Pakistan and Afghanistan against terrorist training camps has been ascribed to many things—including tactics changes, troop buildup, and most recently, improved design of Predator Drone robotic combat units—these factors are not sufficient. We now know from Army Intelligence work that there have been substantial, at times crippling, attacks on terrorist camps in these regions that are not due to any known military or covert activity. We are talking about major professional strikes against groups that have eluded our capture for years and that yet, in a matter of barely a year, have been erased from the area."

"I don't understand," said Kanter. "If not us . . ."

"Then *who*?" said the state department woman. "Haven't you guessed?"

Kanter shook his head in disbelief. "I'm sorry, but you're trying to tell me that you have a group of essentially *rogue* CIA hit squads that are not only bringing down Islamic radicals around the world but are also out-gunning our best marines in the mountains of Asia? That they are doing this using former US training and resources, under our noses?"

The woman from the state department spoke. "Currently, we have no proof of this, but all analysis from the CIA and other agencies places this scenario as the most probable."

"Any *other* scenarios?" Kanter asked.

"Several, including foreign involvement and, of course, the null hypothesis that these are indeed *not* related. However, the potential political and geopolitical ramifications of our working hypothesis are so dire; we must focus on this possibility."

"Don't you know where these people are? Haven't you kept track of them?"

The CIA woman raised her voice. "Of course we know where they are! But many had gone in and out of the program over the years, and there has not been any clear need for constant surveillance of these trainees. Until now. You can rest assured that we are ascertaining the whereabouts of as many of these personnel as we can."

Kanter shook his head. "We'll help however we can, but let me be frank here—this is above our heads."

"That is exactly what I hoped to hear from you, Agent Kanter," stated the deputy secretary of state. "I want you to make it clear to your people that this is a matter best left to other agencies. We do *not* want an obscure branch of the FBI stirring this up accidentally so that the public stumbles on this disaster. We will therefore assign liaisons from the CIA to coordinate any investigative work you perform in this area. We debated asking you to drop it altogether but concluded that the success rate of your group warranted your continued efforts."

"Along those lines, we have a request," the NSA man spoke up. He pulled out a memory stick and tossed it across the table to Kanter. "That drive stores a series of audio files recorded by US Marines in Afghanistan several weeks ago. They were tracking a terrorist training cell, not having too much luck, as it was. One night, their communications team picked up an encoded series of transmissions. Definitely not hostiles— they were using modifications of US military codes."

He let this sink in. To hammer the point home, the CIA woman spoke. "This only further convinced us that we had rogue US forces involved."

"The modifications were clever, but we have enough computer firepower to break down just about any code. We did that, with enormous confidence statistically, and generated the audio file I've given you. Drop it in your favorite MP3 player."

"I don't understand," said Kanter. "How can we help?"

"This is a bit embarrassing. The audio file contains a series of sharp command-like phrases spoken by a male voice. The problem is that we can't make heads or tails out of what is being said. We have a formidable army of linguists at our disposal, Agent Kanter. We have translators covering hundreds of known tongues. We've gotten nowhere. A brick wall. It's definitely not a common Arabic, Semitic, European, or Asian language. Whatever is being said over those coded transmissions is in a language no one speaks on this earth. It might as well be from Mars."

"This doesn't make sense," said Kanter.

"Not one damn bit," said the NSA man. "You have a reputation for solving puzzles, Agent Kanter. You're not linguists, but frankly, the linguists have failed. I believe there's a puzzle here, something we aren't seeing. Not a code, not a trick, something else. Have your go at it."

The meeting ended sharply on that note. Kanter was thanked, charged with maintaining confidentiality, and dismissed. He stumbled out of the building into the bright and warm moonlight of June, dizzy and exhausted from the last hour. More than anything, Larry Kanter was very troubled about all that he had heard. Rogue agents on the loose, assassinations, commando raids on terrorist centers, alien languages, and a political ball of radioactive waste. This was a mountain of a mess.

He was going to kill Savas.

9

Disturbed, Savas watched as the uproar of chatter erupted from the members of Intel 1. Only Angel Lightfoote sat apart from the heated discussion, staring out the window, seemingly oblivious to the turmoil.

Larry Kanter threw up his arms in surrender and thundered over the rest. "That's *all* I have!"

Savas glanced around at the group, at the frustration evident in their faces. He couldn't blame them. Larry was holding back key information, and everyone knew it. Kanter hadn't said a word about the CIA death squads except to stonewall that all the information was classified. *Classified!* Of course it was classified. What were they, preschoolers? They had obtained classified information before. That Kanter was implying it was anything except an obstacle spoke volumes. After everything they had all been through, it felt a little like betrayal.

"Larry," said Frank Miller after some moments, "this smells of cover-up. What is the threat level in this hunt?"

Kanter sighed. "The threat level is very high, and we're hunting for the very dangerous perpetrators of these crimes. We've made connections that are potentially very real, and we need to start from there and work our way out. We have a definite lead. There are these audio recordings, which the NSA believes are communications among our bad guys. The language is not known to any translators in the agency. They're likely farming this out to several places. One of those is Intel 1."

Rideout just shook his head. "This is a weird one, Larry. I mean, what the *hell*?"

"Look, J. P., this is real. It's also complicated, more than I can, am *allowed* to, explain. But it's real. We need to put to the side everything else except this case, which we have been asked to solve—however absurd the pieces handed to us appear to be."

A harsh vibration sounded on the table. Savas reached over and grabbed his cell phone as it slowly rotated on the smooth surface. He glanced at the display, and his eyes widened. He held up a hand and took the call. Kanter and the others waited.

"Rasheed? This better be an emergency." Savas was silent for a moment, then he exclaimed into the phone, "*What?* Tonight? That was *not* part of the deal, Rasheed! You break that deal, and three felony counts will suddenly reappear and net you half a lifetime in jail!" A voice yelled over the speaker, and Savas responded firmly. "You bet your ass I can! And it *will* be your ass. What? You don't *care?* Rasheed, this is crazy!"

Savas swiveled his chair and bent over the phone. "Where are you?" The voice could be heard barking out strained words. "We'll meet there. In an hour—I'll be there! If you value your freedom, you'll give me that hour and talk."

Savas closed the phone and cursed.

"Mother-in-law?" asked Rideout.

"The Sheikh. I don't believe this. He's rabbiting. Spooked to high heaven. I've got to stop him. He's crucial to several operations."

Kanter studied Savas for a moment. "What's gotten into him?"

"Seen a ghost," said Lightfoote, staring seriously at the group.

Savas ignored her. "I don't know. Even the threat of jail wasn't touching him. I've got to get up to East Harlem before he changes his mind and decides to skip our little chat."

Kanter nodded. "Go, John."

Savas stood up quickly and headed to the door. On his way out, he passed Lightfoote, who continued to stare intensely at everyone around the table, her long red hair offset by the growing darkness outside. Rain began to pellet the window behind her, and deep rumblings of thunder could be felt through the walls.

She muttered. "Seen his own ghost."

Her words sat uncomfortably in Savas's mind as he walked out the door.

Water pounded the New York streets as Savas slammed the door of the cab and sprinted into the park. Mothers with strollers dashed madly searching for shelter, and large puddles began to form on street corners with failing drainage. Savas dodged several strollers and seemingly unperturbed jogging fanatics as he aimed for the center of the park. He spotted the pedestrian bridge as he rose over a small hill and danced down the steps along its side, finding himself in a circular garden, complete with vacated benches and a central flower bed morphed into a pond by the rain. To the side, a short tunnel ran under the bridge. He headed for it and the dark shape waiting inside.

The Sheikh had looked better. He normally sported a strange combination of tailored clothes that clashed with the reversed baseball cap and multiple earring studs. Today the hat and clothes were soaked, the heavy gold necklace and wrist chains spotted with water yet still bright, even in the dim light against his dark Arabic skin. The white shirt he wore was nearly transparent, soaked through, and Savas could see the blurred shape of a tattoo on his right forearm. What worried Savas the most was the disarray in his face. The Sheikh was always a cool customer, arrogant in his confidence, his ability to play all sides to his advantage. Today, he looked like a frightened punk.

"You'll have me in my grave, G-man."

"You've been watching too many Capone films, Rasheed." Savas shook the water from his face. "You're too important to be disappearing on me. I need to know what's going on."

"You need to know. You always need to know," said the Sheikh. "What's *going on* is that the network's gone rabid, man. There's a purge on."

"It's not us, Rasheed. You're tagged as mine. No one will touch you as long as you're working with us."

The Sheikh laughed. "*Damn*, man, no one's scared of *you*. You Feds are always three steps behind."

"Caught you, didn't I?"

The Sheikh smiled. "You got lucky. But I mean *going down*. That ain't jail, man. They're *dead*. Bodies just piling up, and no one's fingered, everybody's denying. Likely true, too—everybody's getting hit. If you in the business, you get marked, a price is on your head. No one wants to talk about it. Like the fucking boogeyman."

Savas felt his heart rate increase. More killings? Purgings in the terrorist underground? This was potentially even bigger than he thought. He *needed* the Sheikh to stay where he was! "Rasheed, you don't have to run. We've got protection teams. We can watch your back, undercover. If it gets too hot, we can take you into protective custody."

The Sheikh just shook his head. "This ain't the usual. Boys aren't scared for nothing. Someone's coming after us, G-man, and they ain't interested in business. They interested in dead men. Networks are wrecked. There ain't no credit, no trail, nothing we can see."

He looked around anxiously, water dripping from his cap. The rain continued its downpour, periodic flashes following rolls of thunder echoing against the concrete and stone walls of the tunnel. A small river began to flow through the tunnel under the bridge, soaking through their shoes.

The Sheikh grinned diabolically. "Doing your job for you."

"This is important, *damn it*!" Savas had to convince him to work from within. "We *know* this is happening. We've got to figure out who is behind this!"

"That ain't no interest to me. I done well in this business, and no one's wise to me. But money ain't no good if you're six feet under."

Savas used the only tool he had left: fear. "Do you really think you can hide from them, Rasheed?" The Sheikh's widening eyes betrayed his concern. Savas continued. "Whoever is behind this, they've taken out imams in England and diplomats in New York. They're all over the globe, invisible, *professional*. Like you said, they don't seem to be familiar with the word 'mercy,' or to have an interest in money or negotiation. You're a *player*, Rasheed. For both sides, we know too well, but a player who makes the network hum. *You're* one of those important links. It's not a question of whether you have a price on your head—it's how much, and when they will cash in."

"Fuck you, man!" he shouted, and started to back away.

"You run, and you'll be completely on your own, unprotected and no closer to knowing who is after you. If we can figure this out, we can come down hard on these people, and that will go a lot farther toward saving your ass than trying to hide in a hole. They'll dig you out, Rasheed. Then they'll pull the trigger."

The Sheikh looked like he was near panic; the truth of Savas's words burrowed inside him. He would either break in alarm from the fear or see that the FBI was throwing him a lifeline—a tenuous one, perhaps, but without it, he was helpless in the water as the sharks circled.

The man inched back toward Savas. He grasped the line.

"What do you want? I don't have much time. They're on to me. Too many small things; can't explain it. But I know."

Instinct. Savas exhaled softly. "You're to keep your eyes open. We'll assign a team of undercover agents to shadow you. If what you say is true, you'll be the trap."

"I'll be the fucking *bait*, man."

Savas leveled his gaze at the man. Honesty was essential. "Yes, Rasheed. You will be."

10

Pants Henry lay in an alcohol-induced daze on a hard park bench.

A cool breeze stirred through the darkness surrounding him, rustling leaves and pieces of litter along the sidewalk, searching for morning. The boiling New York summer had not yet triumphed over the spring, and the city had still to warm to its deep tissue of concrete and metal. A rare and soft stillness rested over Manhattan. A good time to sleep it off.

A beige moon hung over the East River, and a winking handful of stars forced their way through the moonlight and the orange haze of streetlamps. Pants breathed slowly on his bench in Dag Hammarskjold Park in Midtown, a brown paper bag on the ground next to him, a pushcart and several bags of cans and sundry objects to the side. After so many years frequenting this park, he was nearly a decoration. The locals tolerated him, and his one intact pants leg, as best they could.

The moonlight darted through the metal grid of a park sculpture that rose from the middle of the plaza. Six spidery pillars of black iron climbed toward the heavens from foot-tall concrete blocks, and six filigreed arches curved upward, intersecting at a small ring to create a netted dome. The moonlight danced through this meshwork, alighting on Pants's haggard face, beard, and the thin wire transmitter/receiver running from ear to mouth. Soft static bursts escaped from the device as he quietly responded.

"Eagle 7, this is Alpha center." The language was guttural, vaguely Germanic, uninterpretable to anyone who might have overheard.

"Copy," Pants whispered in the same tongue, his eyes cracked open imperceptibly.

"Report."

"Plaza is clean."

"Remain in position. Delta team has exited the target zone. Surveillance has been redirected. The gardeners are planting. Estimate less than ten minutes. Situation is nominal but critical. Execute extreme caution. This is it, Eagle 7."

"Roger, Alpha center."

Pants knew that ten minutes was more than enough. The city block at Second Avenue had been re-created in the deserts of the Southwest, the operation rehearsed more times than he wished to remember, with too many different scenarios, too many failures and unexpected events encountered. Nothing could go wrong tonight.

That was why, when he saw motion at the far end of the park, training took over, and the outcome was never in doubt.

He watched as two young men stepped into the plaza. Their voices were loud for the hour, alcohol a likely culprit. They appeared to be fair-skinned blacks or Latinos, with loose-fitting jeans, sharply cut shirts revealing strong muscles, and not a few thin-edged scars. Unmoving on the park bench, Pants was not surprised to see the black-and-gold tattoos. *Latin Kings*. Fallen from their heyday, broken by police and changing times, their members were still feared. He would need to be focused.

"Alpha center, two unidentifieds, moving toward the garden. Latin Kings. Moving to intercept."

"Roger that, Eagle 7. Mission critical. Sanitize the plaza."

"Roger, Alpha Center. In progress."

He rose slowly from the bench, an old bum seemingly both drunk and hungover. He reached down for his paper bag and shuffled toward the middle of the plaza, walking slowly beneath the iron dome, grasping bars to steady himself. The two Kings slowed, still laughing, but many nights living near death's edge had sharpened intuitions that preserved life. There was nothing unusual about the wino in front of them— Pants had made sure of that—but still they slowed. Pants understood: that place of unreason that awakens in the face of danger whispered deep within them.

He made himself appear oblivious to their motions, stumbling forward and talking to himself and to the brown stone-tiled walkway at his feet. Approaching within ten yards, he raised his head, babbling nonsense and quickening his gait. The young men slowed and stared at each other. They seemed amused, an initial sense of caution replaced with a smirking mischief. Pants watched as the man on the right reached into his pocket and pulled out a short knife, grinning.

The youth's smile faded. *Can't hide the eyes.* Pants knew the young man did not see the clouded eyes of a drunk; he saw those of a hunter.

With surprising speed, Pants spun into action. From underneath his shabby coat, he removed a handgun, a silencer protruding from the barrel. Without hesitation, he aimed and squeezed the trigger twice. Two soft spits melted into the soft June wind blowing through the park, followed by the wet impact of a human form dropping to the ground. Even as the first figure began its descent to the hard pavement, Pants rotated his arm a few degrees and fired again. The head of the other man arched backward as the second shot exploded near his heart. Both bodies lay crumbled on the ground.

Pants paused, listening, the gun still and upright, his body tense, his head cocked at an angle. From one of the bodies came a soft moaning. The first target placed his hands on the ground in front of him as he tried vainly to rise. Blood covered his chest and hands; his face looked pale. Posture erect, motions sure and controlled, Pants stepped toward the prone man and aimed the weapon.

"No . . ." the young man whispered, seeing the barrel pointed at his head. He dropped straight down as a shot blew apart the upper right corner of his forehead, spraying blood and bone across the cobbled walkway. Pants knelt down and checked the other body. Satisfied, he glanced around the plaza carefully, also scanning the windows of surrounding buildings, then spoke into his microphone.

"Alpha center, this is Eagle 7. Plaza is sanitized. Repeat, plaza is sanitized."

"Roger that, Eagle 7. Gardeners have seeded the area. Exit plaza and proceed to rendezvous with flock."

"Any disposal, Alpha center?"

"Negative, Eagle 7. Unnecessary, and there's no time. After tomorrow, your little mess will be the least of their worries."

"Roger that. Eagle 7, out." Pants resumed a stumbling gait and slowly made his way down the plaza walkway toward First Avenue. There, he turned left, uptown, glancing back only momentarily at the dancing currents of the East River. Somewhere, he knew, those currents were carrying the body of the real Pants Henry, who was finally at rest.

Far more intently, he followed the lights alongside the river, staring up at the towering form of the United Nations building at the river's edge.

11

Traffic rushed like swarms of locusts across Second Avenue. *Swarms of large, cheap, ugly metallic locusts,* thought Fahd Shobokshi, aide to the Saudi Counselor, as he stepped over a fresh pile of dog excrement left by some undoubtedly charming member of this filthy city of infidels. Fahd Shobokshi hated his job. He hated being away from his homeland. He hated having to fawn over the pompous and idiotic head of the Saudi Consulate in Manhattan. He hated the small and poorly furnished hole they called an apartment in this city. He hated living in this nation of sinners and in this chief city of Satan, where a righteous man could not walk two blocks without having to turn away from pornography. He hated the dinners overflowing with Western dishes, the long hours of tedious paperwork. Most of all, he hated the mornings when he knew he would be dressed down by the counselor for being late. Today, he was late again.

The street sign blinked to "walk," and Fahd dodged the rushing cab as he stepped across the street. There was one thing he did like about the city, and that was the—what did they call it in Urdu? *The kulfi wala.* Yes, he liked the kulfi wala, he thought pleasantly, as a stinking and sweating American jogger bumped into him. If it made him even later, then he would gain much and lose little. His dressing down was already assured. At the corner of the plaza, the cart was there, as it was every working summer day. The short little Pakistani would be there, too, with his terrible but wonderful kulfi. Fahd had come to love the mornings and his kulfi—so superior to the dripping and too-thick ice cream these Americans preferred. A day felt incomplete without it.

He stepped up to the cart and smiled at the man. These Pakistanis were good people, but they were barely Muslims. An inferior race still tainted by their roots in paganism. *But Allah is merciful, and he offers his mercy to all people who follow his precepts.* He paid and took his plastic bowl and spoon and began to eat, tasting the cool of the ice milk in the warming June sun, pausing long enough outside of 866 Second Avenue for a final moment of peace before the day began. He glanced over toward the plaza. *Police.* There were several, and they had begun to fence off a region of the park. *More crime in this murderous city.*

He glanced up at the tall building, its black-glass windows filled with floor after floor of United Nations' representatives. It was a rather imposing building, sucking the light out of the nice little corner between the tree-lined plaza and the small park across the street. He'd rather wait outside, especially on a nice day like today. But he could not. He took a deep breath. He was late already, and pausing outside would not benefit his situation.

A moment later, he watched the door to hell open in front of his feet.

He felt turned inside-out in the middle of a fire, pummeled by stones and bathed in rushing air. His ears ached from an assault by a multitude of sounds, as if submerged in water. He reached up to touch them, then pulled his hands down. With blurred vision, he saw that they were covered in blood. Suddenly, his back erupted in a spasm of pain, and his eyes focused. He was lying on the street surrounded by broken glass, nearly underneath a large truck parked on the west side of Second Avenue.

I am across the street. How? Through the wetness of the blood in his injured ears, he began to filter sounds. Alarms, many of them. Building alarms, car alarms; he could not tell. Voices screaming—commands, exclamations. Cries for help. His eyes could see only a brown haze, a thick cloud of dust like a choking fog surrounding the block. Cars were overturned or crushed by what seemed like enormous slabs of concrete. Glass was everywhere, and flakes like confetti rained down from above.

He tried to stand. The pain in his back was paralyzing. He tried again, groaning from the effort, and finally made it to his feet. His left arm was not working; it hung limply at his side. *I cannot feel it.* He looked down to realize that he was covered in bloody ash. One shoe was missing. *Merciful God, what has happened?*

He limped forward over what had been the busy street. No cars drove there now. Thousands of shards of glass covered the roadway. He heard sirens, choruses of sirens blaring, it seemed, from all directions. Glancing forward, across the street, he gasped. The cloud of dust was still amazingly thick, a sharp rain descending like sand. It had cleared enough, however, to leave no doubt. A gaping hole was carved out of the earth. Fires ranged along the crater, in nearby vehicles, in the trees of Dag Hammarskjold Park. The corner of Second Avenue and Forty-Sixth Street was a giant hole, a black pit of nothingness opening its maw to drink the dust above it. The building, *his building*, a tower of polished black glass and steel, filled with workers from twenty different nations, was simply gone. Blown and dispersed into the air of New York.

For several seconds, he could not move. Police cars and fire trucks arrived at the scene, and the sounds of chaos flowed over his shattered ears like water in a sea cave. A hulking fireman in a mask rushed toward Fahd, shouting at him and pointing across the road, telling him something he could not understand. Fahd nodded dumbly, turning left to retreat back across the street. He glimpsed the pushcart he had visited this morning, in a place and time far from this one, in another world. Next to the overturned cart lay a body unmoving. A small dark form. His Pakistani friend.

Fahd stumbled over debris in the road. He looked down to right himself and noticed an irregular object. He stared in horror. He began to shake. Below him was the face of a woman. *Not her head, dear Allah, not her head.* Three-quarters of her face was removed from the rest of her body, an eye along with distorted and grotesque lips and cartilage from the nose, tattered bits of a forehead, all soaked in blood. He heard it now, crashing against his bleeding eardrums. Screams and screams and screams of terror. He looked around, turning in every direction, edging away from the demonic mask of death near his feet. The screams grew louder and louder in his head, and he turned to look but could not find the source of the voices. Only as he began to limp maniacally across the road, no longer caring what he stepped on, glass or flesh, did he realize that the screams were his own.

12

John Savas stepped up the curb onto the sidewalk in front of 26 Federal Plaza. He wore a dark suit and sunglasses, and carried a coffee in one hand and the *New York Times* and his briefcase in the other. As was clear to anyone who knew him, the tension of the last few weeks had begun to extract a toll. His shoulders sagged slightly, and behind the sunglasses, his eyes were bloodshot from lack of sleep.

He swung into the main entrance of the FBI building, keeping his coffee level while dodging exiting and entering figures, rarely taking his eyes of the page he was reading. He glanced up at security, nodded toward the well-known faces, handed off his items, went through the required checks, grabbed his items, and found his place back in the article as he approached the elevators.

Several figures were waiting in line. He smiled, glimpsing a young woman with waist-length red hair. Today she wore a bright-green dress complemented by red sneakers, and stood apart from the crowd waiting for the elevators, staring straight up at the wall to her left and seemingly caught in another trance of some kind. Savas glanced back down at his article and slowed to a stop behind her.

"Greetings, Kemo Sabe," the young woman spoke.

"Someday I'm going to learn how to sneak up on you, Angel."

"I doubt that, John."

"Yeah, so do I."

"You look like shit."

Savas laughed. "Thanks, doll. I'm looking forward to the weekend and a little rest."

"Sorry to hear that," said Lightfoote, moving toward the elevator.

Before Savas could process her words, the bell rang and the doors opened.

As soon as Savas stepped out of the elevator onto his floor, he knew something was wrong. The normal rhythms of work were completely out-of-whack as agents darted from place to place among a din of rising voices. Already he could see Kanter in the back pointing and shouting commands; then, spotting Savas, he called him over with an imperious wave of his hand.

"See you soon, Captain Overlord, sir," Lightfoote said sweetly.

"What?" asked Savas distractedly, but by the time he turned to look, she was already flitting across the room. Savas spilled his coffee over his *New York Times*, cursed, and marched forward after dropping both in the trash.

Kanter was in prime form. Already his tie was askew and his receding gray hair hung in growing disarray. A fire burned in his eyes, and his jaw jutted forward, signaling that he was in the crazed problem-solving mode that made him so skilled as an administrator, as well as such a pain in the ass. Kanter didn't waste any time getting to the point.

"This is it, John!" he said, grabbing the ex-cop's arm in a vicelike grip and dragging him across the room. "No drill. We have a bona fide event right now in New York City."

"What?" sputtered Savas. "An attack? Today?"

"That's right. Looks like it's down by the UN—not the UN proper, thank goodness. We have some confirmation on that, at least. But in the immediate area. Set your team up now, John. I want everything you can get on this pouring in ASAP." Kanter left his side and stormed off toward another team.

Savas headed toward the Operations Room for Intel 1. On his way he banged on the office doors of his group members. "Let's go! We need to move right now to the OR!" Of his six team members, only the angular form of Matt King emerged.

"I supposed from all this chaos that we must—"

"Shut it, Matt. Mail me the essay. This is real. Let's move." Savas turned and nearly crashed into the hairy form of Hernandez.

"Manuel, please, to the Operations Room. This one looks real, and we might just burn through all the wires you duct-taped together. I need you in there making sure we fly straight; you got it?"

"I'm on it."

"Please don't tell me we're running any beta versions of anything."

"I live by a don't-ask-don't-tell policy for software, John."

Savas stared harshly at the ceiling for a moment. "The system better not crash." He pushed past Hernandez and felt him following behind as they headed to the Operations Room. Along the way, they were joined by J. P. Rideout and Frank Miller. The four strode into the OR.

"OK, where's Rebecca?" asked Savas, glancing around the room with some anxiety. Over the last few years, he'd come to count more on Rebecca Cohen than on anyone in the group. Her sharp mind, grounded personality, and holistic way of thinking kept the team focused with the right perspective. She was also a whiz with the crises system Hernandez had set up. Today would be a bad day for her to call in sick.

"I'm here, John," she said, whisking into the OR. He breathed easier.

"All right, now if we can only get Angel in here, we can start to break this thing down."

Hernandez tugged on his arm and pointed across the room. Savas followed his hand to the end of the half-moon desk. Lightfoote sat there; somehow she had entered before they had come in, or perhaps she had floated in like some ghost without anyone noticing. As he looked at her, she paused her furious typing to raise a hand, eyes still on the screen, giving Savas the thumbs-up.

Aside from Savas and Hernandez, the remaining members of Intel 1 were busy logging in and bringing up the system. Awaiting commands from Savas, some were already running the analysis software.

"OK, folks, all I've got for the present is that there was an attack Midtown East by the UN. Rebecca, let's bring up the police and fire data. Angel, can you get a live satellite view up?"

An enormous projection screen was draped over the far wall, some ten feet in front of the table. It flashed to life, showing five smaller subdivisions superimposed over a larger background. One screen, corresponding to Lightfoote's terminal, blinked and came to life, displaying a view from space. It quickly zoomed into the island of Manhattan just south of the Queensboro Bridge. Smoke obscured a region of several blocks near the United Nations building. Other screens flashed and showed a stream of text—emergency bulletins from several New York City agencies.

"Excellent. Rebecca, why don't you run the link to Larry's office and dump the live feed. OK, what do we have folks?"

In the time it took him to say these things, several of the other screens flashed on, revealing varied scenes. One was cutting between local and national coverage of the event on television. Another was funneling information from Internet search engines through one of Manuel's algorithms.

"Explosive device, John," Cohen called out, processing the information and integrating it faster than anyone. Lightfoote cut in, "Second Avenue, near the plaza. Can't see through the smoke."

An altered image of the scene displayed in false color revealed no obscuring smoke but rather illuminated solid structures—buildings, cars, and rubble—in an eerie green.

"Filtering it through the IATIA satellite, looks like a hole ... there!" King called out. Several intakes of breath were heard over the clacking of keyboards.

"Damn," said Savas. "Something was blown to hell and back."

Immediately, another image of the area occupied the screen controlled by Rideout. It showed the same region, in real color and without the hole.

"SAT photo before the bombing, sometime last week," Rideout chimed in. "It's the corner of Second and Forty-Sixth Street."

"OK, people, what is it? Let's find out what was in that hole."

Cohen leaned back. "John, fire department chatter confirms what we're seeing. There was a massive explosion. There is some severe damage, and there are reports of many injuries and secondary carnage from car fires and falling debris."

"Well, they've come back to visit again, folks, that much is clear. Anyone know what the hell they hit yet?"

"Got it! It's a UN office building. 866 Second Avenue," said Rideout. An image flashed, showing a tall, black-glass building. "Damn. I'm getting one international office located there after another: representatives from Ecuador, Greece, Guyana, Honduras, even the Saudi General Consulate . . . they're spread out on different floors and offices."

Miller muttered, "I don't think it's gonna matter what floor those poor bastards were on."

"No, indeed," echoed Savas. "OK, so, what we have is an attack on UN personnel, a UN building for all practical purposes, with enough shit to take the entire building down."

"Structural damage to neighboring buildings is minimal from both the SAT and chatter, John," said Cohen.

"OK. Your point?"

"Well, they didn't use airplanes this time, that's for sure," said Miller.

Cohen nodded. "This was a surgical strike, John. Whoever did this managed to obliterate an entire building in midtown Manhattan without much collateral damage. Unless they got supremely lucky, we're looking at some very highly skilled munitions work."

"I guess they've been busy in those caves all these years," said Savas, turning toward the screen. "Manuel, what do we have in terms of munitions analysis?"

"Ah, John, that isn't exactly anything I know much about or that can be done easily with software. We'll need to farm this out to forensics."

"Yeah, figured. But that means we're waiting as usual to sift through the aftermath. This is in real-time, folks. OK, what else can we pull out of this?"

"CNN, Fearless Leader," said Lightfoote.

Her terminal cut to a live broadcast from the news organization. A reporter stood before a mob of people kept at a distance by police and fire department personnel, who themselves were partially obscured by pouring smoke. The reporter's words were barely audible over the sound of sirens and voices.

". . . about half an hour ago, Brian. This is as close as our crew was able to get. As you can see, there is simply an incredible amount of smoke, and the building lies in complete ruins. Onlookers report an enormous explosion, or series of explosions. One elderly woman said the ground shook and she nearly fell."

"Doesn't look like Second Avenue to me . . ." started King.

"It's not," said Savas. "It's not even New York. Go to full screen, Rebecca."

The image grew to fill the entire projection screen. People were running in all directions while the reporter continued speaking. Savas grabbed a chair, flipped it around so that its back faced him, and sat down as he listened to the footage. His hands gripped the chair back tightly.

"I'm sorry, Brian, it's just chaos here; I can't hear you. Let me repeat, there has been a major explosion at the Saudi Arabian Embassy here in Washington, DC. None of us can get close enough to see what's going on, but from what we can see, it seems that the embassy has been severely damaged . . . of considerable power. . . . Police and fire crews . . . uncertain . . . injuries . . ." The transmission was breaking up slightly. King used this moment to speak.

"John, I've got this on the SAT."

"Put it up."

The green-colored image occluded a portion of the news feed. Next to it, King superimposed a photograph of the Saudi Embassy from space. In the false-color image that cut through the smoke and clouds, the results of the explosion were obvious to all.

"My *God*, the whole thing's gone," said Rideout. "Just like here. This is like some 9/11 replay. They're hitting us in New York and Washington at the same time."

Rideout's words were like blows to the stomach. Savas felt himself become unhinged in time. *Towers like sand crumbling in the wind. Falling, falling slowly, a million tons of concrete and metal . . . and flesh and bone. Police beneath, young officers, daughters . . . sons. Beneath a mountain falling . . .*

Cohen's voice became a lifeline.

"John, you're not going to believe this."

Savas's eyes, unfocused and in another time, turned toward her and became completely alert. She was holding a cell phone.

"One of the agents guarding the Sheikh is on the phone. They lost him. Two of them are down. Somebody took them out, and the Sheikh bolted. Our man is wounded. He doesn't know if the Sheikh is alive or dead."

13

The group sat still in the dim lighting and bright screens of the Intel 1 crisis center, listening silently to a cell phone message play over the speaker in the room. They heard a strained voice, winded, the man obviously hurt and struggling to speak.

"They knew we were there," he panted. "Shots came—Jones and Richards went down. I think they're dead." He coughed, a harsh and grating sound. "I'm hit, but I can move. The rat ran. I tried to follow," he paused, out of breath, requiring several seconds to speak again. "Couldn't keep up. Trace my cell. I need help. Losing blood."

Cohen stopped the playback. Her voice was soft and flat. "We have an ambulance on the way."

All eyes in Intel 1 turned to Savas. On the screens were the continuing images of the terror attacks: flashing lights of emergency vehicles, smoke, and statements to the press from US and foreign government officials. A voice called out that Kanter was on his way down.

"All right, people, we literally have the world blowing up around us. Let's think carefully but quickly." Savas paced around the room, talking as much toward the floor and ceiling as to the members of his team. "We have major attacks in New York and Washington, coordinated attacks, unlike anything since 9/11. The FBI, the White House, the nation will demand that the majority of our resources be focused on these attacks—and they're right. So, unless Larry countermands me on this, I want most of you busting your asses to get everything you can on these bombings. However, if anything, this ambush on our protection squad convinces me that we are onto something. It may be too late—the Sheikh may be dead. But we don't know that. I'll work with Frank to try to locate him, intercept him, and bring him in if he's not already flower food. Any objections?"

"Damn inconvenient timing!" barked Kanter, who was standing in the doorway listening. "Your contact surely excels in planning, orchestrating his near murder right as we scramble to cover this nightmare!"

"Someone may indeed have a sense of timing, Larry, but I don't think it's the Sheikh."

Kanter waved off Savas's anger. "You and Miller go, and try like hell not to get yourselves killed if you find him—these boys out there are *not* playing around. Meanwhile, Intel 1 will be a little short-staffed but will sacrifice increasing amounts of their lives, or at least sleep, to make up the difference." Kanter turned toward the group, focusing on Rebecca. "Agent Cohen, I assume that you have no objections if I elevate you to temporary group leader in John's absence?"

"No, Larry, of course—"

"Good. Because I've got more calls than I have call-waiting circuits, and I don't have time to babysit you people. Your job is to figure out what the hell happened, who's responsible, and, if possible, have them in custody this evening."

"We'll do our best . . . sir," said Cohen.

Kanter frowned and stormed out of the room.

Savas looked at the ex-marine and sighed. "OK, Frank, you and I will carve out a little corner of the OR. The rest of you—Rebecca has the wheel."

Cohen nodded but instead walked over toward Savas and pulled him aside. He blinked. She almost looked angry.

"John, you were unconscious after Indian Point for *two days*. You suffered radiation sickness and a broken rib. Do you think you need to be chasing this street punk and those assassins down while all the rest of this is going on? Is this mission really that critical?"

"Yes, I think so. Something important is tied into this." He tried to calm her. "Look, we'll be careful, like Larry said. We know there are some nasties buzzing around this one."

She just stared at him disbelievingly. "Sure, zero to sixty in 5.4

seconds, crashing explosives with a forklift in a radioactive death cell. Was your monster truck trick careful, too?"

Savas was taken aback. "Rebecca, I did what I had to there! Those explosives were rigged to blow. The cooling rods were completely exposed!"

Cohen nodded but with a frown on her face, her eyes distant. "John, it's not the details. It's the pattern. This is becoming a habit, don't you think?"

"What is?"

"You nearly getting yourself killed on every case."

Savas looked away. This was a direction he didn't want any conversation to go. Not now, with buildings coming down and contacts on the run. Not with Rebecca.

Miller delivered him. The muscled agent strode up to the pair. "John, let's move. Manuel let me have the keys to the car, and I'm bringing up the tracking system. Let's see where he's running."

Savas avoided Cohen's gaze and followed the ex-marine. Maybe the Sheikh wasn't the only one running.

There was a counterpoint of activity in the room as the majority of Intel 1 continued to focus on the unfolding terrorist attacks. Savas and Miller commandeered a terminal and went to work tracking down his contact.

"Manuel has transferred control of our communications software, John," Miller announced, typing furiously on the keyboard. "I *think* I know what I'm doing with it. Look—*here*! His phone has a GPS, and we can track him. He's in Queens, apparently not moving—assuming, of course, that it's him alive with the phone."

"Try the cell. If he's stopped running, he might answer."

"Punching it, using your number as the caller," said Miller. "I'll run a general scan on the phone as well."

The digital tones of the dialed number played over the small computer speakers. There was a click, and a voice answered.

"*Fuck you*, G-man!" came the welcome. "A lot of good your muscle did me."

"Shut up, Rasheed!" yelled Savas into the computer microphone. "We've got agents dead who were covering your ass! We need to come in and get you."

"You'd better!"

"We will!"

"They know; it all started after I talked to you."

"What started? Who's *they*, Rasheed?"

"Fuck that! No time! I need protection! Your men are down, useless. I need to come in!"

"OK, Rasheed, we know where you are."

Miller covered the microphone and whispered to Savas "John, so does someone else. His cell's being tracked."

Savas felt a surge of adrenaline. "Who?"

"Checking . . . no one legit!"

Christ! "Rasheed, you've got to hang up and call me from another cell, a new cell, prepaid, or a pay phone. Your cell is tagged. They're tracking you."

"*Fuck!*" The phone went dead.

Miller turned to Savas. "He'll move from there; he's smart. He'll call us when he's got another phone."

Savas nodded. "I hope so. Meanwhile, we know where he is, so let's get there."

"Yeah," said Miller, "before someone else does."

14

The drive to Queens became an exercise in patience in the face of panic. Law enforcement had locked down all of Manhattan—bridges, tunnels, airports. Getting on or off the island required long waits through the stalled traffic and repeated discussions with police and national guard personnel to achieve clearance. Miller drove, and Savas could only boil inside as he played through multiple scenarios—most ending up with the Sheikh dead before they could get to him. He also did not forget that they were heading into a covert warzone, where unknown ciphers were playing a deadly game of cat and mouse. He had two dead agents, and a growing list of downed assassination targets, to remind him.

He reached over and removed his pistol, placing it on his lap. In a quick series of motions, he lifted the weapon, pressed the magazine catch, and let the cartridge drop onto his legs. He pulled the slide back and inspected the chamber to ensure it was empty, then allowed the slide to spring forward. He pointed the gun toward the right side of the car and pulled the trigger. The click was clear, smart, and drowned by the sound of tires over the Queensboro Bridge.

"You planning on breaking it down on the way over?" asked Miller wryly, his eyes on the road, the speedometer approaching sixty.

Savas shook his head. "Figured we may be reloading today, Frank. Wanted to have a peek at things inside."

Miller nodded. "Shot placement is everything. I've seen guys unload and hit an assailant with more than ten rounds in the wrong places. The man just kept firing. Even without drugs, a determined man can take a lot of incidental damage and fight through the pain. Got to unplug the battery—heart, lungs, major organs."

"I know, Frank," said Savas, but the ex-marine continued.

"In the war, in Afghanistan, I saw shit you wouldn't believe. I've seen a two-twenty-pound pile of Special Forces muscle drop dead from a piece a shrapnel no bigger than a needle. I've seen men drag themselves with half a leg blown off, still firing, screaming obscenities, until they dropped from blood loss. The worst are the religious nuts, the jihadists who believe every dead American is another virgin in paradise. I've seen those bastards filled with ammo, and they keep coming. Human, of course—just got to hit them in the right place." He shook his head sharply, as if trying to shake the visions out of his mind. "Seen the opposite, of course—young Arab kids who take a shot in the leg and learn the hard way that their faith was abstract. Those fall fast. Bunch of bawling kids on the side while you deal with the maniacs."

"Sounds like hell, Frank."

Miller smiled sharply. "I've heard it called so. When you're there, it just is what it is."

Savas's cell rang out, and he picked up.

"Rasheed? Where are you?"

Miller concentrated, trying to hear the words spoken on the other end. Savas continued. "OK, we're almost there. We're going to pull up near the Astoria line. You'll see a black town car, FBI written all over it. Yes, I know! But it's all we had access to! In case you didn't realize, all hell's broken out in the city today!"

Savas continued after the voice spoke for several seconds. "If you *are* being followed, we'll have you covered. Come up Thirtieth Avenue toward the subway line. We'll be hidden close to the station, near the car, but we'll see down the street for a long way. Anything suspicious and we'll move on it."

Savas closed the phone.

"One of the subway stations, John? Kinda public for this."

Savas paused a moment, deep in thought. "I know, but I needed a place he could identify and get to fast, without confusion. Also, it will be harder to pull anything off in a crowded place."

Miller raised his eyebrows. "If they do, we could get some collateral damage."

Savas nodded, his face troubled. He had accepted the risk but was burdened by it anyway. *The location—so close to the church. Why did I choose to meet him there?*

"He was clean?"

"Said he was using a pay phone." He turned toward Miller. "I can't believe his cell was being tracked! Who has that kind of access, Frank?"

"Phone companies and select government agencies, John. You know that."

"The CIA hit squads? Damn it, I don't believe that, Frank!"

Miller shrugged. "No one else could have that access, John. No one."

"To pull off all these kills, they'd need worldwide access. It doesn't make sense."

"Well, someone's tapped into US communication networks, all to track down this one guy. Either they really want him, or they have a kind of casual access that is frightening."

"He's not that important."

"Then we ought to be worried about who we are dealing with, John."

They rode the rest of the way in silence.

The Sheikh was due to be on foot, moving up the street toward the station from the west. After checking the platform, Savas and Miller quickly descended from the elevated tracks above Thirty-First Street. Miller sat down at an outdoor café and was the perfect model of a relaxed two-hundred-and-thirty-pound marine enjoying the fine June weather. Savas took a more awkward position, slowly gazing over the newspaper stand in front of a deli. Soon, he had run out of papers to stare at and began to examine the produce out on display when he noticed a movement from Miller's direction.

The marine had spotted their quarry first and rose from his seat, heading toward the street crossing. Savas's cell vibrated as Miller sent an alert to his phone. Across the street and halfway down the block, weaving erratically, was the harried figure of the Sheikh. *Oh, Christ!* Savas tensed instinctively as he realized that the man was nearly running. He and Miller locked eyes for a moment, the communication enough, then both began to cross the street in the direction of their informant. Savas reached down and felt for his gun in his side holster, hidden behind the side of his suit jacket. He continued to zero in on the Sheikh, while scanning the sea of people behind him.

The hunter was hard to miss. A tallish man rounded the corner at the far end of the block, and, like the Sheikh, he moved too fast, counter to the normal flow of pedestrians. Savas heard Miller shout from the right. Both men pulled their guns and began sprinting toward the Sheikh, who had nearly reached the corner. Several people began to scream, and Savas waved them out of their way.

"FBI! Everyone clear the way! Clear the way!"

The pedestrian traffic parted like the Red Sea, some people dropping to the ground, some rushing into buildings, most running either right or left of Savas. Savas saw the Sheikh and waved him down.

"Drop! Drop down!"

The Sheikh dropped. His action, and the parting crowd, exposed the figure pursuing him. A gun was in the assassin's hand. As the killer sprinted, he steadied the weapon, aiming it at the Sheikh.

Savas braced himself against a lamppost and fired. Gunshots exploded from his and Miller's weapons. People screamed. Bullets whizzed past him, sending shards of shattered concrete into the air.

The battle was brief, the assassin caught in an unexpected crossfire. Savas watched him stumble and fall backward. His weapon arm struck the sidewalk, sending the gun rattling behind him.

"Frank, the Sheikh!" screamed Savas. Miller dashed forward to the prone figure of their contact. Savas approached the downed killer, gun steadied in his hands and aimed forward. Four shots had found their mark: two in the chest, one to the gun shoulder, and the last either a graze or partial-penetration head wound. Savas knew the wounds were life threatening. But the man was *alive!* Miller came up to his side with the Sheikh in tow, who spat out curses.

"Shut it!" yelled Savas, as he pulled out his cell, mashing several buttons. "Getting medical help here as soon as possible. We aren't losing this bastard! He's our key, Frank. I promise you, one way or the other, he'll lead us to the truth."

The man mumbled several words, then suddenly came to consciousness. For a moment he looked confused; then he seemed to place himself and his situation. Even seriously wounded, he managed to attempt an attack. Savas, uninjured, was more than ready, and he forced the man back down. The killer relaxed, having spent most of his available energy. Savas grabbed him by the shirt collar.

"Nice try, asshole. While you're awake, you should know that you have the right to remain silent. Anything you say can and will be used against you in a court of law. You have the right to have an attorney present during questioning. If you cannot afford an attorney, one will be appointed for you. Do you understand these rights?" The man whispered something Savas could not understand. "I'll take that as a 'yes.'"

Suddenly, before Savas had even released his grip on the man, an impact blew open the man's forehead, showering the three of them with blood. Stunned momentarily, they didn't move. Then Savas turned quickly toward Miller.

"Get him down! Get him—" But it was too late. As Miller reached over to grab the Sheikh, a loud slap sounded, and their contact arched his neck, a shot blasting through his spine and brainstem. He dropped instantly to the ground, his vital processes immediately halted. He was dead.

"No, *damn it!*" shouted Savas, as he drew his fists up sharply and pounded the hard concrete. *The trap had been reversed!* Another assassin had been waiting or in pursuit. He finished the job on the wounded killer, then turned his sights on the Sheikh.

Guns drawn, Miller and Savas scanned the general direction from which the bullet had originated. No further shots followed. The second assassin was gone.

"He shot *him* first." It was Miller's voice. The ex-marine was staring at the body of the dead assassin. "As much as they wanted your contact dead, they wanted more to make sure we didn't take that killer."

Savas nodded, the implications dawning on him. He slowly stood up, his palms numb and clenched, one feeling strangely pricked. He turned his hand over and opened his palm. Gleaming yellow in the sunlight was a golden necklace, torn unintentionally from the dead assassin's neck. Fresh blood stained the gold links. At the bottom hung a golden pendant. It was a strange object, shaped like an anchor, and unlike anything Savas had ever seen.

The harsh face of a bird was carved in its side.

15

In the fading light of the June evening, John Savas watched the old women file out of the church in Astoria. A sea of black with gray caps, they walked or shuffled, some limping down the steps toward the streets. In the midst of the black tide, there were the more nimble steps of the young, small islands lit with bright colors in the midst of the older generation. Vespers was over, the last prayers of the day having been read. Soon, the cantor himself walked out into the falling night. Gazing up at the gold-painted dome and the neon-white cross, he lit a cigarette, crossed himself, and stepped down into the night. In seconds he was lost in the swirling currents of New Yorkers flowing across the busy streets.

After several minutes, when it was clear that the church had emptied, Savas stepped out of a black Lincoln Continental. His polished shoes slapped the pavement as he made his way toward the steps. He wore a black suit, formal yet unimpressive in its make. Functional. His shoes clacked up the stairs to bring him before the entrance, where he crossed himself and pushed one of the doors open slowly, peering inside. Satisfied, he stepped through completely and let the door close softly behind him.

Inside the church, a palpable stillness hung in the air along with the remaining incense. It was always like this, he thought, taking comfort from the fact. That period after the service when no other human being was around seemed to him the most holy, devoid of the voices and noises of men and women, yet still *full* with what he could only think of as the spirits of the worshippers, or the angels themselves still lingering. The space held a thoughtful, prayerful silence more pregnant than the chanting itself. He dropped several coins into the slot underneath the rows of beeswax candles, rows of varying lengths and thicknesses beside the icons at the front of the narthex. He took two candles and lit them from those already placed in the sand, thinking first of his son, then of his ex-wife. He crossed himself again, kissed the icon of Christ, and stepped into the nave.

The lights were very low, and the candles around the body of the church shone brightly. He could smell the incense now. Father Timothy was stowing away his vestments. He looked up, squinting at the visitor in the pews.

"John?" his voice echoed in the dim air between them. "John Savas?"

"Hello, Father."

The priest smiled. "John! It's good to see you after all these years."

"I wasn't sure that it would be," he replied.

The priest frowned. "Of course it is! Let's not have any such nonsense from you about this." The priest came forward. John Savas took his hand, kissed it, and crossed himself. The priest tried vainly to pull his hand back and wave the traditional gesture away, but he submitted to it in the end.

"Father Timothy, I've come for confession. That is, if you have the time tonight."

The priest stood suddenly, still and serious. He gave Savas a long look. "OK, John, give me a second. I was just putting everything away. Please, wait for me in the corner, by the icon of Saint Nicholas."

Savas nodded and walked over to the left side of the nave. There, from just above the floor to more than fifteen feet up the side of the wall, was the icon of the great ascetic from Anatolia, now western Turkey, his brown robes flowing from sandaled feet to the receding hairline at the top of his head. Savas always found it amusing how Western Christians had taken this harsh monk and dressed him up in a red suit, strapped him to a sleigh with reindeer out of the pagan Northern myths, and made him so fat it was hard to imagine him ever fasting. This was the man who had slapped a heretical bishop at the First Council of Nicea, after all! As a child, Savas never quite felt like telling his friends that underneath the icon in his church, in a golden case about the size of a breadbox, were the bones of Santa Claus himself. It was likely that any explanations of the veneration of relics would have failed to bridge this cultural divide.

Father Timothy bustled over and laid a prayer book on a marble handrail. He gestured to a chair, but Savas shook his head. He'd been sitting too much, analyzing too much, until his eyes were blurry. He'd stand for this.

"Behold, my child, Christ stands here invisibly receiving your confession. Do not be ashamed and do not fear, and do not withhold anything from me; but without doubt, tell all you have done and receive forgiveness from the Lord Jesus Christ. Lo, He is before us, and I am only a witness, bearing testimony before Him of all things which you say to me. But if you conceal anything from me, you shall have the greater sin. Take heed, therefore, lest having come to the physician, you depart unhealed."

It was a routine Savas had known since his days as an altar boy. Yet now it was alien, because he was alien, because he had come and gone through a place that had changed him. He did not know anymore who he was, or who God was. The priest sat down in the chair. He had aged significantly since John Savas was a boy, and it showed in his movements and in his stamina.

"I'll make this short, Father. Not that I'm happy with myself or anything. But there are things that are real and important, and I need to say them. Most important, I suppose, is that I don't know anymore if I believe in God."

The priest showed no outward sign of surprise or dismay at this admission. He merely replied after Savas's long pause, "Go on, John."

John Savas looked up at the icon of Saint Nicholas. *Who was he? Who am I?*

"I'm serious about that, Father. I don't disbelieve. But I realized that the idea of God I had in my mind couldn't be real. I mean, the idea from my parents, priests, Sunday school teachers, friends, and family—

the myth we were all accepting, I just can't believe in that anymore. Whatever God is, it's not this simple, orderly, Father Christmas idea so many have. I really don't know if there is a God. I certainly don't know the nature of God. I don't know how to trust any man to tell me what the truth is."

Father Timothy gazed at him in silence, impassively. After a few more moments went by, during which time Savas had not spoken, the priest nodded slowly, as if to himself.

"John, I'm not going to tell you to make a pilgrimage to the island of Tinos and crawl up the hill on your knees to the Church of the Megalohari. I will say that you are at a most dangerous, and yet promising place. Dangerous, because your soul stands on the edge of nothingness into which it might fall, forever to be lost. Promising because only there can you truly reach out to the Mystery that is God."

"Father, I don't feel like I'm reaching out to anything. I can't see anything leading me anywhere. If there's a cliff, I won't know it."

"John, you are reaching out, or you would not be here tonight. I would ask you not to turn away from prayer, if you can do that. That is your link to God."

"OK, Father. I'll try. But I don't know who or what I'm praying to."

The old priest smiled. "None of us truly do. When we do, we are either entering sainthood or staring at a false idol."

The priest stood up from the chair and opened the small leather-bound book he had brought. Savas was surprised, as he had not expected the priest to accept his confession. But habit was long in him, and he knelt down before Father Timothy, who placed the stole over his head.

"O God, our Savior, Who by Thy prophet Nathan granted unto repented David pardon of his transgressions, and has accepted the Manasses' prayer of penitence, do Thou, in Thy love toward mankind, accept also Thy servant John who repents of his sins which he has committed, overlooking all that he has done, pardoning his offenses and passing by his iniquities. Unto Thee we ascribe glory, to the Father, and to the Son, and to the Holy Spirit, now and ever, and unto ages of ages. Amen."

The priest finished reading the prayers. John Savas stood and crossed himself. Father Timothy walked him to the door of the church.

"This week's events have brought you here, haven't they?" he asked.

John Savas stared up into the night sky, hearing the rushing sounds of the subway line behind them. "They were the trigger. My life has brought me here, Father. I just don't know where it's taking me next."

16

"Special Forces, served in Afghanistan and Iraq for a number of years," said Rebecca Cohen, reading off the screen. "And get this: discharge code: 28B/HKA—Discreditable Incidents—Civilian or Military. What does that mean?"

Savas turned to Miller. "Frank, any idea?"

Miller shook his head. "It's not good, but it can cover a lot of ground. You could sweep almost anything under that. One thing is sure; he was out of control in some way."

"So, we have an out-of-control former special-ops soldier functioning as an assassin who was chasing down a player in the underground terrorist network. Doesn't sound like a trained CIA operative."

"Not sure he was the assassin," said J. P. Rideout. "Sure, he was muscle hired to kill the guy, but he was *sloppy*. Looks like they needed someone fast and had to settle for poor quality control. When the Sheikh caused them problems, they brought in a second, an *expert*, who got the job done seriously."

Savas sighed. They were back to the death squad idea. The growing mystique behind these kills was becoming almost superstitious. "Look, he was part of something. If these are CIA death squads running around the world murdering people, why hire a flaky ex-SEAL who could blow the entire thing? There aren't enough super-assassins in the world to cover all the territory these guys are covering. It's like a little army. Some soldiers perform better than others."

"Army?" asked Matt King, his eyebrows raised.

"Honestly, people! These aren't superheroes! For the kind of impact they've had—"

"*If* you're right that they are all linked," interrupted King.

"Yes, *if* I'm right, that kind of impact on several continents has to be associated with a large personnel base. There's no other way. When your operation gets too big, you always make recruitment mistakes. I think this is one of them. Besides, rogue CIA assassin teams don't suddenly get all organized and vengeful! This is a group, a *large* group, with a purpose behind it."

There was silence in the room. Savas decided not to press the argument further.

"What else do we have?" he asked sullenly.

Cohen swiveled away from the computer screen and sighed. "That's it, John. Hardly any background. He was discharged four years ago, disappeared off the map, and showed up two thousand miles away from home brandishing a weapon in Queens."

"There's got to be more. This is our only link!" he said in frustration. "Anything on that pendant?"

"No. Why?"

"I don't know," began Savas hesitantly. "Not many men wear jewelry. If they do, it's usually a cross, Star of David, St. Christopher's medal, dog tags. Men tend to wear pendants that have meaning rather than as decoration. That pendant is unusual. Anything unusual can potentially tell us something."

"All we have is an anchor with a bird's face," said Rideout. "Not sure where we go with that."

Savas was ready to call the meeting to an end when Hernandez came bursting into the room.

"John, you're going to love this," he said, dropping a printout on the countertop beside the computer.

The other members of the group drew closer and strained to see the page. Savas picked it up. His brows furrowed as he stared at the strange collection of figures running across the page. After a few moments, he looked toward Hernandez expectantly.

"OK, Manuel, I'm stumped. What is this?"

Hernandez shrugged. "No idea. It was encoded in the big mysterious audiotapes you gave me."

"They're runes." It was Lightfoote. She had wiggled her way in between several bodies, her head almost on Savas's forearm, orange hair spilling everywhere, her gaze full on the page.

"*Runes?*" asked Hernandez, perplexed.

Lightfoote cocked her head at him. "Yeah, roooones," she dragged out the vowel, mocking his question. "Letters. Old. *Magical.*"

"Oh, brother," said Rideout under his breath.

"She's right," said Cohen, staring closely at the paper. "Not sure of the writing system, but look—clearly letters of some kind, with broad strokes and simple forms. Old ones designed not for pen and paper but for carving, wood, or stone."

Savas turned toward the former programmer. "Manuel, where did these letters come from?"

"*Runes*," piped Lightfoote. Savas ignored her.

"That's the craziest part, John. The audio transmission, with the weird language no one understands, it was double-coded."

"Meaning?"

"There was a second message overlaid at high frequencies. I found it by running the message through a Fourier analysis. In general, you would need to know to look for it, or you'd never extract it. The second message is coded, but it's clearly bitmapped imaging. I had to try a few permutations, but once I got the encoding right, out popped this. It's like a page worth of text and a diagram of what looks like a geographical region. These are instructions for the receiver."

He handed Savas another printout, diagrams of a site.

"Looks like an assault plan," said Miller.

"How can you be sure?" asked Savas.

"Style, points of entry, defense lines, observation points—here, and here. I've seen a thousand such drawings. Military style is easy to spot, once you know what to look for. I'd wager this is a plan of attack."

"This is crazy," said Savas. "I mean, hidden messages within messages, written in letters no one can read? Seems a bit extreme."

"What about this doesn't, John?" asked Hernandez. "These guys are *totally* FUBAR. Secret language, layered codes—they set things up so that no one could possibly figure out what they were talking about. Now Frank says they are commando hit teams?" He looked at Miller, who merely shrugged. "*Really* out there, man."

"John," Cohen began, "just why are we looking into this audio? It must be related to the assassinations, but how?"

Savas frowned. "Larry's mum on that. Super spy, top-secret decoder ring material, I assume. I don't think we can find that out."

"Think again," said Hernandez. All eyes were riveted on him. "The map is laid out in precise detail, down to the friggin' coordinates. Convert to longitude and latitude, and *bang*, instant top-secret information."

"And, so *where* is it?" asked Savas with irritation.

"Afghan-Paki border, dudes. Deep in the mountains. No-man's-land of terrorists and drug lords. Nice spot for a military assault plan."

There was a pregnant silence. Savas whistled. "Larry, that bastard. He should have told us."

"Told us what?" asked Matt King in confusion.

"Larry was called up to DC once we raised the lid on a connection between these murders. He came back with instructions relating to those killings, and this mysterious audiotape." A dawning awareness spread across King's face. Hernandez nodded and looked back at Savas, who continued. "That's right. We have a connection not only to isolated hits but to larger, military-style missions in hostile territory. Secretive missions, not using any known military codes. Somebody is *very* serious about their pursuit of Islamic baddies."

He checked his watch. "That's great work, Manuel, even if I don't know where the hell this is all leading." Savas turned to the group. "Folks, this has been fun, but it's been assigned to Miller and me, if you remember. In ten minutes, we're all due in Larry's office for a breakdown on the much bigger story going on around us. Maybe these guys are purging their ranks, but we still have some serious terrorist activity going on, right on our front lawn. Let's minimally prepare, get me and Frank up to speed on the latest that you have, and head on up there."

The members of Intel 1 scrambled. Savas stared at the screen, hardly seeing the ex-soldier's file. In his right hand was a page of archaic runes and an attack map, and running through his mind, the face and pendant of a dead assassin. Did it all fit together? He was sure it did. Somewhere was the key to link these strange bits of evidence and the progression of killings across the globe. In the chaos surrounding them, he hoped they could find it.

17

Savas's mind raced as he listened to Cohen's animated words. Their FBI vehicle crossed over the George Washington Bridge, en route to the New Jersey distribution offices of a military weapons manufacturer. The company representatives had sounded shell-shocked when he explained the reasons the FBI wanted to speak with them. They were also in full denial mode. *Their* explosives? *Impossible.* Well, the analysis had shown it was all *too* possible. These guys had some serious explaining to do, and Savas was going to be there to hear it.

"John, are you listening?"

He refocused. "Yes, Rebecca, sorry. I'm thinking ahead to the meeting today."

"So then, what do we have?"

Savas sighed. "Two massive bombings targeting foreign embassies in separate cities. We've got the UN screaming their lungs out at the United States, and half of their reps booking flights out of the country. We've got the president on TV trying to calm the nation down, trying to calm the whole world down, while offering our jobs to the meat grinder if we don't find out what in the name of God is going on here. *That's* what we've got."

The Hudson streamed by two hundred feet below them. Savas could sense their driver trying to listen in on the conversation. He couldn't blame the man. The world seemed to be burning down. "Still no group has claimed responsibility."

"It's crazy," said Cohen, shaking her head. "There was nothing, *nothing* on any of the watches for terrorist chatter, which makes no sense! Since when does a terrorist organization plan and execute coordinated multicity attacks of this magnitude, pull them off, and all without a sound? In 2001, we had NSA and even German intelligence intercepts of al-Qaeda chatter on the attacks. This time, it was as quiet as the vacuum of space."

"They're also not some bunch of fanatics who learned how to fly planes into buildings or how to rig IEDs," said Savas. "Surgical strikes, surgical bombings that were carried out under our noses, under security, and set up to take out single buildings and no more."

Cohen nodded and completed his thought. "It takes professional expertise with munitions to do something like this. Put that together with the skill in how they pulled it off, and you have a group of terrorists with a talent base we've never seen before."

The vehicle rattled roughly as they transitioned from the bridge to the New Jersey Turnpike. Savas felt his stomach lurch.

"You brought the forensics report?" he asked as the car exited quickly onto the Palisades Parkway. The monotonous gray of the turnpike transitioned suddenly, jarringly into the greens of the New Jersey forests.

"The FBI-CIA teams fast-tracked some results to us, and my initial analysis of the report indicates that it fits very well with the preliminary assessment."

"Mira got them to turn it over so fast?"

"Who else? She sent PDF files to all our secure accounts this morning."

Mirjana Vujanac. Vujanac came from Serbian grandparents. Savas's own Balkan ancestry provided a connection between them, and he also liked her for her basic decency. Ironically, her job as head of the Joint Offices group was to help de-Balkanize the intelligence organizations in the US government, serving as a focal point for interactions between the FBI and the CIA. It was a highly sensitive position, unpopular with both agencies, but Mira was the perfect person to balance the mutual paranoia and ego with her patient and winning personality. This case looked like it would require extended work with the CIA and other organizations. They were going to need Vujanac on this one.

"The initial analysis is solid?"

"Definitely." Cohen had put on her sharp-edged, Euro-style eyeglasses, the kind that always increased a woman's sex appeal in an elegant way. Her expression was serious as she looked over the report, giving her the appearance of a graduate student presenting a paper.

"Looks like a recent derivative of the explosive Semtex was used," she said. "Mass-spectroscopy analysis of numerous samples now confirms this. Same as the prelim report: judging from the molecular weight of the compounds, it's almost certainly homegrown. There are only two plants in the world that make this stuff, both run by the Heward Corporation. This stuff is made in the USA all the way."

Savas glanced out the window as the vehicle slowed and headed off the ramp. The green of the parkway surrendered to the landscaped parking lot that boxed in a six-floor office building.

"Well, we're here. Let's see what they have to say about that."

It was a frustrating half-hour before they sat down in the stale-smelling office. The two had run an obstacle course of security checkpoints for the vehicle and at the front door, temporary ID badges, metal detectors, and finally a walk down a long corridor to the office of a local divisions manager. It was a tranquil space, softly lit and shadowed by tall trees covering the window at one end of a rectangular room. A quiet space for the distributors of the world's most advanced explosives.

As they entered and shook hands, Savas noted the presence of two other men, open briefcases at their sides. The lawyers had arrived. Savas smiled. One lawyer meant denial. Two, limited accountability. The company must have gotten the new report from Vujanac this morning as well.

"Agent Savas, Fred Reynolds," began the manager, the firmness of his handshake doing little to conceal the perspiration on his palm. "Welcome. Please, won't you sit down?"

"This is my colleague, Rebecca Cohen, also from the NYC branch."

The man shook Cohen's hand as well. "This is Michael Ivy and Brian Colbert," introduced Reynolds as the two lawyers stood up. "They are here to help advise me in any legal ramifications of our discussions."

Savas and Cohen exchanged greetings with the men.

"I'm sorry you two found it necessary to come all the way out here," said Reynolds, as they all sat around the conference table. "As we said over the phone, we were happy to come into the city tomorrow."

And give your legal eagles twenty-four more hours to coach you into admitting even less than you will today. "Couldn't wait, Mr. Reynolds. This is as red alert as it gets. National security priority."

The man's face seemed to tighten. "Yes, of course."

Savas nodded to Cohen, who stepped up to the plate. She opened her briefcase across from the lawyers and placed several documents on the table. "Mr. Reynolds, I assume you have had a chance to examine our forensics reports."

"Yes," he began stiffly. "Yes, we have." He glanced at the other two men. "We are prepared to acknowledge that the material used in the bombings came from our nearby factory."

Cohen glanced briefly at Savas. At least they wouldn't have to fight that battle. She made sure. "To confirm our results, this is your newest high-tech explosive, S-47, that matches the chemical analysis?"

"That's correct."

"And, to make sure I understand correctly, you consistently ID each batch of explosive?"

Reynolds nodded. "There are records for every ounce we produce. Each lot is infused with a chemical called DMDNB for identification, and various ion ratios can essentially ID a given lot. We have completed an emergency review of all S-47 produced in the last year. There is not one gram unaccounted for. Everything we've made is either onsite or shipped to reputable governmental sources."

Savas interrupted. "Then how did S-47 residue end up dusting the New York landscape last month?"

Reynolds glanced at the lawyers again. "Agent Savas, we really cannot speculate."

"What about material produced further back?" asked Cohen.

"We are continuing to review our records," said Reynolds. "However, I can assure you, we have exacting standards. We've never lost material, and our customers are limited to United States military and allied governments."

"Could this be an inside job?" Savas pressed. "I mean, could we be looking at *American* terrorists?"

"Again, Agent Savas, I think it is imprudent to speculate at this time."

Savas felt his temper rising. "*Imprudent?* You fellows do realize that we've just had two terrorist bombings on US soil, one of them right across the river from here? *Your* explosives were involved in both of those attacks. Your high-tech, *military-only* S-47 leveled one New York City building and the entire Saudi Embassy in DC."

"Yes, Agent Savas, but, as I stated—"

"You don't see navy mines being used to sink US ships, or army surplus surface-to-air missiles shooting down aircraft in this nation."

"If you will just—"

"If you don't know how your explosives got there, then I think it's high time you started speculating and testing some hypotheses! At the very least, you're going to need some good cover stories for when the press gets hold of this."

Reynolds's face turned white. "If you are trying to threaten me, Agent Savas, I can assure you, we will respond strongly to such harassment."

Savas laughed. "Please, Mr. Reynolds. If you think the fact that an American company is the supplier for the bombs that hit us last month is something the FBI, the CIA, or G.O.D. could keep secret for long, you're more naive than I could have imagined."

"We have supplied no terrorists!" Reynolds practically shrieked. "All our material is accounted for. All sales were legitimate, to verified US government sources!"

Savas leaned forward and locked eyes with the company man. "Then why don't you go explain that to the families of the victims vaporized by your product, Mr. Reynolds."

There was an icy silence as the man broke eye contact with Savas. The lawyer beside Reynolds leaned over and whispered into his ear.

Reynolds seemed to make an effort to control himself, and his face drained of emotion. *Screw this tap dance*, thought Savas. He'd had enough. He apologized to Cohen, rose, and walked out of the room without another word.

Cohen's voice echoed strangely as he stormed down the hallway. "As you can see, Mr. Reynolds, my role is *good* cop. We'll need to set up some very open channels between your company and the FBI for the next few weeks as we work through this."

The sounds inside the building faded as Savas stepped out into the bright sunlight. He exhaled slowly. He knew his fuse was too short. He knew he had to rein in his emotions, even as the events around him pushed every button. He knew these company men were just following orders.

And he knew he wanted to deck one of them.

Arriving back at FBI offices, Savas stepped into the Operations Room of Intel 1. He tossed his briefcase roughly onto a chair and removed his jacket. Perspiration stained his shirt. He sighed and loosened his tie.

"Bad day at the office?" came the words of Hernandez, whose fingers clacked across a keyboard nearby. J. P. Rideout, Mark King, and Frank Miller stood around the computer geek in a semicircle, staring at the screen.

"I'm at the office *now*, Manuel."

"Suits stiff you?"

"Of course. But they seem to sink to new levels of corporate cowardice on a yearly basis." Savas stared at the small gathering across from him. "So, what's the party about?"

"Well, we've got something interesting you might want to see."

Savas walked over to the group. At that moment, Kanter stepped into the room as well.

"John, you're back. I need—"

"Hang on, Larry," said Savas. "Manuel's reeling in some new fish."

Interested, Kanter joined the group. Savas stared down at the screen; numerous time- and date-stamped video images of buildings flitted across his field of view.

"We've had a look at the security cams in a large radius around the site," began Manuel.

"How did you get those?" asked Savas.

"We don't have to go to the sites for the newer ones. Patriot Act II —we're already plugged in, 24/7. We just need to access the relevant minutes from DTO ..."

"Domestic Terrorism Operations," Rideout whispered to Savas, who rolled his eyes. The acronyms never seemed to end.

"...and within hours we can get the footage from thirty local cameras downloaded."

Miller turned toward Savas and Kanter, a serious expression on his face. "Every camera with a clear shot at 866 Second Avenue showed static from the hours of three to four a.m. the night before the bombing."

"What?" said Kanter incredulously.

"I want to make this clear, Larry," said Miller. "Every camera that could possibly have had a shot at recording what happened around the building that early morning had a similar malfunction for the same duration. *Every* one of them."

"Some serious hacking, dudes," noted Hernandez.

"Wait, no security firm noticed this? No one looked into it?" asked Kanter.

Rideout shook his head. "Most of the cameras don't have flesh and blood babysitting them. We get the feeds, but they are automatically routed and stored. Our analysis probably wasn't the first time they had been viewed, but when each individual firm saw the static for their equipment, they likely assumed their cameras were malfunctioning. Happens all the time. Only when you pool together all the local cameras can you see the pattern. No way that's coincidence."

Miller finished. "We're talking about some real pros here, Larry, and some really careful ones, at that."

"So, what do they want?" asked Matt King in frustration. "This doesn't seem to be some 9/11 replay."

"Exactly, and it's these differences we need to focus more on," cut in Savas. "In 2001, American targets, American symbols were attacked by mostly Saudi suicide bombers. This time, the cities may be the same, but it looks like foreign targets, and, as far as I can tell, primarily *Saudi* targets were hit. I don't know about you, but this seems to put a different spin on the whole thing."

Kanter cast a harsh look toward Savas and responded quickly. "OK, we have, as usual, more questions than answers. Who are these people? How and where were they trained? What motivates them?"

Savas turned angrily to Kanter, his simmering frustrations from the day boiling over. "I'll tell you what is motivating them, Larry. *Hatred.* Feelings that cross beyond Islamophobic into Islamopathic. You're tap dancing around the real issue because of warnings from above, but we know about the mystery commando raids in Afghanistan."

Kanter sat up stiffly. "How do you know?"

"Thanks for confirming it." Savas was not done. He looked around at the eyes focused on him. "Isn't it obvious? We're sitting here acting like we have two cases—a string of assassinations of Islamic radicals, and now a major terrorist attack on Islamic targets. It's the *same* group, Larry! They're just upping the ante!"

"Hold on a minute!" shouted Kanter. "John, you're completely going wild here. These attacks are on *American* soil, terrorist attacks in New York, in the *capital*, for God's sake! Your vengeful furies wouldn't strike here, would they?"

"Why not? To them, the enemy is as much here as there."

Kanter stared coldly at Savas. "To *them*, John? Or to *you*?"

Savas felt anger surge through him, but he held his temper. *They had to listen!*

"Larry, I haven't done myself any favors for this argument by my actions over the last few years; I know that. But *think*! If you saw the Islamic nations as the enemy, as a threat, their presence here might be one of the *first* places to strike! Purge America of them. If they are homegrown, well, hitting here would be a hell of a lot easier than doing a job like this overseas, especially in Islamic nations where they would stick out like sore thumbs."

"We haven't even established that there is a definite connection between the *assassinations*, John. It's *all* circumstantial. Now you want to throw this into the mix? How big a conspiracy?" Kanter waved his hands back and forth. "This isn't Dr. No. At least the murder conspiracy had a consistency in targets. These bombings aren't of Islamic radicals. They're the damn official *government* representatives."

"To some, it might be hard to tell the difference."

"*Jesus*, John." Kanter threw up his hands in frustration.

"Damn it, Larry, I'm not justifying this. I'm saying it's a nasty but understandable motive."

"Perhaps you understand this better than I do."

Savas clenched his jaw. He was going to come off as some sort of crazed man no matter what he said. Kanter was right about one thing—they had absolutely no hard evidence to link any of this. His hypothesis was emotional, not fact based.

Frank Miller glanced at Savas as if in sympathy, swept his gaze around the room, and cleared his throat. "I'd like to speak freely on something."

Kanter nearly laughed. "Frank, you aren't in the marines anymore. Shoot. Take a cue from John."

"OK, as John notes, even if it's not connected to the murders he and I are investigating, evidence is pointing toward a homegrown terrorist group, one that might be targeting Islamic sites."

"Yes?" said Kanter.

"I mean, we're mobilizing all the forces of the US government to help protect a bunch of nations that have been quietly, under the table, supporting the bastards who bombed us in the first place." He looked around the room. "I've had friends die at my side in Afghan caves looking for that son of a bitch who was financed by Saudi money, and whose organization was run by Saudi personnel. I'm not sure my heart's in the right place on this one."

A silence fell across the room. Savas looked over at Miller and saw the anger in his eyes. John Savas also felt that anger. It was what had brought him to the FBI in the first place. He felt it every time he looked at a picture of his son.

"Frank," said Kanter thoughtfully but firmly, "these attacks are going to test all of us in some way. I think we need to try to focus on what we're about, and that's law and order. We shouldn't forget that Americans also died in these attacks. But I don't think any of us believe that all the Saudis and other workers in those buildings are necessarily hostile to us, or were involved in anything that had to do with supporting terrorist causes. Now, I'm not saying all of them are clean, but I've been around in this world long enough to know that good and evil are found in every corner. That's my belief, and if I didn't believe that, I don't think I'd care much for law or order. On top of all that, we've got an international incident here, and the repercussions are international. So, folks, this is some serious stuff."

Kanter looked directly at Miller, but Savas knew he was speaking as much or more to him. "Frank, I hear where you're coming from, but around here, we work to enforce the laws of this nation. You understand that, I hope?"

Miller pursed his lips and looked down at his hands. "Yeah, Larry," he said glancing back up, "I do. It's just that things are a bit mixed up inside, is all."

Kanter shook his head. "Ain't that the truth of it."

John Savas closed his notebook as he walked down the hallway from the Operations Room. He and Kanter had stayed for another hour after dismissing the others. Savas was tired and at the stage of fatigue when he knew his thoughts were slow, his logic weak, and his emotions unstable. These last few weeks had drained him—and it was much more than just the work and long hours. Terror attacks on American soil were too raw, *too personal*.

Cohen was waiting for him outside his office. She was sitting at a desk next to a phone, looking like she had just caught something very interesting after casting her line out to the deep sea. He saw how tired she looked as well. Her long hair was disheveled, and she leaned back in the chair. A fire burned in her eyes.

Still so attractive. Savas thrust such thoughts from his mind as he often had over the last few years. He was damaged goods and too con-fused to think in those directions. Tonight he was especially not ready to face anything so complicated as feelings.

"John, about damn time," she said.

"Glad to see you, too, Rebecca," he responded, noting her briefest of smiles, mainly in the eyes.

"I've been waiting to tell you this for over an hour. While you were undoubtedly figuring all this out with Larry, we got a call in about those symbols."

"Runes," corrected Savas.

"Runes. Yes, exactly. That's *exactly* right."

He raised his eyebrows at her tone. "What call?"

"A professor from the English Department at Columbia."

"You cast a wide net."

"Yes. I'm thorough, remember? The poor old man was very excited, and I had a heck of a time calming him down enough to understand what he was talking about."

"OK, so what *was* he talking about?" asked Savas.

"Well, he says he knows what the symbols, the runes mean. Get ready for this, OK? He says they're Norse."

"*Norse?* As in Valhalla and pretentious Wagnerian opera?"

"Precisely. Better still, I sent him everything that we had, including images of the pendant you are so interested in. That's when we hit the jackpot, John." She smiled and tilted her head at a slight angle, triumphant.

"Go on."

"It's also from Norse mythology, an artifact central to much of those beliefs: the hammer of the Norse god of thunder, Thor. The symbol and the runes *match*, John. You've been right all along—there *is* a connection! Not only between the killings but also to the Afghan strikes."

John Savas blinked. "Thor's hammer?"

"Yes. The professor sounds really anxious to talk with you." Cohen smiled at his disbelief, her tongue touching the bottom edge of her front teeth. "I think I want to come along."

18

Fernando Martinez, just twelve years old, weaved and dodged his way through traffic on his small bicycle. The front and back of the bike were weighed down with large wire-caged baskets, loaded with foods from the restaurant that were wrapped carefully in bags for protection. The boy was well tanned from countless journeys through the streets of Caracas; the Venezuelan sun was strong enough even in the winter months to deeply brown anyone spending their hours under its rays. The skies were partly cloudy, the streets full of water and mud splashing against Fernando's legs from recent rainstorms. He could hear the chatter of street vendors and haggling customers as he rode past. He smiled. It was hard work, but it was good to be out, away from a troubled home, feeling the wind on his face and glimpsing the sun through the clouds.

His mother would not approve, but he rode against traffic to cut his trip time, dodging cars and trucks with pitch-changing horns blaring behind him. Señor Moreno would not pay him if he was late. He might not even pay him if he was on time, Fernando reminded himself. His family needed the money; since his father had died, Fernando was the man of the house. So he pedaled fast and did not think about dangers.

He climbed a hill, panting, sweat glistening on his face, arms, and legs. The road leveled off as he crossed through a nice strip of Caracas. Fancier shops, cars, and people lined the sides of the street. Taller buildings, skyscrapers of glass and metal rose around him. This was a place of importance and power. A place of money and oil. Fernando did not know much about the world, but he knew his country was powerful. It had oil, and the sheikh princes from across the seas visited often. His country could talk back to the United States like an equal. He was proud of this, proud of his country's strength to look the bully in the eye.

Ahead were the embassies and banks of the foreign nations that did business with Venezuela and its oil. Fernando liked riding by their protected gates, seeing their guards and security cameras. It was like an American movie. There were embassies and banks from Europe and Asia and the Middle East. He had ridden past them countless times. China and India, and up ahead, the other oil countries, Iran and Saudi Arabia.

Fernando screamed. The explosions were enormous.

A blast of heated air picked him up together with his bike and sent them sprawling on the sidewalk next to an upscale clothing store. The store's glass-front window was shattered inward. Screams and wailing car alarms filled the air around him. The boy lay for several moments on the sidewalk, stunned, his left arm and leg badly skinned and bleeding from being dragged across the asphalt. He felt a small trickle of blood from his scalp. He shook his head, trying to focus and clear the blood from his eyes. Slowly, he raised himself to his feet. Swiping again at the blood, he stared down the road. Smoke and dust billowed toward him. Fires burned in several places. Ahead, he thought he could make out the remains of two buildings, now wreckages on either side of the road.

Sirens grew louder from several directions. *Police.* Frightened, he found his bike several feet from him. It was damaged—the handlebars bent awkwardly, the baskets with the food wrecked. He did not care. He was going home. Señor Moreno could keep his money today. As he turned and rode down the street toward the growing sounds of police and fire sirens, he heard voices behind him. Screams and cries for help.

19

It was a long ride to Philosophy Hall at the corner of 116th Street and Amsterdam Avenue. Traffic was snarled along the West Side Highway from a seven-car pileup, and the driver was forced to cut through Midtown. John Savas glanced outside his tinted windows at the shoppers crowding and crossing the streets at Fifty-Seventh and Madison. The crowds were definitely thinner than normal this time of year, ruining summer tourism and sending more than one business under—one of many repercussions of an urban bombing.

The car lurched forward and shook him out of his reverie. It was challenging to keep his eyes focused outside the car, thanks to the mid-thigh-length skirt Rebecca Cohen was wearing. He knew that if he let himself look for even a moment, he would certainly linger too long to pass anything off as a casual glance.

Her hair was pulled up and fastened Japanese style with two things that actually looked like chopsticks. *Do women use chopsticks in their hair?* he wondered to himself. She wore a white shirt that looked to be standard 1950s FBI, and, sure enough, as if to prevent him from getting any useful thinking done during the ride, she had left the first two buttons open. *Well, it's a hot day.* One hundred and two degrees. She was writing in her characteristically broad script, large, flowing letters that would have taken him hours to form and that she spat out like a typewriter. Savas preferred typing.

He turned his mind back to the case. Rideout and King had compiled information on the professor at Columbia. Fred Styer, PhD in Philology from Harvard, expert in proto-Germanic languages and Germanic literature, Alfred L. Hutchinson Chair of Anglo-Saxon

Studies in the Department of English and Comparative Literature at Columbia University—the titles ran on. A prolific scholar in the 1970s with more than two hundred journal articles and ten books, he was now "mostly" retired, serving as professor emeritus and haunting the hallways of Philosophy Hall at Columbia. He was once considered the greatest scholar on the East Coast in the ancient languages and literature of the Germanic family. Savas just hoped he had a key to unlock this mystery.

After what seemed like an eternity slogging through traffic, the driver finally pulled them up to the building at Columbia University. The entrance to Philosophy Hall was shaded by a plaza built directly over Amsterdam Avenue. Above was a small green park; below, it seemed that the street plunged into a short, dim tunnel right after 116th Street, to emerge in light again half a block later at 117th, right in front of the university's Casa Italiana. Instead of pulling up to the entrance of the building, they followed the old professor's instructions to avoid the construction at the main door and turned the corner in front of the Kent building. They were not sure how they would recognize the old man (photos they had on file were certainly outdated), but it became clear that both he and they were easy marks.

The professor did indeed resemble the photo they had in their files, only older and slightly wider in the waist. He still possessed an enormous beard that spilled over his chest, now much whiter than in the photograph, and, if Savas could bring himself to believe it, perhaps even longer. His bald head and thick glasses were also the same, but today he sported a pipe that gave him the air of an awkward Oxford don. To prove the point, when they stepped out of the car, he waved to them like he was trying to flag down a 737 at Kennedy Airport. Savas waved back, and Cohen stifled a laugh, looking radiant in her amusement. At that point, Savas realized that they looked as ridiculous as the professor did. In the middle of this casual and unconstrained academic campus, their appearance had *FEDS* written all over it.

"Hello, hello, Agent Savas. Welcome, welcome!" Styer repeated, almost gleefully, shaking Savas's hand in a hyper fashion. The old man looked over to Cohen, and his eyes grew large. He smiled and motioned toward her with his head. "Please, and you must be that lovely young woman I spoke with on the phone yesterday . . . Agent Cohen?"

Cohen seemed positively taken. "Rebecca, please, Professor Styer." Savas suppressed an initial desire to not like the man.

"Please, both of you, we'll go to my office. Not straightaway, mind you. They're tearing up the Hall these days, and it's easier to come in through this other building. Follow me."

He led them into Kent, through that building and into a charming green garden abutting Kent and Philosophy Hall. Using a back entrance to the Hall, he took them up a flight of stairs and down a corridor to his office in the Department of English and Comparative Literature. By the time they had all sat down, the old professor was winded and coughing.

"Excuse me," he apologized. "Age shows no mercy."

John Savas looked around the office. It was small, dusty, and filled nearly from side to side with stacks of papers, journals, and books. Behind the stacks were either more stacks, or, if one could make it that far, wall-to-wall bookshelves with yet more books. The professor's desk was old and chipped from years of use. It also was littered with books and papers, a magnifying glass, and a computer that was likely the dustiest thing in the room. Professor Styer was clearly a man of another age. Among the papers, Savas noticed quite a few that showed runes like those decoded from the mysterious communications.

The professor held his thick glasses in one hand and a cloth to wipe them clean in the other. This close, Savas saw how old the man was— clearly in his seventies, perhaps late seventies. His skin was sagging and marked with many age spots. His hands trembled as he wiped the lenses of his glasses. An ancient man to tell them about ancient runes. Savas hoped Styer would last long enough to help them with this case.

Glasses back on, the professor looked out at them, gravitated toward Cohen, smiled delightedly, and asked, "So, my Federal friends, how can I help you?"

Savas flashed a look of concern toward Cohen. Had he gone senile? "Professor Styer, we came here at your request to discuss some runes and symbols that were found in a criminal case, perhaps linked to a series of murders here and abroad."

"I'm not *that* far gone, young man!" he barked. "I was merely opening conversation. I think society has forgotten how to be polite," he said, smiling.

Savas chuckled. "Yes, Professor Styer. My apologies." He pulled out a piece of paper and passed it to the professor. "This is a reproduction of the coded messages we obtained, and this," he said, placing the necklace and pendant in front of him, "is what we found on one of the killers."

Professor Styer glanced briefly at the paper and set it down. "Yes, yes. I've seen it. Agent Cohen sent me all this, you know." He smiled impishly at Cohen. "I told your assistant here what I thought." Cohen smiled.

Savas continued. "So, these symbols we have—you say they are pagan, about pagan gods?"

"Norse gods, to be precise." He reached into his desk drawer and drew out a pouch of tobacco. He dumped the ash from his pipe and filled it while speaking. "The runes—they are very old, predating the Christianization of northern Europe, some of the earliest artifacts dating from a hundred years after the death of Christ. The writing systems are almost certainly older than that. They were used by the Germanic tribes before the Latin alphabet replaced them. This printout, identical, I think, to the one faxed to me, is written in the runic alphabet called the Elder Futhark. This is the oldest version of this alphabet, used for early forms of the Norse language and other dialects from the second to the eighth centuries. It can be found on jewelry, amulets, tools, weapons, rune stones, you name it."

Styer placed his pipe between his teeth and lit it, puffing several times to ignite the tobacco. "Horrible habit, I know," he apologized toward Cohen. "But, to paraphrase George Burns, no one under seventy is allowed to smoke in here." He turned back toward Savas and continued.

"The pendant—one might say 'amulet' in ancient times—is probably the most widespread and best-known symbol of all Norse mythology. Curiously, it also appears in the writings you sent—see, here," he noted, indicating a section of the page with several letters unintelligible to Savas.

"It would be pronounced 'mee-YOLL-neer', spelled m-j-o-l-n-i-r. This is the Norse name for the thunder god Thor's hammer, the greatest weapon of all the gods in Asgaard. It was made for Thor by the dwarves underground—one of their greatest creations. Its name means 'crusher', and Thor would use the hammer in all his battles against the enemies of the gods, the monsters and giants that sought to throw down the ordered reign of Thor's father, Odin, and return the world to chaos."

Savas looked over at Cohen as if to say, *OK, we've definitely come to the right place.* The old man picked up the necklace Savas had handed him and pointed to the pendant with the bird face.

"Mjolnir, my friends. The hammer of Thor. It was often rendered by the Norse artisans in a shape like this, decorated with the face of a raven."

"Are you able to decipher the rest of the writing, or the audio?" asked Cohen.

"I've made partial transcripts," Styer said, passing them a sheet of paper, "but I don't know how much use it will be to you. The audio is Old Norse, a valiant attempt to speak it, I must say. One could quibble with the pronunciations and some of the grammar, but it is quite impressive. College level, you might say, which, it would seem to me, is strange coming from the sources you mention. There was much I could not make out, vocabulary that is modern in origin, I believe, adapted to Norse. There seems little doubt, however, that these are military instructions of some kind."

The knowing look passed between the two FBI agents was not lost on the professor. "I see that I am not too far off the mark."

Savas shifted the conversation. "So, what does this mean, Professor? We have some sort of cult of assassins like the Hashshashin?"

"The Arabic drug-fueled killers from the Middle Ages?"

Savas nodded in response.

"No, Agent Savas, I wouldn't suspect that. These are, if anything you told me is true, anti-Muslim assassins."

Savas continued to press the point. "But perhaps still some modern cult based on Norse religion? Fueled by a fanatical devotion?"

The professor shook his head. "Most modern pagans—unlike

ancient pagans, by the way—are fairly Gaian, Mother Earth, peace-loving aftershocks of the nineteen sixties. This group you are hypothe-sizing—well, they would be something else entirely. Something, in fact, perhaps much more loyal to the character of the Norse legends."

"Could you explain that?" asked Savas.

The professor looked thoughtful. "The Northern peoples devel-oped near the poles, Agent Savas, where for half the year, even light was scarce. The ground was often ice. Life was hard. Their mythology reflected that in many ways. This group you are hunting seems an effi-cient and terrible organization. I will suggest that these killers were attracted to the Norse culture for two reasons. First, and most obvious, is the contrast to the Middle Eastern monotheistic religion of Islam. Their targets are Muslims. What better contrast to Arabic monotheists than Germanic pagans? The second reason, and perhaps the more sig-nificant one, might be the character of the Northern myths themselves."

The professor leaned back in his chair and chewed on his pipe. His eyes closed momentarily. He opened them, glancing toward the ceiling. "The Norse mythos shares many common aspects with the Indo-European mythologies. There are a pantheon of gods and god-desses, many representing similar themes—the sun and moon, of course, the underworld or death, beauty and fertility, strength, the sea, and so forth. They all share a common basis in the creation of order out of chaos, with the gods descending from more primitive elemental forces of nature, the monsters and giants, which seemed chaotic to soci-eties bereft of the miracles of our modern scientific mythos." He smiled mischievously. "The gods seize power and bring order to the world, vanquishing the Titans, or giants, or whatever embodies the forces of chaos in a given mythology. But, of course, as every fragile human being knows, the forces of chaos still strike; our world is swept by pow-erful events beyond us. In such mythologies, this is explained as a con-stant battle between the gods and the elemental, chaotic forces. For the Northern myths, all this reaches a climax at Ragnarök, the Arma-geddon of the Norse legends, a final battle between good and evil to settle the stewardship of the world."

Savas nodded. "But where does that lead us with this group?"

"Where? Honestly, Agent Savas, I couldn't tell you that. But it might be telling you something about who these people are."

"How?"

"Ragnarök, my friends, is the end of the world, as I told you. But it has a special *Norse* quality that makes it contrast sharply with your typical end-of-the-world religious event. In short, all the Norse gods, including Thor and his allies, the heroes waiting in Valhalla for the final battle, what you might call the "good guys" in our Western lexicon—they *lose*. They all die. They are annihilated." He took his pipe out of his mouth and leaned forward for emphasis. "In the Norse mythos, the gods lose, civilization is destroyed, and chaos reigns supreme. From the broth of chaos, it is prophesized that a new creation will arise. But to be enjoyed by others! This organization, whatever they are planning, has chosen a most curious mythology as a symbol. If they take the mythology seriously, and everything you've shown me convinces me that they do, they don't believe their side is necessarily going to triumph and be welcomed into Heaven. No virgins, no pearly gates and harps. Nothing."

"I don't understand," said Savas. "Why do all this, go through all this, without a final expectation of victory?"

"Because they should," said Cohen, looking thoughtful. "It's like Frodo going into Mordor. There was little hope that he had the strength to finish the quest. But it was *right* that he tried."

"Exactly, young lady. Top of the class," Styer said and winked at her. He then leaned back and stared out the window, looking over the small garden they had recently passed. "They do this because they believe it's the *right* thing to do. The gods and heroes of the Northern legends did not despair or, following a more modern sentiment, switch sides, even though through prophecy they knew they were going to be destroyed, that chaos would triumph. No, they fought anyway, not to win, but because fighting for good even in the face of defeat was the right thing."

Cohen raised a question. "Even if this is true for this mythology, Professor, how can we be so sure it applies to this organization?"

The old man leaned back toward the desk and looked shrewdly at

Cohen. "A good question, and, of course, the answer is that we cannot be sure. But someone with this level of sophistication, to organize in this way and then choose these symbols, down to correctly using the writing system and language of an ancient people, is someone extremely invested in this symbolism, Agent Cohen. Anyone with that level of knowledge of Norse mythology would likely understand its curious nature. This theme of Northern courage, a hard courage, grounded not in any hope of victory but only in standing for what is right, has been a powerful force in Western culture, for good and evil. This *character* influenced generations who knew the Norse legends, from Tolkien's archetypal *Lord of the Rings* heroes you just mentioned to Adolf Hitler's perversion of those ideals during the Third Reich." Professor Styer focused sharply on the FBI agents. "Courage to fight no matter what, requiring no hope of reward, only *conviction*. My friends, that makes them a group of a most dangerous kind."

Professor Styer insisted on walking them back to their car. He walked with even more difficulty than when he had first greeted them; the efforts of the day clearly draining him. When they reached the car, Cohen thanked him with a smile and got into the backseat. As Savas moved to follow, the old man grasped his arm.

"Agent Savas, I do hope you know what you have there," he said in a low voice, motioning with his eyes toward the car. "I would keep her close to you."

Taken aback, Savas started stammering something unintelligible. The professor interrupted him. "Oh, I don't mean that! Although, let me tell you, at seventy-eight, there are many more things I regret *not* doing in life than I regret doing. A lady like that doesn't come around often. But that is not what I meant. She's smarter than you are, in case you didn't notice. Don't take that personally. I've taught generations of students, and I know a good mind when I see it. She's got one. You will need her in this. Keep her close." The professor smiled, winked at Savas, then bent toward the car and waved once more at Cohen before turning back toward the building.

Savas gazed forward at the intersection for a moment. *I knew I didn't like that guy.*

20

"Rebecca, do you buy all that?" asked Savas distractedly, his gaze outside the car window as the vehicle began its trek downtown, his mind wrapped in the words of the last half-hour. Cohen was thoughtful as well, but she answered confidently.

"I'm sure everything we heard about the language and writing was accurate. What you're really asking me concerns the speculative portions, the extrapolation of the symbolism to the psychology of the group."

"Yes."

She sighed. "It sounded very reasonable. John, you called it a cult at first, and that is unlikely to be right—who would believe in Norse gods in the twenty-first century? Especially a group as sophisticated and practical as the one you are proposing—a group that has orchestrated the assassinations of more than ten radical Islamic leaders in the last six to nine months."

"And the bombings."

Cohen paused. "The evidence is weaker on that, John; you know it. You only have your intuition, based on your own painful experience and response to 9/11. That's a strength and a weakness—I think you know that. Let's just limit it to the assassinations for the moment."

Savas nodded. "Thanks."

"For what?" she looked at him curiously.

"You're the first person who has taken what I feel seriously, even when you don't feel it. You're at least giving me the benefit of the doubt."

She pursed her lips. "John, I've watched you struggle with this for many years now. Everyone knows your anger, Mad John. Some of us also see the struggle. And the pain."

He looked outside the car again, not daring to engage her eyes.

She coughed. "Anyway, what I was saying is that we have ruthless professionals, not religious fanatics. These guys way outclass al-Qaeda operatives. So, if they aren't religiously invested in this Norse stuff, then they must be invested in another way to have gone to all this trouble. Who learns a dead language and appropriates its culture's symbols? Someone who sees something in it, has extracted something from it, and needs that symbolism in their lives."

"Northern courage?"

"It's the noblest idea of pagan Europe. But I think he's spot-on with the other thing—the contrast to Islam. Whoever started this, there is something driving them. I think you are right about it, John. There's a deep hatred of Islam in all this."

"Then who? People of western European descent, almost certainly, or why all Norse stuff? The killer we encountered was American, so I assume many others are as well. But not the crazy idea of death squads from the CIA."

"Not crazy, John, they existed," noted Cohen. "But you're right. This symbolism, this *crusade* almost, doesn't smell of a government plan that spun out of control. But it does smell of money."

"Sorry?"

"How on earth do you get the skilled personnel, equip them, train them, send them out all over the world for orchestrated assassination work, without enormous capital resources?

Savas nodded. "You can't."

"No, you can't. If you aren't government, you have to be someone with access to just amazing resources, both monetary and, frankly, military."

"Yes, the commando training, the coded messages—it's military."

Cohen turned to Savas, her gaze intense, her mind working quickly. "You have to be well placed financially and logistically. I don't think we're looking for a cult leader, John, not in the normal sense, anyway. I just wish I knew *what* we were looking for."

Savas nodded. He understood her frustration. It was the sense when the puzzle had started to take on some kind of pattern, definition, and yet its overall shape still eluded the mind. As he processed these thoughts, his phone rang, and he reached into his pocket and answered it. The adrenaline flowed back into his body almost instantly. Cohen turned quickly to stare at him. The voice from the speaker was shouting.

"John, this is Larry! Where the hell have you been?"

"Larry, sorry, switched off for this interview. What is it?"

"Get back here now! There's been a second attack."

Even with the sirens on, it was more than half an hour before they reached the FBI offices. People and equipment filled the buzzing Operations Room. Images flowed across giant monitors. Low-level staff darted from office to office with urgent messages. By the time Savas reached the floor, the main story had been fleshed out. He called a meeting of his staff. They convened in a conference room adjacent to the OR.

"Fearless Leader, we have been lost without you," chirped Lightfoote as he and Cohen filed into the room.

"Damn it, Angel." This was all he needed.

"I am a celestial being, and I will forgive your profane words."

I'm going to have to have a talk with that girl. Savas took off his jacket, his shirt soaked in sweat from both the heat outside and the stress within. Miller and Hernandez were the last to file in. *Rambo and Jesus*, thought Savas, *and a nutcase named Angel.*

"All right, Larry's called a meeting in an hour. Fill me in, people."

Matt King donned his glasses and read from notes. After Rebecca, he was the de facto information center for the team. His legal training always showed in his attention to detail.

"At 2:35 p.m. today, two explosions occurred in the Venezuelan capital of Caracas. The explosions occurred at the Saudi and Iranian embassies, apparently completely destroying both buildings. Initial reports have the death toll in the high hundreds, and it is expected to go even higher. Injuries are worse, and the hospitals are overflowing with wounded. Caracas fire and police responders have the secondary blazes under control. The Venezuelan president has already gone on television to calm the populace. The Islamic nations have not failed to notice that there is a connection between the attacks here and in Washington and today's in Caracas."

Miller clarified. "Basically, they're screaming bloody murder about it."

Savas looked around the concerned faces at the table. Only Lightfoote seemed unfazed, drawing odd sketches on her notepad. "All right, in the span of less than a month, we have a new terrorist organization appear from nowhere that has blown up buildings in three different cities, and has begun to upset the global balance."

Rideout chimed in. "Sure has, John. The UN Security Council has called a special meeting. The Arab nations are blaming the United States and allies. Stocks are plunging in all the world markets."

"Well, we've got to keep our heads and not get sucked into this mind job they've worked on everyone else. Terrorism is most powerful when it creates fear. That's its point. Fear is death to the thinking mind. So let's take a deep breath and start looking at what we know."

"Not much. That's the problem," said Miller.

"OK, let's see what information we can glean from the bomb site itself. This is on foreign soil, so at best it's going to be CIA, and that will be slow. The Venezuelans aren't going to be too keen on letting us get our hands dirty down there. The explosives—those are our only lead, and we'll need to make sure we get samples for analysis. You can bet I'll take this up with Larry first thing, although he'll be on it already, I'm sure."

"J. P., I want you and Matt all-nighting this one and monitoring every channel for information from Caracas. Tomorrow morning you get to hand me a report and then find a cot. Angel, I want you . . . Angel?" Savas looked over at Lightfoote staring at the door behind him.

"Leaving on a jet plane, O Captain, my Captain," she said.

"Christ, Angel, what . . ." he turned around and stopped. Just inside the door stood Larry Kanter, along with three other people. One was Mira Vujanac, and where Mira was, so usually was the CIA. Standing next to her was a tall man, thin and bespectacled, stiff and awkward in his formality. He had "bureaucrat spook" written all over him. Next to him stood a man John Savas would never have expected to see and couldn't believe he was seeing.

"John, I'm sorry to interrupt. Could you please step outside for a minute?" Kanter asked, motioning with his eyes that Savas should follow.

Rising slowly from his chair, Savas apologized to his team, who watched with considerable interest as he walked outside. Kanter closed the door behind him, leading him halfway down the hall away from the conference room door and out of earshot.

Kanter stood not five feet from a black man dressed in white robes with a long and thick beard trimmed Islamic style. On his head was a white kufi; the overall impression was of some African imam touring the offices of the FBI. He had a stern face, scarred on one side from what could only have been a knife wound, and yet a strange cheerfulness seemed to imbue his every expression. He was stocky, and a thick musculature without a hint of fat gave him the look of a boxer. He nodded toward Savas.

Savas looked between Kanter and Vujanac. "What the hell is this?"

21

*T*his is Agent Husaam Jordan, John," said Kanter, motioning toward the white-robed man. "CIA. Mira has been in high-level coordination with Langley concerning the recent attacks." Kanter gestured toward the tall, formal-looking man next to Agent Jordan. "Our analysis and identification of the bomb residue picked up an important connection. Husaam has been tracking a series of arms dealers and the shell games they play with foreign governments and commercial US military goods sold overseas. There's an entire black market for military goods that we sell legitimately to other nations, which then turn around illegitimately and resell them for a substantial profit to centralized mafia, weapons dealers who themselves sell the goods to the highest bidder."

Savas looked unimpressed. He could hardly take his eyes off Agent Jordan. "Yeah, Larry, I've heard all this. What does this have to do with these bombings?"

Kanter drew a breath, clearly impatient with his subordinate's tone yet cutting him unusual slack. "Agent Jordan has infiltrated one of the largest of these groups, formerly run by Viktor Bout—you probably have already heard his name, too."

He had. Viktor Bout was a legendary arms dealer, former KGB agent, who had run one of the largest and most profitable organizations in the world. His arrest in 2008 had slowed the trade only momentarily, as others rushed into the void, including new leadership in the organization he founded. Savas was quite aware of all this and was also attentive enough to pick up the warning from Kanter that he had better rein in his anger.

Kanter continued. "Among the many items they offer on the black market—weapons, body armor, even vehicles—are several forms of plastic explosives, including some of the newer, and extremely expensive, derivatives. Explosives with several times the power of previous forms of Semtex or C-4, and with a very high velocity of detonation."

"Perfect for demolitions work," rumbled the deep baritone of Agent Jordan, speaking for the first time.

Kanter nodded. "These items are very hard to get, and it is highly likely that, unless this group stole the material from the plant that made it, which would have been reported, they went through these dealers."

This was very interesting; a potentially important link to the terrorists. If Kanter was right. *If* there was a way to discover the buyers for these materials.

"Agent Jordan and his superior, Richard Michelson, here from the CIA Crime and Narcotics Center, have agreed to work directly with the FBI on this. I've assigned him to your team, John. Husaam will work independently of our chain of command, reporting directly to Agent Michelson, but day-to-day he will be an additional member of Intel 1."

Just great, thought Savas. Kanter looked Savas in the eye and spoke gravely. "I don't have to tell you how important it is that we make some headway on this one, John. We'll need all the help we can get from all agencies. We all need to make this work."

"Larry, can I speak to you privately?" asked Savas, needing an outlet soon lest he jettison all professionalism.

Kanter seemed to suppress a sigh. "Of course, John. Why don't you introduce Husaam to your group and then meet me in my office."

Savas held his emotions in check. "Sure, Larry. Agent Jordan, come this way, please."

He led the CIA man back to the conference room. As he grabbed the doorknob to open it, the baritone spoke. "When we are greeted with a salutation, the person should offer a better welcome, or at least return the same, for God taketh an account of all things." Jordan smiled and extended his hand.

Ah, hell. Savas grasped the offered hand and shook it *very* firmly.

"Nice words," said Savas, turning back to the door.

"From the Holy Koran," replied Jordan.

Savas, doorknob clasped tightly in his hand, stopped and turned slowly toward the CIA agent. "Agent Jordan, let's get something clear, so that we both know where we stand. I don't like the CIA meddling with my group, and no disrespect, but I don't know a damn thing about you. My group works well, and we're one of the best in the business. We've been together a while, and we work like a well-oiled machine. Your coming here, it's like grit thrown in the engine." Savas let go of the doorknob for a second time and pulled up to face Agent Jordan. "You don't know me well, but I don't take it lightly when someone quotes from a book that inspired men to fly airplanes into buildings in my city. Finally, in case the intelligence is fading from the CIA, you might also know that those bastards took the life of my son. So, do we understand each other, Agent Jordan?"

The joyful buoyancy had left the face of Husaam Jordan, but he did not flinch. "No, Agent Savas, not completely. Because you need to know two things about me. The first is that I will always do my best to respect every man I meet, but I will never hide or be ashamed of my religion. Second, I ask you not to judge how much I am grit until you give me a little time to integrate into your team. One thing about me that you will learn—I am a man of justice, as well as a Muslim. For me, they go together. Those who died in September of 2001 were victims of murder, led by extremists that I work every day to bring to justice. It is also said in the Holy Koran, 'Justice is an unassailable fortress, built on the brow of a mountain which cannot be overthrown by the violence of torrents, nor demolished by the force of armies.' I believe that, John Savas. I will work to see that it is so."

For several moments, they stood staring at each other, eye-to-eye, nearly toe-to-toe. Savas clenched his jaw but said nothing. Finally he turned and opened the door to the conference room.

22

"**D**amn it, Larry, you can't do this!"

Savas had officially reached the stage of throwing a fit. He had felt it coming, building up, and had decided to just get out of its way. There were a lot of things you had to put up with in life. A lot of them you didn't. *And some you had to yell about.*

"John, calm down. This isn't going to help the situation," said Kanter as calmly as he could. Standing next to Kanter behind his desk, Mira Vujanac appeared uneasy as she watched the emotional outburst.

"I'm not going to calm down! Do you know what this guy was doing? Quoting me proverbs from the Koran! Do you think I need to hear anything from *that* book? You told me when I came here, Larry, that you hired me because I'd be motivated for this job. What gives me that motivation is the same thing that makes it unacceptable that this representative of that religion be forced on me and my team! I'm not going to allow it!"

"John, that's the last time I want to hear about what you will and won't allow, or, I swear, you'll be finding yourself another place to work!" The veins stood out on Kanter's forehead, and he anchored his hands on his desk, standing and leaning forward. He brought one hand to his face and rubbed his temples. "John, please, sit down a moment."

Savas looked between the two of them and reluctantly took the closest seat. Vujanac sighed softly and adjusted her blouse. She sat on the side of the desk farthest from Savas.

Kanter continued. "This guy comes with amazing recommendations. He's single-handedly begun what has turned into an enormous operation against these international arms dealers. He's used his religion as a screen to work the entire thing, to pose as a radicalized leader of a group seeking to purchase weapons for terrorist activity in the United States. He's just a few steps from setting up a sting operation, and these events have compromised all his efforts. He's willing to work for less than that original goal, to instead try and infiltrate the network to trace the path of the explosives used in these attacks. He is willing to work with us on that to coordinate domestic and international efforts."

"I don't like it." Savas knew he was being obstinate, but it didn't matter.

"Damn it, John, I'm not asking you to like it. I'm asking you to make it work."

"John," said Vujanac softly, "Agent Jordan is an extraordinary man. He's taken a hard route to come to where he is."

"He sure as hell has," fired back Kanter. He picked up a large folder filled with papers and tossed it on his desk in front of Savas. "His file. Read it if you want. The guy grew up on the streets of LA. His mother was a crack addict, his father was gone before he was potty-trained. He joined a gang before he could likely write, rose in the ranks to a high position as an adolescent. Got tossed in jail at one point, found an imam and religion in prison."

Savas rolled his eyes. The last thing he wanted was a feel-good Hollywood story. "So the CIA's recruiting ex-cons now? They that desperate?"

"He was a juvenile."

"Larry, the CIA doesn't hire convicts!"

"Somebody made an exception!"

"They sure did." Savas shook his head. "He doesn't sound like some ex-gang member to me. Speaks like he's Ivy League."

"He is," Mira interjected. "Columbia. His spiritual father was highly educated and insisted Jordan be as well. He was bright enough to master that culture, too."

"Great, now a Muslim elitist spook."

Kanter pressed on. "Lots of these young black kids find Islam in jail. They either get radicalized, or they join social movements for the poor or push civil rights agendas. Well, Jordan felt a call to serve justice, something you don't see too many ex-gang members lean toward. Can you imagine how hard it must have been to get even a single serious look at a job like this? Can you imagine the interviews? He worked hard to erase his past. Some imam funded his college education. He prettied up his speech. He cut all ties with his old life. He knocked on every door until one opened. It looks like nothing stops this guy. He's on a mission, and he's made a serious mark at the CIA."

"John, please," said Vujanac. "We need you to put aside your personal issues. It's hard enough trying to get the FBI and the CIA to play nice. I know this is painful, but we need you to rise to this."

Savas looked out the window at the city. Inside, he felt a war of emotions. Outside, through the glass in Kanter's office, it was utterly still, row upon row of buildings stretching until he could not see beyond them. He closed his eyes and tried to think. He knew they were right. He knew he was being childish, unprofessional. But they did *not* understand how hard this was. It was something he had never expected. The son of a bitch even *dressed* like an Arab! He shook his head and laughed bitterly.

"OK, you two. I can give you this. I have one goal, and that is to bring justice to murderers of innocents, those terrorists that kill our children and hope to see Heaven for it. I'll work with anyone who shares that goal. If he does, I'll make it work."

"Thank you, John," Kanter said with evident relief.

Savas rose from his chair and walked to the door. He stopped and turned around. "Just don't expect me to be friends with the man. He does *his* job, I'll do mine." With that, he walked through the door and shut it behind him.

23

The next morning, Husaam Jordan briefed the team on his long-standing operation. Savas was stunned at how quickly the CIA man had integrated into the group, his extreme professionalism not-withstanding. Muslim or Tibetan monk, he was serious and knowledgeable, and held an intense focus for his work that reminded Savas of the pursuit of a predator of its prey. He also had a strangely winning side to his personality, which seemed to work best with the women in his group. It was clear that the ex-marine Miller was not going to warm easily to the man, and Matt King never warmed easily to anyone.

Cohen was a supporter early on and often came to his side when some of the more hostile members of the group were expressing that hostility. Savas had to admit he was one of those. Lightfoote was positively stuck to the man, showing specific and real interest in another human for the first time in her tenure at Intel 1. She hadn't called Savas "Ruthless Overlord" once today.

Savas, despite his very mixed feelings, was fascinated with what this man had done at the CIA. In the span of three short years, he had built up an undercover operation to infiltrate some of the most powerful and profitable arms dealerships in the world. For each of them, he used the front of an African American radical Muslim who was arming his organization for terrorist attacks in the United States. Whether or not the arms dealers knew or cared anything about this, or believed his intent, was likely irrelevant. They believed that the man wanted to buy, and did buy, and paid promptly in a way that established him and his false group with a strong reputation. It didn't hurt that several major arrests, including that of Viktor Bout himself, had been made in the last few years, disrupting organizations and forcing them to lower standards in chaotic rushes to claim client bases when they restructured. Jordan had taken advantage of this and promised his clients much larger buys in the near future.

For more than two hours, he detailed the organization, its members, foreign bases of operation and contacts, and difficult-to-trace money transfers. It was impressive, Savas had to admit. Impressive and frightening. A black Muslim seeking to become a domestic terrorist through international arms acquisition. The ruse was too plausible for comfort.

The presentation finished, Jordan turned on the lights and sat down. He appeared a bit drained and drank from a glass of water at his side. The room was quiet for a moment.

"Why do you think that this is the source of the explosives?" asked Cohen.

Jordan drank down the remainder of the glass and spoke. "Well, of course, we can't know, but there are not many ways to obtain that grade of explosive. The US government will not sell this stuff to just anyone. It stays with military or, in some cases, is sold to other nations. As you know, that's where the real black market in these things starts, and how our weapons mafia gets its sources. So there may be other ways, but I'm willing to bet that our new terrorist organization used one of these groups as its supplier. Bout's old organization is the biggest and still the best. It's a good place to start poking around."

He looked around the table, studying the faces of Intel 1. "I'm actually curious to know who these people are that went to all the trouble to go for such top-of-the-line materials—really overkill for what they wanted to do."

Savas had known this would come. Jordan had shown his hand from the CIA, down to the last PowerPoint slide. He expected a full briefing in return. Savas wanted to send him back to Langley with a *thank you very much!* and use this potential new lead. But the FBI needed the international reach of the CIA on this, and they specifically needed Jordan and his operation to have any hope of getting close to these dealers. Besides, it was the professional thing to do, and if he didn't, Kanter would cart someone else in to do the job.

"Rebecca Cohen will give you a briefing on what we know."

Cohen stood up, dimmed the lights, and spent the next hour going over everything they had gleaned from the events to date. The forensics reports and details on the bombings seemed familiar to Jordan, likely from previous briefings given by Vujanac or even Kanter. She concluded with the speculation that it might be an internal, American group but was careful to note that there was little solid evidence for that conjecture.

"There are also other, wilder theories," said Savas. He felt the eyes of the group bore in on him. *That was a hell of a thing to open up now.* Why he had done it; he didn't know. Perhaps to seek some form of acceptance, or, less charitably, perhaps to shake this Muslim up a little.

"Yes? What other theories?" asked Jordan after several moments of silence.

"His rogue Valkyries," said Lightfoote cryptically. Savas stared at her in wonderment. Had she spoken to Rebecca?

"It's a possible connection between two cases we've been working on." Savas summarized the worldwide string of assassinations, the use of the Sheikh as bait in a plan gone horribly wrong, and the connection between the attacks in the Afghan mountains and the murders. When he came to the subject of Norse mythology, and the speculation about the group's motivations, Jordan sat upright and still. The information on the more obscure point of the group's unusual name and symbolism seemed to interest him deeply, and he asked a number of intense questions on this matter.

"This Columbia professor," Jordan said, "I think he may be right, and his analysis makes for a very dark view of what we are up against." Jordan nodded thoughtfully toward Savas. "Now I see where you are headed, Agent Savas. You believe that this group is responsible for both the assassinations and these bombings, and that the motivation is the same—a hatred of Islam. Beyond that, a desire perhaps to wage a war against Muslims the world over. By this symbolism, an unending war until Judgment Day."

Rideout cut in. "Come on, people! Look, you've got a terrorist group that is playing to fears in a very effective way. You have a set of assassinations. The only thing connecting them? Scary mythology and some strange occult symbols."

"Pagan," interrupted Lightfoote.

Rideout flashed her an annoyed look.

"Well, trader-man, they are *pagan*, not *occult*," she countered. "There's, like, a *huge* difference."

"Fine. *Pagan* symbols," said Rideout. "This is all Wizard of Oz, if you want my opinion. Some real bombs and guns, and a lot of some ivory tower magician's hocus-pocus to rattle all the cages."

"Rattling the cages is only scary when you're in a cage," said Lightfoote.

Rideout rolled his eyes, his fatigue showing through. "This is what I left seven figures for? What the hell does that mean?"

"Look, enough!" said Miller, steering things back to the topic at hand. "From my vantage point, we have a string of murders and bombings that, even if not related, require our concerted efforts. The question is, what do we do now?"

Matt King answered in his nasal twang. "We track down all the shipments of this material, try to ID the lot used. Mira told us that each lot gets a different ratio of the additives that tag the explosives; we just need to get this material more thoroughly analyzed and figure out where this stuff went."

"Forensics is on that, Matt," said Savas. "But we don't have the equipment for that here. We need some really top-flight mass spectroscopy to ID these batches, and that's got to be farmed out. That takes time."

Rideout sighed and threw his pen onto the notepad before him. "Look, what's the pattern here? I know it's embassies and Middle Eastern oil countries but specifically New York, Washington—I get that. That's front-page material. But Venezuela? I mean, what's that all about? Why not Europe, or China, or the Middle East itself? What's the pattern in these attacks?"

"Well, with only these three bombings, that may be a hard thing to identify," rumbled Jordan.

"Yeah, maybe," said Rideout, "but I think we need to spend some time looking at this. The embassies, the people. Do they share something that we are missing? They must have chosen these targets for a reason."

"OK, J. P., why don't you work with Manuel on that? Let's compile all the data we can on these places, cross-referencing everything."

"We're missing the point here, my friends," boomed Jordan. He looked tired, frustrated, and deadly serious. "We have a good lead that could bring us to contacts that could be one or two steps away from the men we are looking for. This should be our priority."

Savas suppressed an urge to tell the man that, as group leader, he would decide what Intel 1 should and shouldn't be doing. "So, what would you do, Agent Jordan?" he said somewhat tensely.

"This is where my position in the CIA allows me freedoms you do not have. I have reached a decision, Agent Savas. It is a hard one and will ruin years of work, as well as cost tax payers millions of dollars and perhaps some agents their lives. I am going back to Sharjah."

"Sharjah?" asked Savas over the silence. "Why?"

Jordan stared forward, as if glimpsing something in the distance. "You can remember from my presentation—we have established inroads into two of Viktor Bout's primary centers of operation: Belgium and the United Arab Emirates. Bout was pressured out of Belgium in the late 1990s as the press uncovered his shady dealings. His organization never closed up shop there. But the heart of it moved with him to Sharjah in the UAE. There he was coddled by many members of the royal family and developed deep connections to international companies playing with money laundering and terrorism, civil war, and murder. He left behind a well-organized machine."

Cohen took her glasses off and stared at the CIA operative. "Husaam, what do you plan on doing there?"

Jordan paused a moment and took a deep breath. "I may be in the minority, but I take quite seriously the intentions of this terrorist organization and the hypothesis put forward by Agent Savas. Perhaps I have to—after all, it could be a declaration of war against my faith. I believe we must take whatever action we can in order to find out who these people are and how to get to them. I'm going to take my team under-cover into Sharjah, as we have before, but this time to set up a major arms purchase and use that opportunity to break into their organization and seize any records they have on the sale and distribution of Semtex-like explosives."

A heavy silence fell over the group. Rebecca's eyes flashed upward toward Savas. Rideout whistled, adding, "You're likely to end up buried in the sands out there. That's either really damn brave or really damn stupid."

Jordan smiled grimly. "It is written, 'What God writes on your forehead, you will become.'"

PART 2
MERCHANTS OF DEATH

24

A begrimed Caucasian stared across a dusty wooden table at the three Berbers. It was a blistering day, and the sands from the northern Sahara that seemed to invade so much of Algeria bordering on the desert dug into every crevice of his body. His face was deeply bronzed from his time in the sun—time spent coaxing, bribing, and leading these barbarians along the path required. It was one thing to work an act of public violence in a Western nation, or even in a South America nation like Venezuela. Even there, freedom to move around and the mixed-race nature of the population made planning and executing a mission far simpler. But here, in Northern Africa, surrounded by Berber Arabs in a strongly Islamic nation, where custom and language differed far more markedly, he could not work alone.

What one could always count on with these people was that they were as murderous toward each other as toward the West. He had been patient and resourceful. The young Ibadi radicals they had primed were perfect for achieving the mission. Better yet, this splinter group was so ignorant and detached from the rest of the world that the events of the last two months were not known to them, and the plan he proposed had not aroused their suspicions.

The Ibadi were a minority sect of Islam, centered in Oman with pockets in Algeria, with radically different interpretations of Heaven and Hell. They thought of themselves as the only true Muslims. All others were, as he had come to learn with amusement, *kuffar,* "unbelievers." In the last ten years, increasingly radical groups had found inspiration from terrorist organizations like al-Qaeda, and now they desired to exert their violent influence over the world, to establish Ibadi rule. That this meant executing terrorist acts against other Muslims was exactly what he required.

"You will have the trucks ready on the night of the fifteenth," said the American in his poor Arabic.

The older of the three men laughed and smiled broadly, revealing several missing teeth. "My friend, you must learn to speak the language better. Without us, you would get not five steps. Yes, we will have them to transport your men. We will provide real clothes for you," and he laughed again, "not these womanly things you have tried to wear and hide yourself under."

"Then we are agreed, Aziri?" he pressed.

Another spoke. "We do not like that the Ibadi People's Army is to be kept so far from the attack. We are not to be considered children who cannot fight!"

"Aban, I have explained this as clearly as I can. My team works alone. You will bring us into the site. We will complete the mission, and then you will get us out. We are providing the funds, the expertise, and risking our lives for this. We won't do it another way. It is our way or no way."

The three men looked at each other. Aban was angry, but his older brother put his hand on his shoulder. He spoke softly in a local Berber dialect. A back-and-forth ensued, but the older brother held the day. Over the reproachful look of his brother, Aziri continued. "We will accept your offer. The materials you will provide for us. With these things, we will strike again and again into the heart of the kuffar abomination. It will begin with what you will do. You are ignorant, but you do the work of Allah, unbeliever."

"Then make sure it is settled," he said standing, eyeing the three men. "Because we also will not hesitate to inflict a lesson on anyone who tries to interfere with what we do." The three men nodded, convinced by what they had seen of his team to date that he meant what he said.

The American walked out of the small building and into the blazing summer sun. The fools would comply. They were young and filled with fire to strike at the majority Sunni population. This was a chance to do so in a way they could never have imagined before: in the heart of Algeria, at the Great Mosque of Algiers, Jemaa Kebir, built more than one thousand years ago. They dreamed to establish their Berber culture and small sect of Islam, and thereby opened their nation to a worse strike from within. He was happy indeed to hit the mosque, but the goal had been greater, and the Ibadi People's Army would soon find that they had opened Algiers to an attack on another landmark, one dear to all Algerians as a symbol of the defeat of the West. As such a symbol, Mjolnir would hammer it and crush it to the ground. He would see to that. He knew how much was being entrusted to him. He would not fail.

The winds blew, etching sand grains mercilessly over his face. He looked across the desert into the distance, seeing beyond it to the greatest goal ahead. *Another step. Each step brings us closer.* It was all coming together, despite setbacks and delays. He smiled, turned toward the main road, and began walking.

25

The flight to Sharjah was a rough one, far more turbulent than usual, so much so that even Jordan had passed on a recent offer of a meal. The triple-sevens of Boeing were usually smoother rides, and he wondered grimly whether it was a sign of things to come. It had taken him weeks to secure permission for this risky venture, putting his reputation on the line at the CIA. As July ended, he had finally gotten the needed permission, and he prepared his team for what was to come. *As much as they can be prepared.*

The trip was long, more than twelve hours in the air from New York to Dubai City, then a car ride from Dubai to Sharjah, and that was assuming nothing went wrong in between. Right now, his main concern was his team. They were men from every walk of life, from the street to the Ivy League, each a trained CIA operative. All were black; all dressed in Arab garb: white robes and a white African kufi with Muslim-style beards. They looked out of place alongside the Arabs onboard, some of whom were in traditional clothing, many in Western-style business attire; all very different than the African American men sitting together in a group in the middle of the aircraft. These were the men he had trained and honed for the last three years, who had traveled overseas countless times, risking their lives, leaving their families, to build piece by piece, deal by deal a reputation as trusted customers in a black market arms world where there truly was no trust. But where trust could not be found, money and arms did in their stead.

In the facade presented to the arms world, he was Yusuf Abdul-Rauf, leader of a new Muslim extremist group centered in the United States and composed solely of African American members. "A Muslim

Black Panthers," he had explained on several occasions, focused on the liberation of the black people from the oppression of the white Christian power structure "by any means necessary." He sought arms and explosives through deals untraceable by investigative agencies in the United States. He planned to build an army, make a mark with terrorist attacks across the nation. Of course, the dealers cared little why he wanted their merchandise, only that he paid in full and on time. Jordan doubted they believed his organization would do much anyway. They were impressed, however, with his cash and clearly wondered who was bank-rolling his purchases. He only hoped none of them had begun to guess that it was the US government itself behind him.

He traveled with six others. Four of them were muscle, necessary for his real purpose as well as for this well-developed facade. His bodyguards in both worlds, these were operatives expertly trained in combat and defense, and Jordan was always glad to have them around on these missions. All but one were former gang members he had personally recruited. Two were his "money men," operatives trained in finance who had studied the international arms market thoroughly. His Harvard Men, as he called them in jest. Jordan, or Yusuf, was the visionary, the leader who brought these men, and the imaginary hundreds back in the States who followed him, together under a unifying purpose and will.

This team had patiently worked to build respectability as a client in the illegal arms markets, focusing on the one led by the now imprisoned ex-KGB agent Viktor Bout. His team had played a crucial role in the capture of the Merchant of Death, although he had not mentioned this to John Savas and others at the FBI. It was the greatest success of his young career and had earned him respect and authority at the CIA. His infiltration of these networks promised to deliver much more than that over the coming years. Now he was asking his team to travel again and risk destroying years of work, placing all their lives in danger on a hunch that this new terrorist organization was something so threatening that it required drastic action. For all that he was doing, he had better be right. He remembered the prayer in the Koran, in the sura Maryam: *My Lord! surely my bones are weakened and my head flares with hoariness, and, my Lord! I have never been unsuccessful in my prayer to Thee.* He hoped Allah would hear his prayer now.

The final descent toward Dubai was always spectacular, as the golden-brown of the desert and the blue of the sea established a strong contrast, punctuated by the amazing sights of the Palm Islands. These enormous, human-made islands of nearly filigreed projections of sand were clearly visible from the cruising altitude of the plane and upon descent carved out a magnificent decoration in the Gulf spanning nearly three miles in diameter. Close by were hundreds of small sandy islands comprising "The World," an artificial archipelago that re-creates the shape of the continents of the earth, and on which vacation homes, resorts, estates, and communal lands were still being built—a product of endless oil money, some imagination, and what Jordan considered entirely too much time on the hands of the populace.

Jordan and his team disembarked, completely jet-lagged, a strange troop of black Muslims walking like a pack through the Dubai International Airport to pick up a rental car for the drive to Sharjah. It amused him to see the familiar names and icons of Hertz, Avis, and Thrifty rentals amid all the flowing and ornate Arabic script. This part of the trip would be short, at least, and Jordan knew that he and his team would need to get some sleep soon. Tomorrow they would begin a most dangerous gambit.

They were mostly silent driving through Dubai City, each wrapped up in his own thoughts, each fatigued from the trip. Within half an hour, they had crossed into Sharjah proper and were approaching the Millennium Hotel on Corniche Road, its blue-glass face reflecting the bright Middle Eastern sun and the waves of the sea. Check-in was quick. Jordan's Arabic was extremely fluent after many years of training and practice on foreign soil.

In the hotel room, he dialed the number he kept security-locked in his smart phone. After three rings, he heard a tone and then entered a long eight-digit code. A second set of rings was heard, and another tone prompted a second code. A third set of rings was interrupted by a woman's voice speaking Russian.

"Yusuf Abdul-Rauf calling for Mikhail Kharitonov," he replied in the same language.

"A moment, *Puzhalsta*," said the voice. Jordan glanced over at the clock on the wall. It was eleven in the morning. He had called ahead of schedule.

"My American friend," said a strong male voice in heavily accented English. "Happy for you to arrive very good."

"Thank you, Mika. We are glad to be here. I hope things are on schedule for our meeting tomorrow."

"Yes, yes," said the man, sounding almost amused. "We have all as you requested. It is very big order, my friend, and means Mika must work very hard to see all is delivered."

"We understand, Mika. This is important for us. We have all that you asked for. Do not worry."

The voice on the other end of the line laughed. "Yusuf, Mika always worry. That why Mika still alive. Tomorrow, as planned, time and place. You bring and I bring. All is then good, no?"

"Yes, Mika. All is good."

Jordan closed the connection and took a breath of air. The madness would soon begin.

26

T he ride down to the port was a quiet one. Jordan and his team had prepared for this moment for several weeks—in truth, for several years, considering all that had brought them here. After sleeping off the journey, they were up in the early morning considering plans and backup plans, countermeasures and options. Now all their planning came down to execution, and, Jordan knew in his heart, a certain amount of randomness, what others called luck. *But luck favors the prepared.* Part of their preparation was a visit last night from the CIA safe house in Dubai. Their visitors were kind enough to supply them with handguns smuggled into the country, as well as a set of disks, memory sticks, flash drives, and adaptors for the mission to come.

From Corniche Road, which ran through the sands by the Millennium Hotel in Sharjah, it had been a short hop on one of the area's main thoroughfares, Al Ittihad Road, a thoroughly modern highway. Then across a new fourteen-lane, sixteen-thousand-vehicle-capacity bridge, onto the Sheikh Zayed Road, which twisted its way southeast around the center of Dubai, soon to run parallel with the coastline southwest toward the harbor. They passed the World Archipelago on their right, which hardly made an impression this close to the ground. The second and much larger Palm Island loomed somewhere northwest of them as they approached the main port, Jebel Ali.

As they exited E11 and drove on 520th Street, Jordan was again struck by the scale of things in Dubai. With sixty-seven berths and a span of over fifty square miles, Jebel Ali was the world's largest artificial harbor, built over many years in the 1970s. More than five thousand companies from over one hundred and twenty nations made use of this port. A frequent user was in fact the United States Navy. There was hardly a sailor who served in the region who had not visited the port sometime during his tour. The great depth of the harbor and overall width allowed American aircraft carriers to dock, and it was not unusual to find a Nimitz Class carrier with several of its companion boats pier side. Jordan suppressed a laugh. How the arms dealers like Kharitonov loved to do business right under the noses of the United States military forces! How their pride blinded them to the fact that Uncle Sam was aware of everything they were doing, and was using them for the purpose of catching bigger fish—the clients on the other ends of their deals.

Jordan and his men pulled up to the dock number they had been sent and stepped out into the desert heat. Three vehicles were waiting, and Jordan could see the tall, lanky form of Mika Kharitonov standing beside an open car door, several bodyguards flanking him and positioned in the nearby vehicles. The cargo boat behind them, he noticed, was dotted with several shapes obviously toting weapons—what appeared to be automatic weapons. He knew the other guards would also be carrying weapons, concealed, just as Kharitonov knew that Jordan's men were packing. It was like a well-choreographed dance, only with less sexual tension and more potential for chaos and death. Jordan pretended to be blinded by the bright sunlight, taking that time to scope the scene. He spoke quietly out of the side of his mouth to several members of his team.

"Trouble perched high on the boats. We'll need to contain those."

The man next to him smiled tightly. "Looks like we got trouble everywhere we look. We're going to get bloody on this one, Husaam."

"Yeah, we might," he said, feeling a sudden heaviness. The wind gusted and blew grains of sand across their faces. *I'm responsible for these men.*

"Mika, my friend!" Jordan boomed over the sounds of machinery, waves, and vehicles at the port, laughing in his deep bass as he walked rapidly up to greet the Russian. Kharitonov stepped slightly forward, enough to put his guards a few steps behind him—about the same distance that existed between Jordan and his men. They extended hands and shook.

"Good see you, Yusuf. I think you and your men bigger every year. Like Barry Bonds, no?"

"The brothers on the street don't have an easy life. We work hard for what is ours. It shows. You will help us do that."

"Mika happy to help. But Mika more happy when paid. You understand?" he said, with a smile that made Jordan think of what a serial killer must look like before he struck.

"Of course, my friend. Friendship doesn't put food, or vodka, on the table. Kareem!" he shouted over his shoulder. A thinner black man with a goatee stepped up beside Jordan. He carried a slim briefcase, much too slender to contain any significant amount of money. He unlocked the case, opened it, and held it up level to show the Russian its contents. Inside was a small thumb drive.

"Codes and executable," Kareem said flatly, an accountant presenting data. "You have your connection established?"

"Of course, of course," said Kharitonov.

Jordan interjected. "Then why don't we have a look at the merchandise, and as soon as that's done, we'll go digital, my friend."

Kharitonov nodded and signaled to his bodyguards. Kareem closed the case and stepped behind the troop accompanying Jordan as the Russian led them toward the dock and the ramp to board the vessel. As they passed underneath, the men holding automatic weapons gazed down on them and tracked their motion onto the ship.

The boat was enormous, a merchant container ship flying the Greek flag. Jordan knew that the ownership of the vessel was not related to the "flags of convenience" that allowed for easier and cheaper passage, and that the Greeks sheltered numerous such boats. These "box boats" had, over the last century, revolutionized world trade, allowing for highly efficient transfer of enormous amounts of cargo across the planet. More than eighteen million containers journeyed over two hundred million trips per year—and this was the legal material. This early form of the global economy had truly become international, highly dynamic, and

adaptable to maximizing profit. This vessel could have come from anywhere, belonged to anyone, and only the arcane records of the companies using the ships could give any idea to the source of the materials
onboard. That is exactly why Jordan was here in Sharjah and Dubai,
and why today's deal was going to go sour very quickly.

While the boat looked big, Jordan knew that it was one of the
smaller container vessels. The fact that it was docked away from the
land-based cranes was enough to tell you that, even if the presence of
its own small crane to offload the boat boxes didn't. Kharitonov had
his trade down to a science. The forty-foot boxes were rigged with
"quick-entry" latches that opened a specially designed section of the
box, allowing rapid examination of contents. Kharitonov brought
them to one such entry point, unlocked the container, and had his men
pull out a large wooden crate. As they pried it open with crowbars, the
submachine-gun-toting guards closed in behind Jordan's men, sand-
wiching them between Mika's gunmen and the large crate. The men
pulled off the packing insulation, revealing rows of neatly stacked automatic weapons and magazine cartridges. Jordan approached the crate,
reached in, and pulled out one of the guns. It was a sleek, black micro-
Uzi submachine gun. He turned it over, played with the safety, gripped
it in his hands to feel the weight and balance of the thing. Kharitonov
and his subordinates watched in silence as their customer examined the
product.

"The suppressors fit?" he asked himself out loud, removing a
silencer from his robes and attaching it to the barrel of the gun. He
again turned it around and examined it for several moments.

Jordan laughed and tossed the gun to one of his bodyguards, who
caught it cleanly in the air and, as everyone watched, examined the
gun himself, also breaking out into a smile. *Boys and their toys*, thought
Jordan grimly, as he nimbly pocketed two ammo magazines and stashed
them in his robes. One advantage of robes over pants, he thought—far
easier to hide things in those inner pockets. Kharitonov glanced over
at him as he turned away from the weapons container and motioned to
Kareem. Kareem stepped forward and opened the case again. By now,

Kharitonov's men had forged a satellite link to a bank account thousands of miles away.

"The executable runs automatically. You give it your routing numbers and account, and the money is transferred. As before, no strings and untraceable. You should be able to see it immediately. Half now, and half on delivery."

Kharitonov nodded and handed the drive over to the man who set up his connection. He seemed relaxed. Jordan had groomed this man and his organization for four long years, and this was not their first deal. Jordan had been an exemplary customer, never missing a payment or canceling a deal. Kharitonov had grown complacent with him, as much as an international arms dealer could, and Jordan was counting on this. That was why the Russian did not watch Jordan carefully at this moment as he moved slowly along the open crate of weapons. That was also why the Russian did not immediately recognize his peril when his subordinate spoke quickly to him in concerned Russian.

"Yusuf," Kharitonov said, staring at the screen, "transfer not going through." Jordan looked at him, unconcerned, his arms behind his back as he stood at attention. The Russian looked down at the screen, and as he did so, Jordan made quick eye contact with his team. "Not understanding. Yusuf—there is problem?" he asked.

Jordan looked at the Russian grimly. "Yes, Mika, there is."

Several things happened at the same time. Jordan whipped a loaded Uzi out from behind him, a second silencer already attached. He opened fire with several bursts at bodyguards flanking Kharitonov. One dropped immediately as a line of red stains erupted across this chest. The second dove to his right, pulling a weapon out from his belt and aiming toward Jordan. Before he could pull the trigger, his neck snapped back as flesh and blood ripped apart, a barrage of bullets fired by one of Jordan's bodyguards. Simultaneously, the other members of his team pulled out handguns, all with silencers attached, and turned toward the guards behind them. Although the guards held the advantage in firepower, they were too slow to realize what was happening, and Jordan's combat-trained operatives pounced on them like tigers.

The rear members of his team, nearest the guards, had chosen hand-to-hand combat. One had dropped to a push-up position and swung his leg around like a helicopter blade, catching the guard behind the knees and dropping him to the ground. The operative behind him fired four quick shots into the prone man, who did not move again. The second guard found his weapon kicked from his arms as the CIA man drew his right leg in an arc like a mace in front of him. The guard stood there stunned as he watched the man pivot on the foot that had just disarmed him, spinning and turning to bring his left leg like a battering ram straight into his face. A jawbone cracked loudly, and the man went down flat on his back, smacking his head against the boat deck. He did not get up.

Kareem had incapacitated the computer man with several blows, then had frozen Kharitonov by placing a gun to the base of his skull. Kharitonov, who had drawn a weapon and was aiming it toward Jordan, relaxed and dropped his firearm. The four remaining bodyguards, poorly positioned in the crowded region around the boat box, had all been either overpowered or killed by Jordan's team. It was over in a matter of seconds.

Jordan grabbed Kharitonov's computer, placed it in the briefcase, and handed it to Kareem.

"You *insane* American!" Kharitonov spat as his hands were tied with wire behind him. "What is for? You get nothing from this!"

Jordan put the barrel of his Uzi under Kharitonov's chin. The Russian pulled up his head in pain from the hot cylinder. *That seemed to get his attention.* "Mika, what I get is my problem. But if you don't do exactly what I say, I can tell you exactly what you're gonna get." He stared at the Russian coldly. "You understand?" Kharitonov nodded, fear in his eyes. "Right now, that means you make a sound we don't like, I fill you with holes. You try to escape, I, or one of my men, will fill you with holes. And if you don't follow as you are directed, right now, you get filled with holes. Got that?" Mika nodded again, sweat pouring down his face.

"Good." Jordan turned to his men. "Take his cell phone. Get him to the car, grab several of these guns and clips. Load up. We're likely going to need them." Jordan strode through the piles of bodies on the ship deck, and his team led Kharitonov at gunpoint down the ramp and to their vehicles. Two drivers were still in the other cars, oblivious in the noisy environment of the dock to the events on deck above them. They were listening to music and reading, one sending text messages to his girlfriend. Before they could do much more than look up, they were knocked unconscious and dragged aside.

"We go in these three cars, to lessen the suspicion." Jordan designated his two Harvard Men to ditch the rentals. The rest of his team loaded up into the three vehicles of Kharitonov. Jordan sat in the back of one car, his Uzi trained on the Russian as they pulled out.

"Let's pay a visit to a little building in Sharjah," said Jordan. The eyes of the Russian grew large as he understood.

"You have no place to hide. You never make deal again! We hunt you down, to America. You are *dead* man, Yusuf."

Jordan looked out through the window of the speeding car over the bright sands and sighed. "So aren't we all, Mika." He slapped a new cartridge into the Uzi. "What's important is what you do while it lasts."

27

Some three thousand miles away, the August night was cool in Algiers. Despite its nearness to the desert, its location within the Tell Atlas Mountains and its proximity to the Mediterranean Sea dominated this coastal city, giving it a temperate climate that even in the hottest months was never too uncomfortable. The day's heat had abated by the predawn hours, and the wind that blew from the mountains dropped the temperature into the high sixties.

The cool night was a welcome relief to the American and his team, especially since they were dressed in bulky Arab clothing over their combat attire. They had ridden into the city late in the evening, disguised as migrant workers, in several trucks provided and driven by their helpful friends of the Ibadi People's Army. Of course, the man laughed to himself; no one had ever heard of the IPA, and they likely never would. But he humored its young and naive founders. They were a ticket through the Arab and Berber landscape in Algiers, a landscape that too easily could become problematic if they ran into any complications. But no one had paid any attention to yet another group of workers trucked into the city to do its heavy lifting.

They had left the Ibadi drivers with the vehicles beside the foul-smelling piers. His team headed under cover of what darkness remained toward the Great Mosque of Algiers, Jemaa Kebir, a structure over one thousand years old. Two members of his team were posted to keep watch on their collaborators. The IPA members wanted credit for the destruction of this landmark of Sunni Islam. They had fought to be a part of tonight's efforts on several occasions in his presence. He would not have them interfering in what he and his men had to do.

Five commandos from his team were dispatched to the mosque. Among them were two weapons specialists, a communications officer, and two demolition men. They carried enough S-47 to take down five buildings this size. The explosion would ensure a level of carnage that would make a statement the world would notice. The men checked off with their leader and sprinted toward the historical shrine.

The rest had another plan. The American turned and gathered together the remaining seven of his team. This was the team that would be responsible for an act of terrorism even greater than that at the mosque, an act targeting an Algerian symbol of independence from Western powers that even the Ibadi held in high respect. They would never have allowed such an action. Had they known of his plans, they would have likely tried to kill him.

His team searched along the roadway hugging the coastline. Several blocks from the Great Mosque, they found what had been left for them: a van with keys inside, left by "tourists" that evening. They loaded into the van, each man with large packs of S-47, gripping automatic weapons. A driver started the engine and pulled out, heading nearly due south along the road. After a few minutes, they took a southeasterly turn through the nearly empty streets of the city and, within five minutes, pulled up several streets before coming to the square.

At night the structure was an awesome sight. Bright lights bathed the curving concrete arches, inverted so they turned inward, giving the imposing structure a solid and yet otherworldly presence. *Maquam E'chahid*, the Martyrs Monument, was constructed in 1982 to celebrate the twentieth anniversary of Algeria's independence from France. It took the abstract interpretation of three standing palm leaves, forming in their center a shelter beneath which the "eternal flame" burned. Statues of soldiers adorned the front of each leaf where it rested to find support on the ground.

He checked his watch. They were nearly late. In two minutes, team Beta would kill the power to this portion of the Algiers power grid, darkening the lights across a portion of town for a short period of time. Before technicians had located the problem and dispatched crews, their job would be done and the power restored, leaving nothing to trigger suspicion at the site.

Right on cue, the powerful searchlights went dark, and the lights in buildings and streetlamps for many blocks around them went out. The site was nearly totally black but for the light leaking its way over from other portions of the city. The team strapped on their night-vision goggles and sprinted to the monument.

With five minutes to spare on their tight schedule, they piled into the van, backpacks empty, magazines full, the job a silent success. They drove north, back toward the site of the Great Mosque, where they parked the car and left the keys. They sprinted back up to the rendez-vous point where they were met by the remaining members of team Alpha. The news was good from both groups, and they returned to find their Ibadi friends waiting impatiently for them.

"This took too long!" whispered Aziri, his eyes flashing. "You are lucky no police came!"

"Relax, Aziri. The job went well. It is best to be sure about these things and take your time."

The Berber grunted and started the truck as the rest of the team settled into the back of the flatbed. He pulled out along the road, taking the American and his men to the airport for the first flight of the morning. The light of dawn began to break on the horizon. "Yes," he noted, "you are right. It is written: 'Haste is of the Devil.'"

"Indeed, my friend," replied the American, beginning to remove his robes and glancing over to the towering form of the monument sil-houetted against the pale sky.

28

The three gray BMWs pulled into a parking lot behind a row of small sheds, which resembled the sort of structures that an army would throw up—cheap, easy to raise, easy to break down, and yet highly functional with amenities like electricity, heat, cooling, running water, and, in this case, Internet lines. The small buildings were in a fairly undeveloped region of Sharjah, with construction surrounding the lot and the ground dirty and paved only with gravel. Little traffic came in or out. It was a perfect location to escape notice and yet to be as completely connected to the world as any high-rise in Dubai.

Jordan marveled at the arrogance, or ignorance, of these dealers. Did they really believe that Viktor Bout had been apprehended at random, through some stroke of luck by the international community? Did they never consider that their entire operation may have been compromised? Yet they maintained their same base of operations, known for years now to the CIA through Jordan's efforts, and now also known to several international agencies when the CIA worked with them to apprehend their former boss.

He stepped out onto the gravel, hearing it crunch beneath his shoes. On the other side of the car, Kharitonov rose slowly, a pistol pointed at his head, and maneuvered awkwardly with his hands wired together behind his back. Two black men in white robes shepherded him toward the back entrance of one of the small structures. He glared at Jordan.

"I cannot feel my hands, you *bastard*!" he spat.

A gun tapped against his temple reminded him to speak more quietly, and more politely.

"Mika, let's go over this to make sure you don't make us have to kill you," said Jordan, looking around the area. Thankfully, the building had few windows, and the back entrance was not easily visible from within. He stared at the Russian coldly. "You will enter as if nothing whatsoever is out of the ordinary. You will speak to us as clients, making up whatever excuse you have to as to why we are here. You will then take us to where you keep your records."

Kharitonov squinted and eyed him darkly as Jordan's men untied the Russian's wrists. "You are police?" he asked.

Jordan nodded his head to one side, and a large man next to the Russian punched him in his right kidney. Kharitonov groaned but kept quiet as Jordan put his finger to his lips. "*Shhhhh.* No, we're worse, my friend. And that is the last I expect to hear from you except for what I have explained. If you alert anyone, if you take any action, or if the air in there doesn't smell right to me, I'll paint the walls with your brain. Understood?"

Kharitonov grunted between painful gasps of air. Jordan gave him a minute to regain his composure, then issued instructions for his team to conceal their weapons. The additional time allowed for the return of his Harvard Men, who had ditched the rentals, bringing Jordan's team up to full strength.

They all made eye contact, and Jordan turned toward Kharitonov. "The guns are out of sight, but don't let them be out of your mind. You saw what we did to your men. We'll do it again. Remember, my Russian is better than your English, so don't get stupid."

He nodded toward the door, and Kharitonov pulled out a security card and held it up to a reader that beeped at the same time a metallic sound could be heard from the door as the lock clicked. He stepped inside, followed closely by Jordan and the other men.

For his part, Mika Kharitonov acted well. No Oscar, but the show and threat, and very real action he had witnessed, had brought out his inner coward. He led them through what appeared to be very ordinary office rooms, filled with clerks, mostly female, typing into computers and taking calls. Guns were good business, and like any modern business, there was a lot of administration. Several people looked surprised to see him, and even more so the entourage that followed him through the room and down the hall to another room where thousands of optical disks were filed and a lone archivist worked. As he had done in the other rooms, Kharitonov put on a pleasant, professional, if somewhat strained face, and told the archivist to leave them alone.

Jordan's team went to work immediately. Within minutes, they had located the records for all transactions within the last five years. These were no longer stored on the computer, so they pulled and pocketed the CDs from storage cabinets. A USB memory stick was used to store all the records that were present on the computer itself, although Jordan doubted that what they were looking for was there. Kharitonov was clearly as intrigued as he was frightened, but he was forced to chew on his questions as the operatives worked on in silence.

"OK, move it, move it. The clock's running on this one, and we don't know when time runs out," Jordan said, pushing his team.

Within half an hour they were finished. Jordan rounded up his team, the precious data in his own backpack. They headed back the way they had entered, through what looked suspiciously like a call center, and out the back door. Kharitonov opened the door to the outside, stood upright, straight as a plank of wood, and dove to the right and outside the door.

Ambush! thought Jordan, and lunged to the left, pulling the Uzi out as he slid to the floor. The thin walls of the building exploded with sound as bullets tore through the siding and whizzed in through the open door. Two of his team fell with multiple bullet wounds, as did several phone operators near the door. Screams filled the room, and women dropped to the floor or dashed out toward the front of the building, sending papers flying through the office. Still the bullets blasted against the walls, and one shattered the single window on the side of the building where Jordan lay, showering glass over him and the unmoving body of a nearby office worker.

He knew things had been too easy.

29

The day was going to be hot, and the tourists squirmed awkwardly under backpacks, cameras, and overloaded shopping bags along the streets of Algiers. Street vendors hocked their overpriced items as locals smirked at the naive Westerners spending more money than could possibly be justified for the goods. Business was particularly good around the Great Mosque. The combination of history and its nearness to the sea made the landmark a must-see stop on the tourist run.

"*Allahu Akbar!*" Suddenly, a loud, static-filled call rose over the loudspeaker near the mosque. Heads of tourists turned toward the sound, despite having heard it several times in the day already, and five times every day of their stay; it was still an unusual sound to their ears. In contrast, the Algiers citizens seem to give a calm and familiar response, the pious slowly stopping their activities, pulling out prayer mats and laying them on the ground. A tight group of American tourists listened as their guide explained and translated.

"The muezzin is making the *adhan*, the call to prayer," he said.

"*Allaahu Akbar!*"

"God is great!" he echoed in English to the wondering faces.

"*Ashhadu Allah ilaaha illa-Lah; Ash Hadu anna Muhamadar rasuulullah.*"

"I bear witness that there is no other god but Allah. I bear witness that Muhammad is the messenger of God!"

"*Hayya' alas Salaah; Hayya' ala Falaah.*"

"Come to prayer! Come to Success."

"*Allaahu Akbar! Laa ilaaha illa-Lah.*"

"God is great! There is no god but Allah."

The echoes of the haunting Arabic chant rebounded over the streets and cement buildings, reaching out over the harbor toward incoming ships. After a moment of silence, as if in answer, the mosque exploded.

The sound was deafening, the shock wave injurious and stunning, citizens and tourists alike thrown to the ground as rock and metal hurled through the air at lethal velocity. The loudspeaker from the minaret arched high above the road as debris flew underneath it, then reached an apex and took its parabolic dive toward the street below, crushing a street vendor and his cart. The muezzin making the call to prayer, and all the worshippers within the mosque, were never identified in what remained.

Chaos landed along with the loudspeaker, as the able-bodied fled from the scene in panic, abandoning hundreds of injured and dying to their screams for aid. Time slowed down for all who remained, as a false evening fell from the smoke and dust obscuring the sun. Wounded shadows limped through the choking fog of grit, like undead creatures risen from the grave, the horror real and more terrible than any film director's vision.

Finally, muffled sirens were heard as emergency vehicles and military personnel arrived on the scene and worked to impose order over the chaotic remains. Just as they had begun to attend to the wounded and put out the fires, staring with wide eyes toward what was minutes ago the Great Mosque, a strong breeze from the sea sliced the cloud of dust blocking the view, providing a tunnel of vision southward to reveal the majesty and brutal artistry of the Martyrs Monument.

Under the shadow of the monument, a group of French tourists were gathered for a final photograph before returning home from their vacation. What had been a tightly pressed form with twenty smiles facing the camera became a dissolving clump looking toward the northern part of town as a thunderous sound reached their ears and a pillar of smoke began to rise several miles away. The photographer turned to face the chaos, and the sounds of her shutter firing rapidly stuttered in the growing silence. All conversation ceased for several moments, then rose to a higher level as concerned voices sought the meaning of the events. Many were running toward the northern edges of the park that rose up on a small hill above the port, seeking a closer and clearer view of the source of the smoke and noise. Cell phones were pulled out, more photos taken, and many left the monument site to head home or elsewhere.

The French tourists remained close to the monument. They were expecting their tour guide to return and meet them there, under the monument, and lead them to a bus for the airport. None of them would make the return trip.

Three massive explosions erupted around them, the blast ejecting building debris radially from the structure, flailing the tourists to death in milliseconds. Each explosion was centered on one of the three legs of the Martyrs Monument, placed strategically to sever the supports of the tower from its body like a giant's scalpel. Those watching at a distance stared transfixed as time crawled and the great tower appeared to shudder above the disk of debris beneath it, then plunge toward the ground like a spear. The concrete column crumbled as it smashed into the surface underneath, dissolving like dust and throwing a circular plume outward and upward. Within seconds, the great symbol of Algerian pride for independence from foreign rule was gone.

"Anything from Husaam?" Rebecca Cohen asked as she poked her head into John Savas's office.

"No," he replied, sipping from his morning coffee. "The CIA is slow to update us, and they never released his precise schedule. He should have made contact with the Russian dealer by now. I guess we'll hear soon how that went."

Cohen stepped into his office, partially closing the door. "John, I think morale is beginning to slip. It's two weeks into August, and we aren't any closer to finding out who is behind this. Frankly, we aren't sure where to look anymore. Manuel is down to ten percent confidence in his database associations—that's all that's left, and let me tell you, when you are at ten percent, it really is pretty random. J. P. and Matt have taken to bickering for the most part, and Angel has completely withdrawn."

"Well, we need to keep focused on what this is about. They need to see beyond their own frustrations."

Cohen frowned. "John, it's not that they don't. It's that they want this so badly. Larry picked us all in part because we had a commitment, an emotional one, to combating terrorism. That much has become clear over the years. In the past two months, we've seen two horrific attacks, one right under our noses. In our own city! That also brings back so many painful memories, as if it weren't bad enough by itself. The strain is coming because they want to bag these guys. But right now, it's starting to seem to them that their goal is somewhere way out of reach."

Savas winced. He understood. He understood because that was exactly how he was feeling as well. Outside of a few small leads, they had nothing to go on. Nothing at all. What few leads they did have were being pursued thousands of miles away by the CIA, leaving the FBI to await information, search databases, conduct late-night brainstorming sessions over stale coffee. Essentially, twiddling their thumbs. It was time for a mind clearing for all of them, a pep talk of some kind. Savas realized he needed to reset the course for the team.

A loud knock came at the door, and it swung open suddenly. Startled, Savas looked up. It was Rideout. His face was ashen and yet touched with fury. He spoke, slightly out of breath, clearly having raced over to the office.

"John, Rebecca—you'd better come. There's been another one."

30

Cubicle dividers and desks continued to explode around him, and Jordan crawled toward the side of the building and away from the doorway. He placed his back against the wall and brought his Uzi forward, gazing through the room. Women were still running to the far end of the building. Dust and sparks filled the air from the massive weapons assault. He saw two of his men on the ground, likely dead, riddled with bullet holes. Others were crouched down, weapons drawn, looking over to him for guidance. His mind raced. To follow the women out the front seemed the easy solution and also provided the advantage of cover. He and his remaining team could race inside that crowd and seek to escape in the chaos, perhaps commandeering one of their vehicles and heading straight for the safe house.

He rejected that strategy immediately. He knew if he were leading the assault from outside, this would be the obvious response, and Jordan could expect a welcoming gunfire spray should he take that route. Less obvious would be to face head-on the devastating firepower that had just wreaked havoc in the building. He motioned to the back door. His men did not hesitate, he was proud to see. They moved forward with bursts of speed and crouched on either side of the doorway. The firing had stopped. The targets were out of sight, and no doubt an ambush was being readied at the front of the building. Jordan prepared to give the signal to rush through the door.

Suddenly, a man toting a submachine gun darted through the doorway, weapon aimed over the heads of those who crouched low to the ground. The man scanned the room as an operative to his left rolled onto his back into the line of sight of the door, less than a foot in front of the man, and opened fire from the floor. Three shots struck the man in the chest; he staggered backward in retreat and fell onto the ground outside the building. Jordan and his team then leapt through the doorway, weapons firing.

Shots rained around them. Several gunmen had taken cover behind vehicles parked directly in front of the entrance. Another trap, and his men paid a high price. They had the disadvantage in position but the advantage in skill. Jordan sprayed fire with his Uzi toward three gunmen behind one of the cars. Each fell back, one wounded and disoriented, spinning around and firing rounds into the air.

Out of the corner of his eye, he caught the movement of a figure and sensed a hostile intent. He dove to the ground for cover, feeling at that moment a sharp, searing pain in his right leg as the sound of a gun blast reached his ears. He looked down and saw blood darkening in crimson the white of his robes. Behind him he heard a laugh.

"You stupid man," screamed Kharitonov, standing near the entrance with a pistol in his hand. "You think I have no way to send message?" Jordan tried to spin around to aim the Uzi, but his right leg was badly wounded, and he knew he would not make it in time as the Russian raised his weapon and fired. Jordan's shoulder exploded in pain as he twisted sideways. He was still conscious, however, and turned around in time to see Kharitonov arch his back as red bursts exploded out of his abdomen. The Russian dropped immediately to his knees, cradling his stomach and rolling over. The CIA operative who had shot him was then pinned by submachine gunfire against the wall of the building, shaking violently as multiple bullets wrecked his body. All Jordan's men were now down.

He grabbed the Uzi with his left arm and fired on the last of the men behind the cars. His aim was poor, but the Uzi made up in spray for what it lacked in precision. The man fell backward, moaning, crawled several feet, then did not move.

Jordan guessed he had less than a minute. The noise must have alerted the team placed at the front of the building, and they would be racing back at this moment. The bullet-ridden car of the dealer's hit men was less than twenty feet away from his current position. He raised himself to his feet using all his strength and willpower, the pain in his leg flaring bright like a nova in his mind, eclipsing that of his shoulder as he staggered toward the vehicle. It seemed to sway and tilt as he moved, and Jordan hoped he could cross this distance and remain conscious. He turned toward the other two cars and opened fire on them, the tires rupturing.

Reaching the open door, he dropped his weapon, stepped over a dead body, and clasped the frame with his hands, pulling himself around and into the driver's seat. He grimaced, realizing that his right leg was useless. He grasped it with his left hand and screamed in pain as he awkwardly shoved his right foot over into the floorboard of the passenger side.

He was lucky it was an automatic. He turned the ignition and the car started. Using his left foot on the brake, he closed the door and shifted into reverse, then gunned the car backward, smashing closed the door of another car and, after about thirty feet, turning the wheel sharply to the left. The car spun around, and he shifted into forward gear and hammered the accelerator. Shots shattered the rear window, but he was not hit, and within seconds, he was shielded by parked cars and other buildings on the left side.

With his left hand steering, he pulled out toward the highway. Blood covered his clothing, the steering wheel, the seats, and the gear shift. Jordan knew that he was losing blood quickly and would not be able to stay conscious for long. He also knew that men were soon likely to be following him. *The safe house was where?* His mind blanked, his memory blurry and threatening to fail him.

The backpack. He froze, remembering nothing of taking it or what had become of it. He glanced around the front seat of the car and breathed in relief. Somehow he had carried it looped over his left shoulder, and it was wedged in the car against the door. He had the records. The records that would show them the trail to those who had purchased the S-47, their only lead, their only hope to discover the identity of this new terrorist group. He tried to focus. The data in the backpack. It was everything.

Now he had only to reach the safe house before he was run down or bled to death on the highways of Dubai.

31

In New York, a crowd circled a large flat-screen monitor hanging from a wall in Larry Kanter's division. The news station played over and over the footage of the collapse of the Martyrs Monument, narrated by a quickly assembled expert commentary to put the significance in context for the American viewer. All watched in silence, memories of nearby towers falling close in their thoughts. The video was grainy and shook in a jarring fashion, shot from a tourist's handheld device, and yet all the more powerful for it. The footage cut from the tower collapse to the afternoon rescue efforts at the Great Mosque and around the monument. People who appeared to have been bathed in ash shuffled past the camera. Some fell to their knees with arms outstretched, crying up to the heavens. Bodies could be seen lining the roadway.

"Dear God," said Kanter to the hushed room.

"It's them," said Cohen flatly, not taking her eyes off the scene. Tears welled in her eyes. "I don't think there can be any doubt anymore."

"Yes," said Savas. "Same MO."

"Yeah, I'd say," said Miller. "Blow the shit out of some important Muslim building and leave bodies all over the place."

Kanter let their argument pass.

"Someone's got to stop this, Larry," said Rideout. "These are major, major hits, one after the other in a span of months. There's never been anything like this before. Al-Qaeda at their best needed years between each major terrorist attack. These guys are like fucking commandos or something."

Kanter shook his head. "It's unprecedented." The screen showed the wounded being loaded on stretchers, or, more commonly, carried by hand. The footage turned to showing angry crowds filling the streets in Algiers, chanting "Death to the infidels."

"This will turn into World War Three if it keeps going," said Savas.

Kanter turned to face his division members. "OK, everyone. If we all needed any reminders about what we're up against, or why we get up every morning, well," he said, pointing back to the screen, "it's right up there for you to see in full color. Now, I want to call . . ."

He was interrupted by the sound of a woman shouting his name. Everyone turned to see Mira Vujanac running across the room, dodging personnel and desks in her black pumps. Breathless, she stopped near Kanter and Savas.

"Larry, I'm sorry," she gasped. Seeming to recognize herself again, she straightened her blouse and hair quickly. "It's Agent Jordan. The CIA just phoned me. Their base in Dubai left a message. He's critically injured, shot up pretty bad. They don't know if he will survive. He is being flown to an army hospital in Germany." She paused and caught her breath. "They also said he got the records."

"Mira, come with me to my office. Everyone, back to your groups and back to work. Intel teams, we'll update you as soon as we can on this." He took Mira's arm and led her toward his office.

King looked over at Savas. "What the hell did he get into?"

Savas could only shake his head.

"I hope he's alright," said Cohen. Savas turned to her and saw the real anxiety in her eyes. He realized with some annoyance that he shared her concern.

"He's being taken to some of the best military doctors around. He'll be in good hands."

Angel Lightfoote swept beside them and stopped as Savas finished. She turned her head slightly toward him and said in a distracted tone, "He's closer to God now. Much closer."

With that, she turned and walked off toward her desk.

32

Late that evening, Savas was trapped in thought. Rain was pouring against the windows of his office, the darkness outside nearly impenetrable to the eye. As the night drew on, a weight increasingly settled on him, one he could not simply dismiss as related to the cloud fronts rolling in, plunging the city into blackness hours before sunset. The offices were emptied, and he felt a loneliness descend that he had not felt in some time. There were just too many reminders, too many conflicts stirring long-constrained emotions within him.

Jordan's heroics, his very existence, was like a stone kicked off a ledge, leading to an avalanche below. He triggered so many clashing thoughts in Savas's mind that it forced him inward, toward his own demons, monsters he had thrown into a pit and covered but that now stirred inside. *My own private Tartarus.*

He wanted to hate this man. He *did* hate this man in many ways. He could not wrap his mind around how an American citizen could embrace a religion whose practitioners around the world likened his nation to the Devil, burned American symbols, and supported and carried out murder against its citizens. Yet, here he was, this Muslim CIA agent, having risked his life *on a lead*. It was like an immovable object of prejudice was meeting the unstoppable force of a real man's character. In the middle of it was Savas's dead son Thanos and what had happened at the World Trade Center.

The rain worked in earnest against the windows of his office, like some maniacal typist drumming incessantly in the night. Savas opened a desk drawer and pulled out a fraying envelope. He opened its contents. Addressed to Thanos Savas from the NYPD—his letter of acceptance to the force. Savas was not sure who was more proud the day that letter arrived—him or his son. Not one year later, he was sitting next to his ashen-faced wife at the memorial service. He felt his eyes well up with tears.

A soft knock sounded on his door. His lights were off, the lightning like a strobe light flashing through his room. He got up awkwardly, rubbed his eyes on his sleeve, and stepped over to the cracked door.

It was Cohen. In the darkness he could not be sure whether she had seen his face, seen the pain etched across his features, but her expression told him that if she had not, she was clairvoyant. "John, are you OK?" she asked.

"Yes, Rebecca. Just tired is all," he said with difficulty. Crazily, he felt his defenses dissolving, and his emotions, rather than demanding to be further suppressed, were raging all the more to be freed. "Not feeling well. I think I'll head home."

Astonishingly, she placed her fingers to his mouth. Her soft skin brushed his lips, and a shudder ran through his body. He felt like a great wave was rising from the sea, and there was no place to flee from it. With her other hand, she took off her glasses and laid them on a shelf. Looking into her eyes, he saw what seemed to be an endless sea of compassion, focused on him, and it took all his strength to hold back the tears that wished to pour out. He could smell her breath, the scent of her body, its warmth like fingers stroking his skin. Her hair curled over her shoulders, spilling across her chest as she cupped his cheek in her hand and brought his lips to hers. For an instant, it was as if a creature, long split in two and languishing incomplete for an eon, had found its other half. He felt a life force rush through him, a force more than his life or her life alone. A force that promised magic and miracles.

John Savas pulled back, stumbling backward. Cohen looked into his eyes, her own eyes wide and concerned yet filled with longing. He grabbed his coat off the hook on his door and brushed past her, rushing down the corridor. "John, please!" she called out behind him, but he did not turn or respond as he cut past the elevators to the stairway and sprinted recklessly down the steps. When he reached the ground floor, his chest heaving, out of breath, he opened the door and stepped into the alley behind the FBI building. Rain rushed down over him, and he lifted his face to the skies to receive it.

The icon of Saint Nicholas glittered, reflecting the candle flames that lit it from below. A thousand shards of light from hand-placed mosaic pieces, each no bigger than the nails on John Savas's fingers, glinted in the smoky darkness. Each stone was a different color and had been collected by monks and shipped across the seas to churches during the Greek Diaspora: deep reds and blues, turquoise, magenta, gold-plated stones of yellow, white marble. Shaped and placed, up close resembling a pixilated image on a computer screen, merging from a distance into a unified whole. *A window to the soul.*

Father Timothy sat across from him, troubled yet purposeful. His eyes were like the mosaic stones reflecting the dancing candlelight, and his face was lit harshly by the flashes of lightning outside.

"John, I'm not going to quote to you verses on loving your enemies or forgiving your brother seventy times seven. You've read them or heard them so many times that you can't listen to them. But there is one thing I know, and that is that hatred eats at us from within, and if we let it take root, it will slowly burn away at everything we are, and the life-blood of our soul, our ability to love, will die. You have carried a hatred within you for too long. Inside, you know this; you can feel it. You are being asked now to make a choice, John, between taking your life and turning it into a sword, or letting the pain flow through you, so that from that place inside, a stronger love will be born."

John Savas lowered his head to stare at the floor between his feet. He could not accept a sermon; no words would touch the place within him that burned. He knew the priest was right about something; he did burn, and choices were being asked of him. He wondered whether it wasn't, after all, about a choice between love and hate, as simple as it sounded. Tonight, he had turned his back on a woman who had opened herself in vulnerability to him, even for a short moment. It was the most beautiful moment he had known in many years, and yet the fire inside of him would not let him embrace it or accept her love and return it with his own. The fire demanded something different, something harder, where tears did not flow, where vengeance ruled. He felt the church walls closing in on him; felt that God Himself was probing with a scalpel, reaching out from the burning eyes of Saint Nicholas before him. Savas stood up, surprising the priest in the middle of a sentence that he had not heard, apologized, and quickly stepped through the church and into the rain.

The downpour seemed to have only intensified. He walked through the pelting drops and slumped into his car. Ten minutes later, he was standing at the entrance of his apartment building, the rain so thick he could barely see five feet in front of him. Water pooled in his shoes, seeping into every surface of his body. The sound of a car door closing was muffled in the storm. He pulled out his keys, fitting them to the lock, then turning to the side at the sound of approaching footsteps. The light above the door spilled directly over him, and he could see only partially into the shadows on his left. Squinting, he saw a dark form approach, and he tensed instinctively, expecting the worse.

She was as wet as he was, her brown hair turned black by the pouring water and the darkness of the night. Her clothing was completely soaked, her white shirt transparent, revealing the pink of her skin, the swell of her breasts taut against the rain-washed fabric. Even in the rain, he saw that she had tears in her eyes, and she stepped up to him with a sharp desperation cut into her face.

"Rebecca, please, you didn't—" and once again she placed her hand to his mouth to silence him.

"John, please. I shouldn't have come here, I know. But so much has happened, such madness. Let me speak, before I lose the courage. I know you have suffered, and you have tried to find your way back from this suffering. I've watched you, from the first day I came to the Bureau. I watched you try to turn your pain into something good. I've waited for you, John, at first only as a dream, and then with the growing realization that you wanted me, too. I tried to give you your time, but I am built of flesh and blood and needs, too, John. I have my own pains," she spoke, choking back tears. "I can't wait anymore. Tonight I am here for you to make a choice. To choose me, all of me and what I offer you, good and bad, or find your own way in this world without me. I need to offer you my heart, John, to reject it or to take it. I've loved you for too long and for too many lonely days and nights." She stood inches from his face, her eyelashes wet with droplets of rain. "I love you, John Savas. Will you love me?"

Savas felt her cut through him like a warm blade. In that instant, he understood what was being offered to him, and from deep within, he answered, without hesitation, with his whole heart. He wrapped his arm around her waist, and with his other hand cupped the back of her head, pulling her to him.

They embraced. The water poured over and between them, and he held her so tight he could feel her breath escape through her lips. For a short moment, everything that he had built around him seemed to collapse, and his shoulders shook from the muffled sobs he tried to suppress.

They kissed. With the thunder reverberating around them, they kissed deeply like two starved things, oblivious to the storm's rage, knowing a personal shelter, a space protected from all that assailed them from without. Entwined, hands exploring, lips uncovering, breath in gasps, in pain and in ecstasy, with joy and sorrow, swirling wildly in the evening gusts.

33

John Savas awoke to sunlight and a cool breeze blowing in through an open window. He lay on his back; Rebecca's head nestled into his chest, her arm draped over his right shoulder. Her breathing was soft, a rising and falling cadence that stirred him deeply. He raised himself slowly, carefully, afraid to wake her. He wanted to see her face, see that haunting beauty that he now let himself admit he had desired and fought against for years, see it as she slept and in the morning's fresh light.

"Finally awake?" she said, one eye half open like a cat, a playful smile on her face. She rolled off his chest and snuggled into the pillow behind her. He rolled onto his stomach toward her, gazing up into her brandy eyes.

"Yeah, getting old, I'm afraid."

Savas looked at her face, beautiful, and sad, a distant look in her eyes. He thought back over the years and realized that he had been blind to so much. *Blinded*, he corrected himself. *Consumed*.

Cohen turned and tried to laugh. "Now, if you were rich, my inner *shadchan* would be pleased, but I have to quiet her, as things stand."

"Shadchan?" he asked.

"Jewish matchmaker. Think Yente from *Fiddler on the Roof*."

"Ah, OK."

"But in the real world, it's just my dad now. I think he'd be happy that I'm interested in any biped with a Y chromosome. Even you."

Savas smiled. "*Thanks*. Breakfast? I might have something you can stand to eat."

She smiled. "A coffee would be great, actually."

Savas grabbed a shirt, slipped it on, and went into the kitchen. Out of the corner of his eye, he could see Rebecca climbing out of bed. He pushed the button, the clashing sound of beans on metal filled the apartment, and the fresh smell of ground coffee struck him as it always did in the morning. *Smells better than it tastes*, he thought once again. He caught another glimpse of her in the bed. By that point, she had started combing out her hair. *I could just watch her all day.*

She left the comb on the dresser and walked over to the kitchen. The gurgling of the coffeepot was loud now; the pot filled with warm brew. She put her hands on his shoulders. Standing five-foot-five, she was nearly half a head shorter than he was, and as she kissed him, she rose up on her toes.

"Good morning," she said. "I forgot to tell you."

"It's the best morning I've had in a long time, Rebecca. I mean that."

She squeezed his hand, and he embraced her. For several moments he held her close to him. "So," she said, stepping back, "how's that coffee?"

"It's ready." Savas grabbed two cups, quickly checked them to make sure they would pass some minimal health inspection, and, satisfied, filled each about three-quarters. "How do you take yours?"

"Black," she said.

"Me, too." He smiled back at her.

"Let me see what you have in this refrigerator of yours."

Savas thought to dissuade her of the action but changed his mind. *She might as well see that, too.* He sipped at his coffee and walked over to the window, gazing outside and upward to the rising sun. The light was warm, the air fresh on his face. He felt something inside of him, an emotion long forgotten, crushed by years at NYPD, banished by the loss of his son. A feeling he immediately associated with his childhood, nearly excitement, washed through him now as it had not for long decades.

But inside, another voice arose in challenge, from a darker place, a buried place, and for a moment it seemed that the light outside faded and a chill had come into the air. He knew this voice, because he had listened to it for many years now. There was anger in its cry, a hatred that refused any solace or sense of peace. *Leave me alone. For today, let me be.*

He placed the coffee cup on the windowsill and turned to look at Cohen, bent over, head invisible, blocked behind the refrigerator door.

"Oh, *wow*, John. This is worse than I thought."

He smiled, and for the moment, the angry voice was silenced. The older feeling swelled within him: *Hope.* That was the feeling. Simple hope. Could it last? The thundercloud deep inside waited, and he knew it would not be denied. He ignored it. For one day at least, he would remember what it was to hope.

34

ISLAMIC GROUPS THREATEN U.S. AND EUROPE
OVER TERROR ATTACKS
By Thomas Fischetti, Associated Press

Arab nations and their organizations issued multiple statements today condemning the string of Muslim-targeted terrorist attacks and threatened Western nations with economic repercussions if these attacks did not end and the responsible parties were not apprehended.

The Arab League issued a terse statement accusing Western governments of "complicity" and a "willing inaction" in stopping the attacks and finding those responsible. Two hours later, OPEC followed suit, threatening "economic hardship" to any nation "supporting Western terrorism against Muslims." One high-ranking official who spoke under conditions of anonymity said that "Muslims are furious. This has brought even sworn enemies together to fight their common foe. This will blow up in the faces of infidel nations. This will make the oil crises of the last century seem like a celebration."

Spokesmen from the European community in Brussels sought to stave off the controversy, indicating that all possible investigative organizations were active and working diligently to address Muslim safety in Europe and apprehend the terrorists. A White House spokesperson stated that it was counterproductive to threaten the United States when it was itself involved in efforts to solve these crimes. "These attacks have also occurred on our own soil, and we wish justice done as much as anyone," said the press secretary.

The source responded to these remarks. "Words are not enough. It is time for the Western nations to practice what they tell Muslim nations—to stop terrorists. Unless these murderers and destroyers of Muslim holy sites are caught and executed, the West will be held responsible. I tell you now, Allah will rain suffering on your people."

Traffic on the FDR northbound was unusually bad. It was a constant stop-and-go, intermittent motion turning quickly into what looked like a frozen river of vehicles. Tugboats on the East River pushing box-laden barges overtook them on the right. A cabbie darted left directly in front of Savas, pushing his way into the middle lane and forcing him either to slow down or to plow into the yellow car. He felt the symptoms of road rage coming to the surface, but with Cohen riding shotgun, he sighed and let the taxi have its pointless lane change.

After nearly forty-five minutes, they reached the Sixty-Second Street exit and pulled off under the FDR, past a gas station, and onto York Avenue. They found a parking garage on Sixty-Third Street, then walked the five blocks to New York Hospital. Passing the small green oasis of Rockefeller University on the right, the pair turned down Sixty-Eighth Street toward the hospital. Within ten minutes, they were in a recovery room staring down at Husaam Jordan.

Savas's first thought was that he looked well. He had clearly lost some weight from his once hyper-muscular frame, and his right leg and shoulder were still bandaged, but he was alert. His eyes were bright, and he was reading a set of newspapers draped over his legs. As they walked in, he looked up and smiled. His basso profundo boomed throughout the small room.

"John. Rebecca," he said, sitting up straighter. "Here to rescue me?"

Cohen smiled. Savas just shook his head. "Agent Jordan, from what I've heard, you do a good enough job of that sort of thing yourself."

"'Good enough' is a relative term." His smile faded. "It was not good enough for the men I took with me. Good men, who have served this nation well." Jordan gestured to his arm and shoulder with his left hand. "More personally, it was not enough from the point of view of my leg and arm. They have been reminding me of this frequently."

"I've heard that you will be released soon," Cohen said.

"Yes, next week if I have anything to do with it. I have a very aggressive rehabilitation program planned, and I can't wait to start."

A nurse dashed into the room and took the lunch tray he had cast to the side. "Well, you won't be doing anything *aggressive* as long as you are on my floor," she scolded, giving him a disapproving glare. She looked over at the two visitors. "He's been nothing but trouble since he got here."

Savas suppressed a laugh. "Yes, well, ma'am, he's been a load of trouble for a bunch of folks. But I think his heart is in the right place."

Jordan looked directly at Savas, who returned his gaze. It was the closest he felt he'd ever get to admitting that he had changed his mind about the man. The nurse just grunted and took the tray out of the room.

Jordan changed the subject. "So, I hope you have brought me some news finally. After two surgeries, three hospitals, and a week under sedation, I'm trying to figure out where the world is again." He held up a newspaper that showed schematics of the Martyrs Monument and an analysis of how it had collapsed. "I don't suppose our friends from Valhalla have blown anything else up?"

Savas shook his head. "Thank goodness, no, although given what's happened so far, we're all waiting for this month's attack."

"Yes, so am I," said Jordan.

"So is the rest of the world," interjected Cohen. "The president has called a special meeting with representatives from the Arab League at Camp David. The Muslim world from Africa to the Middle East to Southeast Asia is in chaos. Conspiracy theories abound."

"Has anyone warmed to your crazy theory?" Jordan asked.

Savas shook his head. "No. But the CIA death squad idea is slowly dying. They've rounded up most of those who participated. You can count on one hand those remaining."

"Certainly they can begin to see the pattern? The similarities in the assassinations and the bombings?"

Cohen laughed. "Our governmental agencies might not, but the

Muslim world sees the connection. They are blaming the Western nations. Prominent leaders in the major oil-producing nations are calling for an embargo unless this terrorist group is found and caught. OPEC has signaled that it is considering several of these ideas. The world financial markets are in complete turmoil."

Jordan smiled. "Well, I guess I'll be trading in my Hummer for a Chevy Volt."

Savas smiled as well, but Cohen frowned. "It's not just about gas. Few people realize how completely dependent modern society is on oil. Did you know that, at minimum, four out of every five calories we eat come from petroleum?"

Uh-oh, thought Savas, *she's in Berkeley mode.*

Cohen did not disappoint, launching into a lecture about the fragility of the modern fossil fuel economy. It amused him to see her take on the airs of a college protest leader. But her passion was always real, and he had learned to *never* challenge her facts. He also had to admit that she often had a lot to teach him.

Savas was curious. "What's food got to do with oil?"

Cohen sighed. "Food *is* oil, John. At least in this day and age. We have to plow the land to plant, water our crops, fertilize the ground, harvest the crops, process the food, and package and distribute it all over the country. Oil's the primary energy source for all of this. It's the basis for the entire modern world. Now the US and Europe are scrambling to ensure an uninterrupted flow of oil. China and Russia are turning paranoid fast about this."

Savas nodded. "That's for sure. I've already heard talk about using military force to secure our supplies. We're still the biggest kid on the block, but things have changed."

Cohen looked at Jordan. "This is quickly becoming one of the most dangerous situations in international relations in a long time."

Jordan whistled. "So what are you two doing here visiting me? Don't you have some important work or meetings to be getting to downtown?"

Savas nodded. "Well, we did, but Rebecca insisted we come."

"I know your wife and sons were here, but I thought that it was shameful that no one from the FBI had visited a hero after his return home," she said with a smile.

Jordan bowed his head. "A noble woman, John. Don't you forget that," he said, and Savas wondered if it meant more than it seemed on the surface.

"We have a big meeting with the CIA tomorrow," Savas spoke over his own thoughts. "They will present to us the analysis of the shipping records you obtained in Dubai and Sharjah. I'm hoping something useful will come of that."

Jordan gestured again to his wounded limbs. "You aren't the only one."

Savas was silent on the drive back from the hospital. As they crossed the Queensboro Bridge, the falling night in front of them was offset by the skyline of Manhattan behind them, a view always particularly spectacular when driving the opposite direction on the bridge. They were headed to a Greek seafood place he knew in Astoria, but he could not relax for an evening out. Too many things were burning in his mind as he drove. How came to be this man, Husaam Jordan, who practiced, even celebrated a religion that had spawned such hatred and monstrosities? How could any of them stop this new diabolic force that was shattering lives and peace across the globe before the stability of the world itself was threatened?

Not realizing what he was doing, Savas found himself taking the well-known streets in Astoria, but not in the direction of the restaurant. Instead, his car weaved its way to park beside the dome of the Church of the Holy Trinity. He stopped the vehicle and shut off the engine.

"We're walking from here?" Cohen asked.

"I thought we'd make a quick pit stop to see someone first, if it's OK."

She looked over at him quizzically. "OK, who's that?"

Savas sighed. "Thought I'd see that priest I told you about. Father

Timothy. You know, the one I almost shot during church service," he said dryly.

Cohen stared at him seriously. "OK, John. I'd like to meet him. Anyone who can welcome you back after that is worth meeting."

He laughed so hard he thought he might break a rib. "Yes, I suppose. He's the only one of the congregation. I tend to make secretive visits to this place."

She nodded. "I can see why."

They stepped out of the car, and Cohen followed him toward the church and up the stairs. Inside, it was mostly dark, the shadows deep in the dim candlelight. Holding her hand, Savas led Cohen through the church. It was completely empty and silent. She gazed with interest at the large mosaics of saints and biblical stories spread across the walls. As they passed the icon of Saint Nicholas, Savas whispered, "Santa Claus."

"What?" she asked, confused.

"Sorry," he said, smiling, "I'll tell you another time."

He walked up to the left side of the iconostasis and knocked on the door. After several tries without an answer, he turned to Cohen.

"He must not be here."

"Home?" she asked.

"Maybe. But he might be around back, in the garden. Want to go check?" She took his arm and smiled up at him. "Sure."

He led her out of the church and down the steps again, turning toward the right and heading around the building. At the back, a fence ran around the church, perhaps eight feet high and made of metal. Apartment buildings stood on the other side of the fence. Planted at the base of the fence all the way around the church were rows of different kinds of plants—flowering bushes, grasses, even some vegetables. At a point opposite the front doors of the church, directly behind the building, lay a large stone slab with a stone cross at its tip. In front of the slab, on his knees with head bowed, was Father Timothy.

Savas stopped as soon as he saw him, hoping to turn around and not disturb the priest. But the old man had noticed them and stood up immediately, if slowly and painfully, brushing the dirt off his cassock. He looked up and smiled, walking toward them.

"Father Timothy, I didn't mean to bother you.... I can come back..." Savas began.

"Nonsense. John, good to see you," the priest said, putting a hand on Savas's shoulder. The old priest looked toward Cohen.

"Father Timothy, this is Rebecca Cohen. She's part of my team at the FBI."

"Pleased to meet you, Father," she said, smiling.

"You two working so late?" he asked, a twinkle in his eye.

"Ah, well, actually, we are done for the day, and Rebecca had heard me talk about this seafood place, Elijah's Corner, and..." He stumbled over the words.

"Well, I insisted that we go tonight to see if it's all that he bragged about," she finished for him confidently. Savas looked gratefully toward her.

"Yes, yes. The best Greek food is in Astoria," said the priest.

"So, I don't want to bother you..." Savas began again.

"No, no. Just praying at the grave of an old friend," Father Timothy said. "Did you know Brother Elefterios?" Savas shook his head. "He was the priest of the church before I came here. He died nearly ten years ago. He was a monk and lived in that old shack there," he said, pointing over his shoulder.

Savas had always wondered about that small shack as a child. It hardly seemed able to keep the garden tools dry, let alone house a human being.

Father Timothy sighed. "Even after he got too old to run the church and I was brought in, he asked to continue to care for the garden. I said yes, of course. Over the years, this small old man would come out here every day, into his late eighties, tending this garden lovingly. I got to know him well, and came to miss his presence here after his death. Many times when there were problems in the world, or inside the church, I would come and speak to him. He seemed to have this stunning peacefulness about him, born out of prayer or temperament, I will never know."

The old priest smiled sadly. "So, I still come here to speak with him. These attacks . . ." he shook his head. "The world seems poised to begin a terrible spiral of violence that will lead to great suffering. I talk to my old friend. I just wish I could hear him now."

Savas and Cohen traded glances, unsure what to say. "That was why I came, Father. All this has been weighing on me, too. I wanted to ask you to pray for us, for what we are doing."

"John, if you are trying to bring an end to this growing madness, you have my prayers, certainly. But more importantly, I think I can hear the host of saints praying for all the souls of the world as well."

35

On the highest floor of a tower of glass and steel, a man gazed through a large window. His partial reflection displayed a tall and lean form, with pressed gray hair and sharp-rimmed glasses, peering over the sprawling city below him.

Contrasting with the open expanse through the glass pane, where a step would drop him hundreds of feet to the concrete below, he sensed behind him the solidity of his grand office. It was the size of a tennis court, decorated and trimmed with the best that was to be had. Like an anchor, the presence of his enormous cherry-wood desk rooted him inside the room, its bulk framed by the solid sheet of glass revealing the heart of the city.

He pulled on the cuff of his expensive suit, glancing at a timepiece of Swiss manufacture. With mild annoyance, he returned his arms behind his back, clasping them tightly, military-style. The lights were off in his office; he required time for contemplation. Staring into the sky, he counted more than twenty planes in the air at once, small dots like yellow stars moving across the night sky over the three local airspaces. The city appeared like some pharaoh's tomb decorated in one hundred thousand jewels of light, the bridges as streaming necklaces across the waters.

His computer blinked and issued an alert tone. He turned around and stared at it. The screen displayed a security code algorithm, establishing an untraceable connection. Events were moving forward. He took several steps toward his desk and sat in his chair. He pressed ENTER and waited. The image of a chiseled face filled the screen, blond hair and crew cut etched like stone into the LCD.

"Connection is secure, sir," said the blond man.

"You're late, Rout," snapped the older man.

"I was delayed."

"You are ready to proceed, I assume?"

"Yes, sir. Phase One was maximally successful. All targets were destroyed without compromise of personnel or mission. World media and governments have reacted in a panic, and this has had the intended effect. Training for the next several missions has nearly been completed, and all resources and elements are in place. We await your word on this."

"Investigations?"

"There are too many to name or for us to keep track of. Notable are CIA, FBI, MI6, SIS, European groups—China, you may be interested to know, along with Russia and some others. Everyone is scared shitless, and it's not clear if it's the Arabs, or the Western governments that need them, who are more worried. This is threatening to blow up into a real international situation."

"Then let us pour gasoline on this small fire we've kindled. Proceed to Phase Two."

"Yes, sir."

"Finally, the broken arrow in our quiver. We need to make sure there are no connections to us, no way to surmise how we plan to end this. He has gone his own way for too long now."

Rout stared coldly into the screen, no movement of flesh betraying his inner thoughts. "He will be missed, sir. He was a real soldier."

The gray-haired man nodded imperceptibly. "It is a link that must be cut. We cannot afford to leave any bridges intact behind us."

"Understood, sir. I'll see to this one myself."

"As you see fit. We have to make hard choices, Patrick. Good-bye."

The man broke the secure connection, and the screen went dark. He pressed his fingertips together and rotated his chair around to face the skyline once more. Clouds had moved in slowly from the west, and the orange-light pollution from streetlamps seeped upward, giving them a slightly hideous color, like sick flames descending.

It was appropriate, he thought. *Ragnarök is coming.*

36

The morning broke with the last clouds from the evening storm trailing out to sea. The sun rose, slicing through them to give a multifaceted spray of red and orange rays across the sky and water. Philip Jeffrey rolled up the mooring rope and pulled on the halyard, raising the mainsail. The white sheet climbed slowly, and he trimmed the sail to catch the wind, filling and driving the boat forward as the airfoil and dagger boards combined to produce the force of motion. He was quickly under way, as the sun reared powerfully over the cloud line and sprayed its now golden radiance over the harbor.

Jeffrey smiled as the spray of water caught him unprepared. *Thank God I bought this boat.* The irony was that he thought he'd never have time to use it. That was before Liam had called him one fateful night in 2003. He shook his head. Liam's nickname had come from his Irish mother, even though he resembled in appearance and character his father, a Swede; an immigrant family whose son had done more than well.

They had gone way back, to some of the early days of Liam's rise in business, when he still controlled half of the defense contracts for the air force in one way or the other. It was more than just a profitable business relationship—the money to Liam, the promotions to Jeffrey—but a friendship had developed, based on a mutual connection that was rare for men of their ambition. How many nights along the Sound had he entertained Liam and Judy on his older vessel? And the long cruises to the Virgin Islands—those had been special times.

Then a Tuesday in September 2001 had changed everything. Nineteen terrorists flew two planes into the World Trade Towers and brought those buildings down. Everyone changed after that day, but some more than others. Liam became estranged. He had stopped calling and had hardly spoken to him at the memorial service. Rumors circled that he was retiring or had suffered a nervous breakdown. Jeffrey could only guess. After nearly a year and a half of silence, he had begun to wonder whether the pain of that loss had forever separated him from his friend.

But a phone call in late February changed all that. Liam had called and asked to visit Jeffrey at his beach house on Long Island. Like old times. But the Liam that appeared the next weekend was a creature different from the man he had known before. This was a man with a fire lit within that made his previous ambition to succeed seem a faint light. Liam spoke passionately that evening about the world, the evils of nations, and our need to fight, of not using the outdated strategies of the past. He scoffed at conventional war and diplomacy, convinced that radical efforts were demanded.

And Philip Jeffrey had been converted.

Truth be told, he was never a good fit at the Pentagon. His hard-line beliefs about the changing nature of conflict, so in harmony with Liam's own, did not buy him popularity within the changing power structure in Washington. The neocons had such a naive faith in technology! Jeffrey knew that it was men's hearts, as much as their weapons, that dictated the course of battle. What he and Liam saw brewing in the world was a conflict of men more than machines.

"*Patrick believes he can lead the final mission, Philip. I think he may be right.*"

Jeffrey winced at hearing that voice again. The man haunted him, the force of his personality like some apparition scarring his memory. But he knew better than to fight it. It would have its due. For all that Jeffrey knew, all that he had done, his mind needed to wrestle with what had happened. His soul could find little peace.

"*This will take some doing.*"

"*Yes, it will, Philip,*" Liam said, rising and lifting a small object from his desk. He passed it between his hands, the metal glinting in the soft light. "*Are you ready to put this in motion?*"

"This will not be so easy, my friend. And in the end, my career, a long and honorable one, might I add, will be destroyed."

Jeffrey closed his eyes, feeling the wind on his face, salt spray crusting his skin. He lost himself in time.

"Do you doubt our plans?"

Jeffrey laughed briefly. "No, of course not. The top brass have all checked their minds at the door of the Pentagon, anyway. I don't belong anymore. Any day now they will give that fool Texan his war."

Liam straightened quickly, then took the metal object and hurled it against the wall. It struck the paneling and entered, splintering the wood and lodging deep like an arrow.

"We have a blind cowboy for a president!" he spat. "A puppet advised by slow-minded and greedy fools. They cannot even focus on the abomination that orchestrated these acts of murder! They chase and they chase after dreams inspired by their politics. And miss the larger target! The heart of evil of which this diabetic coward is only one foul seed." He walked over to the wall, grabbed the object, and pried it free with a single, swift tug. "No, my friend, we will not aim so low as that."

Liam's eyes burned into Jeffrey's mind. His words seem to reverberate and echo. "It is said one must beware the vengeance of a patient man. Philip, we will be very patient. Our organization will be hidden, slowly established in every major target nation on earth—no matter how difficult to penetrate. Only when we are ready, when we have trained an elite force, acquired the weapons and tactics we require, and developed our plan thoroughly, will we strike. And by then, it will be almost impossible to stop us. Then blood will be had for blood, and more. Then fire will rain from the skies."

Jeffrey stared grimly forward. "Yes, and like Prometheus, I will bring you that fire. Hell, my liver's shot anyway. I'm ready, Liam. You will need patience. This will take time. But it will be done. You know my beliefs."

Liam nodded and returned to his desk, placing the metal object back on its stand. The light glittered off the glass bottom, serving to highlight the metallic arms on which the object rested. The arms came together at the top, forming a cup-like loop, from which the thinner end of the object *hung. The metal of the tip thickened from the stem to a much wider girth near the end of the shape, flattening, forming a sharp point in an otherwise flat surface. Carved into the face of the metal was the head of a raven. Jeffrey looked at the object and felt vaguely troubled. From this angle, it did indeed resemble a hammer.*

A seagull's cry startled him, and he broke out of his reverie.

"I'll never be free of you, Liam," he spoke to the depths of the sea.

Liam's proposal was audacious, insane, and brilliant. Jeffrey was swept up by it and terrified at the same time. But when his old friend left, he knew that he would help fulfill that plan. He had engineered his transfer to Ward County, North Dakota—*North Dakota!* Minot Air Force Base was the perfect seat of operations for what he needed to do. For four years he worked to engineer one of the greatest betrayals in the history of the United States. A betrayal of the country he had fought for, and would die for, because to save it from itself, from its foolish citizens and leaders, drastic action must be taken. And he had pulled it off, an act that had cost him his job and his honor in the military community. Now he was a disgrace, the truth of his crimes hidden from the public. Were Jeffrey in medieval Japan, he would cast himself on his sword.

Instead, he sailed. At sea, the land faded and the world of men became something that seemed almost small. When the waves rolled on and on to the edge of sight, it was almost possible to forget the shame, and perhaps even the guilt, for what was done, and what was to come. Every great action extracts a terrible price. On the waters of the Atlantic, Philip Jeffrey was sailing to find his soul.

The wind was a strong ten knots north by northwest. He tacked his course northward, seeking the middle of the Long Island Sound. The July sun was already beginning to warm the boat and his skin considerably. *Damn the melanoma*, he thought and steered his course.

Behind him rose a disturbance in the peace he had found at sea, and he turned toward the sound. A boat could be seen at some distance, closing in on him quickly. It was odd. Powerboats didn't usually come out this far, and rarely had he seen one moving at such high speed. As the boat approached, he could see it wasn't the coast guard but what looked like a dock-bound party boat, right down to the tinted windows. Whoever was piloting the thing was reckless as hell. While he couldn't imagine that his good-sized catamaran was not visible to the other boater, he wasn't taking any chances. He went into the spacious cabin and sat down at the two-way radio, powering up to contact the other skipper. The radio was malfunctioning, issuing only static. *Odd.* He had checked it only last night. After several minutes of fiddling with the knobs, he gave up. Electronics were not his strong suit.

The sound of the other engine was now very loud, and, as he exited the cabin, he could see the boat slow down and approach the left side of his own boat, matching course and speed, much too close for comfort. A figure could be seen standing on the starboard deck, grasping something in his hands. *What in the world is he up to?*

The sounds of automatic fire erupted from the motorboat. Philip Jeffrey arched back, his face in shock, his chest and neck exploding in bursts of clothing and crimson. He fell backward, close to the cockpit, hitting the wheel and causing the boat to lurch. The powerboat pulled aside as the catamaran turned sharply into the wind and the sails began to luff. Jeffrey lay in a growing pool of his own blood, grasping at the railings. A searing pain across his midsection, chest, and neck clouded his vision, and he slipped and struck hard against the deck.

Time streamed at the surreal pace of a dream. Sensations were confused, as if he were cast into the sea itself, drowning and sinking, unable to stop falling. After what seemed an eternity, he opened his eyes and found himself clutching the railing, the open sea beneath him. He realized that the boat was no longer moving. Fighting against weakness and a terrible nausea, he turned over on his back. The sky was a bright-blue now, the sun sweltering, and he squinted at its light. For a moment, the light was blocked, and Jeffrey saw a shape above him, broad shoulders and a head in the way of the sun. The figure raised his arm, pointing a dark object at Jeffrey's head. A gunshot rang out over the open sea.

The gray-haired man tapped his keyboard, and the screen in front of him went dark. He swiveled around in his chair and faced the window and the city once more. There were choices to be made, and only some were able to make them. With those choices came sacrifices. In the end, that was how wars were won.

"Good-bye, my friend," he whispered to the darkness.

37

The rising sun cast a light that seemed harsh and unforgiving. The three agents were exhausted. Coffee mugs and scattered boxes of Chinese food and donuts littered the desktop. Hernandez brushed his long hair out of his face to better see the screen. Savas thought his computer whiz looked like a particularly disheveled tumbleweed after a windstorm. Cohen rested her head on her hands, her mouth pursed.

The eyes he saw reflected in the screen told a different story. Dark circles and bags hung under them, yet each pair burned with the intensity of a hunter on the chase, catching the scent of prey. Their bodies were slung at angles showing fatigue, but they willed their minds into focus after an elusive target that was for the first time coming into view.

"I'll be damned," said Savas.

Hernandez whistled. "Yeah, man, crazy shit. I thought it was too much that those records connected the dealers to GI, but this . . ." He chuckled. "Husaam hit the jackpot."

Cohen nodded. "I'd say we now have motive with the means and opportunity."

Savas agreed. "One hell of a motive. I didn't think it would be like this. You two did some good work digging this out."

"So, what do we do now?" asked Cohen.

Savas straightened up and sighed. "It's time to bring this to Larry."

"He's got a big powwow with the CIA this morning, dude," said Manuel.

"I know. All the better." Savas stood up, still staring at the photograph of a woman on the computer screen. "This changes everything."

"John, what's going on? I'm in the middle of a meeting!"

Kanter stood up from his desk with a look of intense displeasure on his face. Across from him sat Richard Michelson, the lanky and pale head of the CIA's Crime and Narcotics Center. At Kanter's right was Mira Vujanac, who looked startled and concerned. Next to Michelson sat a thick black man in a white robe and kufi—Husaam Jordan. Jordan seemed fatigued, sporting a sling and a cane beside him.

"Larry, this can't wait, and it's for everyone present to hear," said Savas, casting his gaze across those gathered. He ushered in Cohen and a nervous Hernandez. Kanter let out an exasperated sigh.

"This better be important, John."

Savas stared back. "It is. Manuel, can you pull up the data on Larry's screen?"

The wall beside Kanter was essentially one large LCD monitor. Savas knew his boss was an information junkie, constantly monitoring the work of Intel 1, especially during a crisis. He hoped to fully engage him now. Hernandez activated the touch screen, and Kanter enabled access. Soon a list of cargo manifests and other shipping records were displayed, along with photographs: a man with silver hair and a stunning woman in her late forties.

"Let me just clarify this for you," began Savas, as the others in the room strained to decipher the details on the screen. "As you know, both of our agencies have been poring over the records obtained from the Dubai arms dealers."

Jordan rumbled, "The CIA hasn't made very much progress." Savas saw Michelson's face tighten. "I'm glad Mira's efforts have helped distribute those files. I was beginning to think I'd taken metal in vain."

"No, not in vain at all. It's buried, but it's there. A clear connection. The S-47 was sold in bulk three times over the last five years. In each case, a maze of shell business and offshore bank accounts, all essentially untraceable and bearing the mark of a highly organized operation, transferred money to our recently deceased arms dealers."

Irritably, Michelson interrupted. "Yes, this is nothing new. The CIA has identified these money-laundering fronts as well. They've buried their tracks in that labyrinth."

Savas smiled. "Not well enough, Mr. Michelson. Guess they didn't count on anyone turning Rebecca loose on the data."

Cohen smiled a little shyly as Savas continued. "It took some doing, but together with Manuel they found their way through the false accounts and companies. The sales are linked to something very real. Bottom line: these explosives were moved to cargo ships flying various flags, but each and every one of them was sailing under the management of Operon Shipping."

Kanter frowned. "What's Operon?"

Savas walked to the screen beside Manuel. "That's where this case takes a big turn, Larry. Operon Shipping is a company wholly owned and managed as a subsidiary of Gunn International, the single most powerful defense contracting corporation in the world." For emphasis he tapped his index finger next to the photo of the man on the screen.

Eyebrows across the table were raised. Everyone had heard of GI, or Gunn International. GI handled everything from weapons shipments to aircraft design, a multibillion-dollar enterprise headed by the reclusive William Gunn, a man legendary for his iron-willed governance and secrecy. Linking GI and William Gunn to the terrorist attacks was like shaking a can of nitroglycerin. The stunned expressions from everyone in the room reflected this.

"GI?" said Kanter, as much to himself as to Savas. "Wait a second. John, that's a big jump from Operon to Gunn International."

Michelson nodded. "Based on circumstantial evidence."

"There's more. Manuel, pull up the construction site images."

The screen filled with satellite images of desert lands. Two photos, dated more than a year apart, were juxtaposed.

"These are images from the Nevada desert, taken of identical sites. Notice the buildup and subsequent erasure of structures?"

Kanter nodded. "Yes, and so? Why are you focusing on these? What led you to these images?"

"The phony shell companies. Once we had the link to Operon Shipping, we searched for any other activity from these entities. Turns out they outsourced several construction projects in the American Southwest, but the records are another wild goose chase. Nothing tied to anything concrete. Oh, to be sure, there's work that was done. Up pop buildings and landscaping a year or so ago, but now it's all gone. Erased. Like it never happened."

"What the hell, then?" asked Kanter, perplexed.

"Military exercises." It was Jordan.

Savas smiled, exchanging a glance with Cohen. *The man was quick!*

Michelson stared at his employee. "*Military* exercises?"

Jordan shifted his weight to reposition his healing leg. "What do you do before you rig international monuments with S-47? To pull those missions off—complicated, secretive missions of high precision—you have to be prepared. You have to run simulations. These people are military-level precise in what they do, and I'll bet you that they train like Special Forces as well. For all we know, most of them *are* ex-Special Forces troops."

"I'll be damned," Kanter whispered absentmindedly, staring at the images.

"What are you saying?" Michelson asked with poorly concealed irritation.

Savas turned to the CIA official. "That these 'construction jobs' are terrorist training sites. Like those in Afghanistan used by al-Qaeda, but right here at home, hidden in our own backyard, run by Americans, and at a far higher skill level."

"That's crazy," began Michelson.

Jordan decided to up the ante. "And, furthermore, funded to the hilt by none other than Gunn International. I think you'd find, if there were any trace left, which there won't be, that these construction companies were all assembled, equipped, and run by personnel from former GI subsidiaries."

"You don't have any evidence for this!" shouted Michelson, to everyone's surprise. He paused to collect himself. "As you are all likely aware, Agent Jordan is an excellent field man, but one that I and many of his superiors feel is too often overzealous in his pursuit of action in his nation's interests. We should all step back and realize that at present, there are no ties whatsoever with Gunn International or any illegality. There is no reason to believe there would be any motive for there to be one."

Mira cut in. "Exactly. What's the motive here? Why on earth would one of our biggest military contractors be transporting illegal explosives and training terrorists to attack Muslims?"

Savas stepped back to the board. "It turns out that there might be a motive." The image of the striking woman grew large on the screen. Savas swallowed. He felt vertigo descend on him again. Images of falling towers and the face of his son threatened to paralyze his thought processes. *Focus, damn it!*

"On 9/11, an accountant with J. P. Morgan traveled to the former World Trade Center," he stammered, finding it difficult to get the words out in a professional manner. "She was in a meeting in 1 WTC on the 102nd floor when the plane hit. She made a series of calls to a cell phone number listed to an owner in New York City, and then to the police and fire departments. Due to volume, her calls were not answered at police or fire, and the private number she called did not pick up. At approximately 10:28 a.m., the time of the North Tower collapse, all calls from that number ceased. Her name was Judith Rosenberg. She was the wife of William Gunn."

There was a long silence.

Kanter shook his head, his expression sympathetic. "John, there are a lot of people in this city, and I'd wager at many international corporations, who lost someone they loved that day." He looked uncomfortable saying this to Savas, but he continued. "Do they all have motive? Do you? We can't go all wild conspiracy theory here and tie rogue shipping companies to terrorist training camps for a vengeful CEO."

Savas felt crestfallen. Kanter wasn't buying it.

"Well, I say we can," boomed Jordan.

"Agent Jordan," began Michelson, "we have already—"

"I say we can and *should*," interrupted Jordan. "Something smells wrong here. Whoever is bankrolling this thing has the pockets of a bin Laden, and his fanaticism, too. I think GI has something important to do with this, and I think William Gunn needs to be examined more closely than he has been."

"Nonsense!" shouted Michelson. "We are professional organizations—both the FBI and the CIA. We don't try to muscle powerful companies or individuals—companies and individuals, I should remind you, who have served their nation well and helped to protect us from these threats from abroad for years! Certainly not because of some half-baked hunch!"

Mira tugged at her diamond pendant and glanced up. "John, I don't want to be difficult, but, assuming you are right about this, where would we even start? And how? Gunn is a Howard Hughes—secretive, paranoid, and retaliatory. His ruthlessness is legendary. And GI is a giant octopus. It's like saying this case has something to do with China. How do you find a needle in that haystack, the proof you need? This haystack is a powerful force that isn't going to let itself be searched, especially if there is a chance for legal action and embarrassment."

Hernandez, quiet until now, fired back. "We have shipping records linking GI to an international arms dealership! *That's* a place to start."

"Not realistically," said Kanter. "You have to see the legal angle, Manuel. So what if these gunrunners used an Operon ship? How much did Operon know? Was it a local smuggling problem or something broader? Nothing connects this in a way we can pursue right now, to GI or to anything else. Hell, I'm not convinced GI had *anything* to do with it. Do you know how many boats they run at any given time? It must be huge. If we move now, we'll just make fools of ourselves."

Savas felt the moment slipping away. "We can at least follow up on the shipping leads! We know where these boats docked; we can try to trace the shipments from there."

Kanter nodded. "We can certainly do that, John. Our good friends at the CIA can help us here, as this goes outside the country and our jurisdiction," he gestured with his eyes toward Michelson and

Jordan. "From that we can get names and locations, hopefully trace these things back to the buyers. This will get us closer, and, I think, provide us with harder evidence should we need to move on GI in a more serious manner. Whatever the circumstantial story you've put together," he said, gesturing to the flat screen, "there is *nothing*, no reason to think GI was involved beyond being duped, and it would be impossible to take that company on without a powerful case to give us powerful warrants."

Mira finished. "Besides, it is not as if there are many options with respect to Mr. Gunn at our disposal, as it is."

Jordan smiled. "Sure there are. Walk up to the man and lay the cards on the table. Call him out. In that moment, you'll know from the eyes."

Michelson sneered and laughed. "A lot of good that will do. Your antics in Dubai wrecked a decade of CIA operations and left a trail of bodies that we are still trying to smooth over with the UAE government."

"He got the records, didn't he?" Savas found himself speaking, to his own surprise. Jordan eyed Savas, more intrigued than grateful.

Richard Michelson flashed an angry glare toward him. "Indeed he did, Agent Savas. So might have ten other plans he ignored in his anxious pursuit of the mission. The CIA is not in the habit of inducing international incidents for small gains. Nor will anyone authorize any such rash actions on American soil, I would wager."

Savas smiled. "But the CIA doesn't have authorization on US soil, if I remember correctly."

"No, it doesn't," said Kanter firmly, his tone imperial. "But I do. And I say this line of discussion has gone too far."

38

Savas paced silently in his office. They were moving through September without an incident, and the stress of wondering if another attack would hit had him exhausted. There were long hours poring over the shipping records, information on Operon and GI, William Gunn and several other executives, other CIA and FBI information. Correlating, looking for patterns. Finding curious hints but nothing solid.

Kanter had decided to take the conservative approach and continue to follow up on the shipping information. This was the rational move and would certainly lead them eventually to the buyers and the source of the explosive orders, one way or the other. It was the "eventually" that had Savas worried. How much time and how many more attacks could the international community take before something cracked? Wars were often started for the stupidest of reasons, when international tensions were high and mistakes in judgment were made. As Cohen had made very clear, oil was the lifeblood of the modern world, and if its flow was impaired, nations would respond as they felt necessary to preserve it. If things did not resolve soon, John Savas knew, there would be war.

Just thinking about Cohen, even in this context, was comforting. She had left earlier, keeping to their plan of schedule separation at work. Savas was pleased that, despite the fact that they were together nearly every night, it seemed no one had an inkling of the situation. And while it rankled him to have to hide their affection, the time wasn't right, and it was the last thing they or the group needed.

There was a knock, and he half expected to see Cohen's silhouette in the doorway. Instead, it was Larry Kanter. He looked exhausted. "Mind if I come in?" he asked.

"Sure, Larry. Have a seat."

Kanter walked over and dropped into the chair. "This has been a real pain in the ass working with the CIA, John," he began, tilting his head back onto the chair and staring up at the ceiling. "It's an expensive deal, in terms of how much information we get and how many years of my life are lost."

Savas chuckled. "I'm glad it's you and not me."

"Well, truly, pity Mira. She has to act the diplomat with that zombie Michelson nine to five. Only through men like him can bureaucracy prevail." Kanter laughed. "Although it is a kick to watch him and Jordan have their polite disagreements. I tell you, if I were in a tight spot, I know who I'd want next to me."

Savas listened attentively, wondering what had really brought Kanter to his office this night. He didn't pay social visits, and he didn't need to talk to the crew to unwind.

"But a man like that," continued Kanter, "a good man, it should be noted, whatever you think, John—he can undo himself. Especially in a job like this. If he transgresses too many unspoken or, in his case, even spoken rules, he can find himself moved to the agency equivalent of Siberia, or even out of a job."

Kanter paused and leaned forward to look at Savas. "Take, for instance, that scandal a few years ago with that guy, what was his name? Herr. Dale Herr."

Savas felt an iced blade softly scrape up his neck. *Dale Herr? The man who scandalized FBI with sex tapes with coworkers? Is this example a coincidence, or is he trying to tell me something?*

"Wow, did that thing ever blow up in our faces! Taxpayer money not catching bad guys, that was for sure. Since then, it's gotten worse than having the Bureau run by nuns as far as how forgiving they are of in-house romances." Kanter looked him in the eyes. "You know what I mean, John?"

This was no coincidence. Kanter was sending him a message, a very strong one. *How did he know? Who else knew?* If the Bureau knew, Kanter wouldn't be here now: some random cog would be announcing to him a formal investigation of policy violations. He could take some comfort in that, at least. *But for how long?* He brushed that aside; Kanter needed a clear response. Savas had to make it very clear.

"Yes, Larry, I know exactly what you mean," he said, not taking his eyes off Kanter. "But a man like that, he's a free man, not a wheel in the machine here, like Michelson. He won't sacrifice who he is for the agency, for any agency, any government or any man. That can spell trouble sometimes. But, it is also the reason he has been so spectacularly successful. Like you said, he's the kind you want with you when it's bad."

Kanter looked at him for several moments, nodded his head, and stood up. "Yeah, that's it, alright. I like the man, in all honesty. Reminds me of you a bit, if you don't mind me saying. I don't want him to change, either. The only thing I'd say to him, if I had the chance, is *be careful*, and don't give the zombies any more reasons to take you down."

Kanter walked to the door, opened it, and was halfway out when he stopped and turned back. "Oh, I've been meaning to ask—how's Rebecca?"

"Rebecca?" said Savas. "She left some time ago, I think. She's a workhorse, as you know, a real asset in everything we do. Why?"

"Oh, it's just I haven't seen her for a while. She used to work late a lot more often. I could always count on you and Rebecca being here late into the night trying to crack a case."

Savas smiled. "Well, she's been turning in earlier. I think the stress of this case is getting to her some."

"Well, I think that's true for all of us, John. Good night." Kanter stepped out into the hallway and walked down the corridor.

39

Headlights and the growl of an engine cut through the peaceful sounds of a forest in upstate New York. A dark Hummer bounced along a gravel roadway that hugged the shore of an expansive lake, the water black and silver as it reflected the moonlight. The large vehicle came to a full stop, small rocks raining in soft sounds as they fell from the deep tire treads. At the edge of the roadway was an old wooden bridge, supported in part by metal girders underneath, yet sagging all the same and seemingly too fragile to handle the weight of the vehicle.

Inside the truck, behind dark tinted windows, a blond man frowned. His harsh features and short-cropped hair added a stern frame to the scowl he wore. He always hated playing dice with that bridge. It should be modernized, brought up to specs. But the man he had come to visit had always refused to do anything about it, for sentimental reasons. That was the problem with him, his great weakness and strength, the driver told himself. His heart gave him the power of vision and steadfastness to do great things, but it also clouded his mind and made him vulnerable to attack or wrong decision. The scowl turned to a sneer that was almost a smile. *That's why I exist.* Patrick Rout knew he suffered from no such vulnerability.

It was a spectacular property. The bridge led out over the water to a small island in the lake. Two houses, a main structure and guest lodge, had been built on the island over one hundred years ago. They sat surrounded by trees and well-manicured shrubbery. Several docks extended into the water for recreational activities, and the western end of the island had a small boathouse. This is where his commander had come with his wife on many occasions. It was her favorite retreat, and it was still a special place for him because of that. Isolated, unusual, pristine, and beautiful. The driver scoffed. *That's what you do when you've got more money than many nations. Buy your own damned island!*

He shifted, accelerated, and drove across the bridge. Within thirty seconds, he had entered the circular driveway, passed the spraying fountain filled with live fish, and pulled up to the porch that framed the front entrance. A trim man with gray hair and glasses was already waiting for him at the bottom of the steps.

The CEO greeted him. "Thank you for coming. I know this is an inconvenience at this time, but with things moving as fast as they are, I wanted to speak to you personally to consider these new developments." Rout nodded and let the man lead. "Please, it's a nice evening; why don't we talk outside?"

Outside? Perhaps these new developments had spooked him more than he let on. *Is he really worried about surveillance? Or is this part of his vacation home persona?* It was better that his wife had died. The man needed the edge her death had given him to lead this battle.

They walked along the side of the small island, a path having been made for lazy excursions, and the wooded regions stopped some twenty feet from the edge. The stars shone very clearly and brightly this far from any streetlights, forming a milky whiteness in the central band across the sky from which the galaxy had gotten its name. There were few sounds: a soft wind, the water lapping the rocks ringing the island, and the insect sounds of the night.

The CEO continued. "Things have been penetrated faster than I had expected. The probing of the Operon businesses—this was FBI?"

"As far as we can tell, but they are not the only ones."

"Meaning?"

"We aren't sure. Someone, not FBI, and not easily marked. Perhaps an international group, but it's not Interpol."

"Then who?"

"It might even be the CIA," he said. "Recent events point that way."

"Explain."

"The Russian dealers, the ones in Dubai, they have had a major incident. We just learned of this. Many in the leadership are dead. Our contacts—and a lot of money between parties—heard rumors that their operation there was hit recently, very violently. If that is true, records may have been retrieved, connections revealed."

The CEO stopped near one of the rickety docks and turned to face Rout. "CIA?"

"There is no hard evidence, but there is enough circumstantial that it has me wondering. There is an active field house there that many have speculated was involved with the Dubai government in the arrest of Viktor Bout. There has also been a lot of chatter from sources about CIA involvement. But nothing solid. Even if they weren't involved, if the records were stolen, they could simply have been sold."

"Can they trace Operon back to us?" asked the CEO, staring out over the lake.

Rout frowned. "I don't believe so. The bank trails are all but impossible to follow: no connections to anything illegal. Operon is a subsidiary. Even they can't know all the smuggling that occurs inside their system."

The CEO turned quickly, his expression suddenly hard. "What worries me is not the likelihood of exposure. We've controlled for that as well as possible. What worries me are the people searching. I'm sure we are insulated from the organizations—bureaucracies are lumbering and clumsy. But individuals within the organizations, well, *that* is a different story. All it takes is one devoted person, and they can unravel the best defenses. We need to find out who is looking and why. We need their names, their histories, where they live, and what shoe size their children wear. Do you understand what I mean?"

Rout kept his smile in check. "Yes, sir, I do."

"Good. See to that, then. We need to contain this and not lose our focus on the next mission."

"Regarding the mission, sir, the Brits have begun guarding the site."

"How many?"

"We aren't certain yet, but it appears to be a British Section—a small infantry unit of about eight soldiers."

"Soldiers?" he asked with interest. "They are taking this seriously."

"Indeed, and it will complicate the mission significantly to have to neutralize that many trained men readied in defense of the structure. But we are making plans to solve that problem, and to do so without alerting their command structure, which, as you realize, is the complicated part of this."

The CEO's face hardened. "I don't care what it takes. I want that target hit, and hit hard."

"It will be, sir."

"New York?" he asked.

"No, sir. Nothing. Since when did Homeland Security anticipate anything real? The other sites show no suspicions."

He nodded curtly. "It would not do to lose even one. A harsh statement will be made. The map will continue to be drawn all the way to the desert sands."

He paused, looking out over the water, the soft breeze ruffling the gray hair that shone in the light of the rising moon. His more kindly smile returned. "Now, come inside, and have something to eat."

Rout suppressed a sigh. He'd rather get back to work.

40

For Savas and Cohen, things had become far more difficult in Intel 1. Their everyday interactions had always been somewhat restrained, a tension constantly between them, but it was one they both controlled within their separate and private shells. Intimacy had unleashed emotion that was freely expressed outside the office but that was caged again each morning. She passed by and he smelled her, heard the fabric of her clothes rustle as her body shifted positions, caught a glimpse of her eyes or saw her smiling and laughing with others. Each time it was a struggle to remain detached and distant. He longed to put his arms around her, both to relieve his need for her touch and also to claim her as his in front of others. It was primitive, and it was sublime.

Savas did not know where this would lead. His life was complicated enough without a constant deception. They agreed to keep their affair secret until she could transfer to another department, and that would not be until this case had reached some kind of ending point. For each of them, it was too important.

At the end of the day, the pattern was reversed. Each left separately, trying to stick to previous work patterns. This was difficult, because in the past, they had both tended to work later than the others and would often find themselves the sole members of Intel 1 working into the night. With their new circumstances, this was a dangerous pattern, so one started leaving earlier than the other, and both, despite their desire to work on the case, ended up spending less time at work and more time with each other. Competing needs, to be sure, but intimacy had been denied both of them for so long that it took some precedence.

This night, Savas had arrived an hour after Cohen. Her apartment was a mansion compared to his tiny studio in Queens. She swooped out of the kitchen and into her bedroom. Savas heard the sound of her closet door opening, unmistakable rummaging noises, an object falling and a grunt, then the door closing once more. She came out toward the dining table, her hair somewhat disheveled, grasping an old bronze candlestick holder. It was unusual, a style Savas had never seen before. There were two holders for candles, spread apart by about a foot and a half, each supported by a curved and decorated arm that arched up like the beginning of a heart-shaped form from the base. The base itself was also highly decorated, with prominent symbols carved into the bronze. He was sure they looked like Hebrew letters.

Cohen looked toward him expectantly. "So? Do you like it?"

"It's pretty. Is it something special?"

"It's a Maurice Ascalon, an *original*." She took some candles she had shoved into her pocket and set them in place. She frowned at his lack of understanding. "Maurice Ascalon was one of Israel's most famous sculptors. He was famous in many areas but especially decorative arts. This was my mother's. She gave it to me a few years before she died." Her voice trailed off, and she stared into the distance for a few moments.

"Anyway, they were packed up in the closet, and I haven't used them since. It's not that I would have had a reason anyway. I don't really hold to much tradition—something that always made her sad."

Savas could see the pain in her face but did not understand. "What do you mean?"

"Oh, I'm sorry, John. These are Shabbat candles."

"Like Sabbath?"

She smiled. "Shabbat is *the* Sabbath, John. The Jews invented it, so we ought to know," she said in an amused voice. "It's nearly sunset, so I got it about right, even if I forgot the flowers. She always had flowers. Friday evening meals, my mother lit the candles. We would have a special meal, and, when we were little anyway, we couldn't do anything fun. All the electricity was off, so no TV! My father, as man of the house, would say the prayers to welcome the day of rest after the candles were lit."

Savas looked distinctly uncomfortable, and Cohen laughed. "Don't worry! My feeling all nostalgic doesn't mean you have to get religion tonight, John." She lit the candles and whispered something he could not catch. She stood tall and recited.

"*Barukh ata Adonai Eloheinu Melekh ha-olam, asher kid'shanu b'mitzvotav v'tzivanu l'hadlik ner shel Shabbat.*" She paused and closed her eyes.

"It means: Blessed are You, Lord, our God, King of the Universe, who has sanctified us with His commandments and commanded us to light the Shabbat candles."

She turned quickly and went into the kitchen, returning with a tray holding the food she had been preparing. "And now, we eat."

Cohen placed the tray on the table and looked at him. There were tears in her eyes and rolling down her beautiful cheeks.

41

The September night was cool and misty in Morden, a south-western suburb of London, home to the Ahmadiyya Muslim Community. A cloud sat on the earth, and the air was a prickling vapor of water droplets that obscured vision beyond ten or fifteen feet. Street-lights seemed to be standing at attention with ghostly haloes around their heads.

Situated on more than five acres of land, the Baitul Futuh Mosque displayed a proud and powerful facade. Able to accommodate over ten thousand worshippers per day in three prayer halls, its interior filled with a gymnasium, multiple offices, a library, and television studios, it held claim to being the largest mosque in Western Europe. It was a statement to the people of London, and the world, that this Muslim community was to be taken seriously. The Ahmadiyya faithful repre-sented a splinter sect of Islam, condemned by orthodox Muslims as heretical, and also by Western groups as harboring fanaticism and anti-Western sentiment. The Baitul Futuh, or House of Victories, was a defiant answer to all these doubters.

The parking lot in front of the mosque was deserted. Only a single military-standard personnel truck was parked in front of the structure, its color faded to gray in the darkness and fog. A minaret drove skyward for over one hundred feet, but this evening it was lost as it plunged into the gray, and the top of the silver dome began to blur. Several weary-looking soldiers stood at positions around the structure, weapons in hand or lighting cigarettes and cursing their foul duty to guard the property of a group many considered to be enemies of their nation.

One soldier cupped his hand over his lighter and puffed. He

glanced toward the parking lot as streetlights suddenly went dark, plunging the area into near total blackness. As the flame went out, a small red circle the size of a pencil eraser danced over his forehead. For a moment, the laser light hit his eyes, blinding him as had the flame. Before he could understand, a soft pop was heard some thirty yards away. Instantly his head arched back, blown open, and he dropped to the ground with a loud thud. Several of his mates turned toward the sound, but before they could even complete the motion, a near simultaneous group of muffled retorts sounded around the mosque. Each of the soldiers fell. A sudden rush of dark shapes flooded over the steps like a polluted tide. Dressed in black from head to foot, only their eyes showing through masks, they quickly grabbed the downed soldiers and dragged them off the concrete around the mosque, several bending down and washing the ground of blood and remains. Riflemen rose from the fields and parking lot around the mosque, shouldered their weapons, and approached the others.

At that moment, two soldiers stepped out from inside the mosque and froze before the sights and sounds of the shadowed men around them. One grabbed for his weapon, but a shadow was on him from the side. The dark shape seized the soldier's gun arm in one hand, extending it with the weapon grasped tightly, then drove his palm into the back of the elbow, breaking the joint. The soldier screamed and dropped the weapon just as the dark figure drew back his palm and struck the soldier in the neck, shattering his windpipe. The man dropped to the ground, choking and gasping for air, unable to scream further. Beside him lay the other soldier who had stepped outside with him, an empty expression in his eyes, his neck twisted strangely to one side.

"Move these two out!" hissed one of the cloaked figures. Like the others, the two bodies were dragged away from the structure. A van had pulled up next to the military vehicle, and the bodies were loaded into it. Black bags were taken off the van and distributed to several masked figures who busied themselves pulling out dark bundles from the bags and stripping off their clothes.

Others moved around the mosque, placing devices that they camouflaged in various ways—with mortar and tile that matched the surface of the mosque or as electronic devices, some even resembling the cameras that were already in place around the building but that had ceased functioning several minutes previously.

Within thirty minutes, the scene had nearly returned to normal. The dark shapes were gone from the deep fog, like undead wraiths that crept back into the mists. A small group of false soldiers in uniform patrolled the site, glancing up only momentarily as streetlights winked back on, throwing a ghastly light over the building. Cameras mounted around the mosque turned on and began to transmit once again. At the end of the parking lot, a brown van turned out onto the road, its head-lights off, only the red of its brake lights flashing momentarily like two grim eyes fading in the mists as the first light of dawn began to pale the evening sky.

Across the Atlantic, in Manhattan, the sidewalks were almost empty after midnight, and the streets around Ninety-Seventh contained only a handful of cabs and late-nighters. Few noticed that the streetlights along this side of the block up to Third Avenue had gone out. None noticed the darkly clad figures passing by a large structure, quickly darting out of sight, one by one over a span of five minutes. Inside the high fences, a building at a twenty-degree angle from the Manhattan street grid loomed upward yet was still dwarfed by taller apartment buildings around it. The building was squat, broad at its base, with sheer walls and a modern style tapering to a large black dome. It had been said that the geometry of the structure, founded on a repeating pattern of square units, followed Islamic law, which forbade the representation of natural forms. Atop the dome, on a spire, rested a crescent moon. A minaret rose next to the building, nearly in the middle of the block of land but open and easily visible to Ninety-Sixth Street. A sign outside read: "Islamic Cultural Center of New York," but the place was better known to many as the Manhattan Mosque.

Within the fences, no one from the streets could see the dark figures quickly traversing the traditional exterior court that led to the entrance of the mosque, or the shapes gathered around the minaret, placing objects along its sides. Shapes entered and exited the mosque carrying loaded backpacks that appeared to be much lighter on their way out. Within forty-five minutes, all activity ceased; the dark figures were gone, and the corner displayed nothing out of the ordinary. Even the streetlights were back on.

Finally, across all of Europe and Africa, the morning sunrise drenched the lands. In a suburb of London, a tired-looking troop of soldiers drove off early, a little before the arrival of the morning shift, and disappeared, never to be seen by any regiment in England again. In Finland, Friday worshippers prepared to make the long trek to one of the handful of mosques in this northern country, grateful for asylum and a chance to worship in this new land. In Nigeria, the spires at the tops of the four minarets of the Abuja National Mosque lifted majestically toward the heavens in the orange light. Approaching from the main highway, the sun rose behind the stunning building, casting it in a dark shadow, a silhouette of a giant dome and four spears. Morning sounds played over the capital of Abuja and mixed in with the sounds of the *adhan* called out over the city by the muezzin.

42

Cohen sat down beside Savas at the table and smiled. By the calendar, it was nearly a week since he had shared that special Sabbath meal with her, but in the growing madness around them, his sense of time had begun to blur.

However absurd, he knew she loved the way he looked in the mornings. His hair, flattened and disheveled from the night's sleep, had always refused to obey even the roughest of brushings. Only after he had showered and shampooed could there be any management. Coupled with his unruly hair, she noted impishly that he had the shell-shocked look of being half-asleep. She said it gave him the expression of a little boy just slightly lost. She kissed him as he grumbled and drank his coffee, and stretched over to turn on the television.

Savas's face hardened almost immediately, and the boy and the lovable expression vanished, replaced by something hard and hurt.

The scenes on the television were horrific. The British police and military had carved out a zone beyond which the public and press were excluded. Inside this region, the remains of a large structure could be seen burning brightly and belching skyward a plume of black smoke. Emergency responders rushed back and forth, carrying body after body. Pools of blood were easily made out as the runoff water from the fire hoses diluted them. Crumpled figures, blasted and burnt carcasses littered the site—men, women, children.

Children. Savas stared at the horror in front of his eyes as a reporter gasped out words in a British accent.

"Simply unimaginable carnage at the former site of the largest mosque in Western Europe. The mosque, the entire structure, is completely gone and burning as I speak to you. The death toll appears to easily be in the thousands. This attack happened on the holiest day of the week for Muslims, Friday, during the mosque's busiest time at noon prayers. Men, women, and many, many children lie dead behind me at this horrific, horrific site of England's, of Europe's, most terrible terrorist attack in history."

"Oh, God . . . John?" Cohen reached over and took his hand. He held hers but did not take his eyes off the screen. Savas reached over and turned up the volume.

The reporter continued. "Sources have reported that a section of British soldiers has been in place for several weeks guarding the mosque. Like several other Islamic sites in and around London, the government has acted proactively to try and protect them from the new and terrifying terrorist organization that has been targeting Muslims. Many are asking how anyone could have planted the enormous amount of explosives needed to destroy this building under the noses of the military."

Savas looked at Cohen. "You know what today is?"

A dawning of understanding lit her eyes.

"Rebecca, today is September 11." Savas looked back at the screen. "This attack has been very deliberately chosen for today. My God, Rebecca, this isn't going to be the only one. I know it. I feel it in my bones. They will hit multiple targets today to make a point— remind the world of the multiple attacks on 9/11. Today is going to be from hell."

As if to respond to his terrible intuition, the coverage cut from the scene of devastation in England back to the station's main desk. A well-coiffed woman with blonde hair and a fashionable scarf spoke almost hesitantly.

"Sorry to interrupt, Donald, but we have breaking news. Reports are pouring in that there have been two more bombings. I repeat, two more bombings of mosques in different parts of the world. Several reports are coming in from Nigeria, that there has been a bombing there. We also have word of a bombing in Finland. A mosque there has been attacked. We have a report live from the capital of Nigeria. . . ."

"John . . ." Cohen looked at him, pain in her eyes.

"I'm sorry. I didn't want to be right. But I knew I was. I'm going to get showered and dressed. We've got to get in. I won't be long." Savas stood up from the table and headed down the hall and into the bathroom. He shaved quickly, not bothering to notice the nicks and blood. He showered even faster and was out and dressing before ten minutes had passed. It dawned on him as he buttoned his shirt that he was processing sounds, sounds invading his swirling thoughts of past and present, death and destruction. *Sirens.* It sounded like ten or twenty police cars. He darted to the window but could see nothing. However, it was unmistakable—the well-known Doppler shift of a siren approaching, then drawing away as it passed. One after the other after the other.

"John," Cohen called. "You'd better get in here."

By the time he reached the kitchen, he did not need to see the scenes of destruction at the edge of Harlem to know what had happened. The target he did not guess. He had forgotten about the Manhattan Mosque—the Islamic Cultural Center of New York, thought by some to be a potential incubator for radical Islamic elements. No terrorists would be stepping forth from Ninety-Sixth and Third anytime soon.

A reporter spoke hurriedly, shouting over the sounds of a helicopter. "This is the Traffic Cam in the Sky, news every hour, on the hour. We have diverted location to the Upper East Side." A camera showed the geometric lines of the New York City grid, and at one corner of a block, what seemed to be a volcanic eruption of smoke pouring into the sky. Around the site like bugs circling honey, a flashing light show of fire trucks and emergency vehicles contrasted with the dark cloud climbing from the blaze below. A voice cut in over the reporter in the helicopter.

"We are going back to footage in Nigeria. . . ." On the screen appeared a split image; on one side, the giant mosque as it had appeared before the explosion, with its four minarets intact. The other side showed the same building, live, now with a single minaret standing and the rest of the structure reduced to rubble, fire, and ash. More scenes of carnage followed from the capital city of Nigeria. Savas stood nearly breathless watching the wild, panicked expressions and motions of emergency workers tending the wounded, many beyond help, scattered over the field of vision provided by the camera. The news reports darted back and forth, from Africa, to Finland, to England, and back to New York. It all began to blur in his mind, rubble and smoke, sirens, hysteria, blood, and fire. *So much death.* Men and women struck down. The old and the young. Mothers, fathers, daughters, sons.

Sons. The images before him began to merge with his own memory—two towers falling like sand to the earth, burying thousands, choking downtown Manhattan. *The death of sons.* The death of a young police officer who had made his father proud, giving the greatest sacrifice for his city and never knowing why.

His fists were balled tightly, and tears dropped from his eyes, yet his eyes still had nothing soft in them. A wildness burned there, a primitive urge to strike at the creature attacking the young, stealing life from those who should never have been buried by their parents. A shout broke him out of his trance.

"John, please!" Cohen was standing next to him, shaking him. "John, stop this; come back!"

Savas fought through the nightmare in his mind. He turned to the counter and grabbed his wallet and keys. "I'm sorry, Rebecca, I've got to go."

"To work?" she asked, hesitantly, afraid of the look in his eyes.

"No, not to work." He looked forward, seeing something far off. "I'm going to Gunn International. I'm going to do what Jordan said we should do. I'm going to confront that bastard and look into his eyes. I have to know, Rebecca. I can't wait for the wheels to turn in this matter." He motioned toward the television. "I don't know if the world can wait for this damn machine to do its job. These guys are ten steps ahead of us. If we play inside the rules we've set for ourselves, it will stay that way."

"John, please, think about this," she said, grabbing his face in her hands, staring up toward those wild eyes. "You'll have no authority; you'll be potentially in violation of the law, vulnerable to charges of harassment. They might not even let you in. What are you going to do, break down the doors?"

"If I have to."

"John, even if you find something, these actions might sabotage any legal recourse we have against this man and whatever organization he might be running. You know this, John. You can't do this."

Savas smiled bitterly. "Rebecca, what I know is that we are losing badly, and while we lose, people are burning alive. I *can* do this. I *have* to do this. Someone has to." He stared at her silently for a moment.

"Until today, my damn rage and quest for revenge blinded me to seeing what was so obvious. Every time these bastards would take out some jihadist, I was cheering them on. They were doing what we could never do. I didn't want to know what I should have known, to see what is so clear." He grabbed her shoulders firmly but not forcefully.

"They were destroying the monsters and becoming themselves the very things they sought to destroy. I hated the jihadists for taking the lives of the innocent. Of my son. But God, Rebecca, look at this," he said, gesturing toward the television. "The streets are lined with children's bodies. They are no longer fighting the enemy. They *are* the enemy. They have become everything they seek to destroy." He let go of her shoulders. "Someone has to stop them."

She stared a moment into his eyes, shaking her head, but she knew what she saw. "Then I'm coming with you."

Savas looked at her in disbelief. "Absolutely not! It's enough for one of us to go crazy and jump off the cliff. I will not let you endanger yourself, your career, for what I'm forced to do."

Cohen slipped on her shoes and grabbed her bag. "If you don't let me come with you, I will call the FBI, the NYPD, and Gunn International and warn them of your coming. They'll wall you out before you get into the building. Take me or forget going, John."

Savas didn't know whether he felt angry or touched by her hard-headed bargaining. "All right, you crazy woman. Let's go. But you let me do all the stupid stuff."

"Agreed. And I'm *your* crazy woman, stupid man. Don't forget that."

43

The ride through Midtown was eerily devoid of the usual traffic. Two terrorist attacks in four months in Manhattan had had a profound effect on the city. Within ten minutes, Savas had parked his car in one of an unusual number of open spots along the side of the street, a block away from the fifty-five floors of steel and blue glass that was Gunn Tower.

He was curious to find himself putting money in the meter. He had the quarters piled high in the small storage area underneath the CD player and radio. The human mind was a mess of contradictions. He was about to enter without a warrant and confront one of the world's most powerful CEOs. Rationally, he knew that he might walk out under arrest and would no longer need his car, perhaps for a long time. But he found himself unable to let go of the old habit of tending to the vehicle. He looked over at Cohen, who gave him a quizzical look as he paused, staring at the meter.

"Well, we don't want to get a ticket or anything," he said dryly as she put on her sunglasses.

They entered the enormous lobby of Gunn Tower, passing through a revolving door set in a solid wall of glass. Inside, the ceiling was at least fifty feet above their heads, with stairways and escalators leading to multiple overhanging layers that held general social functions, including restaurants and stores. The floor was of polished blue-green marble. Light poured into the lobby from outside, filtered into a bluish hue. Savas felt like he was in a giant aquarium. On the open second floor, a small museum dedicated to the Gunn family and their accomplishments was advertised by a sign. Modesty was not on display.

One hundred feet in front of the entrance was a security checkpoint that screened those headed back toward the main elevators. Armed security guards flanked the metal detectors. Pleasant-looking women stood on each side, checking ID cards for personnel. Cohen looked over at Savas, her glasses hiding the anxiety he could feel emanating from her.

"OK, now what?" she asked.

"We exploit the power of the federal government."

Savas walked up to the long marble counter beside the security checkpoint and addressed a young woman who smiled and welcomed him to Gunn Tower. Savas opened the leather case for his badge and showed her its contents.

"Agent John Savas from the FBI," he said curtly, pleased at the instant shift in demeanor from the woman behind the counter.

"Yes, sir, how can I help you?"

"I've been sent from the downtown division to follow up on a lead. It involves some international shipments by a company owned by Gunn International. This is a sensitive matter, and I am instructed to speak only with Mr. Gunn himself. Could you please tell me how I can go about seeing him immediately?"

The woman stared dumbly, clearly out of her element. Her mouth hung open for a moment; then she closed it, shifting weight to one foot and pushing her hair back behind her head. She glanced at the unmoving, expressionless figure of Cohen in her sunglasses, then back at Savas.

"Sir, I really don't know how to help you. I just work for general Lower Floor Management. I can't connect you with Mr. Gunn or anyone in his level. You'll have to make an appointment with him yourself, sir," she finished, her long nails playing with her buttons, her expression anxious.

"Ma'am," began Savas, "I hope I've made myself clear. I am from the Federal Bureau of Investigation, here to chase a lead on a very important international crime case. My superiors here and in Washington believe that Gunn International can shed light on a series of heinous crimes, including those of murder and terrorism. I am expecting full cooperation from Mr. Gunn and his company. Why am I not receiving it, Ms.... ?" Savas nodded toward Cohen, who reached into her purse, pulled out a small voice recorder and clicked it on. "Of course, you have the option to call a lawyer before speaking with us," Cohen added dramatically.

Whatever calm the woman had imperfectly maintained was shattered. Savas doubted she felt her job was worth this sort of trouble. "Please wait a minute, sir," she said, staring at the voice recorder. "I'll get my superior."

Three minutes later, a harried-looking man stepped over with the young blonde and stared skeptically at the FBI agents. He took off a pair of glasses that then hung from his neck. "Marcia tells me that you are FBI? Can I help you?"

Savas again held out his badge, which the man examined, and repeated his story. The man shook his head. "Agent ... Savas? Yes, well, certainly there are more formal ways to establish a meeting with Mr. Gunn rather than traipsing into his building and demanding an audience. Why don't you have your bureau chief call over and do this properly?"

Savas leaned forward and put on his irritated face. "I'm sorry. I did not get your name." Cohen leaned forward slightly, pointing the voice recorder toward the man.

"Richard Carter, but I don't see how—"

"Mr. Carter, I don't think your employee here has impressed upon you the seriousness of this case," Savas interrupted forcefully. "We are pursuing *time-sensitive* leads in an international arms smuggling and terrorist case, linked, if you must know, to a series of attacks around the world in the last few months, including two here in New York City. One of those attacks happened today not forty blocks north of this grand tower. We have reason to believe that other attacks are planned, and that they may be prevented only by timely action. So don't tell me that we need to waste the precious time we hardly have to follow a train of niceties to speak with your lofty CEO!"

The man's faced turned ashen as Savas mentioned the links to the terrorist attacks. Savas saw this and acted quickly to exploit it. "Things are moving too fast and are too dangerous to play games, Mr. Carter. We need all citizens to work with us on this, or the next attacks will be worse."

The man put his glasses back on and nodded vigorously. "Yes, yes, I apologize. Horrible, what has been happening. Please, this is unusual. Let me contact Mr. Gunn's department and convey your request."

Savas nodded in a satisfied manner. "Mr. Carter, that is the right thing to do. What a true patriot would do."

The man nodded awkwardly and hustled over to a set of phones. The woman apparently felt more comfortable with her supervisor and followed him closely, leaving Savas and Cohen alone.

"You get all that?" he asked quietly, motioning with his head toward her voice recorder. "That was sheer genius."

"No," she said flatly. "I don't think I've changed the battery on this thing for two years." Savas made a quick face indicating how disappointed he was. Cohen stared at him through her dark-brown sunglasses. "What a true patriot would do?" Savas waved her off as Carter hurried back over.

"Agent Savas. I have spoken with the floor administrative assistant in charge of general issues for several offices, including Mr. Gunn's, sir. She was most upset with this request, I must say," he continued, sweat now beading on his forehead. "However, I managed to impress upon her the seriousness of this matter. She has agreed to speak with you upstairs, although, regrettably, she cannot offer you a meeting with Mr. Gunn today."

Savas smiled at the man. "Mr. Carter, you have done a service to your country, a country that is under attack. Thank you for getting us this far. I will remember your help in this matter." The man smiled both anxiously and modestly, then turned toward Cohen, his smile fading under the relentless gaze of her sunglasses and expressionless face.

"Please, right this way, follow me." Carter gestured, stepping toward the security line. It was the express route through the line, up the elevators, and to the fiftieth floor of the building. The doors opened revealing a lower, standard-height ceiling, fluorescent lighting, and a large desk not more than ten feet in front of the elevator doors. Behind the desk sat an older woman with a stern face, talking into a Bluetooth headset and typing on a computer. She motioned for them to wait.

Carter led them up to the large wraparound desk and waited quietly. Savas was in no mood to wait. He checked his watch and spoke to the woman.

"Ma'am, which way to Mr. Gunn's office?"

She continued talking and typing but held up one finger, indicating for him to wait. Savas began to walk around the desk toward the hallway on the right. "It's alright, ma'am," he said, as her eyes widened and she began to spin around in her chair to follow him. "I'll find it myself."

Richard Carter looked stunned, and Cohen made a motion to follow Savas. The woman at the desk stood up and called after him. "Sir! You cannot go back there! Sir! Stop! Mr. Gunn is busy! He cannot see you now!"

Savas turned to Cohen. "Stall her." The hound at the desk would not be so easy to cow as Carter had been. Savas knew she would have security on him within a short span; Cohen might buy him a few minutes. Out of the corner of his eye, he noticed Cohen moving to intervene as Carter was speaking excitedly to the woman, waving his arms.

Savas strode purposefully down the hallway, passing offices and conference rooms. *Always appear confident.* A lesson he learned bluffing his way to buy booze as a teenager and as a cop in an armed standoff on the streets. The big man's office would be easy to find, likely at the end of the hallway, most likely protected by another guard dog. *There.* The hall opened to a larger space filled with another large desk. Behind it sat a young woman. Behind her and to the left was a magnificent door, cherry wood by the look of it, built thick and carved with adornments. The woman was on the phone, a concerned expression on her face. *Word has come from the front lines*, thought Savas.

She stood up, the phone still to her ear. "Sir, I'm afraid I will have to—"

Savas flashed his badge. "FBI, ma'am," he said pushing past her and her objections and opening the door.

It was a magnificent office. Larger by far than anything he had seen or even imagined at the FBI, decorated with very expensive furniture and paintings. The wall opposite the entrance was not a wall but a room-length window opening out to the heart of the city. Behind an enormous and beautiful wooden desk sat a man Savas had only seen in FBI photos and on the Internet. Tall, thin, silver hair framing a hard and handsome face. Set in the middle were two burning gray eyes.

"Mr. William Gunn?" asked Savas, bursting into the room.

Gunn glanced up from his computer screen with an angry look. He hit a key sharply and stood up to face Savas.

"What is the meaning of this?" he asked.

Savas heard a fluttering behind him, and the young woman from outside rushed in front of him and faced Gunn.

"Mr. Gunn, sir, I'm sorry!" she began breathlessly. "I tried to keep him out. He's come through Jennifer and from below and won't listen and . . ."

"Calm down, Marianne," he said, turning toward Savas. "Who are you, and what is going on here?"

Savas smiled. "My name is John Savas, Agent John Savas from the FBI." He went through the age-old movie scene and flipped out his ID. Gunn registered no distress and appeared, if anything, intrigued.

His assistant chirped behind Savas. "Mr. Gunn, sir, security is on its way. They already have the other one."

"Marianne, please, a servant of the people is here. Call off security. Another agent?" The woman nodded. "Please go and bring him here as well. Something important must be on the minds of these agents to have gone through such trouble to speak to me." He turned toward Savas. "I wish you had contacted me first and avoided all this bother. I am a rather insulated man. It helps me maintain my focus."

He motioned toward the chairs in front of his desk. "Please, won't you have a seat?"

This is one cool customer. Savas nodded and sat down as Gunn moved back around his desk, entered a few keystrokes into his computer, and sat down.

"Please tell me how I can help you today."

Savas stared directly at him. "Today, in four locations around the world, terrorists struck mosques, blowing them to bits along with all the people in and around them. One of those attacks happened just uptown from here at the Manhattan Mosque."

Gunn nodded slowly, eyeing Savas coldly. "Yes, I have seen the footage. Terrible. The second attack in our city in just a few months."

"Yes, one of many since the first attack in June that have been linked to a terrorist organization called Mjolnir."

Gunn stared silently. "I'm not familiar with the name."

"Few are."

"How have you traced this *Mjolnir* to the bombings, Agent Savas?"

"Not only bombings but a series of assassinations of prominent Islamic radicals, as well. They are a very busy organization. One thing that we have linked them to through our forensics team is the plastic explosive S-47."

Gunn shook his head and raised his eyebrows. "S-47? I'm sorry, Agent Savas, I don't know much about explosives."

"It's a very new form of Semtex, more powerful, more versatile. The details are not important. Traces of this material have been found at every bombing site associated with Mjolnir."

At that moment, Savas heard sounds at the door behind him. Gunn rose and asked his secretary, "Marianne—this is the other agent?" Savas turned to see Cohen standing in the doorway, her hair disheveled, her blouse untucked and wrinkled. He winced to think of the security guards manhandling her.

"Yes, Mr. Gunn. She was in the custody of our guards, and I brought her back up as soon as you requested."

Gunn walked chivalrously toward Cohen and motioned to the seat beside Savas. Cohen, her glasses gone, straightened her clothes and walked stiffly over to sit next to Savas, never glancing in his direction. He understood. She couldn't look into his eyes and maintain her composure.

Gunn returned to his seat in front of the enormous window. Savas motioned toward Cohen. "This is my colleague at the FBI, Rebecca Cohen."

"Pleased to meet you, Ms. Cohen. I am sorry about our security personnel. They are often overzealous in keeping the peace in my building."

Cohen glanced quickly around the room and over his desk. She focused momentarily on an object at his side, then looked into Gunn's eyes. "No need to apologize," she said. "We have been in a great hurry today, and our lack of standard protocol has created some problems."

"Yes," said Gunn, "Agent Savas here was explaining to me. Something about explosives?"

"This S-47 is easily traceable material in many ways, because it is so rare. It can only be found with US military personnel or on the black market in the international arms arena."

Savas stared intently at Gunn, but the businessman showed no reaction. Savas continued. "Agents with the CIA recently ran a sting operation in the Middle East and identified the source of much of the black market S-47. This source had been sold repeatedly to a single buyer, of unknown origin and identity, but the goods were always shipped in the same way, by boat—ships owned and operated by the Operon Company."

"Operon?" Gunn said, searching his memory. "That's one of ours. I see. You have connected the supply of this explosive to one of my companies, and you now wish to trace it further to attempt to identify the buyers, and thus, presumably, the terrorists themselves." He glanced momentarily at each agent before continuing. "Of course, the FBI will have full cooperation from Gunn International on this. Unfortunately, I know little of the day-to-day operations of the many subsidiaries and contractors we have. But I will personally see to it that those who do, will work with the FBI and the CIA and whoever requires information from us to help apprehend these terrorists."

Savas stared at the man. This was not what he had expected. He had been so emotional this morning, he believed he would confront the man, and the truth or an obvious lie would come out, be forced out. He had come here, navigated the obstacle course on passion and adrenaline and street smarts, and hit Gunn with the facts, only to find a calm and cooperative citizen. *Was Husaam wrong? Am I wrong?*

He looked into the eyes before him—cold, icy-gray, and unrevealing. *Eyes of a predator*, he thought. No, his intuition, his gut, whatever it was that had saved his life on many occasions on the street told him otherwise. There was something profoundly unsettling about William Gunn, and Savas felt that he was sitting only feet away from someone calculating and murderous.

Cohen spoke up. "We were concerned that this connection to your company, Mr. Gunn, might go further than the use of a shipping company." The CEO turned slowly toward Cohen, and Savas felt his stomach tighten as the cold eyes fell on her.

"I'm sorry, Agent Cohen, could you be more explicit?"

"Yes. There have been enormous financial transfers in these arms purchases. These levels of monetary exchange and the financial machinations that made them possible, and difficult to trace, could only have been accomplished by individuals with enormous capital and financial dexterity. We are concerned that perhaps someone within your company, at a much higher level than that of a shipping organization, might be involved."

My God, this is bold, Rebecca! She faulted *him* for being reckless today?

The CEO eyed her very closely. "That is a very serious concern you have raised, Agent Cohen. Rest assured that we will seek to root out any such person, should they exist, and work closely with you to do so." He looked at his watch, then back at the two FBI agents.

"I'm sorry to be rushing you, but I have a very important meeting with the visiting ambassador from China. As you know, China is becoming an increasingly important business partner for much of the world, and Gunn International is no exception. I cannot keep the ambassador waiting. Is there anything else I can help you with?"

"One other thing," Cohen continued. "This terrorist organization has a fascination with the Nordic myths. Do you know of any such people or organizations within your company who might be involved in such neo-paganism?"

Savas stared at her in confusion. *Rebecca, where are you going with this?*

"Agent Cohen, I would expect every sort of person from the wonderfully diverse city of New York to work under the umbrella of my organization. Such interests do not concern me in general as long as each employee does his or her job."

"We understand that, Mr. Gunn," she continued, "only in this case, such individuals would be highly suspect. You come from a Northern European background, Scandinavian, I believe?

The CEO focused on her impassively. "Yes. My father was an immigrant from Stockholm."

"Do you know what the name of this organization, Mjolnir, means?"

Gunn shook his head. "No. I mainly studied the Greek myths in school."

"It is the name of the hammer used by the Norse god of thunder, Thor."

"Yes, I'm sorry. I do remember reading that somewhere."

"If you were to see or hear this name in any context, in the English translation, or as Mjolnir, or depicted in *any* symbolic form, please let us know."

Savas nearly wanted to jump over and shield Cohen, so hostile and intent were the eyes that looked her over. "Yes, Agent Cohen, you can rest assured that I will."

As they walked out of the skyscraper and into the bright midmorning sunlight, Savas felt the adrenaline rush out of him and the world speed up again. It seemed that he had passed out of a dream state. It was always like this after confrontation. He sat in the car next to Cohen and exhaled, not starting the engine.

"I can't believe we did that, and I can't believe we did it for nothing!"

She turned toward him, her sunglasses back on, and her shaking hands withdrawing from her face. "What do you mean, 'for nothing'?"

"We go there, risk our careers, potentially blowing the entire case if he is the one behind this, and for nothing! He turns out to be happy as a clam to work with us! So cooperative! He played us like fools. And, I swear, all the time I felt like I was sitting across from a serial killer laughing at us."

Cohen stared forward, her face still ashen from the encounter. "We didn't fail, John. His cooperation *saved* our careers, for one thing. For another, he *is* the one behind all this. Trust your feelings."

Savas shook his head in confusion. "Well, that is something! How on earth do you conclude that? My feelings agree, but we came away with nothing."

"Did you look at his desk?"

He looked at her incredulously. "Sure. Hard to miss. Big giant thing, expensive wood. Cost more than my car."

She shook her head, still gazing forward. "No, not the desk itself, but what was on it."

Savas didn't know what she was getting at. "Papers, a computer . . . a few executive playthings?"

"Like the little toy on his left in front of you?"

He shook his head. "No, I didn't see what it was."

Cohen paused. "Well, I did. Small little metal thing, hanging from two metal rods that almost meet. The small little metal thing, John—it was a hammer." She turned toward him. "It was Thor's hammer."

"Oh, my God."

William Gunn returned to his desk after locking his door behind the departing FBI agents. He sat down and typed in several keystrokes. The black screen lit up, revealing the familiar face of Patrick Rout.

"Mr. Gunn? What the hell was that all about?"

Gunn gazed sideways, away from the screen. "Well, it's obvious, isn't it? You were right about the hit on the Russians. They have the connection, and they suspect. My concern was right about fearing someone passionate about this. You didn't see his eyes, but this John Savas is a driven man. And Cohen, well, she *knows*."

"They have no proof! Nothing to go on!"

"No. Of course not, and they will not get that, certainly not in time to stop us."

"We need to make sure of that, Mr. Gunn."

Gunn turned toward the monitor, his expression grim. "Yes, my friend, we do. We need to find out who these agents are. We will have to make some decisions about them soon."

44

OPEC BEGINS OIL EMBARGO CUTTING SUPPLY
TO EUROPE AND UNITED STATES
By Thomas Fischetti, Associated Press

The Organization of Petroleum Exporting Countries (OPEC) announced today a partial embargo against the United States and the European Community. OPEC will reduce oil supply to these nations by 25%, effective immediately.

An OPEC spokesman was quoted by Al Jazeera as saying that "the recent bombings of Islamic Holy sites around the world have left us no choice" but to enact the embargo. In the statement issued, OPEC demanded that Western nations end the terrorist attacks and apprehend those responsible.

Last month, in an unprecedented attack on Muslim houses of worship, terrorist attacks destroyed four mosques in four nations spread around the globe—England, the United States, Finland, and Nigeria. These attacks led to more than four thousand deaths, and followed on the heels of what have become seemingly monthly attacks on Muslims, including attacks in Algiers, New York, and Venezuela.

The White House press secretary issued a stern warning to OPEC. "The president condemns both the terror attacks and the response of OPEC, and cautions OPEC that the United States will not allow its supply of oil to be threatened." Reports placed several US warships en route to the Persian Gulf, and military sources claim that the entire United States military has been placed on high alert. Analysts have parsed the president's words and generally conclude that a full-scale embargo would in short time lead to massive military intervention.

China and Russia have protested US deployment in the Gulf, the Chinese representative to the UN calling the moves "reckless and destabilizing." Russia has vowed to prevent foreign occupation of oil-producing nations, and has placed its own military on heightened alert, according to sources in Moscow. The president has canceled his long-planned trip to India and is returning to Washington. He is expected to address the nation tomorrow evening.

J ohn Savas stepped out of his office and nearly crashed into the muscled figure of Husaam Jordan standing outside his door. Jordan had made a rapid recovery. He still limped slightly and favored his shoulder at times, but it was becoming increasingly difficult to tell that he had been through the ordeal in the desert. Savas assumed that in another month or two, he would be almost fully recovered. He apologized for his carelessness, caused by distraction over events following last month's insane visit to Gunn International. The large CIA agent smiled and clapped him on the shoulder.

"So, how is the investigation going?" he called out.

Savas smiled ruefully. "Which one?"

Jordan nodded back. "Indeed. But I am more interested in one than the other."

Savas could only agree, except that the FBI inquiry into his trip to Gunn Tower was occupying increasing amounts of his time. He had managed to convince all those involved that Cohen had been dragged along with him, and, for now at least, she had been spared the paperwork, meetings, and constant interruptions that an internal investigation entailed. He had also been spared any suspension of his duties or privileges—a rescue effort by Kanter. That was *after* Kanter had first threatened to kill him.

Savas nodded toward Jordan. "You were right."

Jordan cocked his head to one side and half-smiled. "About which investigation is more important?"

"Yes," said Savas, "but more than that—about following the trail of Operon and the shell companies."

Jordan became serious. "That trail is getting cold as we speak. The CIA isn't going to listen to the ravings of two mad FBI agents who stormed an American icon. Gunn practically ran a monopoly in the defense industry for two decades. He's owed more favors in Washington than we can guess. They've tied my hands, John. And it's been too long. Weeks and weeks have gone by. They aren't going to leave anything standing, or anyone connected alive."

"The FBI has twisted itself into a tangle of internal investigation," said Savas with obvious irritation. "Everyone is scared shitless now about moving on this guy. Larry's frustrated as hell, but he is protecting his division. Until this blows over, we're left doing research reports on the Internet. Meanwhile, we wait for the next fall of the hammer."

"Don't give up hope, John," Jordan rumbled. "It is written in the Holy Koran, 'When a man dies, they who survive him ask what property he has left behind. The angel who bends over the dying man asks what good deed he has sent before him.' You have worked for justice."

Savas stared at the black man standing before him, an American, a former gang member, and now a Koran-thumping Muslim. Yet he had come not only to respect Husaam Jordan but to feel a tug of affection for a person who clearly sought justice, who had disregarded career and safety in the service of justice. He just could not reconcile the different parts.

"Husaam, I don't want this to go the wrong way, but there are some things I don't understand."

Jordan stared straight into Savas's eyes, his expression unflinching yet knowing. Savas pressed forward anyway. "I like you. I didn't at first, I have to be honest. Well, I couldn't at first."

"You could not separate me from the Muslims who killed your son."

Savas winced. "You're a good man, a man who sees right and wrong and risks his life for what is right. You can't find one out of a thousand men like that. How can you be part of this religion that gives birth to all these crazed murderers who kill in the name of this damn book you keep quoting? How can Islam be anything but evil for the wars and bombs and wrongs it has caused? I just don't understand it."

Jordan smiled, his white teeth set in his strong jaw, bright against the darkness of his face. "The Abuja National Mosque was a gift from the heavens. If you had seen it, with open eyes, John, not eyes colored with anger, you would have seen its majesty rising into the African sky, its four minarets reaching toward God. Its beautiful dome was a bright star in the daytime sun or a powerful silhouette in the setting orange light at day's end. Muslims have made some of the most beautiful religious houses in the world. For hundreds of years, they preserved knowledge while Europe sank into the Middle Ages and burned witches at the stake, tortured innocents with the Inquisition, and converted by the sword many of the pagans of central and northern Europe. Science, mathematics, and philosophy were preserved, developed, and passed on to an awakening Europe by *Muslims.*"

Jordan opened his hands in a questioning gesture. "When you listen to the great composers of Germany—Bach, Mozart, Beethoven—do you also see in their music the ashes of the Holocaust? When you gaze at the religious sculptures and paintings of Michelangelo, do you see in them the blood-soaked lands the Crusaders marched across? America was founded by people fleeing persecution at the hands of fellow Christians. For the centuries of Christians doing evil in the name of God, how can *you* be one?"

Savas shook his head. "You're using this argument on the wrong man, Husaam. I'm not sure what I believe. I very nearly became violent with the priest of the church where I was an altar boy, and this crazy man still hears my confessions. Confessions mostly about how much I don't know, and how I can't see God."

Jordan nodded. "But my point is that if we are to judge a belief system by the actions of any group that claims to act in its name, every creed that exists or has existed will fall. Just as great beauty and selfless service to humanity has come from Christianity, so, too, from Islam." He paused for a moment, considering his next words.

"John, Islam is very personal for me. I grew up in poverty, abandoned by my parents, rejected by society—both black and white. I joined a gang before I could shave. At least there I *mattered*, I had a family. There was a code of honor and loyalty. The gang gave me a sense of worth and purpose society had denied me. But it was a life of sin. In prison as an adolescent, an imam who had emigrated from Africa was making the rounds. I was ready to hear what he had to say. I was ready to open myself to something larger and to find my place with God."

His eyes had a faraway look. He smiled softly.

"Do you know what the *al-Hajar-ul-Aswad* is?"

Savas shook his head.

"It is more commonly known as the Black Stone."

"Yes," Savas dredged his memory. "The meteorite in Mecca. Where the pilgrims go every year."

"Yes. It is one of the Five Pillars of Islam to make at least one pilgrimage to Mecca in a Muslim's lifetime. There the pilgrims congregate at the al-Masjid al-Haram Mosque in Saudi Arabia, and in the center of this mosque is the holiest site in all of Islam—the Kaaba. The Kaaba is a cube carved out of granite from the hillsides, covered with a black silk curtain decorated with gold-embroidered calligraphy, its four corners pointing in the four directions of the compass. It is the site to which we Muslims pray five times a day."

Jordan's eyes appeared to gaze far off, as if trying to glimpse the site itself. "At the eastern-most corner of the Kaaba is the Black Stone. According to our tradition, it fell from Heaven during the time of Adam and Eve. After the Fall, it was hidden by the Angels until Abraham rebuilt the Kaaba, and then the Arch-Angel Gabriel brought it to him from its keeping place."

Jordan paused for emphasis and turned toward Savas. "Muslims believe, John, that when the Kaaba fell to the earth from the heavens, the stone was *not* black but a blinding *white*. It has since absorbed, year after year, the crimes, the lies, the pain, the torture, the murder, poverty, and starvation—in short, the sins of mankind. The white stone from above turned as solid black as the evening sky from our sins. So you see, Muslims do not turn away from this truth, that we are all both light and dark. Someday, I will make the pilgrimage, the *Hajj*, and I will walk around the Kaaba, find my way to the Black Stone, and kiss it as did the Prophet."

He nearly recited. "I believe that there is no god but Allah, and that Mohammed is his Prophet. Not despite any evils of Islam, but because of its beauties, and its call to submission to God in the face of the evils every nation, every creed, and every person has committed."

Savas held his gaze. "How do we know that the evil itself isn't somehow built into many of the beliefs that claim to save us from them? For all the talk of salvation, there seems to be scant evidence that anyone has been saved by any of these faiths. We keep repeating the same old evils, in old as well as new forms. If religion and faith are real, and change us, and heal us, and remake us, then I have to ask why this is the case. I've called to God, and listened, but so far I haven't heard anything."

Jordan smiled. "But you are honest! How much closer to God you are than so many who deceive themselves. When Muslims, Christians, or Hindus, whoever, do evil in the name of God, they listen not to God but only to themselves, their fears, their inadequacies. At least you will not create a false god to serve your own needs. I will have hope for you yet!"

"That's fine. Hope is good," said Savas with resignation. "Just let's keep the volume down on all this *religious* hoping, if you would."

Before Jordan could speak, Manuel Hernandez came crashing down the hallway, his awkward gait nearly a full run. Too many long hours hunched over a computer screen had given him the dough-boy physique of a programmer, and he panted, struggling for air as he leaned over to catch his breath, his long brown hair hanging over his face and covering it, his brushy beard the only part sticking out from under the hair. He gasped out anxious words.

"John, we've got a situation."

45

Savas rolled his eyes. He wasn't sure he even knew what that meant anymore. "What, another one? Get back to me after the other twenty-three clear, Manuel. I don't have time for another one."

"No, I mean a *situation*," he wheezed out the last word, trying hard to place emphasis.

Savas opened his palms toward him. "OK, shoot."

"We've been hacked."

Jordan glanced toward him, his eyebrows raised. Savas stood there stunned for a moment, trying to come to terms with the implications. "What? I thought you said your security setup was like Fort Knox."

"No, not us directly. Someone hacked into Personnel, Accounting, perhaps a few other departments. I don't know the extent of it yet. Hell, *they* don't even know it happened yet." Hernandez stood straight up now, hands off his knees, recovering from his sprint to John's office. He saw the confusion in the other two faces in front of him.

"See, they *did* try to hack us, and then when they failed, they tried to go through other internal servers—hack into those, use internal networks to find security holes, break into our stuff that way. Well, that didn't work either, as I've walled us off even from the FBI."

"You're one paranoid geek, Manuel."

"Yeah, thanks. So, we're not compromised. But just about everyone I've checked in the building is."

"How long have you known this?"

"Ten minutes, John. I ran over here as soon as I was sure and had some idea about the extent of it."

"Well, that's ten minutes too long. You get up to Larry's office. Tell that bulldog guarding outside I sent you *priority*. Get Larry to write you a get-out-of-Intel-Free pass, and get up to those departments and try to figure out what the hell is going on."

"Timing's what's worrying me," interrupted Hernandez. Jordan looked over at Savas and nodded.

"I mean, right when we start to get a lock on this guy, this Gunn-dude, we get hacked. And, let me tell you, they were aiming for us, John, following the tracks, I mean, of all the offices and groups. These were black hats on a mission. They wanted us."

Savas nodded. "Get up to Larry and find out all you can. Track them through this if you can. Maybe we can find out who or where they are."

"OK. I'm on it. But I'm done running for the day." Hernandez turned around and walked briskly back down the hallway.

"You think it's Gunn?" asked Savas.

Jordan nodded. "This looks like a pro job, and if there's one thing we know about Mjolnir, it's that they are professionals. Only the connection with Gunn would lead a bunch of skilled hackers to focus on you and your people. In some ways, it's just more evidence that we are on the right track."

"Not some random cyber attack?"

"Sure, could be. How many of those do you get a month, and how many get this close?"

Savas nodded, then looked up in exasperation. "I was supposed to meet Frank and Matt downstairs—our last hot dog–stand lunch before the new security regs force the carts a few blocks up. At least the food's fast and I can march them back up here. Care to join me before I run back up into this insanity?"

"Sure," said Jordan. "But I'll go with the potato knish."

Savas groaned inwardly. *Pork and Muslims, oil and water.* He smiled to cover for his gaffe.

"OK, let's go. I've got to eat something before we go into red alert again."

It was a sunny, early-October day, crisp and even slightly warm under the sun. Savas stepped out of the FBI building, squinting in the bright light. If it weren't for all the chaos, it would have been nice to be outside on such a beautiful fall afternoon. Jordan followed him down the stairs to the pavement, his eyes scanning the area, an old survival instinct that would never leave him, no matter how safe the neighborhood. Savas spotted Frank Miller first. That was always easy; the ex-marine was about as wide as a standard refrigerator. Matt King provided a striking contrast. His lanky form, slouched posture, and bookish demeanor set him apart. However, both were equally enjoying the hot dogs on this fine day. Each was looking toward Savas with an air of feigned annoyance.

Miller waved them over. "I thought you said you'd meet us down here at noon, John," he said, ripping off about half the hot dog and bun, then speaking through a full mouth. "We've been here twenty minutes waiting for you. The hot dogs were getting old, I'm afraid."

"I thought they weren't biodegradable," mused King.

Savas smiled. "I'm sorry, guys, but we have a small situation upstairs."

Both rolled their eyes and groaned, almost in stereophonic harmony. King shook his head. "I think making partner would have been easier than this job. What now?"

"We were hacked." Savas paused to let it sink in. King nearly choked on his food as Savas continued. "From what Manuel says, half the building was hacked, and actually, we were not, thanks to Jesus's ultra-paranoid, super firewall. But someone, according to him, someone good, got into several systems in the building, trying to use those to get to us."

"To us?" said Miller.

"Apparently, yes, we were the target. Manuel is running around up there trying to get a handle on it, and that is what we all get to go do as soon as we insert those indigestion tubes," he said, waving toward the hot dog stand. Jordan came toward them, holding a knish.

"Holy shit," said King. "This is pretty freaky stuff, John. This, and all the Gunn stuff; you think it's connected?"

"Yes," said Savas. "So does Agent Jordan."

"I don't think too much of coincidences in this business," Jordan said.

Frank Miller nodded. "Well, that raises the stakes some. Cops chase robbers, but these guys are scary folk. They chase back."

Savas was momentarily aware of a flash of light, a movement of red across his chest. Miller, closest to him, focused intently on the red circle. Suddenly, he lunged toward Savas like a lineman about to pummel a quarterback. Time seemed to grind to a stop. Stunned, Savas saw the huge former marine actually become airborne as he dove toward him, his coffee and hot dog seemingly suspended in midair.

There was a soft whizz through the air and a simultaneous explosion of fabric over Miller's shoulder. A cloud of red mist burst into the air. Miller crashed into Savas's chest, smashing the wind out of him and sending them both plummeting toward the hard pavement below. Miller landed on top of him and rolled to the side, clutching his right shoulder. It was soaked red with blood. Savas struggled to catch his breath.

"Ahhh, *fuck!*" screamed Miller, raising himself to a crouch and motioning with his good arm for Savas to stay down. "Keep low, John! Sniper!" Miller gasped out. "Crawl behind that parked van! *Damn!*"

The pavement exploded as several more rifle shots were fired. People were screaming and running in various directions. Jordan had pulled out a pistol and was crouched beside the FedEx van, looking up toward a building across the street.

Miller screamed out, "Damn it, John! Move to the curb, by the van. The shots came from that building across the street!" Miller paused, inhaled sharply through his teeth. "He can't hit you if you move. So move!"

Savas came to himself enough to get on his hands and knees and crawl over to the van. He heard Miller and Jordan talking rapidly.

"I think it's the roof of the corner building," Miller gasped.

"Yes," said Jordan, "I saw the gunman. He took two more shots and that exposed him. He ran back from the roof after that. He's either going down through the building or going to hit the fire escapes on the older structure around the back. I think it's the last—too easy to get caught inside." Jordan looked over at Matt King, who had also taken refuge behind the van and was shaking violently even as he held out a weapon.

"Matt—stay here with John and shoot anyone we don't know or who gets close to him. He was the target, and we don't know if there are other snipers. Meanwhile, call an ambulance for Frank, then your offices. Get some people down here if they aren't already on their way. I'm going after this guy."

King had only a second to respond with "OK, but..." when Jordan, gun still in hand, sprinted off across the street with his slight limp, leaped onto and across the hood of a taxi barring his way, and was out of sight.

Jordan crossed Broadway—not so broad this far south on the island and down to a one-way street—and ran across the opposite sidewalk, crossing Duane Street and heading toward the corner of Broadway and Reade. People jumped back from him, a sprinting black man dressed in Islamic garb, gun held aloft and pointed toward the skies. Who knew what was going through their minds? *I just hope the cops don't arrest me*, he thought.

He darted around the corner and sprinted up Reade Street, his mending leg stiff and throbbing. Dropping from the fire escape halfway up the block, a man landed on the pavement, hitting hard and catching himself with his hands. As he regained balance, he looked down the street and saw Jordan; their eyes locked. The man turned, drawing something dark from his belt behind his back, and sprinted up the street. *Lost the rifle, heading toward Church Street, armed with handgun.* Jordan sprinted after him.

The figure crossed Duane on the east side of Church, then disappeared, hidden by a building. Jordan sprinted harder. Every second out of sight meant the suspect could be lost. Jordan nearly crashed into a couple pushing a stroller. The woman screamed, but he pivoted out of their way and continued toward Church Street. The alley was in shadow from the buildings, and Church was lit brightly from the sun in comparison. Instinct took over as he approached the corner. He raised his gun, and as he stepped into the light, he crouched and scanned around him.

The crouch saved his life. A retort from a gun sounded as he heard the bullet whiz over his head, a store window next to him shattering, screams and an alarm filling the air. His prey had waited, expecting a figure the height of an average male to emerge, and in haste had not adjusted his aim properly, missing Jordan by inches. He rolled across the pavement, shielding himself behind a parked car. *Fool!* If the man had used his time getting away and not trying to kill him, he might have escaped easily. Jordan darted up, just in time to see a figure sprinting across the road and heading south. *Chambers and Church subway stop!* Jordan knew where he was headed, and if he made it there, he'd be lost in the underground labyrinth.

Jordan was nearly out of breath when he reached the subway station. He leapt down the stairs, sending one man flying and cursing behind him. When he reached the turnstiles, his heart sank. A figure had jumped them and was racing down the steps. If a train was waiting or came soon, he'd be lost. Jordan darted forward, screaming at people and waving his weapon. It was very effective. He moved through the dividing mass of people in line, jumped over the turnstile to several angry cries, and flew down the steps at a reckless and dangerous rate. His leg was on fire, the pain beginning to distract him. Jordan pushed it away, focusing on the chase.

The subway stop was a flood of humanity, like sardines in a can. He scanned the area, back and forth. He knew he wouldn't be able to see the man he was chasing, but if his quarry continued to panic, he would be doing the one thing he shouldn't in a crowd like this—he would be moving. *There!* He saw first the ripples in the crowd as someone pushed his way forcefully through. The sniper was about halfway to the next stairway, but Jordan knew that this was not his goal. The tunnel wind had begun, indicating an approaching train. In this density of people, Jordan realized that he would never reach the killer in time, and if he got on the train, the odds of continuing the chase successfully would drop precipitously. So he did the only thing he could think of in the moment.

"Allah be praised!" he yelled, springing on top of a bench and brandishing his firearm. "Everyone down, *down* or I will kill all infidels!" He fired his weapon at the ceiling. People screamed, and a great horde of them dropped straight to the ground. His quarry continued to panic, and instead of dropping as well, concealing himself in the crowd, he reached behind his back to pull out his weapon. Jordan crouched on the bench, steadied, and aimed. The man raised his weapon. Jordan pulled the trigger twice in succession.

Both shots were true. They struck the man solidly in the chest, and he shuddered, disoriented, discharging his weapon into the air and crying out as he fell. Several more people screamed, as did the train brakes as the lead car blasted out of the tunnel and into the stop, a rush of air flowing into the chamber. Jordan leapt down from the bench and raced across as people crouched in terror. He kept his weapon turned on the man but drew it up as he came close.

The gunman had collapsed and was sprawled on his back, blood soaking his chest and sputtering out of his mouth as he coughed. One of the bullets had hit the heart or a major artery. No longer a threat, his gun lay beside his hand on the ground. Jordan felt his stomach turn. The man was near death. His shot had done more damage than he had intended.

He bent down on one knee and grabbed the man's denim jacket. "Who sent you?" he barked out.

The man looked up, his eyes swimming at first, then focusing for a brief moment. "You will lose, *Muslim*," he whispered, the word a curse in his mouth. "Mjolnir will strike, and strike soon. Burn, and burn again in hell." His eyes rolled back, and he became heavy as his muscles completely relaxed. Jordan let go of him and clenched his fist. *No!* It was not to be helped. He had done all that he could. But it had not been enough.

"NYPD—*freeze!*" the shout was from behind him, the sounds of shoes running toward him unmistakable. "Hands up in the air! Now! Now! Now!"

Jordan placed his gun down and raised his hands slowly over his head. As the officer threw him on his face and cuffed him, he had a brief flashback to the many arrests he had endured as a young gang member, the last one leading to his imprisonment—and to his salvation at the hands of a Muslim cleric. It didn't matter, he thought, as he felt blood leak from his nose. He had failed today. *What will tomorrow bring?*

"You terrorist *bastard*," said the officer standing over him, with his knee in his back. "We'll soon have you shipped somewhere nice. Where I hope they electrocute your fucking balls off."

"I don't believe this! Right in our front yard!" said Larry Kanter, standing outside the FBI building, watching the ambulance pull out with a sedated Frank Miller inside. "Is he going to be OK?"

Savas followed the flashing lights. "Yeah, Larry. It ain't pretty, but it's only a shoulder injury. He's lost some blood, but Matt's the same type, and he insisted on riding with them just in case. The emergency responders gave Matt some flack, but took one look at him and his badge and eased up."

Kanter nodded. "Good, good. Let's get back up now and figure out what the hell is going on. We've got an assassination attempt at our front door, hackers breaking into FBI networks—this is going down as one of our really good days."

"You believe me now?"

Kanter scowled and looked away. "I guess I don't have much choice. These bastards pretty much made the argument for you. *Damn!* I should have listened to you earlier, but I just couldn't swallow something that big, that impossible. I don't think the powers-that-be will either, not even after this. But we'll deal with it."

Savas didn't respond immediately. Finally, he looked at Kanter. "The bullet was meant for me, Larry. Frank stuck his shoulder in the way, threw *himself* in the way to get me out of the line of fire. He's bleeding now instead of my heart being blown out of my chest."

Kanter's jaw tightened. "John, we all know the job brings dangers. We might think as analysts we are protected from the worst, but today you see differently. We are fellow soldiers in this war, and Frank has seen enough war for all of us. There are two kinds of soldiers, John. Those who will take a bullet for the platoon, and those who won't. You see which one Frank Miller is."

Savas nodded. Kanter motioned for him to walk in. "Now, we've got some responding to do on this. First, we've got to put a security team on you right way. More than ever it looks like Gunn must be behind this. You were the one to confront him. He's focusing on you."

Savas's stomach tightened. "Larry, I wasn't the only one there that day."

Kanter looked him in the eye. "Yes, John, I know that. I've got men heading over to her apartment as of fifteen minutes ago."

46

William Gunn switched off the television feed and glanced out over the sea of clouds below. The white ocean seemed to stretch forever, even to the edge of the horizon as viewed from this height. Waves seemed to be embedded in the cloud blanket, giving it the appearance of some heavenly body of celestial water, frozen in the moment. He glanced up above the plane, where the sky seemed to darken ever so slightly and lose its blue, and where, if he looked closely enough, he imagined, one might make out the brightest stars.

A man approached Gunn's private section of the aircraft and knocked on the wall next to the curtain separating the compartments. "Come in," said Gunn.

It was Rout. "Mr. Gunn, sir. We will be arriving in half an hour. We have arranged for several different limos to depart simultaneously, and will switch vehicles three times, with cars following behind to search for tails."

"Good. Have you seen the footage from today's missions?"

"I have, sir. Spectacular successes both in Sudan and on the airliner. The preliminary work has now been set, and every mission a success. The pattern is in place, and the final point is waiting to be added."

"It is time we revealed ourselves, then. You have the press package readied?"

"Just give the signal."

"Today. Send it to all the major news organizations. It is time to prime the trap for the final stroke."

"It will be done."

Gunn nodded. "Have you been debriefed on the failure in New York last week?"

"Yes, sir. A poorly executed mission. The resource was apprehended, but he died of wounds before he could be brought into custody. He was a blind and could have told them little of practical use."

"We will make another, more thorough effort soon."

"Sir?"

"The information we obtained from the FBI—a break through their computer security—has proven very useful. We were unable to penetrate his division, however. There were some very significant security safeguards in place. But we were able to reconstruct the organization and obtain extensive information from other computers about all personnel of relevance."

"He will be a much harder target now. There will be security on his person and place of residence, and he will scramble his travel and schedule."

The CEO nodded. "Yes; that is to be expected. A harder target but not unreachable. They still cannot connect things to us, and our friendliness with the FBI allows us to steer the research into Gunn International and Operon, effectively slowing them down considerably. Besides, the list of targets has expanded dramatically. I think another strategy is in order.

"We will need more assets in New York," Rout added.

Gunn sipped from a glass of brandy. "It would be better to bring in our mission units."

Rout nodded curtly. "Yes, but we cannot bring them back for this mission without jeopardizing the other."

"I understand. They are to return for the final mission training. We'll run New York with what we have here. The primary teams need to be fully briefed on the details of Ragnarök."

"Yes, sir. You will oversee the transfer to Mexico?"

Gunn smiled. "Yes, personally. When the day comes, I will also see that ship launched toward its goal. I want to be there, close enough to touch the thing." He laughed. "Consider it the closest I get to superstition. A blessing, if you will."

Rout responded with little more than a raised eyebrow. "Understood, sir." He then spun around and walked through the curtains back to his seat.

47

WORLD MARKETS PLUNGE AS OPEC
DECLARES FULL OIL EMBARGO
By Brandon Lewis and Thomas Fischetti, Associated Press

Stock markets in Asia and Europe fell dramatically as the Organization of Petroleum Exporting Countries (OPEC) announced today a full embargo of oil to Europe and the United States. These actions followed the latest in a series of brazen terrorist attacks on Muslim targets. These attacks, more than one a month across Africa, Europe, North, and South America, include the Great Mosque in Khartoum and the downing of an Iranian Boeing 747 that killed more than 400 people en route to South America. An organization, calling itself Mjolnir, claimed responsibility for these and a series of attacks against Islamic targets, releasing a statement and video announcing its intentions to escalate a war of terror against Islamic peoples and sites.

The recently formed joint United States and Europe Task Force on Oil (USETFO) issued a warning that oil supplies would be maintained by any necessary action, and called upon the OPEC nations to remove the embargo by the end of the month. High-ranking officers of NATO and the US secretary of state were present at the press conference, indicating to many analysts that the full force of the US and European military was behind the official statements.

The Russian president, visiting China on an emergency trip many have speculated has been related to the growing international crisis, issued a warning at a press conference in Beijing that foreign aggression in the oil-producing countries would not be tolerated and would be considered "an act of war" against all countries relying on the supply of oil.

Standing beside the Russian leader, the president of China noted that US ships heading to the Persian Gulf were in violation of international law and posed a serious risk of "global destabilization."

Mjolnir is being described as a "Western" terrorist organization due to its use of Nordic religious symbols and its stated purpose of attacking Islamic nations and culture. Muslim nations have demanded the apprehension of the terrorists and the cessation of attacks before they halt the embargo. European and American antiterrorist organizations have said that they are working diligently to stop the group, but so far have seemed impotent in the face of the escalating and continued violence.

Savas finished cutting the tomatoes and tossed them along with the cucumbers into the large wooden bowl. He quickly diced an onion and sprinkled the bits over the growing salad. Going to the fridge, he pulled out the large white tub of feta cheese, opened it, and cut out a medium-sized hunk that he placed on a plate. With his bare hands, he crushed the cheese into small morsels over the salad, washing his hands afterward. Finally, he grabbed the olive oil and spread it luxuriously over the contents of the bowl. A country Greek salad with make-do, store-bought produce. Nothing would come close to his grandfather's garden in Thessaloniki, where the bright Greek sun, the earth, and the green hands of a man who cared would always yield crops far superior to the products of agribusiness that landed in the supermarkets. But it would have to do.

He gazed outside the window in the kitchen, and, not for the first time, wondered when a coherent red light of a laser targeting scope would dart across his chest, the glass in the window exploding, and a bullet tearing through his flesh. The night was silent except for the muffled roar of a motorcycle and the sounds of Cohen showering in the next room.

He placed the salad on the table and returned to the kitchen to check on the lamb. It had a bronzed texture, so he turned off the oven and the oven light. The sound of the water faded, and he heard the shower curtain slide open. He resisted the urge to go see her. There was nothing sexier or more beautiful than a woman wet and dripping from the shower. *Or from a rainstorm*, he reminded himself.

Following the attempt on his life, much had changed—seemingly for the better. The investigation of his conduct toward William Gunn had ended, as enough of the decision makers at the FBI had decided that perhaps all this was not so coincidental. The cyber attack on the FBI had certainly helped his case. Once it was clear how much confidential information had been breached, an entirely new investigation into lax computer security had begun. By the time Jordan had obtained a governmental get-out-of-jail-free card, Savas was off the hook internally. But the relief was muted. He had a price on his head.

The FBI decided to keep a constant watch on both him and Cohen. This had at first panicked them both, as they thought it meant they would not be able to see each other for the duration. But it had turned out wonderfully once Kanter had suggested that it would conserve resources to keep them together at all times. This was something of a double-edged sword: they had a complete lack of freedom in their activities outside the apartment and the FBI, but a freedom from the constraints of hiding their relationship. Cohen had suggested that they hole up after work at her place. While the guards outside the room were a nuisance, they were finally afforded a strange sort of normalcy in their relationship. "Now we can finally go to work together, *darling*," she had joked one morning. Yes, with the caveat that they go together with the hulking shapes of Agents Robertson and Smith.

Breaking him out of thought, Cohen walked into the kitchen, and once again, John Savas felt the complete power of her beauty reduce him to a small singularity that radiated only awe. Her long hair cascaded over her shoulders, and she had quite unfairly worn the "monkey shirt"—a tight number with a brightly colored monkey spread in undulations over her chest. Once, when they had walked through a park in late August, she had worn the shirt, and he had asked that night whether she had intended it to draw his attention to her breasts. She had laughed at him. "John, not everything revolves around sex." He had tried hard to digest that one.

She saw his admiring gaze and smiled. "OK, this time I *did* wear it for you to look at my chest," she said impishly.

Savas smiled. "So, I have permission?"

She laughed and kissed him. "Let's try some of that salad."

Cohen walked to the table as Savas brought out the salad and the lamb. "It's too much for the two of us, but I'd rather save some for tomorrow and not invite in our well-armed shadows."

They ate in silence for a few minutes, each content in this mundane activity that nonetheless seemed as deep as any world event that had crashed on them in the last five months. Finally, Cohen spoke through the stillness.

"Frank is going to be OK?"

Savas put down his fork and exhaled. "It looks like he will. There was a lot of deep-tissue damage, so his racquetball game is never going to be the same. But he'll get most of his range of motion back, or so the doctors tell me anyway. At least we got Husaam out of lockup without too much trouble. What a mess!"

"God, John, it still runs through my mind every day. If it weren't for Frank . . ."

He cut her off. "But he was there, love. It's torture to think through the possibilities. I'm here, and we just have to keep our wits about us now."

"Nothing more from the sniper?"

Savas shook his head. "No. Same pattern as the other one. Ex-military, served in an antiterrorism unit. There were reports of behavior toward enemy combatants that led to formal disciplinary action. Seems that lots of these Mjolnir soldiers have some strong hatred for Muslims, Rebecca. Gunn must have recruited such men."

"So we just play it cool with Gunn?"

"That's how they want it. Filtering it through Larry's evasions, it seems there is still enough debate higher up about messing with Gunn that they are going to slow down, which makes sense from another angle—he's still working with the FBI. The hope is to find enough about Operon, or get lucky and strike gold in looking into Gunn International itself, that we'll find what we need to take this thing down and stop whatever they're planning next."

"John, something is troubling me about all these attacks."

"You mean besides all the death and destruction?"

She gave him her sharp look. "Yes. They don't make sense. OK, sure, they are all Muslim targets and Mjolnir is out to destroy Islam—motive is there. But why do you go out bombing random mosques across the world, or, come on, a civilian airliner? How is this going to bring down a religion of over a billion souls?"

"I don't know, but it's sure shaking up the world. The Islamic nations have gone ape-shit, embargoed us, and we've sent a bunch of ships toward the Gulf threatening them and scaring everyone that World War Three is on the horizon. *That* part of their plan seems to be working."

"OK, yes, that is something, but couldn't that be done while still hitting more strategic targets? Government buildings? Leaders of nations? These targets are so random, so haphazard. Why not more professional-type targets for such a professional group? They began with assassinations that followed such a pattern. Then this."

"Maybe we don't know what their aims are."

Cohen shifted her weight forward, put her elbows on the table, and clasped her hands under her chin. "That's exactly what I am getting at, John. We are missing something. These guys are too smart, too careful, too *thoughtful* to appear so scattershot."

"Sometimes revenge isn't logical, Rebecca. Sometimes it's just mean and crazy."

She shook her head. "John, I don't think so. They are too cruel, too ordered, for simplistic revenge. You said it best—Gunn is like a serial killer. There is something cold, calculating alongside all that hatred. Some pattern, however demented. We're missing something that is pointing somewhere."

Savas heard the anxiety in her voice and reached out to take her hand. "Where then? What do you mean?"

Cohen stared out across the room. "I don't know. Somewhere dark. To something bigger, much bigger."

She squeezed his hand so tightly it nearly hurt. "John, I'm scared."

48

Michael Inherp watched the docked boats bob in the waves of the Gulf of Mexico. Night had fallen on New Orleans. *Not the old New Orleans*, he reminded himself, full of swagger and slum, of music and magic, of Mardi Gras and murder, of artists and pimps. It was a wounded shadow of the once great city, left alone to rot after Hurricane Katrina in 2005. Lights danced on the sea stretching out before the dock like those in a van Gogh painting, the rigging of sailboats nearby like muffled bells playing to the rhythm of the waves. *Calm before the storm.* He closed his eyes, thinking about the tempest to come.

A small freighter waited hungrily at the dock. It was an unusual vessel, thoroughly modernized, down to tinted black windows and highly sophisticated and expensive radar and communications equipment visible from the outside. Inherp had seen the inside and knew the outside told only a superficial tale. For several days, he and other soldiers of Mjolnir had passed on and off the boat. Men with purpose and haste and intensity foreign to the rhythms of the port.

Inherp continued to scan the port as part of his guard duty. He watched an old fisherman prepare his boat for the night's expedition. This was not the first time the old man had worked his boat during Inherp's watch. Stooped, a gray beard visible from a distance, he had seen unusual activity at the strange boat. Inherp doubted the fisherman thought long on the issue. This was New Orleans, after all. He displayed no real curiosity. He prepped his boat and cast out. Night after night. The old man seemed to have a different pace, a sense of the sea, its rhythm, its long heartbeat and toll of a lifetime. Inherp suppressed a bitter laugh. *Not like us, are you, Gramps? With our machines and power, flaunting our disrespect for the great waters of the world.*

This night, the activity was particularly brisk, and Inherp knew the man had seen much, even inadvertently. *Seen too much.* The old fisherman had been working when the very large crate was pulled along the dock on an extended trolley. The old man had perked up when the crate rolled by, its mass flanked on each side by armed men. He had cast a glance or two as the men wheeled the crate to the freighter, which was equipped with a small crane. The men had secured the crate to a harness, and the crane had pulled the crate upward, out of sight. The old man had worked late one night too many.

It happened so quickly the old fisherman never understood. Inherp watched a shadow rise behind the fisherman. He had only an instant to recognize the broad end of a silenced weapon raised as several muffled spits sounded over the splashing of waves against the dock. The old man lay on the deck of his boat, nets tangled around his arms, a pool of blood forming around his head.

Inherp bowed his head for a moment. The rigging of the sailboats rang like church bells in the thickening night.

Later, onboard, he was ordered to sequester the large crate below deck. He and his fellow soldiers worked very carefully and secured it tightly. Next to the crate, he and the others stood at attention. A tall, thin man descended a narrow set of stairs above him, bowed to fit within the lower ceiling, and straightened to full height when he reached the last step and entered the room. He wore a dark-gray suit, his silvery hair set tight on his head. Money, power, and influence seemed to radiate from his person, as well as something more feral, something that Inherp could feel and that kept him even more tightly at attention. *William Gunn.* Inherp felt stunned to be in his presence. Following behind, a powerfully built figure with blond hair emerged and now stood a few feet to Gunn's left. This man had a sharp crew cut and the face of a tested warrior.

"Open it," said Gunn.

Inherp jumped to obey, and within moments, he and the others had revealed what lay within. Gunn stared at the long, black object inside with a terrible fascination that sickened Inherp. The CEO stepped up and rubbed his hands along its smooth contours. It ran nearly twenty-one feet in length with a diameter of about two and a half feet. Wings jutted outward from its midsection, spanning over ten feet. The very design of the thing reeked of threat and death. It was a predator like the world had never seen.

"AGM-129 ACM cruise missile," said the older soldier, matter-of-factly. "Average speed that of a jet plane at five hundred miles per hour. Range—two thousand nautical miles. Payload—a W80-1 variable yield. She flies fast, she flies low and unseen, and delivers one hell of a punch at the end."

Inherp noticed that Gunn did not take his eyes off the black missile. The men around him looked distinctly uncomfortable. Finally, the CEO stepped back and addressed the soldiers.

"When you have delivered the package and it is secured, we will begin training for our most important mission, one that will spill fire on our enemies and forever change the world. You men will be part of that mission, a strike at the heart of fanaticism in the world with a weapon the gods themselves didn't possess."

He glared intensely across the faces, and Inherp felt the man's eyes burn into him. Gunn turned and marched quickly up the stairs. Although Inherp felt a massive tension leave his body, the night had only just begun.

After the leaders had left the room, Inherp and the other young recruits assembled the crate again. As the wood began to cover the black monstrosity within, Inherp hung back from the others, using the crate's sides to partially shield himself from their view. In his hand he held a small metallic and plastic object, and he pointed it at the missile several times discreetly, finishing quickly and ensuring that he remained hidden from the other two soldiers. Finally, he pocketed the object and assisted in the final steps of securing the crate, boxing in the beast once more.

Afterward, he ascended and stood looking across the bow to the waves below. He felt sick inside and turned his face to the wind. Cool air swept across his face as the ship motored out to sea in the quiet of the night. He touched the cell phone in his pocket. It held information that the world had to see—and had to see soon. He knew that somehow, he had to live long enough to make sure that they did.

49

Savas entered the Operations Room. As always, there was an assault of visual information from the many monitors mounted on the walls—a strange FBI version of Times Square. J. P. Rideout called to him from across the room.

"John—we've got the specs on that plane and the initial analysis of the explosion. This came from the US Navy. They were right on the scene and recorded most of the useful data we've got on this." He called up several figures on one of the screens showing a large commercial jetliner, 747, and several incomprehensible schematics depicting the analysis of the blast.

"J. P., can you give me the Cliffs Notes version?"

"Yeah, sorry. I don't understand half this stuff myself. Bottom line—this was not an accident. A high-yield explosive device was employed, likely contained in the baggage compartment. How it got past security is anyone's guess. S-47 isn't easy to detect, but they wouldn't have needed anything so sophisticated to bring that plane down."

"Was there any wreckage recovered?"

"That's still ongoing. There will be some, but that Boeing was blown to bits. There appears to be some remains of the tail section, but it's deep now, and it will take at least another few weeks until the navy can get the necessary equipment out there—that is, if they aren't diverted to the Gulf."

Savas shook his head slowly. "Yeah. It's a magnet right now for large ships with men and guns. This whole thing is starting to reach critical mass over there."

Rideout looked up from his terminal. "You think this is going to lead to war?" Several heads swiveled over in their direction. It was a question on everyone's mind.

"Well, it doesn't look good, but I'm not the one to predict the choices of nations and armies. I sure as hell hope not. If it does, it won't be some little police action like Nam or Iraq—no offense to you guys, who saw blood spilled there. This is going to be something big, something where we can't even bring the bodies back. If Russia and China get involved, who knows where it will go. Mjolnir's wet dream."

Matt King piped up. "The mosque in Sudan—same MO. Same results from forensics. Your little visit didn't dissuade them from using S-47, or from anything else, it seems. There were riots again in Khartoum, and the American Embassy was firebombed. Molotov cocktails and the like. Luckily, we evacuated our people last week. It's definitely not a good time to travel with a US passport."

"Or to live near any Muslim holy site of any significance," said Savas.

Frank Miller nodded, wincing from the pain in his shoulder, his arm in a sling. "That sure as hell is true. The question is, where will they strike next? We've been banging our heads against this for months, but there's no rhyme or reason, no pattern."

Savas and Cohen exchanged glances. "No," Savas said. "Nothing. No structure, pattern, nothing we can get our hands on to predict and prepare."

"There's something . . ." Angel Lightfoote whispered as much to herself as to anyone in the room.

"Angel?" asked Savas. "You think you see something?"

Lightfoote stared forward, shaking her head. "There's always something."

He sighed. They remained in the dark, powerless, while a panther stalked the world—and stalked him and Cohen. They kept waiting for the hammer to fall.

Husaam Jordan stepped into the room and approached Savas. "John, we think that Gunn has left the country, probably for Mexico or somewhere in Central America."

"What?" William Gunn leaving the country, and not flying to a big bank in China or Europe, made Savas very uneasy. "Field agents last had him in New Orleans!"

"He lost them quite effectively, it seems. He's been using a number of decoys. Our contacts at the ports place a man who fits his description, as well as an unusual amount of activity, at a cargo ship several days ago. Right around that time, there was a shooting at the same port that occurred the night that ship left harbor. We've been able to track the numbers on the boat back to an old discarded model once used by Operon several years back."

"We need a better team down there," Savas said dejectedly. "You spooks are doing our job for us. OK, assuming that this is not a coincidence, why does that mean he's out of the country?"

"CIA contacts in Mexico, John. This boat docked several days after departure, south of the border. We've sent a team, and they will check it out, but I bet all traces of Mjolnir will be gone."

"Assuming he was on the boat, what the hell is he doing there?"

"Not vacationing," the Muslim said flatly.

PART 3
PILLARS OF ISLAM

50

That night Savas lay next to Cohen, unable to sleep. He glanced over at the clock—it was three in the morning. His mind was obsessively examining the scant data and unproven hypotheses that characterized the investigation. There had to be a pattern to the attacks, something that would help them understand their structure and purpose, and from that, to know where Mjolnir would strike again. Did any of this have to do with Gunn's departure for Mexico? Why would he leave in such a clandestine fashion? How would they unearth the evidence required to link him to these crimes?

He rolled over on his side. If he stayed like that too long, his back, battered during his days on the force, would cramp, but he needed to look at her. She slept peacefully, her lips slightly parted, a slow and soft rhythm to her breath hardly disturbing the quiet of the night.

A sudden sound broke the peace. His head darted toward the bedroom door. The sound was muffled, shielded from the bedroom by a hallway and several thin walls, but it was unmistakable. Several sudden and harsh spits, an intake of breath, and the soft thud of a body falling against the wall. *Outside.* He pulled off the blanket, jumped out of bed, and ran to the chest of drawers. He pulled out his handgun, checked the clip, and popped the safety. The moonlight shone through the windows, bathing his naked form in a silvery sheen. Every muscle was tensed, and he listened a moment without moving. *Click.* The bolt lock. Every nightmare he had had in the last month was coming alive before him.

He jumped back to the bed and shook Cohen. She stirred, opened her eyes, and was about to speak when he placed his hand over her mouth, holding his gun hand to his own with an outstretched finger over his lips. She snapped to an alert state, her eyes large, instinctively pulling the sheet closer. He shook his head, motioning to her not to speak and indicating that she should get down behind the bed. Cohen was an amazing FBI agent, but she was an analyst, not made for violence. Savas had seen plenty on the streets, especially during his early years at NYPD. But these were the trained assassins of Mjolnir, not common criminals. *I cannot lose her.*

The door crashed open with a thunderous noise, the drag chain snapping and flying across the living room. Savas dove through the bedroom door landing on his shoulder and side on the floor of the hallway. Absorbing the impact, he steadied his firearm and aimed in front of him.

He saw two dim shapes entering the apartment, weapons in their hands. *Two.* But he had the advantage of surprise.

He opened fire from his prone position at the closer of the two shapes; the other was still coming through the doorway. Three rapid shots from his pistol. The figure crumbled, let out a hoarse shout, and dropped to the ground firing wildly and shattering a mirror on the wall over the couch. Instinctively, Savas rolled right and into the bathroom, and a second later the wooden tile of the hallway exploded as several shots tore through the floor. He pulled his feet inside, stood up to steady himself, and prepared to dart out and fire on the second assailant.

It was unnecessary. His assailant found him.

Suddenly a dark shape appeared in the doorway. Savas swung his arm to divert the man's weapon hand, and several shots exploded against the tile of the bathtub. He brought his own gun forward, but the assailant was both fast and strong. Savas's wrist was pinned by the gunman's left hand and twisted backward so hard he cried out in pain and dropped his gun. The man brought his gun across his body as a bludgeoning weapon and struck Savas in the jaw, crashing his head into the wall. Partially stunned, yet running on the adrenaline of survival, Savas was able to bring his left arm down like a hammer, smashing the weapon out of the man's hand. The gun clanked heavily as it hit the floor tiles.

Cohen screamed his name. *No! Hide, hide, hide . . .* Savas felt the impact and deep swelling pain as the man crashed his knee into his testicles, and a flurry of fists impacted his abdomen and face, sending him crashing backward through the shower curtain and into the bathtub. His back was nicked by several broken shards of tile lying in the bottom, and he crumbled into the fetal position, wracked with pain. He watched helplessly as the man reached down, picked up his weapon, and aimed it at him. *Rebecca, run . . . please, run.* His vision blurred as he bordered on the edge of consciousness.

Two loud explosions shook him to alertness, and he felt a spray of blood as the chest of his assailant burst open, two bullets passing through his body and embedding themselves into the tile above the bathtub. The assassin fell to his knees with a heavy thud, then slowly pitched forward onto his face. The killer's body began to spasm. Savas gazed forward and saw another shape in the frame of the doorway, a man, arms outstretched and ending in a pistol.

"Agent Savas, sir?" came a young voice. "Are you OK?"

An hour later, Savas put down the phone and placed the ice pack back on his jaw. *Ice packs all over me*, he thought ruefully. Cohen sat across from him, her eyes bloodshot with dark circles under them. Her expression was pained. He could guess what it was like to look at him right now. At least the presence of all the FBI agents in the house should help calm her.

"It's OK. It's just not going to be pretty for a while."

"What did Larry say?" Her voice was nearly devoid of emotion. *Shock.*

Savas motioned to the door. "Well, the agents outside—it's the worst. Shot dead right next to the door. We were saved because Larry had another team downstairs. I didn't even know. They were monitoring everything. Apparently they had installed microphones around the place, as well as the communications equipment the two out in front were plugged into. They knew the second the hit took place and got their second team up here as fast as possible. I'm going to tell Larry that the basement is too damn far away for an effective response."

"Who were they?"

"You can guess," said Savas. "Prints are in the Armed Forces' database. Professionals. Who else could it be?"

Cohen nodded and pulled her robe around her. She looked cold, he thought. He just felt too awful to get up and move over to her. *Give me a minute, Rebecca.*

"Larry says we'll move to a safe house soon. You'll need to pack up. Maybe we should have done this earlier. After the cyber attack, they knew everything about us, including where we lived. Protecting the apartment was fine, but it wasn't enough. We need to hide out for a while, baby. These guys want us dead for real."

"John, if that man hadn't come in when he did . . ."

Savas finally did stand up. He drew a sharp breath. There are just places a man ought not to be hit. He took two steps and pivoted onto the couch next to Cohen. Glass shards from the mirror had been roughly cleared off, scattered across the Persian carpet she had bought only a month ago. He put his arm around her as her shoulders shook.

"It's OK, baby. We talked about this, remember? Don't think about what might have happened. I'm here. Hurting, but here." She looked over and smiled at him, and he brushed a tear from her eye. "But I think I'm going to have to remain celibate for at least a week."

She laughed softly at this. Savas kept up his charade of nonchalance and smiled back. He forced himself to remain motionless when he needed to shake. He kept his own tears to himself—as well as his thoughts. Inside, he shook with fear, fear that mere seconds had separated Cohen from death. He shook with the shame of the truth that he had failed to protect her. Only her presence next to him gave him any calm. *At least she is safe and will be safer soon.*

William Gunn walked outside a small airfield in Mexico. The runways were barely within the specifications he required, although they would not likely meet FAA approval for the laden cargo planes that were the predominant traffic. But safety was not his primary concern. The looser regulations and minimal scrutiny from any regulatory bodies made this the perfect location from which to work. The overgrown grass and its mesmerizing patterns blowing in the wind also gave it some modicum of charm as well. He spoke to the large man walking beside him.

"My main concern is the trail we are leaving. We were exposed with Operon, and we must be sure to end our reliance on former elements of Gunn International."

Patrick Rout nodded. "I understand, sir. It was extremely convenient in the beginning, but its exposure required the hard-to-anticipate breach of the arms network itself, which is something we will continue to have to rely on."

"I understand the rationale, but the CIA's efforts have shown us the flaw in that reliance, and we must make sure we are completely detached from any such elements in the future."

"Yes, sir."

"The use of the modified cargo plane?"

"We have recruited well. The engineers did a remarkable job in bringing significant stealth technology to the aircraft. I have seen it tested—in flight—and it works beautifully. It's too bulky to be invisible on radar, but the signal will be low. If they don't know precisely where to look, they won't see us."

Gunn paused and gazed out over the field of grass. They were so close, and everything had gone according to plan. The nations had reacted with even more panic and fervor than he had anticipated, practically ensuring complete chaos and war after this mission. The final phase of their grand plan was in motion. Soon the Western armies would once again flow into the Middle East, and the Hammer would strike the Arab nations soundly at their most sensitive point. A new era would begin. William Gunn needed to make sure nothing got in the way.

"Perhaps it is time to take a new tack in New York."

"Sir?"

"Our efforts have been unsuccessful."

Rout stiffened. "We are nearly ready to strike hard, Mr. Gunn, as planned. Changing the operation now, I believe, is a mistake."

Gunn shook his head. "I don't mean overall. I refer to Savas. He has proven very elusive. Perhaps a more indirect course is required."

"Indirect, sir?"

"We are fairly sure now that there is a relationship between him and the Cohen woman. Our recon supports this conclusion strongly."

"Yes, sir. She will be targeted for elimination."

"I believe this to be a mistake. With her death, we risk granting him tremendous motivating force. However, were we to take her alive, she would become a powerful deterrent to his continual involvement in their investigation."

"Perhaps."

Gunn remembered painfully the last time he had seen his wife. "I know something about the man. He will not wish to lose someone else in his life that he cares for. Bring her here."

"Yes, sir."

"Good. Precautions, no more. They are not close to us in any significant fashion. But they are the closest anyone has gotten. Very soon it will not matter what they or anyone else does. The world will be far busier trying to contain the spreading fire."

51

D r. Anthony Russell entered his office at 8:30 a.m., precisely. If asked, he would have said that he was a classic obsessive-compulsive personality, kept in check by therapy and occasional medication, and that such business was his own, thanks very much. Not a single item in the room could have been described as dusty, out of place, or in need of repair. The blinds had been cleaned for the third time that month only yesterday. The air filter systems were regularly replaced. The carpet needed looking at—he would see to that later today.

Whatever his idiosyncrasies, Dr. Russell was a highly respected figure in psychiatry at Fort Marshall, and, in fact, among all of Army medicine. His attention to detail was exactly what was required in observing patients, as well as in prescribing medications and monitoring their effects. But what made Dr. Russell truly stand out was that he just plain cared about US soldiers more than anyone else did.

In the early 1990s, he had begun several unique studies to examine the psychological trauma and syndromes afflicting veterans of the first Persian Gulf War. What he had learned there had been invaluable, if insufficient, for treatment of the far more terrible trauma soldiers faced after the Iraq War. A combination of multiple tours of duty, guerrilla warfare with terrorist tactics, and shoddy commitment to veteran care post-duty had left one of the most damaged generations of US military personnel since—well, since as long as he could remember, and that included Vietnam.

These things made Anthony Russell angry, but he was far too composed—some might say uptight—a person to ever voice such anger in a conventional manner. As the third generation of men in the Russell family to serve proudly, his loyalty to the military was absolute. That which he could not speak up about he sought to address through his work. This partially explained the mountain of effort, the numerous programs and studies for veterans that came from his initiative. He hoped in the end, he might make a difference.

He placed his briefcase in its precise location on the desk, wiped the computer screen with a dust cloth, and switched it on. First task in the morning was e-mail, and there was usually lots of it. He scrolled through the lists—so many invitations for speaking engagements, pharmaceutical company offers that he knew amounted to little more than bribes for their products, and the occasional penis enlargement advertisement that slipped through spam filters. *How creative they could be with spelling*, he thought.

Near the end of the list, an e-mail caught his eye. It took him several seconds to place the name and account—Michael Inherp. He had not heard from the boy since he had left therapy several years ago, simply disappearing, never giving explanation or motive or plans for his future. This had disturbed Dr. Russell. It was certainly a rash thing to do. Inherp had served two tours in Iraq, during which he had seen an IED turn his best friend inside out, stood by as a group of crazed soldiers sodomized a young Iraqi teen, and hidden his sexuality from the men around him who constituted his closest family during those traumatic periods. He was not accepted at home—gay men were still beaten in some parts of the country. All these things were very hard on a man who loved his country, who signed up to fight for it after 9/11. *Where was the boy now?*

He opened the e-mail and scanned the contents. As he read, his face constricted, his eyes squinting even behind his glasses, as if he wondered whether he was reading the text correctly. Finally, he took his glasses off and rested them precisely on his desk, rubbing his eyes. He stared out into the space of his office for several silent moments, recalling the text of the e-mail.

Dear Dr. Russell,

I don't have much time, and it is important that you believe me. Several years ago, I joined the organization known as Mjolnir. I know you have read about them. They promised me a chance to protect America in a way the Army could never do. They have been smart, not like what we've wasted our money and blood for in Iraq, sir. They want to destroy our enemies.

At first I believed, along with them. But something has happened that has changed that. It's important that you believe me. They are planning something terrible. They plan to use a stolen weapon, not conventional, in their next attack. I've seen it. It's real. I've attached photographs of the missile and the serial number.

Please, you have to believe me. Show this to Army Command. To someone. Anyone. I'll do what I can, but I'm only one person. They are serious. They will do this. I don't know where or when, but it's a Muslim target, like all the others.

You helped me when things were dark, and I'll always be thankful. I am sorry to have let you down. But this is more important than me.

Yours, M. Inherp

The photographs showed what indeed looked like a missile inside a large crate, followed by several close-ups of the serial number. *A nuclear weapon? Is he delusional?* His mind raced. Certainly a lost nuclear weapon would have been front-page news. It was impossible. The military had exacting standards, and the press would eat this up as the country and world went into a panic. *Maybe that's what they had intended to stop?* Could the US government hide something like this? It was beyond credibility.

It could be a delusional episode, he told himself, perhaps born from his deep conflict in loving and hating the military. That could have generated a fantasy that he was correcting the mistakes of the military, his need to join the terrorists to "complete" his mission, and his human side taking over in warning him. *Could he have faked the images?* Of course he could. It was easy in this day and age of image-editing software. *But not the serial numbers.* There was a way to address the veracity of his story. Russell shook his head. Dare he bring this up in a serious fashion to the army? Some dent it would make in his reputation if this turned out to be the hoax of a disturbed soldier.

"Michael, what in God's name has happened to you?"

52

Anthony Russell fingered the handle of his briefcase nervously. The secretary had told him the general had been on a very important conference call. Russell had no doubt of it, but the waiting was agonizing. He had known Lieutenant General Fred Marshall for twenty years. The general had become nearly a father figure to him, part of the community that had watched his career develop from a committed therapist to a full-blown researcher and advocate for combat veterans. Marshall was also instrumental in the progression of Russell's career, using his influence at various stages to secure funding and promotion through the ranks. He had on more than one occasion referred patients to him who had failed all other treatments. He had even gone so far as to solicit Russell's opinions and reviews of many of the army's pre-combat training procedures for soldiers, as well as for post-combat care. Russell drew a deep breath. The general had championed his causes, leading to many important changes in how the army handled the trauma of combat. There had been no way to repay him.

Today he felt at a loss for how to prepare for the scheduled meeting. In a few minutes, he would walk into the office next to him and try to make a case for a stray nuclear weapon, the existence of which had been provided by an admittedly mentally unsound former patient. Russell knew the general would hear him out, but he also knew that the general could only believe this was a hoax. *The US military lose a nuclear weapon?* It was unthinkable. And if the unthinkable had happened, it would not be a secret. They would have mounted the largest search imaginable. Russell could not defeat the logic either. All he had was his professional intuition developed over a span of several decades.

The door swung open, and the general ushered in the psychiatrist. Russell tried to put his emotions aside and focus on the issue at hand.

"General Marshall," Russell began formally.

"Anthony, it's good to see you again!" The general gave him a strong handshake and motioned him to sit.

Russell managed a smile. "I would agree, General. But, under the circumstances, I find myself mostly in an agitated state."

Marshall nodded and took a seat behind his desk. "I understand. Then let's get straight to business. Tell me what's going on again. To be honest, your phone call was a bit unsettling."

"I anticipated as much. But all I ask is that you hear me out. Not only for the potential seriousness of what I have told you, but for my years of service to the armed forces. I dared not take this to anyone else at this juncture. I needed someone I could trust."

Marshall nodded again while Russell continued. "I have told you about the e-mail I received and its contents. I have brought them here on a CD-ROM rather than e-mail them to you." Russell handed over a jewel case to the general. "I would rather not spread it beyond my own e-mail account for obvious reasons—that is both for patient confidentiality as well as the sensitivity of the contents. I have removed from the material contained on the CD any clear reference to the individual."

General Marshall stuck the disk into the tray of his computer. "I understand. So tell me, Anthony, you see this kid as sound enough mentally to trust these amazing statements?"

"Honestly, General, no. I do worry about his mental state. However, I must be clear. He had never evinced any sign of delusional psychosis. Moderate depression, anxiety, but nothing beyond that. I can't speak to what has happened over the last year, however. I have felt in a bind on this. My decision to come to you was based on our long relationship, so if this is a product of a troubled mind, no damage is done. However, if there is some truth to his incredible story, it would be too important not to try to look into it in some fashion."

"Yes, of course" the general mumbled, somewhat distracted as he examined the images on the disk. "Well, if it's a hoax, Anthony, the missile looks very convincing. Air Force cruise missile, aircraft mounted." He squinted at the screen. "Oh, now that is interesting. Like you said, we can read the serial numbers. Not too bright if he's making this up, I must say. Easy to verify, although. . . . That *is* very interesting," he trailed off, staring at the screen. After a moment he glanced toward Russell. "Anthony, please remind me where he served."

"Iraq. Infantry."

"He's never worked with weapons systems, missiles, conventional or nuclear?"

Russell shook his head. "No, not that I know of. He wasn't qualified. Why?"

The general looked back toward the screen and spoke. "This is *very* interesting. For a man who wasn't trained with such weapons, he seems to know a lot about serial number format. As someone who has, and whose memory is quite good, it appears to me that he has nailed the digit structure almost perfectly in this image."

Russell felt his stomach tighten. As much as he would hate to ruin his reputation, the alternative—that he was right—was even more frightening.

"He claims he is a member of this terrorist group, Mjolnir."

"Yes, so you mentioned." The general glanced once more at the computer screen, took off his glasses, and placed them on his desk. He turned again to Russell, his expression serious. "I think I need to make some phone calls."

Russell replied stiffly, a chill running through his body. "Yes, sir."

53

Blake Morrison walked out to the mailbox and opened it. *The usual*, he thought: several bills, a pile of catalogs seeking to burst the box, and an assortment of random junk mail. The sun arced over the surrounding hills on its way downward, half-concealed in clouds and throwing off bright beams of light alternating with shade to create a complicated woven pattern in the dimming sky. *Sunshine.* Something he might be able to enjoy if he weren't working so damn hard writing code all day long.

A gray VW Jetta pulled up the street and came to a stop in the driveway across from his house. *The Agent. Everyone on the block knew The Agent*, he thought with some annoyance. How anyone came to know he worked for the FBI had been forgotten, but everyone knew. The man didn't deny it if asked, but he didn't offer much either. *Keeps to himself*, would be the nicer way to put things. Morrison preferred *arrogant* and *aloof*. The man never participated in block or neighborhood activities, rarely spoke with his neighbors. Always seemed to have important things to do, more important than the ordinary Joes he lived around. Morrison had spent a lot of time speculating on just what his neighbor did for a living. He had spent even more time speculating on what he did in his home. He never once had seen a woman go in or come out of that house. He had on occasion seen men. For Blake Morrison, that was enough. *Damn pervert's a homosexual*, he told himself for the fiftieth time as he closed the mailbox. He watched The Agent step out of the Jetta, grab his briefcase, close the door, and try to avoid eye contact with him. *What do you have to hide, Agent Man?*

Morrison shook his head and turned back around. If there was one thing he couldn't abide, it was those homosexuals. Invading all decent neighborhoods, television, schools, forcing their morals on the rest of America. He walked slowly back toward his house, looking over the Victoria's Secret catalog addressed to his wife.

His next sensation was of flying and darkness. When he regained consciousness, it was with the taste of hard concrete in his mouth. He opened his eyes and saw that he was facedown on his sidewalk, perhaps ten feet from his porch. A strange crackling sound seemed to fill the air behind him, and the ringing of numerous car alarms invaded his consciousness. Or were those screams?

He stumbled to his feet, blood covering his face, the left side of his head numb and feeling swollen. His left arm hurt. Yes, those were definitely screams. He turned around slowly and had trouble interpreting what he saw. Across the street, where a small ranch-style home had once stood, there was a raging fire. Smoke billowed into the air, and debris littered the weed-covered lawn, apparently raining down as far as his own manicured front yard. The VW Jetta was a shell, as if it, too, had been blown apart by some incredible force. People were pouring out of their homes, some screaming, some speaking on cell phones, many looking bewildered and shocked. He suddenly realized that he must have been one of them.

"Blake, what the *hell* is going on?"

He turned around and saw his wife standing in the doorway, her initial expression of confusion replaced by one of shock. He simply stared at her.

"Blake? What happened to you? My *God*, is that Mr. Kanter's *house*?"

Morrison said nothing, turning around slowly to look at the burning remains. The Agent. Fire. There was no way anyone was coming out of that alive.

Mira Vujanac got off the bus and walked briskly up the street toward a small brownstone. The light had dimmed fast in the city once the sun had gotten behind the buildings, and Vujanac hated to be outside at night. Twenty years ago, when the city was much less safe, she had been mugged and raped at knifepoint near the park. Despite years of therapy and more money than it cost to send her children to college, she had never been freed of the fear of walking the streets after dark. She clutched her bag as every stranger passed by, focused almost maniacally on the small black gate that protected the tiny space in front of her door. *Still plenty of light*, she reminded herself and yet accelerated her pace.

Suddenly, a dark shape appeared from one of the stairways on her right. Mira reacted instinctively, her past attack having given her a heightened sense of threat, so that she identified the hostile intent in the movements before she was even conscious of it. She reached into her bag and pulled out her mace spray, turned and aimed as she had been taught in her self-defense classes, and sprayed.

The man was too fast. He had anticipated her movement and, with his left arm, swatted away her right, knocking the can of mace from her hand. With his right, he brought up a dark object, a gun with a long and large barrel. *Oh, God, not again.*

Angel Lightfoote walked along the bridge in Central Park, looking down and watching the slow passing of autumn leaves floating on the murky waters of the pond. She passed the couples strolling by holding hands, wrapped in fall jackets, and shielding their faces from the strong wind. Many stopped to stare at her: a waterfall of orange hair, long white dress down to her bare feet, and no jacket. She didn't mind, even if she did notice. There were more important things.

Lightfoote sighed, staring at the trees of the park, leaves turning, soon to become silent skeletons. Winter was a dark time for her, and she dreaded the sleeping of the plants and the sense that life was frozen, stilled, and hidden from view. In that winter bleakness, the concrete of the city no longer seemed so sterile. In fact, she might even prefer it to living things that had been silenced by the cold.

She turned to leave, to return home before the night fell. She began to walk but stopped suddenly. She cocked her head to one side and

stared, as if listening intently. *The animals are quiet*, she thought. Lightfoote had always been able to hear things, see things, sense things that
seemed unavailable to everyone else around her. She had struggled as a
child, not realizing that those things she knew effortlessly were invisible to others, and that she had to be careful to pretend not to notice
them or risk alienating other people with her strangeness. Joining the
FBI, she had found for the first time a usefulness for her strange sensitivity. She didn't fool herself—everyone still thought of her as *different* and kept a certain cautious distance. But for them, she was at
least *useful* on many occasions, when she was able to intuit or connect
facts to answers that others could not.

Something is wrong. She felt it in the air flowing over her, in the
strange silence from the living heartbeats she sensed around her. *They
are afraid.* Lightfoote realized that she, too, was afraid, and that she was
beginning to feel the source of the others' fear. Something close, something hostile, something *murderous* approached. With growing panic,
Lightfoote finally began to realize that it was seeking her.

She spun in several directions, trying to see what this thing was and
from where it approached. But the bridge and surrounding region were
empty, save the scattering leaves and the sound of wind.

Run, Angel. Run.

A voice spoke intently in her mind. All her body felt the urge to
flee, and in a single instant, she gave way and raced down the bridge
toward the park exit. At that moment, wood splintered from behind
her and the voice called out harshly. *You cannot run away.*

Angel ran faster. Her white dress flowed out from her body as
she raced, pieces of wood exploding inches behind her. She leapt onto
the broad handrailing of the bridge and dove through the air. She felt
weightless as she drifted down like a white leaf on the wind and plunged
into the green mass of water below.

The phone calls kept rolling in. John Savas sat in his office, shocked and
disbelieving. Across from him, Cohen sat in a chair weeping, nearly
hysterical and overcome with grief. As he put down the receiver, he

brought his hand to his forehead and squeezed, a headache pounding, crushing him like a vice. Unbidden, his mind scrolled through the names: *Larry, Mira, Matt . . . Manuel*. All confirmed killed, *murdered*, one call after another bringing in horrific news, inducing nauseous baths of emotion and shock. The FBI was scrambling to locate the remaining agents of Kanter's division and the parallel division chiefs. It was a nightmare of proportions he had never imagined.

"That was Morgan from Johnson's division. Manuel was found burned alive inside his car on I-80."

"*Oh, God!*" Cohen burst out sobbing, anger and despair haunting her face. "Please, John, it has to stop. *Please.*"

Savas didn't care anymore who saw them together. He walked over and reached around the chair back to hold her. Everything they knew was collapsing around them.

"What are we going to do?" she asked, burying her head in his shoulder.

"I don't know, Rebecca. I don't know. These guys are real monsters. They're ripping open our bellies today."

The door pushed open slowly, and they stared in shock at the stained and soaked white dress that draped the body of Angel Lightfoote. She smelled of a swamp, and greens and browns polluted the once bright colors of her dress. Her long hair was matted and snarled, hanging in tangled clumps from her head. Her hands were bloodied and bruised, as if they had suffered some blunt-force trauma. But she was alive.

Cohen leapt up, nearly knocking Savas over as she ran to embrace Lightfoote. "Angel, Angel, Angel!" she cried holding the battered woman in her arms. She pulled back and stared into her face, tears on her cheeks.

Lightfoote smiled faintly. "Hi, Rebecca."

Savas stood and walked over to the two women. "Angel—my God, what happened?"

Lightfoote cocked her head to one side and seemed to look out into the distance. "Evil," she said simply. "Something evil wanted to kill me. It shot at me. I dove into the water and banged on a rock. I didn't get up until I had swum far enough away."

Cohen stared mournfully at Lightfoote. "Angel, it's been horrible, everyone . . ."

"Is dead," finished Lightfoote. Her expression didn't change.

"We don't know that!" Savas interrupted. "We have numerous . . . confirmed deaths, Angel. The entire department is being decimated. Larry's dead—killed by a bomb at his house. Several heads of other divisions that have been involved in the case. For us, Matt and Manuel. There are reports that both my apartment and Rebecca's were broken into. Frank managed to overcome his assailant, who fled. J. P. is only alive because some drunk teen plowed into his car in the early morning, setting off the bomb underneath. We don't have any word about other targets."

"Two, at least, in CIA," rolled the booming voice of Husaam Jordan as he entered the room. He had a bruised face and an ice pack on his right eye. A fire burned in his left.

Cohen put her arm on his shoulder. "Husaam—my God. You're hurt."

"You should have seen the other guy," he said grimly. "Actually, I would not recommend that. They're fishing him out of the East River as we speak."

Savas stepped toward the CIA agent. "They have targeted CIA? How?"

"There must have been enough unsecured information in the bowels of FBI computing connecting our groups. Many at the CIA felt it was a mistake to enter into these collaborations. I don't think even the worst critics could have anticipated how deadly a mistake it would be."

He stared intently at Savas. "John, the time has come to move, and move quickly against Gunn. I don't care how we try to sell it, but this should give us the ammunition we need."

Savas shook his head. "Husaam, I'm sure we can make a strong enough case that Mjolnir is behind all this to convince anyone. But we have nothing, nothing at all directly linking Gunn. Now he's out of the country. We have no reliable information where he is!"

"A warrant to search his office, his house, anything."

"That takes time."

Jordan scowled. "As you see, time is running out."

"Yes, sir. That's affirmative, sir." Air Force colonel Jim Cranston nodded vigorously, staring at his computer screen. "Only those two—General Marshall and an army doctor named Russell. We've punted this up to State, and they are moving now to bring those two in for control of this situation. It is understood that all information flow outside of approved channels must be stemmed."

A voice on the other end of the line spoke rapidly, high tension in the voice. Cranston responded. "I can't answer that one, sir. I know the general consensus is that we need to open this up to other agencies, and now with the possibility that it's in the hands of a terrorist organization—*this* terrorist organization, in particular—I think that voice will become nearly unanimous."

The colonel listened intently and nodded. "I believe that is true. But it will be beyond our influence at that point. I think they will judge the possibility of leaks a necessary risk. You know my long-standing position on this. I think it's been a grave mistake from the beginning to keep this buried."

The voice on the other end spoke again, and Cranston shook his head. "No, sir. It's a perfect match. There are no doubts. Serial numbers, make, appearance. 'Dial-a-yield,' five to one hundred and fifty kilotons. A blast up to ten Hiroshimas. It's our broken arrow, sir. In the hands of the devil's minions."

He spoke for several more minutes and hung up the phone, running his hand across his nearly bald head. He stared in front of him. His computer screen displayed the washed-out image taken from the cell phone of Michael Inherp, the long metallic tube of the missile dominating the screen, the numbers printed on its surface: small yet clear. The colonel stood up and walked to his window, staring into the night.

God help us.

54

Three dark shapes rested against the glass like spiders on a wall. Gunn Tower rose mercilessly into the Manhattan sky, the spider shapes dwarfed and vulnerable beside its might.

Jordan released his grip on a suction cup and removed a small disklike object about the size of a Frisbee from his belt. The suction cup remained firmly fastened to the glass, and he placed the device against the building to the right of him. A bright light shone as sparks flew, and within seconds, an ellipse could be seen in the once perfect glass surface. He leaned over, breathing heavily from the exertion, and pounded on the circle. After two strikes, the glass broke inward, leaving a hole in the building. This action was repeated several times as his men repositioned themselves around the growing hole in the glass surface. Finally, Jordan scaled with the suction cups to the metal above the hole and attached a much larger cup into which a secured rope had been fitted. The rope dangled down beside the hole. He grasped it tightly and swung himself inside.

He landed inside a dark office, followed quickly by the rest of his team. He spoke in hushed tones to the others. "We are on the fourth floor, east side of the building. A stairway is around the corner outside this room. It will take us to the floor we are looking for."

He walked to the door. Although it was locked from the outside, it was simple to open from within. Around the corner they found the stairwell and began a long assent, punctuated by intervals of deactivating security cams. Their labored breathing echoed as they passed more than forty floors. Jordan's legs burned from the lactic acid buildup, and he limped slightly as they progressed, the wounds from

Sharjah not completely erased. After forty floors, they felt as if their hearts would explode in their chests. Finally, he halted at the fiftieth floor. For a moment they each caught their breath, their legs shaking, sweat pouring down their faces behind the ski masks.

"We'll pause a minute," said Jordan. "I'm sorry we couldn't take the elevators. They require keycard access and have video monitors. The office is down the hall."

They walked stiffly but silently through the floor, stopping at an elaborate wooden door. It, too, was locked, and the men spent several minutes closely examining the door and its frame.

"Look carefully," said Jordan. "We don't want to trigger any alarms."

Finally, one of the men motioned the other two toward the bottom of the door. Using tools from his belt, he dug around the frame and into the drywall, eventually freeing several wires.

"Good work. Let's deactivate this."

Jordan examined the wires and cut one of them. Satisfied, he nodded to the others who picked the lock on the door. Inside was an enormous office, and at the far end, along a wall of glass, an oversized desk with a large flat-screen computer monitor on its center. Jordan approached the monitor and knelt down, removing a computer tower from underneath the desk.

He unplugged the computer from the power supply and quickly removed the screws in the case, lifting it and placing it to the side. The motherboard and graphics card glinted in the moonlight streaming in through the windows. He motioned to the other two.

"Search the room, photograph anything you can't take, search the files. We need to be out of here in an hour."

The other two responded quickly and circulated throughout the room, examining desk drawers, closets, filing cabinets, and looking behind and under every object. Jordan meanwhile bent over the computer and got to work.

He grounded himself with a wrist strap to the chassis and reached around to disconnect the computer data ribbon from the hard drive. With a screwdriver, he removed it from the metal rails and set it on the desk. He reached into his backpack and removed a device that had its own data ribbon connected to what looked like another hard drive. He connected the hard drive to the device, and the device to AC power. Immediately, a red light went on, and the sounds of drive access could be heard. He then joined the other two men in sweeping the room.

Fifty minutes later, the device on the desk went from red to green, and he walked over and disconnected it. Reversing the previous procedure, he reinstalled the hard drive and closed up the computer, replacing it under the desk. He stuffed the items back inside the pack and shouldered it, stepping from behind the desk and toward the door. He motioned for the other two to follow him.

One of the men gestured to the door. "They'll know we were here."

Jordan smiled. "After the window damage we did, there is no avoiding that. But we got what we came for. Let's hope it leads us somewhere."

"We were never with you on this one, Husaam."

"I'm a lone wolf. Besides, who would be foolish enough to come?"

55

Cohen stared blankly at the rush hour traffic. The black limo carrying her home was just one more of thousands of cars trapped in a giant parking lot called midtown Manhattan. The driver had discussed with her bodyguard whether to put on the flashing lights, but they had both laughed, realizing that in the current gridlock, they weren't going anywhere no matter what they did. She glanced over at the man assigned to guard her life. Who was he? Did he take seriously the task and risk placed in front of him? Could he really understand the ruthlessness of the organization that sought her life?

The guard traded macho banter with the driver, also an armed bodyguard. Cohen did not really feel safe with these two men, so confident in their prowess, so unappreciative of the true risk she felt every moment. It had only been a week since the horror had descended on her life. Mjolnir had sent its assassins into their lives and had brutally taken people she had known and worked with, had come to care for and support, for so many years. She fought back the tears as she thought of each one, murdered so cruelly and coldly, only because they dared to try to investigate these killers.

Larry Kanter had died in his home. Matt King died quickly, a bullet to the head. Mira was never to share another crazy story from her days as a child in a Serbian village. Or Manuel. Sweet, clumsy Manuel. If he had been securing *all* the FBI's computers, they would never have found his name, his place of residence, or known where to place the bomb that incinerated him inside his car.

Kanter's superiors had insisted on round-the-clock security now, and no one in the division could travel together in order to prevent multiple fatalities from a single attack. The coldness of the logic was unsettling. She hated being separated from John in this way. More than anything, she needed to be with him everywhere now. FBI agents in the movies were like police officers—always ready to tumble with the bad guys. The truth was, many were just like her—analysts, smart, book-worms, and not expected to encounter violence, despite the general training they received at the academy. The last week had stunned her, shaken her life apart. Even the power of the FBI could not shield her from those who hunted them.

Suddenly, the driver's side window exploded. Blood and glass shards sprayed across the front seat as the driver's head ruptured, snap-ping to one side, then crashing on the steering wheel and causing the horn to blare continuously. The car lurched forward and crashed softly into the cab in front of them, eliciting a set of expletives audible within the limo.

Cohen screamed. The agent next to her drew his gun and opened the door in a quick motion, stepping outside and raising the weapon. Cohen watched in horror as his gun arm was pinned against the roof while a foot kicked him across the face. Several shots were fired into his frame, his body convulsing and dropping to the ground.

She pulled back against the door next to her, as far away from the driver's side and open door as possible. Suddenly, her door opened from behind her, and she fell out onto the road. Around her, people were screaming and running from the scene. She felt the barrel of a gun against her temple as a firm hand held her by the hair. She closed her eyes and prepared to die.

"If you wish to live, say nothing, do nothing but what we tell you. Do you understand?" an emotionless male voice spoke into her ear.

Cohen opened her eyes and nodded. It didn't make sense, but he had not pulled the trigger. She was still alive. She planned to do what-ever she had to in order to stay that way.

"Then get up and move with me to that alley. Quickly!" Cohen saw the gun gesture toward a dim alleyway on the left side of the street. She got to her feet and walked quickly with the man at her side. She dared not look at him nor at the other men busy around the car. The man walking with her kept his gun in his hand but lowered it, keeping it as hidden from view as possible.

As she stepped on the pavement, a muscular man blocked their way and shoved the man walking beside her to a stop. He had come out of a shop, a bag in one hand, not yet understanding what was transpiring around them. He had noticed Cohen and the forceful treatment she was receiving. A knight in shining armor.

"Hey, buddy, what the hell's going on here? You giving this lady trouble?" Cohen closed her eyes. Several shots rang out, and she felt a push. She opened her eyes to keep from falling over the prone figure that had just dropped to the sidewalk. More screams erupted from the street behind her. *Please, God, help me.*

As they entered the alley, the man pressed her hard until she was practically running to the other side. They passed by trash bins and refuse, discarded machinery, and many things she had no chance to process. Within a minute, they exited into the sunlight again, and the man waved her over to a beat-up white van. The back doors swung open as two men jumped out, dressed in utility workers' uniforms. They led her quickly into the van as the man who had dragged her this far spoke into a mouthpiece and surveyed the area. Suddenly a loud explosion from down the alley rocked the block, and pedestrians turned toward the sound in shock. Many raced over to the alley or down parallel streets to find out what had happened. As the doors closed and Cohen was left imprisoned within the walls of the van, she understood. There would be no one to see her pushed into the van, no one to follow them from the events a few moments ago. The men she had seen around the car had rigged it to blow, and the explosion, death, and chaos would make it simple for her abductors to make a clean escape.

The doors opened again, and the man entered. She saw him clearly now, a young man with a military haircut, blond, dressed in nondescript clothing. He carried with him rope and duct tape. The sounds of sirens and screams filled the air outside the van.

"Don't make a sound and you'll live," he said as he bound her hands behind her and tied her feet together. Tears trailed down her cheeks as he affixed the tape over her mouth and pushed her onto her back on the padded floor. The van lurched forward into the streets of New York.

John, please, help me . . .

56

Jordan was bleary-eyed from hunting through thousands of files—text files, e-mails, log files—trying to glean some hint of Gunn's whereabouts from the rip of his hard drive. He had probably ended his career last night by breaking into Gunn's office, but the time for niceties had passed.

He had wondered whether the man was so secretive that he left nothing behind, no trace, even on a computer that he must have assumed was utterly safe from prying eyes. On more than one occasion, he wished he had Manuel Hernandez from the Savas group with him now—that man knew a thing or two about computers. But William Gunn had seen to it that Hernandez and many others would never be walking the earth again.

In the end, the sleepless night had been worth it. Gunn had not been careful enough to delete from the disk all records of his activities. Jordan gazed at the failing afternoon light with a mixed feeling of dizziness from lack of sleep and elation. Now he knew where that bastard was. What he was doing in Mexico was still a mystery, but the secrecy of his trip and the ruthlessness with which he had sought to crush the investigation told Jordan that this was not an idle excursion. It had purpose written all over it. Where Mjolnir had a strong purpose, there was death waiting.

He swirled the coffee around in his cup but decided he'd had enough caffeine and cold bitterness for one night. He glanced over toward the bedroom door. Vonessa was asleep, exhausted from several days of caring for two sick boys. His grip tightened over the mug. Some would say he was a negligent father for taking the risks he did.

Part of him agreed with them. But another part could not back down from what he felt was his responsibility to the world, to all families, to himself. There were times that demanded risk and sacrifice for the greater good. This was one of those times. He knew what he had to do.

There was little point in going through the motions. After what had happened, the conservatives in the organizations would descend, locking up any fruitful or bold action, giving Gunn too much time. No doubt this was part of the CEO's plans. *Well, my friend, you have a surprise coming.* Jordan was tired of reacting. Time to bring the fight to Gunn.

He opened his laptop and entered the password. He called up a website and entered in the information. Soon he had purchased a round-trip ticket to Mexico. He had some packing to do and arrangements to make once he was south of the border. Most of those plans involved acquiring weapons. He looked back toward the door. He'd call Vonessa's mother to come over. He'd apologize. He'd make it up to them when he got back.

57

Savas looked across the faces sitting around the table. In part, it was a painful exercise. So many faces he was used to seeing at such meetings were not there. Everyone else had been assigned separately to safe houses under FBI protection under orders from Andrew Bryant, the acting head of Kanter's division, until further notice. Things had become confusing—superiors from both the FBI and the CIA were present. Organization, especially at the FBI, had been disrupted, and the hierarchy was clearly in flux, all parties uncomfortable and unsure how to proceed. But most significantly, the presence of high-ranking officers from the air force gave a certain gravity and sense of expectation to the meeting. Something was happening, beyond the mess of the last few weeks. Savas waited and observed.

"We want to thank our colleagues from the CIA and the air force for being here today," began Bryant. "As you will soon find out, they have some pretty serious things to tell us about."

Bryant cleared his throat and gazed around the room. He hardly knew these people. He knew he was not ready to deliver this news. "I won't try to sugarcoat anything for you. We've been through fire since this entire investigation began. We've watched some damn good agents die, and we've worked our asses off to get to the core of this case that is part of something so big it's shaking up the world. What I'm here to tell you now, what these representatives from the air force are here to tell you now, is that it's all about to get a good bit worse." He gestured toward the military men. "Gentlemen?"

The two officers sat together at one end of the table. They were in full uniform, *dress uniform*, Savas noted. They had a set of folders in front of them but spoke without consulting the papers within them. One of the men began to speak, and what he said chilled Savas to the bone.

"Thank you, Agent Bryant. We haven't had time to get to know all your staff, but what we have to say must be said quickly, and we are needed back at our headquarters to continue our end of the investigation. We will be available to any of you at any time to work together on this." The man looked over his audience and continued. "In August of last year, a highly irregular event took place at an air force base in North Dakota. Several cruise missiles were loaded on a plane scheduled to fly to Louisiana. That is a common event, transferring weapons between air force bases. On this day, however, several critical protocols were not followed, and airmen unintentionally loaded cruise missiles with nuclear payload."

Several murmurs broke out around the table as FBI and CIA agents glanced at each other and back toward the officers. "Please," interjected the air force man, "let me continue. I will answer questions afterward." He exhaled slowly. "For a period of thirty-six hours, these missiles were not reported as missing and were not secured, as is customary for nuclear weapons. Some of you may remember a press conference last year about the incident."

"Sure," said Savas. "Fumbling with nukes makes me pay attention. But they said that the weapons had been accounted for, never left the hands of US airmen."

There was an uncomfortable silence. The soldier continued tensely. "That statement was not factual."

Frank Miller sat forward suddenly. He had made a significant recovery since the shooting, but the damage to his shoulder had left him with a reduced range of motion, as well as a residual pain that was constantly with him. Miller in a gruff mood was not a pleasant thing. "Not *factual*? You mean a lie? Don't tell me that these missiles took a walk."

The air force man looked Miller directly in the eye. "That's exactly what I'm here to tell you."

Miller exhaled. "*Jesus.*"

"A decision was made to keep this information top secret, and, until recently, even our team investigating the incident was kept ignorant of this fact." The soldier glared around the room, revealing a poorly concealed anger concerning the events described. "The operative term is *missile*, in point of fact. Singular. One cruise missile was unaccounted for."

Savas felt nauseous. "And let me guess, or you wouldn't be here: those devils at Mjolnir have it?"

The military man glanced uncomfortably around the table. "Yes, it appears that is indeed the case. Major Rivers, would you like to take it from here?"

Miller practically exploded. "Hold on a minute! Let me get this straight. Whoever was ghosting this scandal, it never occurred to them over the last six months since Mjolnir began blowing things up that, *just maybe*, last year's fuck-up was their snatch?"

Major Rivers pursed his lips. "There were months of chaos and confusion over those bombings. The organization did not reveal itself until very recently, perhaps for this purpose, to prevent such speculation."

Miller continued. "Don't make excuses for them! Come on—even if these guys are not the sharpest tools in the shed, somebody must have thought about the unthinkable."

"I don't know," said Rivers. "*Honestly.* I simply don't know what was going on above."

Bryant waved his hands and spoke over a growing din. "Look, let's stay focused. We *need* this information, people. Major Rivers, please, the connection to Mjolnir?"

Rivers nodded. "Recently, we received a tip from a former US Army soldier. He contacted an army psychiatrist claiming to have photographs of the missile. He forwarded these images to him."

Savas couldn't help himself. "How in the hell did he get those?"

Major Rivers continued. "This soldier had joined Mjolnir and recently has had second thoughts."

"An attack of conscience?" said Miller sarcastically.

"Apparently so," said Rivers. "The serial numbers were verified with the air force, and we know that it's our weapon. That is where we stand right now."

Miller leaned forward. "Surely you have tracked this man, know where the weapon is?"

The major shook his head. "There has been no further contact with the source. We have sent e-mail messages, but he has not replied."

"*E-mail?*" asked Rideout incredulously.

"OK, let's back off, folks," offered Bryant. "They are here to work with us on this."

Rideout ignored him. "We have a loose nuke in the hands of the most vicious terrorist group in history, and these chumps are trying to find it by *e-mailing* someone? In case these fine gentlemen from the air force haven't been briefed, Mjolnir has killed half of our division here at the FBI! Do you realize that for these guys to have taken a nuke, we will have an event like we've never seen in world terrorist activity? In the midst of the chaos spreading already? *E-mail?*"

Major Rivers shot back. "That is all the information we have! We have top men working on this problem as we speak. We will find this man, and he will lead us to Mjolnir and the bomb. We hope that you can aid in this search. We are turning to your agency to help find him. His name is Inherp. Michael R. Inherp. In these folders, we have his bio and contact information." He looked over at Rideout, who just shook his head. "These are serious times. We all need to work together."

Top men? Savas hung his head. He had been ready for something bad, but this was worse than his worst nightmare. The horror of the possibilities shook him. He missed Cohen more than ever at that moment. He cursed the new security protocols that the FBI had forced on them. Randomized schedules for arrivals and departures. Restrictions on traveling together. *To prevent multiple hits.* If the worst happened, he'd rather be with her and share her fate. Savas blocked such thoughts from his mind. He couldn't wait to see her again.

58

Savas returned to the Operations Room and sat alone in front of a computer screen. He wasn't sure where to go now with this investigation, one that had grown so large, so deadly, so *insane* that he wondered how it could ever move forward now. At least the air force had provided them with fairly complete information. *Or so it seemed.* Savas had to check himself and remember that this was the group that had kept a missing nuke a secret from the entire country. He stared at the e-mail from Michael Inherp, looked over the images again and again. *What am I missing?*

Nothing in the photo seemed to give any indication where the missile might be located. No hint in the e-mail. Why would this kid send this information and not explain how to get there and stop these madmen? Was he taking them on a false lead? The serial numbers checked out. The missile was real. He wouldn't have revealed that unless he was serious. *Perhaps he can't send any more messages because he's been caught.* That last thought worried Savas the most. If Inherp were discovered, he would be dead, and so would be their only link to Mjolnir.

Savas rubbed his eyes and stretched. A sound from behind him made him turn around, just in time to see the approaching form of Frank Miller. The former marine looked unusually haggard.

"Hell of a day, Frank," he said, smiling. His smile faded as he read the expression on Miller's face.

"John, Rebecca never showed at the safe house. Her car was found on Madison and Sixty-Eighth." Savas felt a numbing cold creeping over his body as his stomach tightened. "A bomb. The blast was enormous, killing over forty people in the immediate vicinity. We don't believe that there could be any survivors in the car."

It was as if a blade sliced mercilessly from his neck to his belly, and he felt his intestines spill out over the ground in front of him. He couldn't breathe. His vision began to cloud.

"John!" Miller caught him as he sank to his knees. "John, God, I'm sorry. I understand. We all knew, John. About Rebecca. We all were happy for you two. God, John, I'm so sorry."

The large marine held him in a bear hug, then sat him on the desk. Savas began to feel himself dissociate from his body. *This is not real. Nothing is real.* At that moment, he knew only that he wished to be no more.

The phone on the desk rang. Frank Miller looked from the phone to Savas, unsure what to do. Deciding that he didn't know what to do with Savas anyway, he reached over and picked up the phone. "FBI. Miller speaking."

Miller's face turned white. "John, it's for you. They say they have Rebecca."

Savas felt like a sailor tossed about on a ship in a storm. His stomach was sick as his emotions spun another one hundred and eighty degrees. A surge of adrenaline rushed through him, and he grabbed the phone from Miller.

"John Savas," he spoke hoarsely into the line.

"Agent Savas, Rebecca Cohen's life rests in our hands. You will not trace this call. You will stop pursuing your investigation of Mjolnir. If you wish to spare her a most horrible and degrading death, you will walk out of your office tonight and not return. Do these things, Agent Savas, and you will see her intact once again. She will be under the eye of one who is bringing a new order to the world, and you have his promise. We are watching."

The phone line went dead.

"*You bastards!*" he cried out and threw the phone and receiver across the room. First they let him think he had lost all that was left in life of love and companionship. Now they were forcing him to choose between his heart's commitment to his son, to every life stolen by terrorism, and the life of the woman he had surrendered his heart to.

Choose his commitment to justice or the woman he loved. He felt torn into two pieces, each horn of the dilemma impaling him in agony.

A phone rang on a nearby desk. Miller stared at it and at Savas, who leapt forward and grabbed the receiver off the handset. "Don't you hurt her! Or I swear I'll spend the rest of my life hunting you down until I drive you into the flames of *hell*!"

There was a long silence on the other end of the line. Finally, a deep voice spoke.

"John? This is Husaam. Please, you must listen to me."

59

Savas's mind morphed from crazed anger to confusion. Slowly he sat down and stared forward blankly. "Husaam?"

Miller raced over to another desk and picked up the phone. "Agent Jordan? This is Frank Miller with the FBI. John Savas is also on the line."

"Is John OK?"

"We've had a shock. Rebecca Cohen has been kidnapped, her car found incinerated by a bomb. There has been no contact with her or her bodyguards."

Savas interrupted, his mind raw but focusing. Hearing the Muslim's voice had brought him back. "Husaam, Mjolnir contacted us by phone—they say they have Rebecca. I haven't spoken to her to . . . confirm, but I believe them. They have her, and they want to shut me and my investigation down. If I don't, they will kill her."

Jordan rumbled on the other end. "You can't do that."

"I'm in a pretty tough place right now, Husaam. I can't let them kill her."

"John, I have to tell you something," Jordan began.

"Wait," interrupted Savas. "It can wait. You need to hear this. Things are far worse than we ever feared." He sat up straight in the chair. There was no way to explain the insanity. He would just say it. "Tonight we learned from the air force representatives that Mjolnir has acquired a nuclear weapon."

The silence lasted nearly ten seconds. "Husaam?"

"How did they get this? How does the air force know?"

Savas nearly laughed at the absurdity of it all. "It's one of *ours*. One of our own damned weapons. Somehow the air force screwed up and didn't secure some cruise missiles."

"Cruise missiles?"

"Yes, only one was lost in the end but with a payload of ten times the bomb that hit Hiroshima. I suppose that's enough," Savas continued. "They've buried this from everyone, if you can believe it."

Jordan practically growled. "I can. How did they find it?"

"They didn't. Some kid, a former US Army soldier, sent in photos with the serial number. He joined Mjolnir several years ago, but I guess this caper was more than he could stomach. But he hasn't returned any attempts at contact. We know the missile is out there, that it's ours, that it's real. We know Mjolnir has it. But we have no idea where or what they are planning and when."

Jordan grunted. "Well, I can't answer the last two, but I know where they are, John. That's why I'm calling. Check your e-mail. You'll find the location. Bit south of the border."

Savas checked e-mail on his cell. "Tampico, Mexico? What the hell is there?"

"Humid summers, petroleum, and General Francisco Javier Mina International Airport, or, more relevantly, some of the subsidiary airfields for cargo planes. Most importantly, that is where William Gunn is right now."

Savas looked over at Frank Miller and shook his head, perplexed. "Husaam, how do you know this?"

The Muslim laughed deeply. "Broke into his office, John. Copied his hard drive. Gunn left that security hole, although I can't blame him for missing it." His voice turned serious. "From what you've told me, something terrible is being planned there. We have to act, and act soon."

"I can sound the alarm and bring in the Feds. Now we know where they are. They wouldn't act on Gunn before, but with the lost nuke, you can be sure as hell they will now."

"Not fast enough. If I had waited for the bureaucracy to function, I wouldn't have the information I have now. And I'm not waiting anymore. I board a flight to Tampico tonight. I'm heading to that airfield."

Miller cut in. "Husaam, if you are right and Mjolnir is there, that is suicide. And you're likely to be thrown in jail for this if you survive it."

"Too much is riding on this, my friends. I can't stay put, waiting until the signal is given. Besides, as you tell me, the call you got said Rebecca is on her way to Gunn."

"That's what I understood," said Savas, the pain returning in full force.

"What do you think will be done once the location of the nuke is made known to the military?"

Savas was silent a moment. "What do you mean?"

Jordan sighed. "Once they finally get the machine moving, it's a potent one. They won't risk that bird getting loose. They're going to rain fire down on the whole area. Massively, even before they send in troops to make sure they recover the missile. No one will survive that assault, John. No one."

60

The private plane taxied from the runway. Cohen sat in the back, her hands no longer tied, her face and lips still raw from the removal of the duct tape. Two men had been assigned to her, meeting her captors at the airport in New York, loading her onto the private plane, and flying with her over the last five hours. They said nothing to her, and she kept to herself. Only her thoughts spoke, constantly, oscillating between panic and complete depression. She had never felt so helpless in her life. She had determined over the last few hours that she was being used against John and the FBI, that her life was in exchange for his stepping back in some way from the investigation. It was the only possible explanation for the fact that she was still alive. Her lease on life was good for as long as she was useful in this way.

She had to smile in spite of her circumstances. *We've rattled them.* She took some comfort in the thought that they had succeeded—to drive them to this. Of course, it had also driven them to murder—horrible murders of people she cared deeply for. That was something that destroyed any satisfaction, and an anger and hatred for these killers, like she had never known, began to boil within her. She had been horrified by the deaths around the world perpetrated by Mjolnir, but it had been far away, images on television, abstract in a way Matt, Larry, Manuel, and Mira were not. They were forces of personality, links in the web of her life. Now they were gone, the men responsible now holding her life in their hands.

The plane taxied to a stop, and the two men onboard stood, bending sharply from the low ceiling. They nodded to her. She understood and got up from her seat and walked to the front of the plane just as the doors opened. She stepped down several short steps onto the tarmac. A moist and slightly cool breeze blew across her, and she squinted in the bright sunlight. The air smelled like a disorienting mixture of kerosene and jungle, and she wondered where on earth they had taken her. *Somewhere south, warmer, and wet.* As if reading her thoughts, a voice proclaimed the answer.

"Welcome to Mexico, Agent Cohen."

She turned to her right, shielding her eyes from the sun. But she didn't need to see the well-dressed, lithe, and gray-topped form of the panther. She would never forget his voice, a voice full of intelligence, nuance, and ice.

William Gunn walked forward and motioned her toward a set of black town cars parked beside the airplane. He wore expensively crafted aviator sunglasses with mirrored lenses, the cold gray eyes hidden behind them. He acted friendly, almost charming. *Like a snake before the strike.*

"Please, won't you step into the vehicle? We have only a short journey yet to go, but you must be tired from your trip." The two men stood on either side of them. Of course the invitation was a farce. She knew she had no choice in the matter. She wondered why he even maintained this pretense.

A man she presumed to be the chauffeur held a car door open for her. She stepped forward and ducked into the backseat, sliding to the far end against the door. The interior was cream leather, detailed wood paneling trimming the sides. To her dismay, Gunn entered as well and sat beside her. The door was shut from the outside, and the driver got in and started the engine.

"We have prepared a place for you," Gunn said over the sound of the car as it pulled away from the plane. "It is comfortable, unusually so, for this area."

His words were like poison to her. She couldn't hold her tongue any longer, whatever the risk to herself. "Are you also in the business of interior decoration for prison cells? Seems a bit off your normal enterprise."

Gunn sighed and took off his glasses, folding them into a leather case that he dropped into the inner pocket of his suit. He stared forward, his tone one of resigned sadness.

"Agent Cohen, there are always unpleasant situations in life. This is one of those. We have to do what we must because we believe in our cause. It is your misfortune that we needed this means to end the investigation of your department at the FBI, and to do that, we have had to neutralize several of its members. Your relationship with John Savas makes you a valuable asset to us in this regard."

"You didn't *neutralize* anyone. You murdered good men and women who committed their lives to serve their nation and its people. You sit so self-righteously on your throne of power, but you are just another despot enforcing his will."

Gunn turned slowly toward her, the gray eyes sharp as knives and digging into her soul. He smiled. "Your emotion does not disturb me, Agent Cohen. I don't expect you or anyone at the FBI to understand, or rather, to accept the logic and necessity of what we are trying to accomplish. I will not debate it with you. I have seen to your needs and will make your stay here as decent as I am able." He looked forward again as the car was jostled by several bumps on the road. "I do not seek harm for harm's sake. I do not enjoy the deaths I have caused, Ms. Cohen. But I understand something you cannot. I understand that we are fighting for our very survival as a culture, as a people, as a history. Lives must be lost in this fight. As in any war."

The car stopped, and the doors on both sides opened. More armed men waited outside. Gunn stepped out of the car, pressed his suit flat again, and leaned back in to speak.

"We will be calling Agent Savas soon to convince him that you are still alive. Please don't do anything stupid that will prevent us from proving that to him."

With that, he turned and walked off. Cohen looked over to the men who stood outside the car waiting for her. She closed her eyes, trying to keep herself together. After a few seconds, she opened them and gripped the door handle to steady herself as she stood. The men stood in front of a small aluminum shack. Around her were several warehouses and storage yards for equipment and parts, all associated with the airport. The sound of planes lifting off and landing could be heard from behind her. Several men were carting crates from place to place. She stared at them. In another context, they could be young soldiers on a tour of duty. One stared across at her, and she looked into his eyes. They almost seemed decent; one would never suspect that he was a man working to murder the innocent.

Cohen looked away and scanned the remainder of the area around her quickly. Barbed-wire fences encircled them. Between the razor blades and the weapons at the sides of the men around her, she knew that there would be no escape. With that thought, she walked forward to the shack that would be her own personal jailhouse.

For as long as I remain useful.

61

The Van Wyck Expressway was surprisingly empty at this time of night. Savas had made the journey more times than he could remember to John F. Kennedy Airport, but it had always been in daylight, when the Van Wyck was packed and slow. At one-thirty in the morning, it looked like some scene from an apocalyptic film, orange streetlights casting a ghastly hue over the road, the occasional red taillights of another vehicle staring back like demonic eyes waiting for them ahead. They veered right onto the roadway circling through the airport, heading quickly to the far right side to hit the exit they needed. Miller took the ramp, and the dark van pulled up to the JFK Cargo Facilities. The white "FBI" lettering was painted boldly on the blue of the vehicle and shone brightly in the security lights at the entrance gate. Miller drove with Savas riding shotgun, and in the back were Lightfoote and Rideout. A crazy day, becoming a crazier night, would soon get crazier still.

Savas had called in what was left of his team and brought them up to speed on the situation. They had devised a plan as insane as the world seemed to be at the moment. Lightfoote had found that the fastest way to get to Tampico was to hop aboard a cargo flight leaving at three in the morning. The next best path was taking a passenger plane in the morning to the Mexico City airport, then to the General Francisco Javier Mina International Airport near Tampico, or to throw in a third stop in Texas. None of these paths would get them to Rebecca before the evening of the next day. Besides, there would have to be a lot of explaining for all these agents and their firearms to make that journey openly. Calls were likely to be made to FBI headquarters. It could end before it began.

It was Miller who cut through to the simplest, if illegal, solution—stow away on the cargo flight. It was direct, from JFK to Tampico, leaving at 3 a.m. and arriving a little after eight in the morning. Jordan had left already and would likely be at the Tampico airfield around that time. They had agreed to meet up and figure out what to do when they got there. *Simple plan.*

First, they had to get on the plane. Lightfoote and Rideout would lead an "inspection" of the cargo flight. Miller and Savas would stow away during this examination, and Lightfoote and Rideout would somehow convince the crew and guards that the other two FBI agents had already finished and returned to the van. The two would stay hidden in the cargo section for the duration of the flight, jump out secretly after landing, figure out where Rebecca was being held, rescue her, and stop Gunn and his plan. *A perfectly* simple *plan.*

Lightfoote and Rideout would return to their office and sound the alarms. Around that time, the guards assigned to them might be waking up from their drug-induced sleep. Savas had hated slipping them loaded drinks, but except for one hell of a headache, and the wrath of their superiors, they would be fine. At that point, Lightfoote would "discover" an e-mail from Savas that let his FBI coworkers know what he was up to. He said nothing about Jordan. He figured it wasn't his place to nanny him for the CIA. By the time the FBI and the CIA had notified the military, and the president and his advisers had confirmed a course of action, they would have had their chance to end it themselves and rescue Rebecca. He just hoped to God they could pull it off. *You don't know what you're getting yourself into, Johnny-boy*, the voice in his head chided him. *Whatever it is, Rebecca's in it already*, he answered back. The voice shut up.

The van stopped at the gate, and a tired-looking guard walked up to them. He held a clipboard in his hand and sluggishly scanned the side of the van as he approached, then looked through sheets of paper on his clipboard.

"You figure he's looking under 'F' for 'FBI'?" quipped Rideout as Miller cast him a sharp look. Indeed, it did seem to them that this was exactly what he was doing. Finally, a look of dawning understanding crept over his features, and he glanced up with a furrowed brow at Miller in the driver's seat.

"FBI?" the young man said, with no attempt to hide his confusion.

"That's right," said the former marine in a tone Savas was sure would command even the most reluctant of soldiers. "These are Agents Savas, Rideout, and Lightfoote with me," he said, gesturing vaguely toward the back. He flipped open his badge case and continued speaking as the bewildered gate guard stared at the ID. "Son, we have some inside information that some of the terrorists who hit the city last month are transporting munitions using cargo carriers. We've traced them to the JFK terminals. We need to get inside and see your superiors immediately. We've got to stop these guys while we still can."

The guard stood there thunderstruck. "Terrorists?"

"Clearly this is not something you're used to dealing with, son, but we need your most efficient cooperation on this. Please, take my badge back to your station and phone this in. Wake them up if they fell asleep. We need to get in and inspect these planes an hour ago!"

The man stepped back at Miller's tone but looked subdued. "Ah, OK, let me call this in. Hell, I'm not even sure who's on call right now." He stumbled over to the small station. Within ten minutes, the van was rolling into the main section of the JFK cargo terminal.

Savas was amazed at what he saw. He knew JFK was big, but he had never seen a cargo-dedicated area of an airport before. Enormous warehouses extended one after the other, lit dimly by streetlights in the evening darkness. Aircraft after aircraft, narrow and wide-body, upper-deck and belly. Inspection sites and rows of eighteen-wheelers from long-haul trucking companies lined up to unload. In several places, as they sped by, were the refrigeration units for enormous climate-controlled and chilled facilities for shipping perishables. There was even a fairly good-sized animal shelter, clearly designed for animals far beyond house pets, facilities that could easily handle many large zoo animals.

At one of the main office complexes, a man was standing outside waving them over. Miller pulled up the van. "OK, everyone, let's look professional. File out with me. There's strength in numbers. At least intimidation. Give him your most dour looks."

Miller exited and strode confidently up to the man, and the rest followed. Savas and Rideout stood beside Miller, serious and silent. They tried to ignore Lightfoote, who glanced around the terminal in her space-cadet fashion. *We should have left her in the van*, he thought.

The man introduced himself. "Hey—I'm Robert Coon, night manager for the facility. Gerry called in. What the hell—you're FBI? This for real?"

Miller paused a moment, staring at the man, then looked back to the van and its bright-white 'FBI' letters that stood out quite visibly in the light.

"Yes, sir, this is absolutely for real. I don't know what your guard at the gate told you, but we are on a high-priority mission. We have received information that the same terrorist group that has bombed this city twice and hit places all around the world is using *your* cargo terminal to ship its explosives across the country and to Mexico, planning new attacks in several major cities."

"Holy shit!" gasped Coon.

"There's nothing holy about it," said Miller. "We have word that one of these planes bound for Mexico tonight is loaded with such cargo. We need to get into that plane and search the cargo."

The manager pulled out his clipboard and searched through it. *Do they all carry clipboards here?* thought Savas with impatience. The manager flipped through several pages and stopped. "Yeah, there's the flight to Tampico, Mexico, hangar 12A. Is that the one you're looking for?"

"The very one," said Miller. "I can't impress upon you how important this is, Mr. Coon. We need immediate access to that plane. And we need your complete silence about the matter."

The manager looked worried. "Sir, I don't know. You need to have a warrant or something, don't you?"

Savas looked impatiently at the man, like he was a poorly educated schoolchild. "Son, you've heard of the Patriot Act, haven't you?"

"Uh, yes, sir."

"Do you know what it says?"

The man looked caught off guard. "I dunno—something about tapping phones to find terrorists and the like?"

"The Patriot Act is what gives law enforcement new powers to stop terrorists from attacking this country. Phone tapping is just one part of it. Section 3.4 of the act specifically states that federal agents can, upon immediate threat to the nation, perform search and seizure without warrant."

"It says that?" the man asked.

"Yes, son, it does. It also states that interference with antiterrorist activities can be prosecuted as criminal aiding and abetting. I know that's nothing you would have to worry about, Mr. Coon, but it's important that no wrong impressions are given."

The young manager looked positively terrified. He licked his lips and nodded. "No, sir, there's no reason to worry. I'll take you over to the plane myself."

"Thank you, Mr. Coon. Your aid in this matter is greatly appreciated."

The manager walked briskly ahead of them, and the FBI agents followed. Miller leaned forward and spoke in a whisper to Savas. "Section 3.4 of the Patriot Act, John?" Savas looked fleetingly over toward Miller. "Effective section, isn't it?"

They approached a wide-body aircraft. It had an image of an American and Mexican flag, crossed, with the words "TransMexico" emblazoned in fiery red underneath. Robert Coon stopped in front of the plane.

"This is it," said the manager. "It was loaded half an hour ago, or should have been, anyway. It's scheduled to depart in an hour. If you look, the bay is open, and even the lift is still there. You just need to get up in there and you'll see all the cargo."

Savas nodded. "We'll get right to it. We'll be done in half an hour or less, I'm sure. If it's clean, we won't hold things up, I promise." He turned to the others. "All right, let's move in."

One by one, they ascended the lift into the belly of the cargo plane. Inside were rows of stacked crates with hardly the width for a person to walk through. All were labeled in English and in Spanish, housing items from foods to equipment.

"He's not checking up on us," said Miller, glancing back down.

"All right," said Savas. "Let's find us a place to hide out. Once we're in place, the rest of you hang out a few more minutes, then head back down and try to convince the man that we've already left the aircraft."

Rideout looked over at Savas. "And if he isn't buying it?"

"Well, we'll just have to play it on the fly."

Twenty minutes later, Robert Coon walked back out toward the plane. He was uneasy about this whole thing. Patriot Act or not, he wasn't in the habit of letting people wander onto the planes at night, FBI, CIA, or NYPD. He had gone back into this office to look through the manuals, but he couldn't find anything to help him figure out what to do in this situation. However, he wasn't about to wake up Sammy for this. He'd tell him in the morning. *I'd better not get into any trouble.*

As he approached the plane, he saw two of the agents, the girl and the thin one, walking back from the aircraft. The man waved him down.

"Mr. Coon," said Rideout, "we've finished our search, and I'm happy to report that there are no items out of the ordinary that we can identify. It looks like our lead was wrong. I want to thank you for your help in this investigation. It's a dangerous world now, and we've all got to work together to protect our nation." He extended his hand toward the man.

The manager nodded, shaking hands with the FBI man. "OK, no problem. I do what I can. So, where are the other agents?"

Rideout gestured toward the van. "They already headed back. Now, Mr. Coon, I just need a little information from you before we leave, for our investigation. Agent Lightfoote, would you join the others in the van and wait for me?"

Lightfoote smiled and nodded, and practically *skipped* back to the van. Rideout wanted to scream but turned the attention of the manager quickly away from Lightfoote.

"Mr. Coon?" he began, removing a notepad. "Let's start with your full name, OK?" The two walked toward the office door. Rideout glanced briefly back toward the plane.

Fifteen minutes later, Rideout opened the door to the van. Lightfoote was in the front passenger side. He closed the door and exhaled.

"I don't know how, but we did it. Hopefully, John and Frank will go undiscovered until they land in Mexico. Meanwhile, you and I need to head straight back and sound the alarms. If you think this was a hard act, convincing the FBI and the CIA and who knows who else that we weren't involved with this is going to be a wake-up call."

Lightfoote smiled and reached over and squeezed his arm. "Oh, I don't worry, J. P. This was easy."

"Easy?" he said, staring at her incredulously. *Sure*, he thought. *Skipping easy.*

At 3:15 a.m., a wide-bodied cargo airliner, owned by TransMexico, lifted off the runway at JFK Airport. Inside, it carried an assortment of perishables, canned goods, liquor, farm equipment, and two stowaway FBI agents headed to confront the terrorist organization Mjolnir.

Several thousand miles away, three hours after the cargo plane had departed Kennedy Airport, a black SUV sped down a highway in eastern Mexico. The driver didn't seem to notice the reading of the speedometer, now pushing past one hundred miles an hour. The large vehicle trembled at that velocity, and the heavy metallic objects on the passenger seat bounced continuously. Jordan glanced over and pushed the weapons toward the seat back, then refocused on the road. The paling sky began to turn a purple-red and then, slowly, a brighter and brighter orange. Finally, a great flaming orb erupted in front of him on the horizon, and he slipped on a pair of sunglasses. His vehicle aimed straight for the orb, and he followed its mark, like some demonic inversion of the shepherds being led to the Christ Child. Only he was not a shepherd, and he carried not gifts but automatic weapons, and what waited under the point of the star was not a Holy Mother and Child but the minions of the damned who sought to bathe the world in fire.

62

Cohen stared out the window. The rising sun turned from a deep red to a yellow-orange as it climbed over the horizon. A strange-looking black aircraft was being fueled under the morning rays. She was no aviation expert, but it was clear the plane was an altered version of a standard design, with several modifications built into the underside of the aircraft. A long tubular extension ran nearly the length of the body underneath, with a set of thin payload doors that seemed ready to open in flight and release their cargo to the world below. The exterior seemed coated in an unusual material, and even the sun was absorbed, its light unable to reflect from the surface. A portal into the night seemed to have opened where the aircraft stood.

A morning mist from the humid lands rose off the vegetation in the distance, and dew covered the surfaces of the aircraft and runway. She observed a platoon of men guiding a long crate up a loading ramp and into the belly of the plane. They walked solemnly, as if marching in a long funeral procession for a beloved statesman. Beside the ramp stood three men at attention. Two were stout and of military bearing, dressed in fatigues, one older than the other. Between them in an expensive suit, with reflective aviation sunglasses strapped to his grayed and angular head, was CEO William Gunn. He watched impassively, and yet every muscle in his body seemed taut with a hidden energy. The three watched the crate being loaded onto the plane and remained unmoving as the soldiers finished, then walked back down the ramp and lined up in formation behind the fuselage.

She pulled herself away from the window. *What was that all about?* The entire scene felt ominous to her, and she wondered what was held inside the cargo they loaded on the plane.

Cohen sat down, exhausted, legs crossed and eyes bloodshot, staring at the door and window of her prison. She had slept fitfully in the makeshift bed they had rigged for her—not a cot exactly, but not a bed. Even if she possessed a king-sized mattress and springs it would have meant nothing last night. She had tried all the possible escape routes—the windows on either side, the door—but each had been effectively barred and locked. After an hour of blistering her hands, she had given up. A refrigerator held cheap foods and drinks inside. She had not touched it. She had simply grown more subdued, waiting until her captors would call on her again.

The door burst open. Cohen jumped up and pressed her back against the wall. A young man she had never seen entered, and he closed the door quickly. He turned around, and instantly she changed her mind—she *had* seen him recently. He was the man who had stared so intently at her the other day after she landed.

"Ms. Cohen?" he asked.

"Yes. Who are you?"

He took off his hat. "My name's Michael Inherp, ma'am. I'm sorry for all this, but it's Mr. Gunn's doing, his plan to keep you here and stop the FBI and others from trying to stop the mission."

Cohen was stunned. Who was this kid, and how did he know so much? What was he doing here?

"You know a lot about this, Mr. Inherp."

He looked around the room quickly, then back at Cohen. "There's not time to explain it all. I'm the one who wrote to the army to tell them about the missile."

"What missile?" *The cargo?*

"You don't know?" He looked bewildered. "There's no *time*. Please, you need to come with me now. FBI and CIA agents are almost here now, and there is no telling what they are going to do. They could get you killed. Not too much longer from now, the air force is going to be bombing this place. We've got to get you *out*."

Cohen felt the nauseating vertigo that combined a lack of understanding with a threat to one's life. "Please!" she said. "What are you talking about!"

The soldier sighed. "Ms. Cohen, this is Mjolnir. They have a nuclear missile they just loaded on a plane. They're going to use that missile. I notified the military just before sunrise. They told me FBI and CIA agents were already on their way, and that I had to warn you and them that the air force is going to bomb this airport to all hell as soon as they can get here. The rest of the airport is evacuating, and it's a miracle they haven't noticed yet. *Please*, we've got to go, *now*!"

He reached over, grasped her hand, and began pulling her toward the door. Just at that moment, the door opened again, and the form of another soldier entered, holding a plate of food and staring downward as he balanced the tray, still unaware of Inherp's presence in the room.

"Breakfast, Ms. Cohen," he began, glancing up and momentarily looking confused at the sight of another soldier in the room.

Inherp kicked the other soldier between the legs. The man hunched over, and inhaled in pain, and Inherp removed his sidearm and brought it down sharply on the man's skull. He crashed to the ground, orange juice and toast spilling over the floor.

Inherp turned and grabbed Cohen's hand again. "*Now!*" he cried.

Terrified, Cohen exited the building with him. They sprinted down the side of the fence away from the loaded plane. She had no idea where they were going or how this soldier planned to get them out of there without Gunn or his troops stopping them. *And FBI coming here? Who? Why would they come if the military was going to strike? My God, can he be right? A nuclear weapon?*

As they ran, the earth shook suddenly. Cohen stumbled from the tremor. She looked behind her. A large fireball erupted from a hundred yards on the other side of the plane. A plume of fire and black smoke rose into the air. They both stopped and stared back at the sight.

"Well," said Inherp, the wind blowing the smoke across the airfield, the place beginning to look like a war zone. "I guess your friends are here."

63

Jordan stood by the storage building, shielding his eyes from the flames. What was left of the fuel truck lay scattered across the tarmac, tendrils of fire reaching outward in several directions, threatening buildings, other vehicles, and the airplane. *Close, but not close enough.* It had been a wild idea. He had coordinated with Savas and Miller once they arrived, communicating over cell phones. They knew that they were hopelessly outnumbered, but their main goal had been to disable as many troops as possible, create a distraction, and damage the plane. *Well, at least I got the first two done.* Indeed, troops were running around in total confusion, and many had been killed instantly by the explosion as Jordan had announced his presence and drawn nearly a dozen in pursuit of him past the fuel truck. But the plane was the most important target, and it was out of the blast radius, still guarded by at least ten well-armed soldiers who were now on high alert.

When they had arrived, New York had reached them on their phones. Wonderful invention, the modern cell phone, he thought. A brave new world that rendered half the old tactics in action and espionage obsolete. They had learned that Inherp had contacted the army about the missile, the location, and the plans to load it on a plane and use it very soon. Perhaps the FBI and the CIA were angry about their going AWOL and trying to run the thing solo, but right now they were the only assets the government had in the area. They were scrambling fighters from nearby bases, but by the time they got airborne and made it to the site, the plane could be gone. Jordan had seen enough of it to know that it would be lost soon if not followed by eye. The plane had been converted into a stealth craft. How Gunn had recruited the expertise, found the materials, and pulled it off, he had no idea. But the man was resourceful, with deep pockets, and obsessed, and it looked like he had forged his own private invisible bomber. This thing would fly low and be invisible to radar. It would not exist in the air. They couldn't let it get off the ground.

He reloaded his weapon and opened his cell phone. He had to get Savas and Frank Miller on the line. Time was running out.

"What the *hell* is going on?" William Gunn stepped out of the hangar as his lieutenant raced over. Fire rose into the sky from the explosion, and the noise of automatic weapons could be heard echoing across the airfield. His second-in-command bolted up beside him carrying a machine gun.

"Mr. Gunn, the worst we could have expected. We are under attack, and the plane narrowly missed being destroyed by the explosion. It looks like it was a fuel truck. There are attacks on soldiers, but haphazard, so I conclude it is a very small force, but they are determined to blow up the plane. They *know*, William."

"*How can they know?* This is crazy!"

"The main airport has evacuated. The pilots have been denied permission to fly. That can only mean one thing—a strategic strike is coming, airborne, no doubt. Somehow the mission has been compromised, sir. We may have only minutes."

Gunn thought quickly. He had to salvage their most important strike.

"Then we get the plane in the air now! Fuck air traffic control. If they've shut the airport down, the skies will be empty. They can't track the plane once it's in the air. Tell them to go, *now*!"

"Yes, sir! But we have to get you out of here. I've already called the helicopter. It's en route. I'll give the pilots the go, tell them to forget pre-check, and get the hell out of here. Then we run to the chopper landing pad."

"Tell the pilots to go, but I also want you to get over to the plane and make sure that no one in that firefight is able to damage it. Work with the soldiers, pin down whoever the hell is doing this!"

"Yes, sir, but you will not be protected!"

"I'll take the car the long way around to the helipad. I'll be fine. That missile is what matters now. We can't jeopardize this mission! Go! You'll meet me at the chopper as soon as the plane is in the air!"

"On my way!" The soldier sprinted toward the billowing smoke and the sound of gunfire. Gunn turned and walked quickly toward a row of cars near the building, his jaw clenched.

They were too close to fail now!

Savas placed the cell phone in his pocket. He felt like he was going mad in the middle of this chaos, coordinating multiple phone calls with the FBI and this Mjolnir soldier turned ally. The fire was spreading and igniting flammables in the hangar near the fuel truck. *This could get completely out of control.* The heat was searing, and his eyes were watering from the smoke. He leaned against the metal siding of one of the storage buildings near the fence and yelled over to Miller.

"This Inherp—he has Rebecca, Frank. As far as I can tell, we're on the wrong side of this inferno, and he's two buildings down waiting for us. We just need to get across and past the soldiers guarding the aircraft before they fill us with bullets."

Miller nodded. "The good news is that we have a lot of smoke for cover. Have you reached Husaam?"

"No!" shouted Savas. "He's not picking up. I don't know if he can't hear in this chaos or if he is engaged. He said he would bring that plane down. It looks like the explosion failed. Once we find her, we need to regroup and form a plan to stop them from getting that missile in the air. Let's move and try again when we find Rebecca."

Miller stood up, then crouched and kept his body low. "Through the worst of the smoke, John. We're probably going to asphyxiate, but it will be nearly impossible to see us in all this."

They both sprinted forward into the smoke and fire, weapons raised and at the ready. Plunging into the black cloud, Savas held his breath as long as he could. Soon he had to inhale, and he nearly choked, his eyes watering, the fumes burning his lungs. *I'm coming, Rebecca!* If he could only make it that far.

64

The engines on the aircraft changed pitch and throttled up significantly. Jordan looked over toward the machine, watching men
scramble on and off and around the thing, confused, uncertain what to
do. *No. They're going to get it out while they can! No!* He couldn't allow
it to leave, but he saw no way to stop it. In an instant he made a decision
and sprinted with his automatic toward the aircraft.

Two men were removing the wheel-stops from underneath the
plane. Most of the soldiers were heading away from the aircraft. He
was fortunate. They had assumed that they would leave their vulnerable
position as the plane left and engage in the firefight erupting around
them. *John and Frank.* Jordan knew they would need help, but he also
knew that far more people might depend on him *not* helping them at
this moment, and getting to that plane. Two of the soldiers slowed,
noticing his sprint to the aircraft, which had slowly begun its taxi. The
loading ramp had not even been drawn up, although it had started to
rise. He was perhaps twenty yards from the plane now. He could reach
it before takeoff.

The soldiers turned slowly, at first stunned to see this man shoot
like an arrow toward the craft they had just abandoned. Jordan lowered
his automatic and sprayed a line of fire across them as he ran past.
The two men had begun to aim their weapons but were caught in the
spray, each hit by multiple rounds. They pivoted following the impact,
then fell toward the ground, one rolling in agony, the other still and
unmoving. Jordan turned his attention to the ramp, even as he heard
the screams of men now alerted to his presence. Ten yards, five . . . the
plane made a slow pivot toward the main runway, and he closed the

remaining distance and leapt onto the ramp. There was hardly room for him, and he quickly rolled into the body of the plane as the ramp slammed shut and locked.

Jordan raised himself on his stomach and aimed his weapon. There was no one there. He paused for a moment and caught his breath. His leg was throbbing. He must have smashed it in the leap onto the ramp. He rolled over as quietly as possible and looked down. Blood stained his thigh next to a large rip in his robes. Red spread slowly across the white of the clothes. He raised his leg to his chest and gasped in pain, but he saw that the laceration was not too deep. He would be able to function for some time, but the leg had just recovered from previous injuries.

He got to his feet slowly, gingerly, keeping low. The aircraft had picked up speed and was taxiing toward the beginning of the runway. Takeoff would occur very soon; Jordan was sure of that. He needed to find a more secure place to position himself until they reached a more stable altitude. The last thing he needed was to be incapacitated at this juncture. He crept into the main cargo chamber as silently as possible. There was an interesting division built into the plane. Instead of a single cargo chamber, there was a split into two sections, divided by a sealed wall with a door. *Is this for when the missile is lowered into the under section?* he wondered. Right now, it didn't matter. He saw the large crate in the center of the hold. To the side was netting of some kind attached to the walls of the plane. He limped over to it and painfully inserted himself into the netting, using the ropes as a set of straps to stabilize him during flight. Just in time—he felt the plane turn ninety degrees as the engines throttled up. The pilots had reached the runway.

Several dead soldiers lay between the two metal storage buildings behind the hangar. Miller and Savas raced across the area as gunfire erupted around them, the ground exploding as countless bullets rained down. A crossfire raged from the point they sought, as Inherp sprayed bullets toward the source of the gunfire. The shooting slowed considerably but continued. As they reached the back side of the building where Inherp hid behind a corner for shelter, Miller cried out in pain and stumbled forward, crashing hard but rolling behind the shed. Savas was right behind him, slamming into the wall beside Cohen and Inherp. She grabbed him and held him tightly, but both then turned toward Miller, who had crawled up beside them.

"Frank!" she cried out. "Are you OK?"

Miller swore like a sailor. "Tell this shithead of yours that I'm *done* saving his ass! *Fuck!* John, you're a gift of holes for me." He pulled out a large ka-bar knife from his belt and ripped open his pant legs. An ugly rip ran along his calf, and blood poured out of it profusely. Miller grimaced.

"Well, at least this time they won't be digging any damn metal out of me. It's just a graze. A deep fucking graze, but a graze. Now we need . . ." His voice trailed off, and he stared into the sky.

"Frank, what's wrong? Wha—" began Savas.

"Quiet! Listen!"

Savas closed his eyes and focused on the noise around him. Two distinct sounds became clear. The first was the roar of an airplane reaching speeds for takeoff. The other was the unmistakable sound of helicopter blades approaching.

"The missile!" Savas yelled in frustration.

"It's gone, John. Look!" Miller gestured toward the sky behind them, and Savas saw a black shadow climb into the air and begin a slow roll to the left. "There's nothing we can do now. We'll just have to wait and hope the air force intercepts." Miller stood up against the metal wall, gasped in pain, and spoke through gritted teeth. "But we can try to take care of something just as important."

Savas looked confusedly toward Miller. "What?"

"Gunn. The helicopter has got to be coming for him. They got that plane off the ground quickly, and not just for our attack, I don't think. They know they've been compromised, and they're trying to get their chieftain out of harm's way."

Inherp turned toward them. "He's right! There is a helipad at the far end of the cargo section—that way!" he gestured. "Maybe three minutes. If he gets away, the missile is just the beginning! Please, I know this man. Stop him! Before it's too late."

Savas looked down at Miller's leg. "Frank, can you make it?"

Miller tried taking several steps, but he crouched down, almost falling, and cried out in pain. "Damn bullet's cut through the muscle, John. I won't make it in time. You and Inherp go. I'll stay with Rebecca."

"No," said Savas. "I'll go alone. You'll need him to hold them off, Frank." He turned and kissed Cohen, then looked up to Inherp. "You've kept her safe today. I'm asking you to do it again."

"Of course," replied the young man.

Frank pushed Savas forward. "John, shut up and get over there! The damn bird's almost here!"

Savas could hear the approaching craft much more clearly now. He gave one more look to Cohen and sprinted off toward the landing pad.

Miller's cell phone rang. "Yes?!" he called loudly into the microphone. As he listened, his eyes grew large. "What? Yes, I can, but, wait!" He looked increasingly shocked, and he called out, "Wait! Husaam? Are you there?"

Cohen and Inherp looked toward him. He stared at them with a stunned expression. "Well, I'll be damned. Husaam—he's on the plane."

"How did he get on the plane?" Cohen asked.

"No damn clue," answered Miller. "But he says we need to get the air force to call him immediately. He says he needs to know how to deactivate a nuclear warhead."

65

The takeoff was a rocky one, and the netting that was secured to the wall did not promise the smoothest ride. The plane had begun to level off as he ended the call with Miller. Until they got the required expertise on the phone to him, he had a lot to do. First, he had to get to the missile. The crate was large and the wood thick. He would need tools. He shook his head. He would *really* need tools once he got it open.

He stood up and disentangled himself from the netting. Scanning the cargo hold, he knew the necessary tools would have to be onboard. There was no way they would take this thing up for its mission and not be ready to keep it absolutely serviced, or to change its settings, if the need arose. Aside from the crate, the cargo hold was mostly empty. This plane had little purpose in its preparation outside of this arrow of death. He wondered how long he had until the soldiers of Mjolnir came back to check on their cargo.

There. In the corner, near the dividing wall in the cargo hold, was a metallic box on four wheels. *A tool case.* He limped up to the case and confirmed his suspicion—an elaborate tool set, with equipment he knew and much he had never seen and could not guess its use. As a gift, lying on top of the box, were several sets of large iron crowbars. He supposed all those able-bodied soldiers worked together to open the crate. He grabbed one and struggled over to the missile.

Despite the pain in his leg and the fatigue he was beginning to feel from the loss of blood, within a little over five minutes he had the top and side panel off the crate—enough to access the missile to open it up and reveal the warhead inside. *With the right tools.* Holding the crowbar in one hand, he limped back toward the metallic box and was about to open some of its top drawers when the door to the chamber opened up. Jordan and a Mjolnir soldier stood face to face, not more than five feet apart. Both were surprised for an instant, but Jordan reacted faster and swung the crowbar up, striking the man underneath his chin. His head snapped backward, and he fell to the ground unconscious. Jordan himself almost fell over; the stress the movement put on his wounded leg was nearly too much. He righted himself, then walked over to the door and closed it. There was no lock. However, there was no doorknob either, just a rectangular handle jutting toward him; the door itself opened outward. He grabbed several crowbars and wedged them inside the metal handle and across the divider beside the door. It worked like a barricade in an old castle—as the door was pushed forward (or pulled from the outside), the bars caught on the metal handle and the wall, preventing further movement. It would not hold long. *But perhaps long enough.*

He wheeled the tool cart over to the missile and parked it next to the warhead. *Now, how on earth did one open this thing?*

Andrew Bryant paced in the Operations Room at FBI headquarters. Angel Lightfoote and J. P. Rideout were there with him, as were several other members from Larry Kanter's former division, as well as representatives from the CIA and the US Air Force. Everything had happened so quickly, *too quickly*, but he knew that was the nature of every crisis. For better or worse, it was now centered at the FBI—Savas and Miller, and Mjolnir kidnapping Cohen, had seen to that. This made Kanter's Operations Room as good a congregation point as any. Live feeds to similar crises management teams at the CIA, the air force, and the Pentagon had been established.

Two monitors showed live satellite feeds from the airport. What had been much easier to see a little while before was now mostly obscured by smoke pouring from a large fuel fire. The dark plane identified by Inherp was nowhere to be seen.

The phone rang. Bryant pivoted quickly and watched as Rideout ID'd the call. "It's Inherp," he said flatly.

"Pick it up, then!" snapped Bryant.

Rideout did so. The call went live to speakers in the room. A computer broke down the speech in real time and flashed it on one of the monitors in front of them.

"This is Michael Inherp." The sounds of automatic weapons could be heard over the sound system. "We are under heavy fire from Mjolnir troops. I am with Rebecca Cohen and Frank Miller. Miller is wounded in the leg, and John Savas has left us to intercept a helicopter coming in to land. We presume it is here to evacuate William Gunn."

An air force major looked at Bryant. "Fifteen minutes until the fighters can engage."

Bryant nodded and spoke into a microphone around his neck. "Inherp, this is Andrew Bryant, FBI. I need to know—"

"Wait!" interrupted Inherp. "The plane has taken off. I repeat, the plane has taken off. It is loaded with the missile. Husaam Jordan is on the plane."

Heads turned and voices mumbled beneath the background sounds over the speakers. The air force major spoke. "Inherp—are you sure? The missile is onboard?"

"Yes, sir. I saw it loaded myself."

"Do you know where they are headed? What is their target?"

"No, sir. Only something important. Something game-changing, sir. Mr. Gunn believes it will cause a world war with the Muslim nations."

"*Damn it*, Inherp!" yelled Bryant, "we need to know where this plane is headed."

"Please, listen to me! Agent Jordan is on the plane. He just called Agent Miller. He must be with the missile. He needs experts to tell him how to disarm it! If we can't shoot the plane down, we can deactivate the missile!"

Voices spoke rapidly over each other in the room, over the phone links with CIA and the Pentagon. Faintly someone could be heard over the speakers asking for a phone.

"Everyone, listen to me!" came the strained voice of Frank Miller.

The room became quiet. "We need someone from the air force to find an engineer, *right now* and conference call him in to Jordan. We're under heavy fire, and we need to move out! He's the one you need to speak with. Get a man on the phone to him!"

The line went dead. A rough voice came over the speakers. "This is General Jim Richards. I am instructing all air force personnel hearing this near me and elsewhere, down to the janitors, get me a weapons engineer with the expertise for this warhead, *yesterday!*"

The air force officers got on their phones and exited the room to make their calls. Bryant placed his fingers to his temple. This was all getting out of his control. Out of the corner of his eye, he saw the large monitors flash. He looked up. The satellite feeds were gone, replaced with a flat map of the world. Red dots were appearing in several places across the globe.

"Hey, where is the satellite feed?" called one of the CIA agents. Bryant looked around with irritation. *What the hell?*

Rideout glanced over toward Lightfoote, who was furiously working her keyboard. "Angel, is this you?" She continued work but nodded slowly up and down, not taking her eyes off the screen. "Angel, we need to focus on Mexico. Can you switch it back over?"

An air force officer back in the room shouted over him. "Tell her to get that satellite feed back up! What the hell is she doing?" Red dots were popping up in several places, and red lines were being drawn between them. Lightfoote appeared oblivious to the rancor around her. Rideout looked at the screen and understood.

"She's marking out the locations of all the attacks," he said.

Bryant shouted, "How is that relevant now? Damn it, Rideout, I've had just about enough of that little freak! Override her! Get the satellite feed back up *this instant!*"

Rideout spoke in a measured tone. "Andrew, I've learned to trust Angel's strange but often very important contributions. That's why Larry brought her in." He turned to his new boss. "I'm going to give this a few minutes. The satellite feed isn't going anywhere." Bryant glared at Rideout, who stared right back.

Across the world map, red marks appeared. New York, Caracas, London, Sudan, over the South Atlantic—digital thumbtacks at each of the sites of Mjolnir bombings. Red lines were now connecting nearly all of them, creating a shape with some clear sort of structure, but one that was not identifiable to anyone in the room.

Bryant shook his head. "I don't see anything of worth here, Rideout. This meaningless cartoon drawing is wasting our time. If you don't cut this back to the feed, I will have someone remove her."

"Wait!" Lightfoote shouted, holding up one hand while continuing to type or use the mouse with the other.

Bryant was about to walk over and remove her himself when a digital image appeared on the screen, superimposed over the world map and the web of lines linking the attacks. The image was by now familiar to all in the room—an anchor shaped emblem, but flat at one end and curved to a point, a long shaft sticking out from that end. It was clearly a relic, old metal carved and weathered, the end of the shaft broadening out like the hilt of a sword, the face of a bird carved into the end. It was Thor's hammer.

Lightfoote manipulated the image, first turning it partially transparent to reveal the map underneath it. She then rotated it ninety degrees counterclockwise, resized it, and distorted it in each dimension slightly until the handle of the hammer rested on North and South America, the shaft extending across the Atlantic Ocean into Africa, and the head of the hammer landing on the Arabian Peninsula, with the sharp tip like a pointer centered on Saudi Arabia.

"What the hell?" said Bryant.

"It's pointing where, Angel, Mecca?" said Rideout.

Lightfoote rotated around, the large monitors behind her glowing with the image of a god's hammer laid across the earth. Her eyes were large and bright.

"Not pointing, J. P." She looked across all the faces. "Smashing. The hammer is smashing."

The air force major was back in the room. "You mean they mapped out the shape of that thing in their attacks? Pointing to Saudi Arabia? Why on earth?"

Lightfoote shook her head again. "*Not* pointing. *Smashing*." She looked over at Rideout for help.

"*Oh, my God*," he said. He turned to Bryant. "Get me Husaam on the line. *Now!*"

Bryant looked stunned. "What is this about?"

Rideout looked at Lightfoote, and she nodded with her eyes large, her expression serious. He spoke flatly. "I know what this attack is all about, Andrew."

66

Jordan shook his head. He was glad he had learned firsthand from his former gang how to take apart cars—a skill used more than a few times for stealing them. To his astonishment, he had, within the span of less than twenty minutes, managed to open up the missile housing and expose the warhead. The missile was long and sleek, aerodynamic like an arrow. The warhead was fat and dull, like a huge bullet the size of a laundry basket, housing the radioactive materials in a manner that would lead to the optimal explosion. The "physics package" was connected to the rest of the missile by numerous wires and circuits, and now Jordan knew he was completely out of his element. He was also nearly out of time.

"Where the hell *is* the engineer?" the gravelly voice of their mission leader called out near the cockpit, his eyes darting around in annoyance. He prided himself on an optimum of organization: each piece in its place at the right time for every mission. The engineer had gone back to make sure all systems were nominal on the missile. A nontrivial issue with what they had onboard.

They had all sat through the long briefings prior to the mission. Mjolnir engineers had employed a number of work-arounds to defeat the multilayered safety systems on the missile and warhead. The military had become very good at making nuclear weapons impossible to detonate accidentally. Safety systems prevented fire, external explosion, or impact from triggering detonation. Safety codes and environmental detection systems ensured no warhead would go off unless it had been properly programmed with secret codes *and* had been delivered in the way intended—in this case, fired from a cruise missile. Unless the proper acceleration, altitude, and pressure readings were in place, the bomb would not detonate.

Of course, they planned to use the cruise missile as the delivery system—it was perfect, and engineers had easily programmed it for the desired coordinates. Defeating the arming safety measures had proven far more difficult, however. Stealing the missile was one thing, nearly impossible. But stealing the codes *was* impossible. The "permissive action link," or PAL lock, was a real bastard: multiple-code, six-digit switch, limited-try followed by lockout. Their cryptologists didn't have the luxury to get it wrong. But Gunn had recruited some extremely talented people. The engineers had rigged something that had bypassed the PAL lock. He didn't care to understand how. They said it worked; the missile was armed, although now in a fairly unprotected state, he had been told. Many of the key safety systems were no longer operational. *Best not to drop the thing*, he thought with a smile.

The engineer was to keep babysitting it. *So where the hell was he?*

"I'll go have a look, sir," said a soldier next to him.

"He should have reported by now." The leader released his belts and headed off down the plane to the dividing door.

Rideout yelled over to Bryant. "We've got him conferenced in from Minot. The line's not secure."

Bryant waved his hand dismissively. "That's been cleared already. Put him on."

Rideout nodded toward them. "Captain Edwards, can you hear me?"

A voice spoke with a moderate static component. "Yes, sir. Loud and clear."

"This is Andrew Bryant with the FBI. We have senior officers at the Pentagon, the CIA, and the air force listening in from several locations. You have been briefed?"

"Uh, yes, sir. I'm to talk a man through the disarming of a W80 warhead mounted on a cruise missile."

"That's it."

"Sir, is this a drill?"

Bryant looked over toward the air force men. They exchanged looks but remained silent. A familiar voice was heard over the line.

"Captain Edwards. This is General Richards, Pentagon. Listen to me well, son—this is *not* a drill. We have an AWOL nuke in the hands of some very bad men, and we have a few minutes to walk a CIA agent through disarming it. We don't have time for more background. I need your very best, young man."

There was a short silence on the other end of the line. "Understood, sir. You've got it."

Bryant continued. "We're connecting with the agent now. Everyone, hold on."

Jordan heard the noises of the door being pulled and the voice outside the door. *How long do I have?* He figured five minutes at best before they forced the door open. Right at that moment, his phone buzzed, and he pulled it from his pocket. *Thank goodness for satellite phones!*

"Husaam Jordan, this is Andrew Bryant with the FBI—"

"Just tell me—do you have someone to walk me through this?"

"Yes, Agent Jordan. You need to know something first. We have determined the target for the missile. It is the Saudi Arabian city of Mecca."

Jordan was stunned. *Mecca?* The holiest site in all of Islam. His stomach turned as a realization dawned on him. "The Hajj," he whispered. There could be more than two million visiting Muslims in Mecca performing the pilgrimage at this moment, plus another two million from the city itself. A massacre in fire of four million souls, a destruction of the center of Islam. A horror without precedent that would spawn horrors of retaliation across the world. "Tell me how to disarm this thing, then. Now!" he shouted.

Bryant continued. "Air Force Engineer Al Edwards on the line. Go, Edwards."

"Agent Jordan?"

"Listen, I don't have time to tell you everything. I've taken several photos with my cell and sent them to Rideout at the FBI. Have him put them up and you can see what I've done."

Rideout cut in on the line. "Husaam—that's not going to work. He's in Minot, North Dakota. He can't see the monitors. Edwards, you by a computer?"

"Yes!"

"Your e-mail, I need it now!" shouted Rideout. The captain told him. "Log onto your account, I'm forwarding the images."

Jordan spoke through the pain in his leg. "I don't have a lot of time."

"Got them, sir. Let me have a look."

Jordan was startled by a loud crashing sound. He turned to the door. Someone on the other side was repeatedly yanking on the handle, and the crowbars were being smashed into the door and the wall. Already one seemed about to fall loose from the handle. He knew it was only a matter of time before the vibrations knocked them all out.

"Edwards—I'm here with the missile near a bunch of hostiles, and in about two minutes they are going to be through the door and on me."

"Yes, sir. You opened it up well. Wow. They've run around or rewired nearly all the PAL circuitry, but the way they've done it, all the strong and weak safety systems around the exclusion zone have been bypassed, too. What a mess!"

"Speak English!" shouted Jordan. One of the crowbars made a clanking noise as it fell to the floor. He could hear shouts on the other side.

"Sir, it means that the warhead is sensitive now to detonation by impact or even electrical surge. That's one unstable nuke you have there."

"Just tell me how to disarm the thing!"

"It's not going to be easy with what they've rigged, and you need to ground yourself. Even a static charge and that thing will blow. OK, first, you need—"

Suddenly there was a loud noise on the speakers—first a crashing sound with metallic elements, then several staccato bursts.

"That's gunfire," whispered Rideout.

The air force major stood up from his chair. "Oh, God."

Jordan fell backward, his shoulder and chest covered in blood, his hand barely holding him upright next to the missile. *Not enough time.* The pain was nearly overwhelming. The door had been yanked open finally, and two men had jumped into the chamber. Jordan had the advantage, however. They had to negotiate through the door, climb over the body of the soldier he had downed earlier, and take the time to scan the area for him. He shot down both but not before taking fire from a third soldier on the other side who had ducked back. Jordan thought he had hit him, but how seriously, he didn't know.

"Husaam!" shouted Rideout. "Are you there?"

Jordan righted himself and grabbed the tool cart with both hands. The front of his white robes was soaked red, and he felt dizzy from the loss of blood. He leaned on his elbows, aimed his weapon at the door, and spoke into the phone.

"Not much time now. I'm shot, badly. More coming. There isn't time."

"Agent Jordan!" shouted Bryant. "You must disarm that weapon!"

Jordan's voice was barely a whisper. "No time. The Hajj . . . the Fifth Pillar . . . I wished to go . . . God be merciful for my failure . . . tell Vonessa, good-bye."

"He's not going to make it," whispered Rideout.

On the plane, Jordan reached into the tool crate drawers and pulled out a voltmeter. He ripped the wires out of the device and stumbled to the missile, crashing against the side of the crate, his blood smearing the porous wood.

Suddenly a new round of gunfire broke out. The Mjolnir mission leader had leapt through the door and over the bodies of the other soldiers. His left arm was bloodied, as was his stomach, but he willed himself back into combat. He took aim and fired a burst into the Muslim's back. Jordan arched in pain and cried out. Miraculously, he held himself upright for another moment and inserted the wiring onto the circuit board as the soldier labored over to stop him.

"Get off the weapon!" he roared.

"I bear witness that there is no god but Allah," Jordan whispered to the circuitry, his legs buckling, sweat pouring over his face, "and Mohammed . . . is his Prophet."

He then connected two regions of the circuit board with the leads. There was a small spark, then a terrible light.

"We've lost the signal," said Rideout.

"Damn it, get him back on the phone!" shouted Bryant.

Lightfoote was crying, staring up at the ceiling. Rideout walked over and held her. People were speaking over each other, and Bryant simply roared again.

"Get him on the phone!" shouted Bryant. Lightfoote looked at him and shook her head. Bryant was about to shout again when he was interrupted by a voice over the speakers.

"This is General Richards. US military satellites report the detection of a nuclear detonation signal in the air above the Gulf of Mexico. I am told that the location is within the cone of probability for the aircraft that took off from Tampico airport. The explosion is almost certainly the stolen weapon. We will end this crisis call now and work within our individual organizations. The president has been informed at every stage of this and is now aware of its resolution. We have a brave man to thank for saving millions of lives."

The line went dead. Lightfoote wept uncontrollably in Rideout's arms. Everyone in the room sat in stunned silence. Finally, recovering his composure, Bryant tried to mobilize his team.

"OK, people, it's over now. Let's get back to work."

Rideout stared at the screen in front of him, the image of Tampico airport back online from the satellite feed.

"No, it's not over yet."

67

Savas stepped out from behind the stacks of boxes. His face was begrimed with the smoke and sweat of the chaos of the last hour. He was panting, nearly out of breath, having sprinted from his position beside Cohen and Miller. The acrid smell of petroleum and fire left his throat raw, but every muscle was primed and alert for what lay before him. He drew his weapon as he approached.

Gunn was walking confidently toward the helicopter, which had landed not more than one hundred yards in front of them both. A distance of fifty feet separated the two men. Savas aimed his firearm and shouted out over the whirring sound of the blades.

"Stop right there, Gunn!" The CEO paused and turned around to face Savas. "Don't get any closer to the helicopter. I'll kill you if you do."

Gunn hardly even blinked. "I highly doubt that, Agent Savas."

Savas laughed and held the gun steady. "And why is that?"

"Because you are an honorable man, and here I am, unarmed, soon to turn my back on you. Will you discharge your weapon into my back?"

Savas stared into the cold, expressionless eyes before him and took several steps forward. "You have millions of lives in front of your own weapon. You aren't unarmed, and I promise you, I'll shoot you in the back, in the front, or in the ass, if I have to."

"Effective and crude point, Agent Savas. But you really should put the gun down. Your son, Thanos, would want you to."

Savas felt his stomach tighten. "You leave him out of this conversation, Gunn, or I'll kill you for sport."

William Gunn did not flinch. "But that is the truth, isn't it? Your son's death drove you to fight the madmen and their beliefs. My wife died that day, Agent Savas. She died someplace near your son, having fallen one hundred floors, doubtless in terror, pain, and panic, to be smashed and crushed, her body so broken that only fragments remained to be identified by DNA analysis. I, too, resolved to fight the monsters that caused this, and fight them we both have."

"You murder the innocent, you bastard! You are no better than they are."

Gunn displayed the first mild hint of anger. His nostrils flared, and his jaw set tightly. "In war, we do not blame the defenders for killing the aggressors, Agent Savas. In war, it becomes necessary to take innocent lives at times to protect many more lives. Do you recall the bombs that leveled Germany and brought down a madman? Yet our actions were too late for six million Jews. Would not it have been better to take one hundred thousand more lives of German innocents to have prevented that? The madmen of 9/11 and their organization are not rightly our focus. They are only a single branch of a tree with deep and strong roots. Those roots and the trunk are the barbaric religion of Islam, a religion that marched by the sword across the deserts of Arabia and the sands of Africa, to the very doorstep of Europe."

Gunn shouted over the helicopter, his words growing in volume as he spoke. "Now this beast reawakens after centuries of sleep and threatens to devour the world. Europe and America will wait until thousands, millions, entire civilizations fall as once before to Mohammed's armies. *I will not.* I will strike back—not at a leaf, or a branch, but at the heart of this vile plant and wound it to its core. I *owe* her that. As you owe it to your son."

Savas listened uneasily. He felt dizzy, standing on the precipice of his own thoughts and soul, looking down into the abyss that called and tempted him even now.

"That is why I am here, and that is why you could be here with me, instead of holding a gun to my face. You have tortured yourself with delusions that protecting Muslims from me is the same as protecting us from them. That cannot be more wrong. We are the defenders, John

Savas. We wage a war of survival against a many-headed beast. But we do not chase the heads stupidly. We bring fire to purge the creature from the world."

Savas shook his head, keeping his gun raised and aimed. "You cannot set fire to the world to rid it of weeds."

Gunn took another step toward Savas, his eyes earnest, his tone nearly pleading. "Join us in this fight! There will not be any real change in your design, only in your means. A change in means is required for any hope to exist that order can finally defeat chaos."

"This isn't a Norse myth, Gunn! This is real! With real nations, real people, real chaos, and death you are bringing. If you do this thing, it will burn out of control."

Gunn stepped forward. "This thing we do is but the first step, Agent Savas. Do you think we have built this organization only to blow up a few mosques and deliver one bomb, however potent? Our attacks, together with the world war to come, will ensure the total destruction of the Islamic threat."

Savas could hardly believe what he was hearing. "You are a madman."

Gunn clenched his jaw. "Perhaps. I cannot waste more time with you. I know still that you will not stop me here. What I plan is too important, too close to your own desires. If you kill me, and you take from the world the hope for the deliverance that I will bring, you will betray your nation, yourself, and everyone who died at the hands of these murderers. I know you cannot do that. Put the gun down, Agent Savas. You will not shoot me." William Gunn turned around and walked briskly toward the helicopter.

Savas shouted. "Don't make me do this!"

Gunn did not pause or turn around. Savas struggled to pull the trigger. He saw himself in the shape that walked away from him, understood the man's pain, the knife's edge that separated them and their choices. Few could understand that pain, and the anger born of helplessness, the mad desire to strike back in fury. All of that burned like acid within the soul.

But he had already found himself in that darkness. He would not return. Savas aimed the weapon carefully.

Suddenly, a vehicle came speeding onto the tarmac, and a black town car flew recklessly across his field of vision, coming to a screeching halt between him and Gunn. A blond man leaped out, and Savas reacted instinctively to what he saw by diving toward the ground. The older soldier landed sure-footed on the asphalt with a machine gun in his right hand.

Gunfire erupted around Savas as he rolled desperately to escape it. To his amazement, gunshots also arose from behind him. The bullets suddenly ceased exploding around him. The assailant had fallen against the hood of the car, clutching his chest. He lay back, sliding slowly down the curve of the hood, and dropped to the concrete surface with a slap.

At that moment, Frank Miller came limping slowly onto the scene, his leg bloodied, his face black and covered in soot, an automatic weapon in his hand. He was followed by Cohen and Michael Inherp. They stood, discombobulated, staring back and forth between Savas and the retreating figure of Gunn, not understanding the dynamic. Then, the three watched John Savas stand up, aim his weapon, and pull the trigger.

The single gunshot was nearly swallowed in the noise of the helicopter. William Gunn arched his back, paused a split second, then crumpled to his knees on the tarmac, rolling slowly to his side. The helicopter pilot panicked, and throttled up and away from the site, leaving a blast of air and the strange and heavy silence that follows exposure to loud noises. From the distance, they watched Savas walk forward toward Gunn and kneel beside him.

Blood pooled underneath the CEO. The bullet had been well aimed, entering near the heart. Gunn gazed upward at Savas, his eyes partially glazed over in pain, life draining quickly from his body. His mouth moved slowly, his voice soft on the air.

"*Why?*" he gasped.

Savas stared sadly at the dying man. "I will *fight* the monsters, Mr.

Gunn. I will not *become* one. You became the worst of them all, and I had to stop you."

William Gunn slowly released a final breath, his eyes rolled back into his head, and he spoke no more. Savas looked up to see the others approach. He stood and embraced Cohen tightly.

"Oh, God, John." She looked down at the body. "He's dead?"

Savas nodded, pulling her away from the lifeless form, and turning her to face the sea. "But he died a long time ago."

They held each other, gazing up into the blue as the sun reached higher into the sky and morning moved toward afternoon. Suddenly, there was a strange sight. Another light grew in intensity in the blue, until it became a bright star vainly trying to rival the sun. The four stood there in the blowing wind, the sounds of flames and sirens ringing, smoke pouring across the airfield, watching the display of two stars seeming to rise in the eastern sky.

"Well, looks like something went wrong with their plan," said Savas. "Detonated a little too soon." He smiled at the others. His grin faded at their somber faces.

Miller spoke first. "Husaam was on the plane, John. He jumped on as it left for takeoff."

At that moment, several fighter planes blasted low over the airfield, shaking the ground with their sonic vibrations. They flew from the west heading out over the sea, pulling up into the sky between the two suns, as the smaller star quickly dimmed and surrendered its pretenses to the brighter light.

Savas closed his eyes. *So many deaths. Yet, so many deaths prevented.* He looked down at the body of William Gunn—mastermind, wounded titan, madman. He thought of Husaam Jordan—Muslim, once an object of his hatred, who sacrificed his life for so many. He glanced over toward the car where another deluded soul, misled by William Gunn, like so many others, had just lost his life.

The ground was empty. Savas turned around and drew his weapon, while Miller and Inherp looked over cautiously. But there was nothing to be seen. The body of Patrick Rout was not there.

68

TENSIONS EASE AFTER TERRORIST PLOT FOILED
By Brandon Lewis and Thomas Fischetti, Associated Press

The new month began with hopeful signs across much of the world. The US government's dramatic thwarting of the terrorist plot to use a nuclear weapon helped to restore relations between Western nations and the OPEC countries. With the lifting of the oil embargo, stocks around the world recovered dramatically, and military buildup in the Persian Gulf was reversed, decreasing tensions in what had become a highly volatile situation.

Anger still boils underneath the surface in many countries, however, as leaders express dismay that the United States could allow a nuclear weapon to be stolen and not report the incident. With the explosion above the Gulf of Mexico, the current administration has been left scrambling to explain its silence, and congressional leaders of both parties have called for a thorough investigation.

Meanwhile, questions still remain about the mysterious terrorist organization called Mjolnir. The revelation that the terror group was headed by the internationally known businessman William Gunn has stunned people across the globe. His death at the hands of FBI agents has not calmed fears, however, that the organization has been defeated. "There are too many loose ends, too many unknowns," said Congressman Derrick Cholon, chairman of the Foreign Relations Committee. "Gunn kept the governments of the world in the dark. He's dead, but is Mjolnir?"

The FBI has issued no comment on this topic, but anonymous sources report that there is concern that the terrorist organization will

*re-form, and perhaps begin again its campaign against the Muslim
nations.*

*For the moment, most nations seem to be breathing a sigh of relief
that the attacks have stopped, and that the escalating crisis has been
defused. Even Cholon expressed optimism. "For now, because of the
brave sacrifices of so many, we have reason for optimism for the coming
year."*

The cold December wind whipped through the coats and scarves
of the onlookers gathered outside the mosque in Queens. The
fading light of the day cast a grayish pall over the group as the sun
plunged behind the cityscape. Several hundred people stood before a
symbolic *kafan*, the ritual cloth folded neatly, the body of the deceased
never to be recovered, vaporized by an atomic blast. An imam led the
prayers, with the deceased's family, his wife and two sons, brothers and
sisters and parents behind him, and friends and other relations behind
them.

Savas stood close to Cohen in the sharp wind. For them, the service
was also a remembrance of all those friends and coworkers who had
died at the end of the last year. Near them were Rideout, Lightfoote,
and Miller, along with several others from the FBI and the CIA who
had known Jordan and had come to pay their respects.

They were not so far from Father Timothy's church in Astoria.
Savas thought about the people around him—Muslim, Christian, Jew,
black, and white—and he closed his eyes and said a prayer that this
society might be given a chance to continue its mad experiment in tol-
erance. He opened them and listened to the words of the imam.

"It is said in the Koran: Every man shall taste death. Only on the
day of resurrection shall he be paid his wages in full. No one knows
what it is that he will earn tomorrow: Nor does anyone know in what
land he is to die. Only God has full knowledge and is acquainted with
all things. When the angels take the lives of the righteous, they say to
them: *'Salaamun Alikum*, Enter Paradise! because of the good deeds

that you have done.' Today we pray for a man who has done great deeds and who offered his life for the lives of many—our brother, Husaam Jordan."

There were muffled sobs and tears all around. Savas looked over and saw the two young boys, perhaps three and five. The older of the two was weeping; the younger appeared dazed and confused, afraid in this mass of strangers—his father nowhere to be found. *Sons taken from fathers, and fathers taken from sons.* He whispered something to Cohen; she nodded, and he quietly stepped away from the ceremony. He had yet to make his peace with God.

After the crowds had dispersed, Savas stood alone beside a rocky drop-off looking over the East River. *Not really a river,* he thought, *but the sea.* He had always been drawn to the sea. *The Greek blood.* His eyes squinted against the sun and the gusts of salty breeze, as he gazed over the snow-crested waves and the white flashes of boats in the distance. The imam stepped to his side.

Savas looked him over. A tall and thin black man in his late sixties, trimmed salt-and-pepper beard, proud of bearing yet bookish, rectangular eyeglasses on his face. Like Jordan, he wore the flowing white robes and the African kufi on his head. This was the man who had found Jordan in prison, then a violent gang member lost in a world of crime and death. He had shown him the light of Islam and had changed a young man's life forever. The imam had sponsored Jordan's education in prison and his college tuition when he was released. He was more a father to Jordan than the man who abandoned him when he was a child.

"Husaam told me that you are Greek, yes? Christian?" he asked. He still spoke with the accent of his native Nigeria.

Savas laughed. "Well, holding on by my fingernails. Father Timothy might be the only reason I still go to church."

The imam nodded. "Yes, Husaam also told me this. Go to your priest, Agent Savas. Go to your Book. At such times, we must seek the will of God."

"I'm not so sure I like God's will. Whatever it might be."

The imam bowed his head. "You lost your son. There can be no greater loss for a father. Madmen of Islam took him from you." Savas tightened his jaw yet said nothing. "But now these Western madmen have taken a son of Islam, a son to me as much as my own son, one I pulled from the fire of his lost youth. A son for a son. Some would say a debt has been paid."

"They would," Savas echoed, gazing out over the water, his eyes fixed far to the horizon, as if seeing into a great distance. He spoke quietly but firmly. "But I can't look at it that way. Not anymore. Not after all this. That's the sort of thinking that got us into this mess in the first place. Husaam and my son, they were good men. Good men taken by men who didn't deserve to breathe the same air they did. Anyone who would take them steals something from the world. Two sons were taken."

He looked over to Jordan's widow, Vonessa, and the two boys standing in the grass, then turned back to the imam. "But I see those two boys in the grass. Two sons were given. I don't know what kind of *fair* that is, and it's not one that satisfies me very much, but right now, it's all I have." John Savas turned from the edge and walked back across the field toward his car, and to the silhouetted form of Rebecca Cohen in the failing light.

EPILOGUE

The freighter cut through the waves with tremendous momentum. The craft was weighed down by its stacks of cargo, giving it a heavy sail en route but a respectable profit at harbor. The captain of the craft looked down from the piloting room at the tourists who paid money for a "freighter cruise," a relatively new and low-thrills way to take to the seas. More and more captains were entering this market, and it allowed them to pocket substantial extra cash.

The cruise passengers were usually the very young, lots of college kids, low on cash but high on adventure, eschewing fancy and expensive cruise boats for container packing freighters. He was glad to see them. Not only did they bring him money he wouldn't have had otherwise; they brought some youth and vitality to a job that was as monotonous as any he could imagine. Besides, the young girls were something to look at in their miniskirts and shorts.

The captain's gaze paused and lingered over the group. He focused on the one passenger that did not fit the pattern. The man was older, in his fifties and traveling alone. He came onboard with a limp, and he seemed in poor health. But he was an imposing man, built like a tank, with a blond crew cut and a hard face that made even the captain uneasy to look at him for very long. He had asked the strangest questions, insisting that he had to know whether the boat would take a certain route, underneath the site where that plane with the bomb had exploded. The captain told him there was no debris to see, but the man had waved him off, saying he knew that.

The captain shook his head. There was no point in concerning himself too much with any one passenger. In all his travels, he had come to know clearly that there were all kinds of strangeness in human beings.

The wind picked up strongly, and it was cold even in the January Gulf weather. Many of the others went inside for shelter. The blond man did not stir. He simply gazed into the sky as the boat motored on.

ACKNOWLEDGMENTS

I t took four years, over a thousand query letters, three major rewrites at the behest of critics, and a last-minute break to find an agent and publisher for this, my first novel. I would like to express my heartfelt thanks to those who made it all possible. After numerous agents either passed without comment (or return mail!), or shrank from the controversial subject matter, my thanks go to Sara and Stephen Camilli for their belief in the story and skillful representation in an increasingly topsy-turvy publishing world. My sincerest appreciation goes to my editor, Dan Mayer, of Seventh Street Books for his time and energies in bringing the novel to press in its best form with Prometheus Books. A similar "thank you" to Julia DeGraf for her work in copyediting the manuscript. To my family, especially my wife, Nina, my daughters, father, and mother—thanks for taking the time to read and comment on what certainly must have seemed a strange and doomed endeavor on my part. And finally, to all who contributed your time, thoughts, and support—you know who you are, and you have my deepest gratitude.

ABOUT THE AUTHOR

Born in the Midwest, Erec Stebbins has pursued diverse interests over the course of his life, including science, music, drama, and writing. He received a degree in physics from Oberlin College in 1992, and a PhD in biochemistry from Cornell University in 1999. Alongside his scientific interests, he is a maker and player of the Native American–style flute, and he has continued to pursue writing for his love of dramatic storytelling. *The Ragnarök Conspiracy* is a novel that took root in him after he witnessed the destruction of September 11, 2001, from his Manhattan apartment. He currently lives and works in New York City as a scientist and professor in biomedical research. For more about the book and Erec Stebbins, visit www.ragnarokconspiracy .com and www.erecstebbins.com.